TREACHEROUS

CARTER KIDS #1

CHLOE WALSH

The right of Chloe Walsh to be identified as the Author of the work has been asserted by her in accordance with the Copyright and Related Rights Act 2000.

All rights reserved. No part of this publication may be reproduced, stored in a retrieval system, or transmitted, in any form or by any means – electronic, mechanical, including photocopying, recording, or by any information storage and retrieval system – without the prior written permission of the publisher, nor be otherwise circulated in any form or binding or cover than that in which it is published and without a similar condition being imposed on the subsequent purchaser.

This e-book is licensed for your personal enjoyment only. This e-book may not be re-sold or given away to other people. If you would like to share this book with another person, please purchase an additional copy for each reader. If you're reading this book and did not purchase it, or it was not purchased for your use only, then please return to your favorite retailer and purchase your own copy. Thank you for respecting the hard work of this author.

Published by Chloe Walsh
Copyright 2014 by Chloe Walsh
All Rights Reserved. ©

Treacherous,
Carter Kids #1
First published, March 2015
Republished, January 2018
All rights reserved. ©
Cover designed by Bee @ Bitter Sage Designs.
Edited by Aleesha Davis.
Proofread by: Bianca Rushton.

DISCLAIMER

This book is a work of fiction. All names, characters, places and incidents either are products of the author's imagination or are used fictitiously. Any resemblance to events, locales, or persons, living or dead, is coincidental.

The author acknowledges all songs titles, song lyrics, film titles, film characters, trademarked statuses, brands, mentioned in this book are the property of, and belong to, their respective owners. The publication/ use of these trademarks is not authorized/ associated with, or sponsored by the trademark owners.

Chloe Walsh is in no way affiliated with any of the brands, songs, musicians or artists mentioned in this book.

All rights reserved ©

*This book is dedicated to anyone who is trapped
in a personal, never-ending battle with mental illness.
To all of you who feel misunderstood, alone, isolated,
and tortured to the point of real and honest to god despair
You are **not** alone.
I feel your pain.
I fight the fight.
And remember your voice is your most powerful weapon
Keep fighting.*

PROLOGUE

3 months earlier
Noah

"*Don't you want to make mommy happy, Noah?" my mother asks, and I nod eagerly.*

I'm seven years old and I want to do anything to stop her from crying. To stop her from marking her body with those horrible crucifixes. I know that when I'm big I will never pray. I don't want to pray ever again. I promise myself I won't. But I don't tell mom that. That would make her sad. I keep it a secret. I'm good at keeping secrets.

"Then climb inside with me," she coaxes, holding the closet door open. Her brown eyes are wild and dark and I'm afraid to get into that closet. I know what will happen if I do. It's a bad idea.

"You're safe out here, mom," I tell her, hoping she'll believe me this time and not get mad.

"Do you want to die, Noah?" she screams, and her face

distorts into ugly mom. Not pretty mom. Ugly mom is mad and scary and cuts her skin with her nails.

"No," I whisper, even though sometimes I think it can't be worse than this...

"You're going to die," she hisses as she scratches her arms. "We're both going to die...like him. Just like him."

"No, we won't," I tell her as calmly as possible. I wish my dad would come home soon. He knows how to make mom feel better. He gives her that special medicine wrapped up in silver foil and she sleeps. Maybe he's gone out to get some medicine for mom?

"It's the devil inside you," she snarls.

Ugly mom doesn't like me. She calls me names and that makes me sad. Pretty mom is much nicer. I hope my dad gets here soon...

Reaching out, mom grabs my sweater and drags me into the closet. "Pray," she spits as her long nails dig roughly into the flesh on my arm. "Pray for your soul, you evil child..."

JERKING AWAKE, I GRABBED MY BED SHEETS AND LAY PERFECTLY still, breathing slowly as I tried to get a handle on myself.

I hated those kind of dreams – the ones that reminded me exactly why I needed to keep doing what I fucking hated most.

The sun shone through my half-closed blinds, letting me know I'd slept away the best part of another summer's day. I had hoped to be up early enough to go hiking with Logan, but obviously I'd overslept – again. I couldn't seem to stay awake these days.

"Noah, are you awake yet?"

My bedroom door swung inwards and Ellie Dennis, my *step-sister,* stood in the doorway, clad in nothing but a bra and thong.

Well, I assumed she was wearing a thong. She was facing me, so I couldn't actually see her ass, but it was a solid guess considering she liked to prance around the house in next to no clothing.

Ellie had her poker-straight, waist-length black hair pulled back in a pony-tail, making sure her curvaceous frame was on full display. "How are you feeling?" she purred in that slinky, cougar voice I hated. It was the voice she used when she wanted something – most often my dick.

I let out a heavy sigh and flinched when a sharp pain ricocheted through my side. "I'm alive aren't I?"

"I missed you, Noah," Ellie crooned. "You were gone longer than usual."

"No shit, Ellie." Usually I worked closer to home and made it back each night, but my last job was out of state and it had taken a week. I finally made it home late last night, and I was feeling every one of those extra days.

Ellie stepped further into my room, walking over to my bed. "By the way, the house next door is occupied. A new family moved in last week."

Rubbing my face with my hand, I let out a sigh. "And you're telling me this because…"

"You know why I'm telling you this," she shot back heatedly, her green eyes flaring like her temper. "Dad says we're supposed to keep…"

"Please stop talking to me about your dad." I didn't need this crap. Not today. Not after last night.

"Do you need a massage?" she asked, smart to change the subject, as she sat on the edge of my bed and leaned closer. Her breasts strained against the tiny scrap of red lace covering them.

"No, I really don't," I replied, entirely uninterested in what she was offering.

Unperturbed by my refusal, Ellie slipped her hand under my blankets and fisted my dick. "Are you sure?" she purred, gliding her hand up and down my semi-erect shaft. "I can help ebb some of that tension inside you."

My eyes fluttered shut, an involuntary reaction to having my dick rubbed. I knew I should tell Ellie to get the hell out of my room, but I honestly didn't have the energy to argue with her. I knew that sounded fucked up and sick, but that was the truth.

Instead, I gently knocked Ellie's hand aside and rolled out of bed before walking stiffly into the adjoining bathroom and closing the door in her face.

"Wow. Rude much, Noah?" I heard her shout.

Thankfully, when I turned on the shower, the noise of the water drowned out her annoying fucking voice.

Every muscle in my body ached as I stood under the scalding hot water, and I had to hold onto the wall to keep my balance. Last night had taken a hell of a lot out of my body. I was pretty sure I'd busted another rib because breathing in stung like a bitch.

Closing my eyes, I tipped my head back, allowing the water to trickle down my face, enjoying the cleansing sensation. With any hope, the water would wash away my memories or, better still, my conscience.

EVERY INCH OF MY BODY WAS ACHING BY THE TIME I MADE IT out of the shower and got dressed. Pain was coursing through every muscle attached to my spinal cord and I honestly didn't know how I was staying upright. I felt like jelly. I looked like shit. I was fairly certain I wouldn't be able to work tonight. Hell, I was fairly certain I needed medical attention.

Pushing my pain to the back of my mind, I made my way down the staircase and headed into the kitchen to refuel.

Popping a slice of last night's pizza in my mouth, I grabbed another and headed out back. As soon as I stepped outside, I heard the sound of a guitar strumming, followed by a female voice singing the lyrics of a song I'd never heard before.

"...I changed my life to make you love me but in the end it doesn't count..."

"...All the tears you saw me cry and now you're gone without a sound..."

I stood stock-still with a slice of pepperoni pizza hanging out of my mouth as I strained to hear her.

"...No more sounds of joy and laughter, just the songs of yesterday..."

"...No more saying babe, I love you because now you're gone away..."

I moved closer to the garden fence, fucking driven by the insane urge to put a face to that voice.

"... And now I wonder just how long it'll take..."

"...For me to say I love you..."

A willowy blonde sat cross-legged and barefoot in the garden next to mine, with a guitar almost the size of her resting on her bare thighs. Swallowing my last slice of pizza, I leaned against the wall separating our houses and watched her play.

"...To another man, another face, another heart, another fake..."

Throwing her head back, her long blonde hair splayed everywhere as she played with her eyes closed, singing at the tops of her lungs, her fingers a blur of movement, and I was fucking fascinated with her.

"...There was a time I would've fought for you...There was a time I would've ignored your cruel words when I overheard you say I wish I never met her..."

"...Not anymore. Not today. I want more. I deserve better..."

She finished her song and placed the guitar on the grass beside her before lying down with her eyes closed and sighing heavily.

Her blonde wavy hair looked like it hadn't been brushed in days. The denim cut-offs she had on were worn to a thread and the white t-shirt she wore was at least five-times too big for her, tied into a makeshift belly-top with a hair clip. Her skin looked like ivory silk, she had a cut on her left knee, a bruise on her right elbow, and I'd never seen anything so fucking beautiful.

She wasn't intentionally sexy... she just was.

I watched her intently as she stretched her arms and legs out, clearly basking in the summer sunshine. I couldn't turn my face away. For some strange reason, the words of Lonestar's song *Unusually Unusual* popped into my mind which was weird as fuck because I wasn't a country music fan.

She twisted her face to one side, opened her eyes, and looked straight into mine.

She didn't look away.

Neither did I.

I just stood there, barely breathing, with a fucked up tightening pain in my chest, as her hazel colored eyes searched deep inside of me, pulling at a part of me I never knew existed.

"What are you doing?" a voice demanded from behind

me, startling me and breaking the weird thing I had going on with the girl over the fence.

The blonde closed her eyes, turned her face up to the sky, and the moment was gone – as was the weird pulling sensation in my chest.

Ellie stepped into my personal space. "Noah, I asked you a question..." her voice trailed off as her eyes followed my line of sight. A harsh laugh escaped from her. "You know you can't, right?" Ellie sneered, glowering over the wall at the girl. "You know what's at stake for us. Never piss on your own doorstep."

"I know," I told her.

It didn't stop me from looking at her, though.

I think she seared me that very first day...because I sure as hell wasn't the same after her.

1

PRESENT DAY

Teagan

My next-door neighbor was certifiably evil – I was sure of it.

When I first arrived here at the beginning of the summer, she had snubbed me and ignored every one of my salutes and *good mornings*, looking through me like I was invisible. That would have been fine by me if it had stayed that way, but it hadn't.

Something changed and I had no idea what that something was, but in the space of a week, her attitude towards me switched from being cool and uninterested to malicious and downright hostile.

In the beginning, I'd forced myself to believe I was imagining her hostility. I mean, she didn't know me, and I'd done nothing to perturb the girl. But this morning, she wound her car window down as she reversed out of her driveway and verbally attacked me. I had very quickly realized it was personal.

Three months later – and with a whole bunch of verbal sparring sessions under our belts– it was clear that Ellie Dennis and I would *never* be friends. Aside from the fact that she'd told me, on more than one occasion, what she thought of me, the girl seemed to deliberately go out of her way to cause trouble for me.

If she wasn't camped outside my driveway, armed with her group of brainless friends, idiot of a boyfriend, and cartons of eggs, then she was cranking her stereo in the middle of the night or spreading very nasty – very unoriginal – rumors about me. Ellie and her little gang of followers had decided to make my life a living hell for reasons unknown to me.

Thanks again for the fabulous relocation, Uncle Max.

Because of my so-called *guardian*, and I used that term lightly, we were the latest family to take up residency on Thirteenth Street, University Hill, Boulder, Colorado, and *I* was the sole target of the bitch over the fence.

And because of my wonderfully unconventional uncle, I was starting sixth year, *senior year*, tomorrow morning, in a brand-new school, with no clue of the curriculum and a serious issue with driving on the right side of the road. It really sucked, because I had a hard enough time fitting in back home in Ireland, so what hope did I have in America, with bears and earthquakes and heat waves, spiders, snakes and tornados?

The worst I'd seen in Ireland was a daddy-long-legs and a bit of rain. I didn't do Fahrenheit, I was a Celsius girl, and anything over sixteen degrees was too much for me.

Considering the abuse I'd endured since my arrival on Coloradan soil, I was more than a little disgruntled with

Max and the fact that he hadn't taken my opinion into account when making a decision that, I don't know, kind of affected *my* life as well as his.

We'd always been more like roommates than uncle and niece, and up until three and a half months ago, our living arrangement had been unfolding beautifully. That was until the night Max sat me down to *discuss* the position he'd been offered as head of the E.R in St. Luke's Hospital, back in his and mom's hometown.

It hadn't been as much of a discussion as it had been a statement. It was happening, we were moving to America, and that was that. The conversation, and our relationship, pretty much went downhill the second the words *'you have to come with me, Teagan. I need to take the position. You don't have a choice'* came out of his mouth.

After a tedious, lengthy, and heated debate, Max had used his get out of jail card, the *'I uprooted my whole life for you when you needed me and it's only fair to return the favor'* guilt trip ensured to make me succumb to almost any demand.

I'd given in with only two prerequisites; someplace quiet to live so I could concentrate on my final year of school, and the absolute guarantee that I could return to Ireland for University next year.

Staying true to his word, Uncle Max leased us this gorgeous two-story situated in the suburbs and surrounded by a well-tended garden, and with a view of the Rocky Mountains that was, in my humble opinion, to die for.

At first the neighborhood had seemed quiet compared to what I had envisioned, and I had *thought* – in my vast naivety – that I would get along with the other neighbors, or at the very least blend in.

Present Day | 11

Well, today was day ninety-nine of operation *blend-in-with-the-locals* and the shit had officially hit the fan.

It was only five in the evening and I'd already been subjected to no less than three verbal attacks from Ellie, a record breaking one-minute long evil glare from her fat father, and of course my daily treat of having our trash can tipped out all over our driveway.

Of course, the nasty pranks and attacks from the girl next-door neighbor didn't bother Uncle Max since he was *always* at the hospital, and I was the one who cleaned everything up. I wished he would spend more time at home with me. I was lonely and it was really shit having to face this crap on my own every day, especially now that the stakes had been raised.

The fact that I'd managed to piss Ellie off by simply breathing seemed inconsequential, heck the Carter brothers living across the street who were so loud at night I could hear them from my bedroom – *all the way across the street* – were a litter of fuzzy little kittens in comparison to my latest problem.

Noah Messina, Ellie's stepbrother, had decided to join her *torment-the-new-girl-until-she-cracks* mission.

There was both a plus and negative side to this latest development.

On the plus side, at least I'd actually done something to deserve Noah's wrath. There had been a fight in their driveway last weekend, between Noah and some other tattooed douchebag, that had progressed into our yard, resulting in the windshield of my car being smashed when Noah pummeled his opponent through it.

Thinking back now, I had to admit that I sort of overreacted when I stalked outside in nothing but a Coldplay t-shirt and a black thong and tossed an entire can of white gloss paint over the hood of Noah's black Lexus in retaliation. It had felt damn good to fight back instead of letting them walk all over me.

On the negative side, Noah hadn't given me any trouble before that night, had barely inclined his beautiful head in my direction – with the exception of that one evening back when I first moved in where Noah and I had this weird staring moment – but destroying his car with paint was like waving a red rag in front of a bull.

He had lost it.

Right there in my driveway, with his t-shirt ripped from his body and blood dripping from his eyebrow, Noah Messina had thrown the biggest man-tantrum I'd ever seen before declaring war on me.

Of course, in true Teagan fashion, I'd goaded him to within an inch of my life.

Right there in my driveway, in my underwear, in front of all the neighbors, I'd gone head to head with the tattooed muscle-head next-door and it had been one of the most terrifyingly exciting moments of my life.

He'd called me a stupid bitch and I'd responded by bitch-slapping his face and calling him a horse's ass. Noah had then backed me up against the door of my car, going as far as pressing his forehead against mine, using his powerful body to cage me in, and I had done absolutely nothing to diffuse the situation.

I'd pressed against him, both our chests heaving, and dared him to go further, showing nothing but defiance even though I knew he could squish me in two if he felt inclined. He had been truly livid, his dark eyes full of dangerous heat, as he stared down at me in obvious frustration.

As mad as he'd been, I still doubted Noah would've physically hurt me, but I never got to find out because Mr.

Carter, the unbelievably hot D.I.L.F from across the street, had raced over and separated us.

Some idiot from the circle of boys who'd been watching the earlier fight misconstrued Mr. Carter's intervention as an attack on Noah. Everything had pretty much gone to shit after that, and a street fight of epic proportions broke out.

After head-butting the douchebag who'd tried to attack him, Mr. Carter had then grabbed Noah by the back of his neck and dragged him away from me, before returning to pick me up and carry me back to his house. Yes, I used the word carried.

It wouldn't have been so bad, but the fact that I'd been partially exposed kind of killed my buzz when he dropped me onto a huge leather couch and I was faced with three Mr. Carter look-alikes, all equally gorgeous, all with a full view of my crotch.

To make a long story short, the cops were called and Noah and I were both asked if we wanted to press charges on each other. Noah said no and that we'd settle it between us, and I, being terrified of uniformed policemen, had earnestly agreed with him.

We then each received a warning and were advised to keep our distance from one another. All three Carter boys, their father, and their bald uncle, had then proceeded to walk me home – all the way across the street – while I tried to discourage one of the boy's, I think his name was Cameron, from setting up camp in my living room.

The only good thing that had come from the whole ordeal was the fact that I'd shown Ellie and Noah that I wasn't going to lie down and let them walk all over me. Screw them. Neither of them had to like me. They didn't even have to speak to me. They just had to fuck off and leave me alone.

I only had ten months left in this place. I'd already managed to survive three months of Ellie's bullying, I could do this. Yeah...I could manage ten months in a brand new school, in a different country, on another continent.

Martin was the only thing I took solace in and, because it was a beautiful day, I decided to go outside and play with him. Grabbing a bottle of water from the fridge, I strolled outside and sat cross-legged in the shade. With Martin resting on my thigh, I began to play.

I should probably state for the record that Martin is made of rosewood and accompanied by six strings. Owned and given to me by my mother a month before she died, my guitar, who I'd aptly named Martin after its maker *Martin & Co.*, was my pride and joy. I would never be the world's greatest guitarist, but I was decent and held a note which kept my bank balance healthy whenever I busked.

Clasping my capo on the third fret, I closed my eyes and allowed my fingers to glide over the strings as I played with note after intricate note, finger plucking my way through my own version of Eva Cassidy's *Songbird*.

I was almost finished belting out the chorus, when a blast of icy cold water hit me full force on the chest, spilling onto my fourteen-hundred-euro guitar and boiling the blood in my veins.

I sat on the grass completely dumbfounded for a moment before jerking to my feet and glowering at the perpetrator over the wall with the garden hose pointed at my chest.

My spine stiffened at the sight of Satan-in-a-bikini and my hackles rose.

There was no denying that Ellie Dennis was gorgeous, could've been Kelly Brook's twin in the curves stakes with long locks of raven colored hair and exotic green eyes, but then again there was also no denying the fact that she was bat-shit crazy.

I wasn't an argumentative person as a rule, but I wasn't a pushover either. If Ellie wanted to spar with me, I wasn't backing down.

"What the hell is your problem?" I demanded as my temper bubbled dangerously close to the edge. "You've been a walking hormone since I moved in."

"You are," she said in a bored tone of voice as she placed one hand on her bare hip, and held an impressive looking iPad in the other. "I don't like you."

"You don't even know me," I shot back in annoyance. "Don't you think you're being a tad judgmental?"

"I don't need to know you in order to make an accurate judgment," she sneered, narrowing her green eyes at me as she leered at me from her side of the wall. "FYI, you're not in the middle of a swamp anymore, Irish. You have neighbors now, so keep the damn noise down."

"Swamp." I rolled my eyes at her. "It's called a bog." Smiling sweetly, I added, "And as far as neighbors go, I'm astounded with your hospitality." I inclined my head slightly. "When should I expect the welcoming basket of muffins?"

"Don't push me," she warned as she pointed the hose at Martin. "You really don't want me as your enemy."

I thought you already were..."Why don't you go and point your hose at something else."

"Or what?" she countered in a spiteful tone of voice.

Or what? "Do you think you're the only person with access to running water?" I laughed in surprise when her brows furrowed. Ha. "You did?" Oh, this was priceless. I was living next door to Barbie.

Reaching down, I grabbed my bottle of water and

unscrewed the lid. "You want a war, Dennis, you've got one." With that I leaned over the chest-high wall and tossed the contents over her head, cackling evilly when she screamed and tried to protect her hair with her iPad.

"You're so dead," she spat as she brushed her hair back from her face. If looks could kill I *would* be dead. "Your card is marked, Irish," she spat. "You're done around here."

"Oh no," I crooned sarcastically. "Like me. *Please* like me. Your opinion means *everything* to me."

"It should!" she screamed. "Do you know who I am?" Her lip curled up cruelly. "You're so finished in school tomorrow." She smiled darkly. "I am going to ruin you."

"I think you should rephrase the question to *do I care*." I smiled. "I think you know the answer to that, but in case you've had too much sun and can't think straight, I'll answer you anyway. *No.* No, I don't care who you are. I've taken your measure and it's pretty clear to me that you're a bitch." Probably the popular girl. The queen bitch. *Be quiet, Teagan. Shh. Don't go any further.* "And stupid." *She's right, I'm finished.* "And ugly." There. I'd done it. I'd ruined my social status from here on out.

"I hate you, Teagan Jones," she snarled. "You're toast."

I snorted as I stared at the brunette over the fence. "I'm toast? I have sun cream on, love, not butter, you're the one baking out here." I was probably as red as a lobster, but I refused to back down from this bully. "And my name is Connolly," I added, annoyed that she called me by my uncle's surname. "Not Jones..."

"Where's my iPad, Ellie?" a deep, throaty voice called out.

Arching my neck, I shaded my eyes from the sun with one hand as I locked eyes on the owner of the voice. I immediately felt like weeping.

Mr. Tall, dark and hated-my-guts stalked towards Ellie

looking mighty fine in his navy swimming trunks and I felt my skin heat instantly. As much of a bastard as Noah Messina was, he was still able to tick all of the man-preference-boxes I never knew I had...

Messy black hair sticking out in all the right directions? Check. Thick, sooty lashes framing eyes as dark as charcoal? Got 'em. A toned, tanned body that could make you come without foreplay? Yup.

Usually I was turned off by tattoos, but Noah? He wore his tags like a boss. Both of his arms were covered in sleeves of intricately designed swivels and loops, and he had this really sexy tattoo of a wolf on his left calf.

"Yeah, it's right here, Noah." Ellie's eyes lit up as she spoke, her voice became husky, and her whole focus became locked on Noah.

Hang on a sec, weren't they brother and sister – at least by law?

Ellie didn't look at him like a sister should. She was looking at him like a predator would its prey.

Hell, even *I* was looking at him like a predator would its prey.

God, it was such a pity they were related. That really sucked. Poison spread in families. But damn he was nice to look at. It was such a shame we hated each other's guts; it kinda meant he was off-limits to me – even in my imagination.

He's off-limits to you whether you hate him or not, idiot. You're in relationship-rebound mode. Remember Liam?

Thoughts of my ex-boyfriend speared through me, bringing with them all kinds of confusing feelings and emotions.

Shaking my head, I pushed those feelings to the pit of my stomach.

I suppose I could sit and cry over a boy who broke up with me because of my whole *leaving the country* issue, and I suppose I could curl up like a wounded animal and make keening noises if I thought about the fact that I put his penis in my mouth about thirty minutes before he gave me my marching orders, but what would be the point in that?

The only person I'd be hurting would be myself. Liam would still be in Ireland, living it up with all of our friends, with my oral-virginity on his notched bedpost, and I would still be here in Colorado, being depressed as well as fighting with the neighbors.

Fuck that.

I was only young once. I'd hash it out with my conscience later. Meanwhile, I had eyes and I liked to look at pretty things. Noah was an asshole, but he was a very pretty one, hence the looking part.

"Although it's probably broken," Ellie added, shooting a meaningful glare in my direction, bringing me back to the here and now. "You can forward the bill to Teagan *Jones*." She purposefully – and wrongfully – said my name like she was naming a horrifically contagious disease. "She's the one who poured water all over it."

My eyes narrowed in outrage. She had some nerve. "You can shove your bill up the highest part of your h..."

"You broke it, bitch," Ellie shot back, waving the piece of technology around like it was a flag.

"No, *you* broke it," I shot back. "When you were drooling all over your brother..."

"That's enough." The warning tone in Noah's voice broke through my thoughts, cutting me off mid-rant and I couldn't stop my eyes from wandering all over his body, drinking him in – every square inch of his body.

His jaw was rough, with a day or so worth of stubble

etched across it, and his body was bronzed from the heat of the sun.

No suntan lotion for him, my mind tossed out and I was suddenly very aware of the pallor of my skin.

Feeling a smidgen of self-consciousness for the first time since my flight landed, I did a mental recap of my current state of appearance, you know, for adolescent-hormonal purposes.

My black Rory Gallagher t-shirt clung to my body like a second skin because of the idiot next-door and her hose pipe. Oh, and the messy-bun I'd teased my overly-long blonde hair into this morning? Well, let's just say the term 'messy-bun' was a kinder way of saying a fuzzy ball of knots.

The flimsy pair of white GAA – Gaelic football – shorts I had on were soaked right through, revealing my gloriously hideous pink granny knickers for the world, and the very hot guy next-door, to see. To finish the stylish ensemble I was wearing, the knock-off Uggs Liam had brought me back from his family holiday to Turkey last summer were drenched right through. My toes were currently burrowing squishy mole holes through the furry insoles.

"Causing trouble again?" Noah drawled in a derisive tone. His gaze roamed over my body lazily before returning to my face, and it suddenly dawned on me; Christina Aguilera had been right all along. Big brown eyes *could* hypnotize. "Nice shorts."

"I'm on *my* side of the fence." Sliding my guitar in front of my body to protect what was left of my dignity, I raised my brow at him. "And nice *lineage*," I added sarcastically.

"So, you play the guitar?" Noah asked me with a smirk.

"No." I stared blankly at him. "*No*, I just like to hold it and look pretty."

Noah's brow rose in surprise. "And how's that working for you?"

"Fantastic," I said through clenched teeth, annoyed at the way he mocked me with his eyes. I knew that sounded stupid, but it was true. He was *laughing* at me with his eyes. "As you can see, business is booming."

"You know, I came outside because I thought I heard an injured animal in pain," Ellie told him as she eyed my guitar. "But it was her. *She's* the headache we've been hearing all summer." How the hell did she ...hang on, did she just call me a headache? That bitch.

My eyes locked on Ellie's smug face and my fingers twitched with the urge to scratch her stupid eyes out. She glared evilly back at me, and the tiny hairs on my arms shot up.

"You're seriously pushing me," I warned her. "Keep going and we're gonna have a problem."

"We..." Ellie gestured between herself and Noah before sneering at me. "Already have a problem. You." She folded her arms across her chest. "So why don't you do us all a favor and go back to where you came from."

I didn't get it.

I seriously didn't freaking get it.

I'd done nothing to this girl to make her hate me so much. It was as if Ellie had taken one look at me and decided she hated me. A part of me wanted to know why, but I wasn't about to verbalize my thoughts on the matter and look weak and whiny. Instead, I glared straight back at her, not giving an inch. "Wow," I mused. "You're friendly."

Ellie's eyes narrowed. "And you're..."

"Didn't your mom get you guitar lessons as a child?" Noah asked in a sardonic tone, interrupting his step-sister's retort. He smirked. "Could've saved me from investing in a pair of earplugs."

"Didn't *your* mom give you a coloring book as a child?" I shot back in an equally mocking tone. "Could've saved yourself a whole pile of money." Shrugging nonchalantly, I added, "You know, from having to pay sweaty, butch men to draw all over your body with needles."

"Teagan," he scolded, shaking his head condescendingly. "I never would've put you down for being sexist."

His words threw me. Threw me and caused my toes to curl. "I'm not," I said slowly, knowing I was walking myself into a verbal trap but couldn't figure out how.

"I pay a very talented, *very* sexy, not-butch-in-the-slightest redhead to draw on my body with needles." I reddened and Noah's smile widened, revealing enviously straight white teeth. "And trust me, Thorn, my tips are mutually beneficial."

Thorn? "You know you should really wipe your mouth, Noah," I snapped, feeling the burn in my cheeks. It was such a pity he had to be a dick. Why did all the hot ones always have to act like assholes? If only he'd kept his mouth shut.

Noah smirked. "I should?"

"Yeah." I smiled sweetly. "You're talking shit."

Resting his arms on the fence, Noah tilted his head to one side and eyed me curiously. "You know your insults are having the opposite effect on me, right?" he mused in a soft tone. "I find your catty behavior a real turn on, Thorn."

"It's *Teagan*," I said calmly, even though I was shaking on the inside. "And what the hell is that supposed to mean?" He was joking. He had to be joking. There was no way I turned a guy like Noah Messina on. He probably got off on naked biker chicks with pierced nipples and tattooed butt-cheeks.

Noah's eyes darkened. "It means you should walk away while you still can."

"Was that your lame attempt at scaring me?" Why the hell was I goading him? I needed to shut the hell up and walk away from this stalemate of a conversation. He was unpredictable and deadly – his actions last weekend had proved that. "Because you'll have to do better than that." *Stop it, Teagan. Shut the hell up.* "Or has all that sun affected your brain and you're too thick to come up with anything better?" I had no idea why I was being like this. I only knew that my words were irking Noah and that piece of knowledge was like music to my ears.

"You're in too deep, *Teagan*." Noah's face broke out in a huge grin. "Let's hope you can swim."

I wondered how it was possible that my brain detested the man in front of me and my body craved him. I was embarrassed at how my body reacted to his presence. "Whatever floats your boat, buddy." Shaking my head, I swung around and walked towards my house before I catapulted over that wall and poked both of their eyes out.

"You know that's two things you owe me for," I heard him call out, followed by snickering. "I take cash, or you could set up a private payment plan with me..."

"You can dream on if you think I'm paying for your iPad or your car," I growled. "The only thing I'm prepared to invest my money in is a muzzle for your sister." *And you.*

"You'll pay," Noah called out from behind me, "One way or another," and his words chilled me to the bone.

NOAH

"You'll pay," I called out as Teagan stalked away. I wasn't serious about the money. I wouldn't take a dime. I'd earn back the cash to pay for my car, but I figured I may as well act like a prick towards her since she'd obviously branded me one. "One way or another."

"I *hate* her," Ellie seethed. "I mean it, Noah. I can't stand that bitch –are you even listening to me?"

No, I wasn't listening to her.

I was too busy watching Teagan Connolly as she strutted her sexy little ass inside her house. God, three months of having her live next door to me and I still felt like slamming my head into the garden wall. Now worse than ever since she'd challenged me, *again*.

I couldn't decide if the girl next-door was extremely reckless or just incredibly stupid. I was veering on the former because it was pretty obvious Teagan had a steady head on her shoulders, and a sharp tongue in her mouth. In the three months she'd been living here, I hadn't seen her in any of the hangouts I spent my time at, which showed she was sharper than most girls our age.

She didn't leave the house much, had never thrown a party next door, but I often spotted her reading under the old oak tree in her backyard. Everything about the girl screamed *mouse*, but she had this fiery temper that I somehow managed to provoke by just being nearby. A lot of Teagan's anger towards me was because of the shitty way Ellie treated her daily, and a small part of me didn't blame her for being a snarky little bitch, but another part of me hated the fact that she was so goddamn judgmental.

Like last weekend for example. I *accidentally* busted her windshield and Teagan had automatically switched on defense mode, even though I'd never intentionally done anything to hurt her.

I was jumped by some sore loser dick from the ring who'd followed me home with a crowd of his buddies, and it was either fight or be fucked over. I'd defended myself and in the heat of the moment, hadn't noticed we'd moved our fight into the neighbor's yard.

When I eventually got the upper-hand and knocked the guy out, Teagan had shocked the hell out of me by stalking out of her house in nothing but a t-shirt and thong with a can of paint in her hands.

The defiance in her eyes as she stared me down before bending over the hood of my baby and emptying the can of paint was something that struck a chord inside of me. I'd never been so angry or turned on in my life.

Pure rage had flooded my veins, driven on even further when Teagan taunted me with her potty mouth and yeah, I'd kind of lost it with her. Problem was, I had an even uglier temper, and Friday night, Teagan Connolly ignited it like no one had before.

When she slapped me and pressed her tight little body against mine, taunting me with that sharp tongue of hers, I'd never been so close to putting my hands on a woman in my life. Except instead of hurting her, I wanted to toss her sexy little ass on the hood of my car and take her right there, not caring who saw us. The urge to be inside her was like nothing I'd ever felt in my life, but before I had a chance to put my mouth on hers, my friend's dad grabbed me by the back of the neck and dragged me away from her.

Teagan had fucked me over big time and it bothered me that I wasn't angry with her. I mean, because of her little tantrum with the paint, I was thirty-five hundred in debt to my boss's mechanic who was holding my car until he received full payment. The worst thing was depending on other people to take me where I needed to be. I hated being in debt to anyone. I had enough of other people's debts to last me a lifetime.

Dammit, thinking about the consequences I knew I *would* suffer because of her hissy fit should have been enough to make me hate her guts. I wanted to, but there was just something about her that made hating her impossible.

Maybe it was the meaning inside that song; the one I heard her play the first time I saw her. Or maybe it was because she challenged me...

"...going to the quarry later?"

Ellie's voice trickled through my mind and I reluctantly turned my attention to her. "What?" I asked in a flat tone.

Ellie's green eyes narrowed as she placed her hands on her hips and glared up at me. "I asked you if you were going to the quarry later."

Shaking my head, I turned back towards the house. "Like I have a choice," I muttered before walking away.

2

NOAH

"You were lucky last night," my stepfather wheezed as he leaned over my shoulder. I was sitting at the kitchen table attempting to eat some breakfast before I joined the ranks of Jefferson High for my final year of high school. Ellie had already left with her friends and I'd be done and out the door a lot fucking quicker if her father backed the hell off and let me eat in peace.

"I won, didn't I?" I shot back before scooping another spoon of cereal up and popping it into my mouth. The oats tasted like cardboard against my tongue, but I knew I needed the nutrition.

"You were distracted," he corrected, pressing his hand down on my shoulder so hard I had to force myself not to flinch. "You can't afford to be distracted, Noah. Not when you're up against the likes of…"

"I wasn't distracted," I managed to grind out through clenched teeth, shaking his hand off. Shoving my chair back, I stood up and brought my bowl over to the sink. "I was fighting above my weight, and I won." I dumped my bowl into the sink and turned to face him. "End of discussion."

George was a short, stocky man in his late-sixties, but his receding gray hair and paunchy stomach didn't fool me. I knew exactly who I was dealing with, and it sure as hell wasn't your average senior citizen.

"Ellie told me you had another confrontation with the brat next-door," he grumbled and every muscle in my body locked up. "Keep her out of our business, Noah," he rasped before dropping a wrinkled brown envelope on the table. "Don't give me a reason to get involved."

I waited for him to leave the kitchen before pocketing the envelope.

TEAGAN

I woke up late for school with a headache from hell, a ponging taste in my mouth – you know the one you get when you've swallowed a spider in your sleep – and a serious case of the where-the-hell-am-I's.

I felt grimy from the unnaturally warm weather. My stomach was up in a heap and my freaking mind wouldn't slow down. I hoped these were first-day-of-school symptoms and not a personality trait I was developing because I was so not enjoying this anxious version of me.

Ugh.

The sound of my uncle's cringe-worthy singing voice boomed through my ears, causing me to shudder in shame.

At thirty-eight, my American-blooded uncle, Maximus Jones–aka Max – had two great loves in life. His work and his niece – me. We'd been together since I was fourteen and my parents were involved in an accident on the way home from a night out in the city. Uncle Max immediately resigned from his job in the states and made the move to the Emerald Isle to look after me when mom died and dad was charged with drunk-driving causing a fatality.

I'd only visited my father a handful of times since mom's funeral. The last time I'd visited Dad was back in May, the day before we left. He was still a broken mess, three years later, and that was about it. In some ways, I felt incredibly sorry for my father, but a huge chunk of me felt it was only fair he still suffered. After all, he was the one who decided to take the risk and drive under the influence. He was the one who'd taken my mother away from me. I couldn't get over that part and a four year prison sentence wouldn't bring my mom back.

But Uncle Max had been wonderful during that period of my life and had made the grieving period as easy as possible for me. He accepted a position in the A&E unit in Galway and took over the lease on my parents' house in Headford so I was able to attend the same school and be in familiar settings.

I always thought that was a pretty awesome thing to do for someone; to just get up and go when someone needed you. But Mom and Max had been incredibly close. Mom, being twelve years older, had practically raised Max until she married Dad and moved to Galway, so I figured looking out for her daughter was Max's way of taking care of his sister. They had two more brothers, Dixon and Moe, but neither mom nor Max had ever said much about them. Just that they were twins and lived somewhere in the states.

So yeah, Max was home. Home to watch my epic-fail of a first day at school.

Rolling out of bed, I stretched lazily before making my way to the bathroom for a shower. Scrubbing my skin until I felt raw, I then washed my hair before grabbing my toothbrush and squirting a healthy dollop of toothpaste on it. Yeah, it was a disgusting thing to do in the shower, and it wasn't something I made a *real* habit of doing, but I was short on time and I liked to improvise.

I dried off in record time before dressing in a pair of stone-washed denim shorts, a plain white t-shirt, and black chucks. Not bothering to blow-dry my hair, I towel dried it as best I could and let it hang loose down my back. The fresh air on my walk to school could dry it, not that I was bothered about it either way.

"Good morning, my favorite niece..." Uncle Max's voice trailed off the second I stepped into the kitchen and his gaze met mine. His pale green eyes narrowed as he scrutinized my appearance with one of his 'what the hell happened to you' looks.

"Don't start," I mumbled as I shuffled over to the fridge. "It's too damn early for niceties." The dark bags under my eyes were no doubt what had caught my uncle's attention.

"Have I missed something?" he asked, eyeing me suspiciously.

Adjusting the cufflinks on his shirt, Max straightened his tie, all while keeping his eyes locked on my face. "You didn't sneak out and go clubbing after I went to bed last night, did you?"

I snorted loudly and rolled my eyes as I slugged some orange juice from the carton. "No need to sneak out," I muttered in a sullen tone before placing the juice back in the fridge. "Not when the club comes to us."

Max frowned. "I'm not following you, Teegs."

"The noise-whores next door?" I stared meaningfully at my uncle.

He stared blankly back at me.

"Tell me you heard them last night?" The fact that they'd been up most of the night pumping music was the reason I was currently in sleep mode and late for my first day. "I can't stand them, Max," I added sullenly. "They're making my life hell."

"You need to stop the bickering with those kids," he mumbled before taking a sip of his coffee. "Stop looking for problems. You said it yourself, you have ten months left here and then you're going home."

"Your point?" I asked dryly.

"My point is get on with it. If the neighbors throw a party then pop some headphones on," he said briskly before running a hand through his brownish-gray hair. "Don't vandalize their cars with paint," he added with a chuckle.

I hissed out a breath and grabbed an apple from the fruit bowl. "Easy for you to say...ugh." I eyed my school bag like the devil it was before begrudgingly hoisting it onto my shoulder.

"I'm heading for my slaughter," I said with a dramatic sigh. "Wish me luck."

"You don't need it," he called out before adding, "I'm working a double shift at the hospital, so I doubt I'll be..."

"Home," I finished for him. He doubted he'd be home tonight.

Yep, that sounded about right.

I always used to like my car, my little three door, bright red Honda Civic, but I hadn't driven it since my fight with Noah last weekend. Max had replaced the windshield, but I was more concerned about my brakes, and the very strong chance Noah could've tampered with them. Maybe I was thinking the worst of him, but it was better to be safe than sorry, therefore my shoes were my current method of transportation.

Closing my front door, I popped my earphones in my ears, stashed my keys in my pocket, and switched my phone onto music mode before setting out on the route Uncle Max showed me.

Rounding the corner of my house, I pulled my straps tighter on my back and mentally fist-thumped along to Taylor Swift's *Shake it off* – a damn good song to listen to before starting at a new school.

One minute I was shaking it off with Taylor and the next I was being mauled by a bear.

A big, huge, brown bear that knocked me flat on my back and decided to maul me to death with his tongue. Guess I wasn't lightening on my feet. "Ouch."

Did bears lick?

Play dead, Teagan, play dead. Bears don't eat dead people.

"Oh my god, I'm so sorry," a soft feminine voice cried out seconds before the weight of the bear was removed from my chest.

Blinking a few times to clear my vision, I adjusted my eyes to the brightness of the sun above me before focusing on the curly haired woman kneeling over me.

"Bear," I managed to croak out. "Run."

The woman smiled and let out a small laugh. "No, not a bear, I promise. Just my dog, Ralph."

Well hell...I'd been sure it was a bear.

"Here, let me help you up," she added and her voice was deceptively soft and...southern? She didn't sound like the other neighbors; namely the evil duo next-door.

Dazed and confused, I grasped the hand of this stranger and staggered to my feet. "I thought he was a bear." I eyed the huge Newfoundland currently sniffing my shoes. "He's big enough to be one."

Now I was no Naomi Campbell myself, 5'5" thank you

very much, but the woman in front of me was tiny, so why in god's name did she feel the need to own a dog that reached her middle in height?

"He's truly very friendly," she said as her cheeks reddened from the effort of keeping a hold of *Ralph's* leash. Tucking a loose curl behind her ear, she stretched her hand out to me and smiled shyly.

My gaze locked on the scar distorting what would have been a truly beautiful face and my gut reaction was to touch my own cheek in reassurance.

She smiled knowingly at my discomfort. "I'm Lee Carter. Welcome to Thirteenth Street."

As in Mr. Carter's wife?

"Teagan Connelly," I mumbled, shaking her outstretched hand as I studied the little woman in front of me. How the hell was she the mother of those giants across the street?

"It's great to see number fifty-eight occupied again," Lee added. "It was such a shame when the Valentine's moved back to Idaho."

Her gaze darkened and my curiosity piqued. "Who?"

"Oh, the family who used to live there," she said with a blush. "Are you starting school today?"

"Yeah, first day as the new girl," I chuckled. "Should be fun."

"What grade?"

"Sixth year." She looked at me in confusion and I blushed. "Senior year," I amended. It was going to take me the whole bloody year to work out the difference in our way of saying things and by then I'd be on a flight back to Shannon. "Lucky me."

"My daughter Hope is in your grade, although you haven't met her yet," Lee said with a smile. "We just got back last night. We've been out of state visiting family for most of the summer."

"Oh cool, I... ah, met the rest of your family last weekend." Shifting awkwardly, I added, "I meant to stop by and thank Mr. Carter again for what he did. He kinda saved my butt with the next-door neighbors."

I wrinkled my nose in distaste and liked my new neighbor even more when she did the same.

"Ellie and Noah." Lee nodded wisely as if she felt my pain. "Hope and Ellie have been at each other's throats since freshman year," she mused. "Noah's different from her... troubled."

I raised my brows in distaste. "Oh, he's trouble alright."

"Mom."

A male voice bellowed and my attention immediately fell on the huge man-child walking down the Carter's driveway. "That douchebag fucked with the shower on purpose. The water's off and I'm cold, I'm wet, I'm fucking late for school and I'm covered in some pink shit that I can only describe as Hope's lip gloss."

Which Carter brother was he again? I could barely tell them apart.

"Did you ask him nicely?" Lee asked what appeared to be her son. Her son on *steroids*. Holy hell. What was in the water around here? Were all the guys in Boulder this... buff?

"*Yes*," the man-child – the seriously sculpted, half naked, wrapped-in-a-teeny-tiny-towel man-child – called back sarcastically. "But I'm afraid I don't speak horse."

Man-child's attention fell on me and he grinned unabashedly. "How's my Galway girl?" he purred with a wink and I immediately remembered which Carter boy I was looking at.

He was the slutty brother.

"Hey, Cameron," I said with a small wave as I mentally scolded myself for giving him that piece of information. I especially regretted it when he began to sing *Galway Girl* at the top of his voice, wrapped in a towel, in his driveway.

"This is bad," Lee muttered under her breath before glancing nervously at me. "Last time this happened I had to take Cam to the emergency room. Colton switched his body lotion with baby oil." Lee winced. "It was awful," she whispered. "He slipped and broke his nose on the side of the bathtub."

I struggled to keep a straight face when I nodded and said, "That must've been awkward."

"Tell me about it." Lee sighed heavily. "I could barely look the doctor in the face when I arrived back at the hospital less than two hours later with a different son. Cam broke Colt's nose in retaliation."

"Yeah," Cam snapped, suddenly serious again as he stalked over to where we were standing and took the bear/dog's leash out of his mother's hand, before pressing a kiss to her cheek.

"Glad you're home, Mom," he grumbled as he sauntered back towards his house with Ralph. "But here's a little warning, you're gonna be minus a son if he doesn't turn it back on."

Lee sighed wearily before shaking her head and following her son back to the house. "Oh, have a nice first day at school, honey," she called out.

I should have felt creeped out that Lee Carter was calling me *honey* having met me less than five minutes ago, but there was something about her. Warmth oozed from her and I found myself grinning like an idiot and waving back at her.

3

NOAH

Please, Noah, I know what you said last time you visited, but you can't do that.

You know what he'll do if that happens and I... I need this.

You can't abandon me like I'm nothing.

We made an agreement. Birthday or not...

You have to do this.

K x

Crumpling the sheet of paper that contained the plea *they* knew I would never ignore, I shoved it into my jeans pocket and inhaled a deep, calming breath, wishing like hell I could punch a hole through something. My head ached from the sheer concentration it had taken me to read the few short words on that scrap of paper.

Reading was hard for me, virtually fucking impossible, and *they* fucking knew it.

I watched a few of my fellow classmates as they chatted happily about school and prom and all that upcoming shit, but none of it moved me. Instead of feeling excited, I just felt hollow inside. I guess that was because deep down inside, I truly wasn't sure if I would survive until graduation.

A pile of books landed on my desk, stirring me from my reverie, followed by the sound of a chair scraping noisily against the lab tiles and then a contented sigh.

"You seem happy considering we're back in this shithole for another year," I stated dryly as I studied the satisfied expression on my friend's face. Personally, I had no clue how Tommy could be so chipper on a Monday morning, but that was just me. I'd never been chipper a day in my life.

Then again, Tommy was probably looking forward to finishing his final year of high school and moving on to greener and brighter pastures. I didn't have any kind of future ahead of me.

Aside from Low, Tommy Moyet was about as close as I had to a brother. He was well built now, but when I first moved to The Hill, he'd been an overgrown skeleton getting picked on left, right, and center by the assholes who roamed the school hallways. When I stood up for Tommy in gym class during sophomore year, when Jason Graham and Layton Brooks were tormenting him, Tommy had pledged his allegiance to me. He was about as loyal as they came.

"You will be, too," Tommy shot back, grinning like an idiot, "when you see the new transplant." He let out a whistle and sagged in his chair before running a hand through his short blonde hair.

"I'm telling you now, dude, she's mine. Don't even think about bagging her."

"Considering I haven't the slightest clue of who you're talking about, you have nothing to worry about," I replied drolly.

Tommy was always like this; competitive as hell when it came to girls. He was under some sick illusion that I gave two shits about who he fucked.

I didn't.

I had one focus and that was f...

"Everybody, this is Teagan Connolly."

No fucking way...

I froze the second Mr. Shaw said her name aloud and my eyes shot to the front of the classroom. I was sitting in the back row, but I had a clear view of her and... Jesus, she looked amazing today in shorts and a plain white tee.

I hadn't realized she was a senior.

"Teagan moved here in the summer from the west coast of Ireland," Mr. Shaw informed the class and, to her credit, Teagan didn't blush or get embarrassed at being introduced to the class. Instead, she looked mildly amused by the whole ordeal.

Then her eyes met mine and the atmosphere in the room changed.

Teagan's entire frame stiffened, her cheeks turned red, and her eyes narrowed on my face.

She gave me her best I-hate-your-guts look and I leaned back in my seat, cocked my head to one side, and told her to blow me with my eyes.

Teagan looked wholly pissed off as she chewed on her juicy bottom lip and, in a sick way, I was thrilled I could get that kind of reaction from her. I was glad that I unsettled her.

Because she sure as hell unsettled me...

For some strange reason, every time that girl put her

eyes on me, I felt... alive. Like someone attached spark plugs to my fucking body and lit me up. Jesus, I felt weird as hell when those hazel eyes were on me. It was probably the anger simmering between us that caused my whole body to go on high alert every time she was close by, but fuck; anger never felt so good.

"Keep her out of our business, Noah... don't give me a reason to get involved..."

George's words of warning drifted into my mind but right at this moment, I couldn't have cared less. Every fiber inside of my body demanded I let that girl get all up in my business.

"Let's make her feel at home," Mr. Shaw announced. "Teagan, you can take a seat in the front – yes, next to Layla."

Teagan didn't move.

She didn't take her eyes off my face and I seriously hoped she would because if she continued to look at me with those fucking amazing eyes, all pissy and cute, I was going to have to do something about it. George was right about one thing. Teagan *was* a brat. A sinfully sexy and audaciously sassy brat.

"That's her," Tommy hissed as he nudged me with his elbow. "Shit, that's her, dude, the transplant."

Teagan, noticing the douche beside me, snapped out of her trance, shook her head, and took her seat at the front of class.

"I have eyes," I snapped, shoving him back. I normally wasn't a possessive guy. I'd never cared enough about a female, and I didn't care about her, but I wanted him and every other guy to stop fucking looking at her like she was a buffet. No, I *needed* them to stop looking at her or I was going to flip the fuck out.

Tommy fell sideways off his chair and landed on the

floor. "You dick," he chuckled, rubbing his arm. "I'm sensitive."

I shook my head as I studied all six feet of the muscular, *sensitive* varsity receiver.

Of course, the class and Mr. Shaw turned around at the commotion.

She turned around in her seat and glanced at me again, causing the hairs on the back of my neck to stand.

Tommy rose to his feet and grinned. "Sorry, Mr. Shaw," he said with a smirk. "But I think I'm falling for her Irish charm already."

The class erupted into a mixture of giggles and wolf whistles, but Teagan didn't take her eyes off mine.

"Forget it, T," I told him as I kept her stare. "She's not for you."

TEAGAN

Okay, so I'd watched tons of movies set in American high schools and I'd read dozens of books, but none of those had prepared me for this... alternate universe.

Back home in Ireland where I came from, at the very most, four or five hundred students filled the classrooms of most secondary schools. But here? I'd never seen the likes of it. At least eighteen hundred students roamed the halls of Jefferson High.

Moving halfway across the world had certainly been a huge lesson in cultural differences. Three hours in and I begrudgingly had to admit that high school wasn't as bad as I had initially thought it would be.

Aside from that one uncomfortable class I'd shared with Noah, I had only received the odd stare here and there in the hallways. Most of the students were wrapped up in their own problems. I prayed it was only one class that Noah and I shared, because there was something about the guy that completely unnerved me. He was intense. The way his eyes burned into mine...

"Hey." A tall, bubbly brunette with a wild head of curls

stepped in front of me on my way out of History, distracting me from my thoughts, and I had to crane my neck up to see her face.

"I saw you talking with my mom this morning," she told me with a smile. "I meant to say hey then, but I was busy trying to drag Colton out of my closet."

She smiled, revealing a set of pearly white, straight teeth, and the clearest blue eyes I'd ever seen. "You're Teagan, right?" she asked as she shifted her books to her side.

"Yeah, and you're Hope?" It wasn't really a question. It was pretty obvious from the dark hair, blue eyes and dimples that she was a Carter.

God, they had some good genes.

"The one and only," she chuckled as she fell into step with me. "What's your next class?"

"I have P.E – gym class," I told her as we strolled out of the classroom. I removed my timetable from my pocket and handed it to her.

"Sweet," she said as she gazed down at the piece of paper. "Looks like we're in a few classes together. So, how's your first day going, Teagan?"

"So far it's been pretty uneventful," I told her drolly, blocking out the image of Noah staring at me with those intense brown eyes. My gaze fell on a group of girls who were staring at us as we walked past. "But ask me again at the end of the day."

"No doubt," Hope chuckled as we descended the staircase to the ground floor, and I had to step behind Hope at one point because the staircase was so jammed with other students.

"You made quite the impression on my brothers," Hope added as we made our way through the main hallway towards the exit. "Colton's particularly smitten. He practically talked my ear off on the way to school, rambling on about you."

"I bet seeing my ass helped sway their opinion," I replied dryly, remembering how close to naked I'd been when I met her brothers. I told Hope about the street fight last weekend and how I'd met her father and brothers. When I mentioned I'd met her uncle, Hope had glared silently ahead and I learned very quickly not to bring the uncle up in conversation again.

As we walked, Hope chattered animatedly about her summer vacation. And it was as easy as that. Hope Carter had clearly decided we were going to be friends and I, being friendless, had gratefully accepted.

While we walked, I had the distinct feeling we were being watched. "This is the *fishbowl* effect," Hope mused, nudging me softly. "Happens to every newbie. Don't sweat it," she smirked. "By the end of the day one of my brothers will have caused havoc and everyone's focus will be on them."

I didn't doubt her.

I barely knew the Carter triplets, but they seemed like colorful characters.

"Teagan, meet Ash." Hope grinned like a madwoman at the stunningly attractive African-American girl who bumped shoulders with her. "Ash, this is Teagan, she moved onto Thirteenth Street over the summer."

"Hey," we both greeted each other.

"So, Teagan, do you have a boyfriend?" Ash asked.

"I had," I told her. "Liam. We were together for three years. He's back home in Ireland. We called it off when we found out I was moving. It didn't make much sense to continue with it when the Atlantic Ocean separated us."

Blah, blah, blah. My words felt like something I'd rehearsed off a cereal box, because they weren't *my* words. They were Liam's... He was the one who'd made the decision. I was the one who'd made a holy show of myself when he informed me of said decision.

"Wow," Ash said softly. She looked genuinely dumbfounded as she led us into the changing rooms. "I thought Hope had it bad."

"What do you mean?" I asked as I unzipped my gear bag and swapped my chucks for my sketchers.

Hope blushed, which I found odd, as she tied the lace on her tennis shoes. "My boyfriend, Jordan," she said in a low tone as if it was some hushed up secret. "We've been together since... Well, since forever, but he moved away a few years ago." Her eyes lit up as she spoke. The girl was clearly smitten. "But he comes back here for me. He always has. And we've... Well, we've made it work."

Ash rolled her eyes and tossed a can of deodorant towards Hope. "What she *hasn't* told you, Teagan," Ash chuckled in a teasing voice. "Is that Jordan is refusing to *work it*."

"Work it?" I shook my head and stared at the two girls in front of me. "Help me out here."

Hope's face was beetroot red and Ash was unabashedly snickering.

"I hate you," Hope hissed.

"And I love you," Ash shot back before blowing a kiss. Turning to face me, Ash's brown eyes twinkled with mischief. "It means..."

"It means I'm a virgin," Hope said dryly as she slipped into her shorts and pulled her hair back in a ponytail.

"Not by choice," coughed Ash.

Hope rolled her eyes. "And Slutty Betty here thinks it's freaking hilarious."

"It's not hilarious," Ash shot back. "It's a crying shame. Have you looked at your boyfriend, like, *ever*?"

And it was during that harmless conversation, as I made my way down the steps towards the outdoor football field with Hope and Ash, that I came to the conclusion I could manage this.

High school was doable and I was even enjoying myself, sort of. That was until I tripped on the second to last step and crashed head first into a wall of muscle before bouncing backwards from the impact.

A pair of tattooed arms shot out and grabbed my shoulders, saving me from my second ass-landing of the day, and I could have groaned in despair when I saw who those arms belonged to.

"You just can't stay away, can you?" Noah smirked down at me. "And here I was thinking I'd have to thaw you out before we came to an arrangement..."

"There's not enough sunshine in the sky to do that, buddy," I shot back as I took a step backwards and desperately tried to ignore the way my skin prickled and heated from his touch.

Hope, who had been standing next to me, gestured towards the field. "I'm gonna go warm up, Teagan," she called out before jogging off with Ash.

Don't leave me with him, I mentally begged them.

I moved around Noah to follow after them, but he stepped in front of me and blocked my path.

I shook my head and went to go around him again, but Noah intercepted my move and blocked my path *again*.

"Move," I told him as I glared up at his stupid, smug face.

He was a good foot taller than me and I hated that he

was using his height as an intimidation tactic. He wasn't even kitted out for gym class, clad in dark jeans, boots, and a hoodie, so why the hell did bother coming down to the pitch?

"I noticed you had your windshield replaced," Noah said as he stepped towards me, forcing me to take a step back from him. I didn't like the way my heart fluttered and my pulse hammered in my fingertips.

That was not good.

Not good at all.

"What's your point, Messina?" I snapped as I stepped backwards. "Hang on..." My gaze locked on Noah's mouth. On what was inside his mouth. "Your tongue is pierced." I hadn't noticed that before now, but then again why would I?

"And?" he drawled, dragging out the word, as he stared down at me.

"And nothing." I shrugged uncomfortably and stepped back. "I didn't realize it before now. That's all."

"Are you sure that's all?" he chuckled, stepping forward.

I wasn't sure that was all. I wasn't sure of anything when he crowded me like this. My brain and my body were on two different picket lines when it came to him.

Noah stepped closer, invading my space, and I felt the fencing around the field against my back. "You kinda look like you want to touch it."

Resting one hand on the fence next to my face, Noah lowered his mouth to mine. His breath fanned my face when he spoke. "Do you, Teagan?" he whispered, brown eyes deep, delicious and locked on mine. "Do you want to touch me?"

Yes, yes, bloody hell yes...

"I wouldn't touch you with a ten-foot barge pole," I shot back, lying through my teeth, as my heart-rate soared.

Where the hell was the teacher?

Why wasn't someone stopping this big dick from attacking me?

And why did a huge chunk of me not want him to be stopped?

I was a seriously messed up seventeen-year-old.

"Just leave me alone, Noah," I breathed, eyes locked on his mouth, on those lips. "You heard the cops; keep your distance."

"I will," he replied, moving even closer to me so that his body was flush with mine. "When you pay me what you owe me." His eyes danced with humor and the way he lazily traced his finger on my bare arm had my body in flames. I shoved him hard in the chest. He didn't budge. *Damn he-man animal...*

"Have you thought of how you'd like to pay me back?" His lips were just shy of touching mine.

"I have actually," I breathed. "And it involves you kissing my ass."

Pulling back from my face Noah raised his brows and smirked. "You want me to do *what* to your ass?" The way he said it, loud enough for our classmates nearby to hear, was disgusting enough, but the sincerity in his voice when he spoke was just evil.

"Bastard." I was fairly certain all the blood in my body had rushed to my face and when Noah stepped closer, I swelled with rage. At least it felt like rage.

Holy hell, my body was on fire.

I was pulsing, actually throbbing *down there* and had to clench my thighs together to get some relief.

This was completely abnormal behavior on my vagina's part considering Liam had wasted numerous nights over the course of our relationship trying to get a response with his nimble fingers to no success.

Nothing. Nada. Nil.

But apparently all Noah Messina had to do was press against me and my vagina welcomed him like the prodigal prick.

I felt weirdly betrayed by my body.

"Don't be ashamed, Thorn," Noah purred before touching my butt cheek. "I can do all types of things to your ass."

I don't doubt it...

"Remove your hand from my ass," I warned him as I dropped my hand to his crotch and squeezed, not hard enough to hurt him, but enough to surprise him. "Or I'll remove your chances of fatherhood." My face flamed and I was the one who was surprised when I felt just how much of *him* was in my hand.

Noah must have heard the promise in my words, felt it in my touch, because he removed his hand from my ass and backed away slowly.

"You're not afraid of me, are you?" he mused softly as he studied my face.

"Should I be?" I heard myself asking, eyes locked on him.

Noah's brow creased and his tone was oddly serious when he said, "You need to walk away from me, Teagan. Before I get addicted."

What the hell?

"Before you get addicted to what, hurting me?" I shot back, truly having no idea what part of my body this bullshit was spewing from.

"Amongst other things," he replied quietly.

"I bet I can hurt you more." I had absolutely no idea why I said that or why I grinned evilly when Noah's face reddened, but my mouth seemed to be suffering from a serious case of verbal diarrhea. "And I've got plenty more paint, just in case the rest of your car needs a makeover."

Noah narrowed his eyes in challenge. "Don't say I didn't warn you, Thorn," he told me as he shot me a dark look that said *I'm not done with you – not by a long shot.*

I was used to having P.E with boys. My old school was co-ed, but one particular boy in my class made the hairs on the back of my neck stand on end.

The way Noah Messina stared at me, smirking maliciously whenever I caught him watching me, was shameless and utterly unsettling. And why was the teacher allowing him to smoke on the side-lines? If we were caught with a box of cigarettes in my old school, it meant immediate suspension.

What the hell was he doing in high school anyway? He looked like he belonged in a gym – or a prison cell...

Noah caught my eye and rubbed his thumb against his fingers, the universal gesture of money, before raising his brows expectantly at me.

Whatever...

Deciding to leave Noah to his broody staring, I gave him the middle finger before running off and joining Hope on the field.

Coach Johnson surprised me when he decided to play soccer and I, in turn, surprised him – and the majority of my class – when I kicked ass.

I grinned like an idiot when I lobbed the ball over Layton Brooks' head and took a shot at the goal. The center-back, Devon Lewis, handled the ball in the penalty box, and Coach blew his whistle, rewarding our team a penalty.

"You take it, Teagan," Layton Brooks panted as he patted my shoulder.

"It's in the bag," I shot back cockily. Layton grinned and shook his cute head before running backwards to join our team.

Positioning the ball, I took a few deep breaths before taking my shot. The football hit the crossbar before coming back out the pitch. I lunged forward and volleyed it. Coach blew the final whistle just as the ball hit the back of the net, courtesy of my foot.

Goal.

Oh yeah, I kick ass.

Our team erupted in cheers and out of the corner of my eye I noticed Noah standing on the sideline having what seemed to be a heated argument with someone that looked an awfully lot like Hope's brother, but I shook it off. I was having a moment and he wasn't included in my revelry.

"Where'd you learn to do that?" Layton asked as he jogged over to congratulate me. "That was fucking awesome. You're sure you're a girl, right?"

I placed my hands on my hips and inhaled deeply, emphasizing the fact that I had breasts and not a penis. I'd heard that particular question more times than I cared to remember because of my ability to kick a guy's butt on pretty much any sports field. *Sticks and stones...* "Last time I checked," I replied sarcastically.

"I didn't mean to offend you." He looked embarrassed. "I've never seen a girl play as well as you. Do all Irish girls play like you?"

"Where I'm from, sport is a pretty big deal," I told him as we walked back towards the dressing rooms. "Most of the girls in my area are involved in sports. There's not much else to do. I played basketball and soccer for my school back home, and then football and camogie for my local GAA club."

"GAA?" Layton looked confused as he handed me his water bottle.

"Yeah," I chuckled before taking a sip. "Have you ever played hurling?"

Again a frown. He wore his frown like a boss. *Cute...*"I brought a few hurleys – the stick you use to play," I told him. "And sliotars – that's the ball you use– with me from home. I can show you sometime if you want..."

A group of girls passed us then, snickering and whispering. "Tranny," one of them snickered.

I rolled my eyes in disgust. "There's a gaggle of geese in every school, right?"

Layton laughed. "Geese?"

I nodded solemnly. "A hissy tormenting group of lookalikes who huddle together in a group hoping to overpower and intimidate anyone weaker than them."

He grinned broadly, exposing a really cute gap in between his front teeth. "So, girls are geese?"

I nodded nonchalantly and shrugged. "Some girls are, sure."

"What are you then?" he asked in a husky voice, stepping closer to me, and I was pretty sure he was flirting with me. I decided I was happy for him to do this since he looked so damn good in his t-shirt that emphasized his complexion. "If you're not one of them?"

"I'm a lone wolf," I shot back with a smile.

"You're all right, Irish," Layton chuckled, his expression sobering quickly when Noah approached. "Lone wolf, meet the alpha," Layton muttered before jogging ahead of me. "I'll talk to you later, 'kay?"

I shrugged. "See ya."

"So, you like to play with balls," Noah said dryly as he stared down at me with his head tilted sideways.

I shook my head and folded my arms across my chest, glaring up at his stupid, beautiful face. "I'm actually a little disappointed with that one."

It was then that it dawned on me... No matter where I lived on this earth, one entity would always remain the same, and that was the stupidity of the pubescent male. It was a comfort, really, to know a dick was a dick no matter what school I went to or which town I lived in.

Shaking my head, I stepped around Noah and strode off in the direction of the changing rooms. "I thought you were more original. My mistake."

"Sweetheart, your mistake was getting involved with me in the first place," Noah called out after me.

"I'm not *involved* with you, *sweetheart*," I shouted back as I stalked inside the gym.

I barely had the words out of my mouth when I turned the corner and an achingly annoying voice drilled through my ears, causing me to look up and mentally groan.

"Ugh," Ellie sneered as she stood in the doorway of the girls changing room, blocking my way. "You're like the proverbial bad penny."

"Yeah, yeah, I keep popping up everywhere." I rolled my eyes and pushed past her and grabbed my bag from the bench.

Swinging around in anger, I marched back to Ellie and stood face to face with her, giving her my best bored expression. "If you're going to try and insult me, then at least have the ingenuity to use some original material." My words were dripping with sarcasm.

"Anorexic bitch," Ellie hissed and I held my hand to my chest.

"Ouch. That really hurt." I sighed and wiped a pretend tear from my eye. "How will I ever get over that one?"

"Stay out of my way, Teagan," Ellie said in an oddly serious voice as she stepped closer to me and out of earshot of her friends. "Stay on your side of the fence, stay away from *him,* and we won't have a problem."

With that she turned on her four inch hooker heels and stalked out of the changing room.

I didn't need to ask who *he* was, and she didn't need to warn me off. I wasn't interested.

I wasn't.

4

TEAGAN

Hope offered me a ride home from school, but I declined when I realized all three of her manchild brothers were traveling with her. They were nice boys, well, Logan was a nice boy, but accepting Hope's offer would involve sitting between Cameron and Colton and I'd had my fill of excitement for the day.

As I strolled down the sidewalk on my way home from school, my mind kept flicking back to the argument I'd witnessed between Noah and that guy on the field earlier in the day. I'd pushed it to the back of my mind at the time, but now I was obsessively going over it. The more I thought about it, the more certain I was that the guy Noah had been talking to was one of the Carter triplets. Which one, I had no clue because they all looked so alike, but he and Noah had looked so intense and this weird feeling kept tapping away in the back of my mind, like a warning.

"Hey, you."

A familiar voice called from behind me, and I swung around and grinned like an idiot when I realized it was the hot guy from gym class. "Hey, Layton," I said as I waited for him to catch up with me.

As he jogged towards me, I took a moment to appreciate just how good looking Layton Brooks was. He was incredibly beautiful for a man. I know that sounded strange, but it was true.

With his black hair shaved tight, his gentle golden-brown eyes, crystal clear skin, and full lips, I had to remember to swallow my spit and not drool on him. "Are you heading this way?" I asked when he reached my side.

"Yeah," he chuckled as he fell into step with me. "So, how was your day?" He nudged me gently as he spoke and I liked that, too. Yeah, he could do more of that. "Make some new friends yet?"

"What, besides you?" I shot back teasingly.

He grinned and my stomach flipped a little.

"I was a given," he chuckled before sliding my bag from my shoulder and placing it on his own shoulder. He winked at me and I was sold. It was official, I loved America. Why couldn't all men be like this one?

"Err, yeah," I mumbled, blinking out of my reverie. "Hope Carter and her friend Ash, do you know them?"

Layton nodded solemnly before bursting out laughing. "I should hope so," he chuckled. "I live with one of them."

I stopped and gaped at him.

"*Ashlynn* is my twin sister," he clarified.

"Well, damn," I mused before picking up my pace again. "It's a small world." Smiling, I added, "They're nice girls, and Hope's family is lovely."

"Yeah," Layton replied uncomfortably. "I still don't know how they can live there," he added before shuddering. "It freaks the hell out of me."

I narrowed my eyes. "What does?"

"That house," he whispered. "You know, because of the murders."

My feet stopped moving.

My heart stopped beating.

"What are you talking about?" I whispered.

Layton frowned. "I thought you knew... Shit," he mumbled before sighing heavily. "Brace yourself, Irish, you may need a whiskey after this."

NOAH

People say your teenage years are supposed to be some of the most memorable of your life.

Well, I didn't want memorable.

I wanted manageable.

Nine months.

Thirty-six weeks.

Two-hundred and fifty-six days.

Reading that letter this morning had severed what hope I'd secretly drummed up for my eighteenth birthday. I knew I had to keep going after reading her words. But I wouldn't do it forever. I'd spoken to Low. He had a plan.

Freedom was within my reach.

I could practically taste it.

All I had to do was be patient, and keep breathing.

Flexing my knuckles, I stared dispassionately at the man swaying in front of me with blood rushing from his face and forced myself to swallow the bile that was rising in my throat. I kept my eyes locked on my opponent's face, not daring to look away, focusing on my target before extracting the final blow.

He dropped to the ground, eyes closed and body jerking. I closed my eyes and swallowed my groan of disgust.
Two-hundred and fifty-six days until I'm free...

TEAGAN

"Thanks a bunch, Uncle Max!" I screamed the minute I stalked through the front door. I knew he was home because his stupid car was in the driveway. Thought he was supposed to be working the double shift? *Oh well, it was on like Donkey Kong.*

Stalking through the hallway, I marched into the kitchen, leaned over the table, and glared at his rapidly receding hairline until he looked up from his newspaper.

Layton was right. I did need a whiskey. I needed several of them.

"For what?" Max asked as he folded his paper and stood up.

"For moving us slap bang into the middle of the Texas chainsaw massacre," I hissed, disgust filling my tone.

Max rolled his eyes and moved towards the sink to wash his mug. "We're in Colorado, Teagan, not Texas."

"Did you know a girl was murdered in the house across the street?" I demanded. "And a man died of suspicious circumstances after *raping* someone in there?" It sounded worse when I said it like that, and I felt like vomiting.

The image of Lee's face flooded my mind and I flinched. "Mrs. Carter looks like someone took a freaking hacksaw to her face."

"Yes, I knew all those things, Teagan," Max replied and that kind of threw me. The tense set of his shoulders and the defensive tone in his voice also confused the hell out of me.

"You knew," I huffed haughtily as I planted my hands on my hips. "So, you knew about all that crap and still moved us here?"

"It's a great location," he replied tightly. "All of that happened over twenty years ago and *none* of it was Kyle or Lee's fault."

"I really think you're missing the point here, Uncle Max," I moaned. "The fact of the matter is *two* human beings died across the road from us in vicious circumstances." I raised my hands in despair. "Haven't you ever watched the Poltergeist?"

He stared back blankly.

"Ugh, forget it." I pressed my fingers to my temples. "I'm going to my room. Which room did you unpack the holy water in?"

"Teagan, stop it," Max told me as he walked over to me and placed his hands on my shoulders. "You know better than to judge people by the actions of others."

"I'm not judging the Carters. I know they're good people," I told him honestly. "I'm just judging how likely we are to have paranormal activity in our neighborhood."

"Oh, for the love of god," Max grumbled and pinched his nose. "The only paranormal activity going on around here is in your imagination."

"Mocking is catching, Max," I told him in a petulant tone. "And another thing, could you please talk to..."

The sound of our front door opening and then slamming shut caused my words to stick in my throat and I did what any ghost-fearing person would do. I covered my face with my hands and froze.

"Teagan?"

Oh god, it knows my name...

"Teagan, I was wondering if I could borrow your trig... Oh hey, Teagan's uncle."

"Call me Max."

He speaks to dead people?

"*Nice* shirt, Max. My dad has that in blue."

Moving my hand away from my face, I let out a sigh of relief to see Hope looking at me peculiarly. "Oh, thank god it's you," I breathed as I clutched her arm in relief. "I thought you were a ghost."

"You're a really weird girl," she mused as she stared at me. "You know that, right?"

I nodded and sighed heavily. "It's an issue I'm dealing with."

5

TEAGAN

"God, I'm starving," Hope grumbled as she carried her lunch tray over to an empty table.

I was coming to the end of my second week as the new girl and getting into the swing of things. I now understood that under no circumstances should I *ever* use the girl's bathroom on the second floor. I still shuddered thinking about who I saw in that cubicle.

Block it out, Teegs...

Repress the image of his hairy ass...

The cafeteria was packed full of students and I followed Hope, taking special care not to drop my tray as I maneuvered between groups of students.

"I could eat a cow." Stopping at the circular table in the center of the cafeteria, Hope pulled out a chair and sat down. "Well, half of one anyway," she said dryly as she removed the plastic covering her beef sandwich.

"How lovely for you," Ash grumbled as she joined us. "I really needed to know that."

From where we were sitting, I could see the same group of girls who'd called me a tranny. This time I could see their leader, and wasn't in the slightest bit surprised to see Ellie Dennis sitting in the center of the gaggle. They were pointing and snickering as animatedly as they had in gym class, and I had a minute of silence for my sex.

"Is there something going on between you and Noah Messina?" Ash asked before taking a sip from her carton of apple juice. "He's been staring at you since you walked into the cafeteria." She chewed a piece of her sandwich and swallowed before casting a fleeting glance behind her shoulder.

"Nothing besides the mutual hatred we share for each other," I grumbled as I my eyes wandered around the cafeteria, reluctantly seeking him out.

My eyes found Noah over by the window and, as if he could feel my eyes on him, Noah looked up from where he was texting and winked at me.

"I think he's hot for you," Ash said with a smirk. "He's been watching you like a starving man watches the cooking channel."

I snorted in disgust. "A man starved for cash more like."

Ash and Hope stared blankly at me and I found myself saying, "He wants money. When he broke my windshield fighting, I kind of retaliated by tossing some paint on his car."

Hope's eyes widened. "You forgot to mention that part," she breathed. "His Lexus – you're the one who ruined his baby?"

I shrugged innocently before adding, "And then I broke his iPad when I poured a bottle of water over his sister's head." I swallowed a bite of my apple and took a swig of water before adding, "Now he wants compensation for the damage. He's an asshole," I growled and then I mouthed the word again slowly so Noah knew I meant him, before itching my nose with my middle finger.

Noah's eyes narrowed and he shook his head as if warning me not to push him further.

Of course I pushed him further, and I did it by taking my car keys out of my pocket and rattling them next to my face before raising my middle finger. I couldn't stop myself from antagonizing him. The thrill was addictive.

"He's *dangerous*," Ash corrected in a no nonsense tone of voice as she leaned forward and swiped a napkin from my tray. "I believe the word you're looking for is dangerous."

"Yeah, well, I can be dangerous, too," I replied as I continued to watch Noah watch me. He wasn't just dangerous... He was treacherous. I tried to ignore the weird tingly sensation that coursed through my body when Noah stared at me, but I just ended up getting more pissed with him because the feelings he evoked inside of me were entirely inexorable. "If Noah or Ellie think I'm going to roll over and let them bully me, then they need to think again."

His brown eyes were locked on my face, his expression intense, and I swear I could feel my body temperature rising from one single glance.

Leaning forward, Hope reached for my hand, pulling me out of the trance I was in. Squeezing it tightly, her blue eyes burned with sincerity when she said, "He's not the kind of boy you should pick fights with, Teagan, and I mean that in the kindest way. He's friends with my brothers, and he's always been polite to me, but there's just something..." Hope paused and let out a sharp breath. "Noah Messina is all kinds of dark and dangerous, wrapped in the body of a sex god."

"Isn't that always the case?" grumbled Ash. Sighing heavily, she added, "Hot boys are mean. Nice boys are gay. The good ones are taken..." She trailed off before casting a fleeting glance around the room. "Every time I look around at the male student-body in this school, I consider becoming a lesbian."

"Give me strength," Hope muttered as she rolled her eyes in despair. "Look, Teagan, babe, from what I've heard, he's the kind of guy who gets off on taking your v-card and then revels in your despair."

"Who said anything about sex?" I grumbled as fierce heat coursed through me. "All I'm trying to do is defend myself, and besides," I shrugged. "I'm not attracted to him." *Liar, liar, pants on fire...*

Ash smiled knowingly at me. "When you're dealing with Noah Messina, it's always about sex."

"So be careful," Hope added quietly. "He's broken more hearts than you've had hot dinners."

My eyes locked on Noah's once more. He smirked, and a cold tremor of unease crept up my spine.

NOAH

Sometimes I wondered if Lee Carter regretted her kids ever meeting me, because I spent most of my time in their home, helping Low and his triplet brothers, Cameron and Colton, raid the fridge and make a general mess of things.

As per usual, the four of us were pigging out in their living room, playing Xbox and wasting away another Friday evening.

"Is it still on later?" Low asked in a quiet tone, eyes locked on my face.

I nodded, not wanting to say much in front of his brothers. I got along well with all of the Carter's, but Low was the one I trusted explicitly. He'd never given me a reason not to even though trusting people didn't come easy to me. Before moving to Thirteenth Street, I'd never stayed in one place long enough to make friends or feel grounded. My father's job had entailed a lot traveling and moving around. It wasn't until my dad died and we moved to The Hill that I discovered what a real family was, because it sure as hell wasn't the one I lived with.

When Ellie's father, George, signed me up as a member

of the gym in the Henderson Hotel when I was fifteen years old, it was one of the few great things he'd done for me.

Of course, he had his own agenda for wanting me groomed and primed, but I didn't care about his reasons. Joining that gym led me to meet the owner's family, who for all intents and purposes had become the family I never had. George had unintentionally given me a lifeline that three years later I still clung to.

"It is what it is, Low," I said calmly as I met his stare head on.

I was sitting on the couch between Cam and Colt, watching them as they beat the shit out of each other in a wrestling game. Across from me, sitting on an armchair, was a pissed looking Logan. I knew why he was mad, and *he* knew there wasn't a damn thing I could do to change it.

I didn't have a choice.

"What *it is*, is bullshit, Noah," Low hissed and I couldn't have agreed more with him.

It *was* bullshit.

My whole life was one complicated concoction of bullshit.

"Boys, will you please take your feet off the table," Lee Carter said with a heavy sigh as she puttered into the living room with an obvious look of dismay on her face. "I just polished in here."

I dropped my feet to the floor and earned a megawatt smile from Lee.

"Thank you, Noah," Lee praised before shooing both Cam's feet and Colt's off the coffee table. "If only the rest of you were as obliging." She tried to keep her expression stern, but failed miserably and ended up smiling lovingly at her children.

"*Thank you, Noah,*" Colton mocked in a feminine tone as he tapped on his Xbox controller.

"*Good boy, Noah,*" Cameron snorted.

Colton waited until his mother left the room before asking me, "So what's going on between Ellie and Teagan?" as he tapped furiously on his controller, eyes locked on the huge flat screen television in front of us. "My sources tell me your sister's got some major beef with blondie across the street."

"Your *sources*," Cam snorted as he leaned forward, concentrating on the game in hand. "Why don't you just say your sister, dude?"

Colt, ignoring Cam's comment, continued his lecture. "She was spreading some nasty rumors today."

"Do I look like Ellie's keeper?" I muttered, even though an abnormal amount of anger bubbled inside of me at the thought of those bitches at school whispering about Teagan. The girl pissed me off worse than anyone else, but that didn't mean I wanted to see her get bullied.

"That's true. She told Amy that Teagan has an eating disorder," Cam grumbled, brows furrowed "And a lot more besides that."

My gut twisted. *Fucking Ellie...* "And you guys are telling me this because?"

"Teagan's all right, Noah," Colt said in a serious tone he rarely used. "She doesn't deserve to be Ellie's next victim."

No, she didn't deserve to be Ellie's next victim.

"You bagged her during the summer, didn't you?" Cam accused. "Ellie only targets the girls you've been with."

"No, I didn't fucking *bag* her," I spat, anger bubbling inside me.

"It would explain why she annihilated your car, dude,"

Colt offered. "There's no worse wrath than a woman scorned and all that..."

"I didn't bag her," I snapped. "Whatever's going on between Teagan and Ellie has nothing to do with me."

"Whatever. *Denial* is a river in Egypt, dude," Cam said with a shrug. "Either you bagged Teagan, or you wanna bag her. There's no other probable explanation for Ellie's jealous behavior."

"I don't have time for this crap," I grumbled, checking my watch as I climbed to my feet. I cast a meaningful glance at Logan. "I'm late for work."

Logan let out a heavy sigh and shook his head sadly. "I'll give you a ride."

"Thanks, man," I replied gratefully when we reached the front door and were out of earshot of his family.

"Doesn't mean I agree with this, Noah," he muttered under his breath. "I don't and I never will."

Low was the one person on this planet who knew what I'd been wrangled into, and he stood by me regardless of the danger a guy like me presented. Our friendship meant a hell of a lot to me, and I fucking hated when he looked at me with disappointment in his gray eyes.

It caused the helpless feeling inside of me to skyrocket.

The entrance leading to the Hub was crammed with cars, bikes, and trucks by the time I made it up there – an hour later than requested thanks to Cam and Colt's stupid fucking conversation.

Hidden from roadside view, several miles down the secluded dirt road leading to the old abandoned quarry, the Hub was the hangout of the immoral and undesirable and was based in an old quarry warehouse set in the mountains that had closed down in the early seventies.

Because of Teagan's tantrum, I was still without a ride and had to rely on Logan. I fucking hated that he was here and had to see this side of my life, and that caused my anger with Teagan for screwing my ride to intensify.

"You should go, Low," I told him, still mentally cursing Teagan as I walked around to the back of the building. "I can find another way home."

"Yeah, that's not happening," Low replied in a dry tone as he followed me inside the back entrance. "The only way I'm leaving this place is with you in the passenger seat."

Every time I found myself back in this dump, which seemed to be more and more frequently these days, something my old boxing coach once told me always reverberated in my mind. *"Keep your eye on the donut, Messina,"* Chancy had rasped out, cigarette hanging out of his mouth as he watched a ten year old version of me getting an ass kicking in the ring. *"And not the hole."*

At ten years old, I hadn't realized how big an impact Chancy's advice would be on my future. But now, with my eighteenth birthday around the corner, I recited those words like a Christian would the bible.

The make-shift bar was bursting at the seams with patrons when we stepped inside. Women were stripping on tables, men were fisting themselves as they watched, and I had to swallow my own vomit as I walked through the crowd with my best friend flanking me, my head held high, and my focus on the donut.

6

TEAGAN

I had always been a fitness fanatic. Nothing to do with losing weight, I just really enjoyed exercising. Working out kept my body supple and my mind content. At least that's how I looked on the outside and felt on the inside.

I'd been a member of the local gym back home in Galway, but since moving to The Hill I'd been lacking in motivation. That had all changed because of Hope – and her sex-god dad.

Yesterday during lunch, when I asked Hope about good gyms in the area she'd texted her dad and within two minutes, I'd been offered a lifetime membership with the gym in his hotel.

Free of charge.

Of course I had accepted and thanked the hell out of her before asking if she wanted to go work out with me on the weekend. Hope had then proceeded to kindly tell me no, not happening. Never, ever.

Apparently Hope didn't *do* exercise and the only thing

that could make her run was the threat of Colton farting near her face.

The second I had walked through the doors of the Henderson Hotel in downtown Boulder, I'd been impressed and a little intimidated.

I hadn't realized the Carter's were rich people. For one, they lived in a middle-class type home, and two, they were about as posh as a rubber boot. But yeah, I would never judge a book by its cover again.

My workout knocked the tension out of my body and by the time I finished, I was feeling like a boss right up until I walked into the parking lot only to find I had not one, but *four* flat tires.

Bizarre coincidence?

I think not.

The knife marks in my tires had Ellie and Noah's stench all over them and I wanted to be the bigger person and walk away, I really did, but my inner child won the battle against my common sense, resulting in a brawl to beat all brawls breaking out the second I made it home... Or at least that's what I had in mind as I made my way home to Thirteenth Street.

I marched straight up the neighbor's porch steps and hammered on their front door. "Get your ass out here right now, you knife-wielding lunatic," I shouted through the letterbox before continuing my door pounding. "I mean it," I screamed, red faced. "I'm not joking around... Whoa...."

The door swung inwards and I barreled into a chest of wet muscle.

"Knife-wielding lunatic?" Noah raised his brow in amusement. "Is that your new pet name for me?"

What the hell had happened to him? One side of his

sculpted stomach was horribly discolored and I momentarily froze, struck dumb as I stared at him.

Was he bruised? Yep.

Did it make him hotter? Yep.

Did I still hate him? Decisively.

Stepping outside to the porch, Noah closed the space between our bodies, towering over me with a cocky expression etched all over his face. "What do I owe the pleasure?"

"Tell your sister she owes me for a set of tires," I informed him in a tight voice as I took a step backwards and regained some personal space. "I'm not taking this shit from either of you anymore."

"*Step*-sister, and what exactly are you accusing us of, Teagan?" Noah asked dryly, tightening his grip on his towel with one hand.

"Oh, I'm not accusing you guys of anything," I shot back, furious. "I'm *telling* you that your sister deliberately sabotaged my car." I kept eye contact with him and folded my arms across my chest. "Or are you the dick who goes around slashing girls' tires?"

Surprise etched his features for a brief moment before the shutters closed. He gazed dispassionately at me for a long time before speaking. "You're a very hypocritical person, Thorn," he said in a tight voice. "You know that, right? Coming over here and tossing around slanderous accusations based on a flat tire?"

"*Four* tires." I balled my hands into fists and urged myself to calm down and not start a brawl with the half-naked sex god standing in front of me. "One of you slashed the tires on my car," I hissed through clenched teeth.

Lowering his face to mine, Noah stared into my eyes. "Prove it," he said with a smirk.

NOAH

"This isn't over, Noah," Teagan hissed as she reached a hand up and tugged on my hair hard and I wasn't sure if I wanted to throttle her or throw her over my shoulder and take her upstairs.

First, she marched her stuck-up ass up my steps and accused me of slashing her tires – something I had not, did not, and would never do – and then she pulled on my hair like a goddamn toddler.

"I'm not taking yours or Ellie's crap anymore," Teagan snarled, chest heaving, her hazel eyes narrowed on mine. "I don't need proof. I *know* it was one of you."

My crap? I hadn't done a damn thing to her. Girl was paranoid as fuck. "Take your hands off me, Thorn," I warned her.

I had no idea what happened to her tires, but what I did know was I was going to lose what was left of my patience if she didn't back the hell up. I was tired, my ribs were aching from last night, and miss prim shouting the odds in my face was something I could do without.

Hot or not, I didn't need this crap from her or anyone else.

Teagan didn't let go. Instead she tugged harder, forcing me to lower my face to hers. "Don't threaten me, you tattooed junkie," she snarled. "I could have you arrested for vandalism to property."

Rage coursed through me as I covered the fist Teagan had knotted in my hair with my own before twisting our bodies around and backing her up against my front door.

"One, I didn't touch your precious car," I told her, getting right in her face. I was so close to her, my nose brushed against hers, but it wasn't lust I was feeling. It was disgust. "And two, don't ever call me a junkie, you judgmental little bitch."

Teagan let go of my hair, her eyes widened in what looked like fear, and I immediately felt like a tool for cussing her out, but then she did something that reminded me of why I wanted to throttle her.

She looked up at me, defiance blazing in her eyes and hissed, "Junkie," into my face before stepping around me and stalking off.

TEAGAN

After my altercation with Noah, I stayed at home brooding for the rest of the day. A tiny part of me worried that I may have wronged Noah, but then images of his step-sister's face infiltrated my mind and I quickly flicked that worry and guilt away. And I wasn't sorry for calling him a junkie, either. The guy was covered in tats, smoked like a chimney, and fought like a ninja on steroids. He had to be smoking something. Or maybe he was right and I was, in fact, a judgmental bitch.

I drove myself crazy all evening thinking about the douche and, thankfully, when Uncle Max left for work Saturday evening, Hope stopped by.

Hope hung out with me for the evening and even cooked us dinner, which consisted of two huge bowls of mac and cheese, before working on some trig homework together. It was after nine when she went home and after showering and dressing into my pajamas, my only plans for the rest of my Saturday night involved chilling on the couch and watching Netflix while doing my very best to eat my weight in chocolate and *not* think about the boy next door.

However, the second I flicked on the television, it became abundantly clear that my plans had been thwarted by the ear splitting rave happening next door.

And that bitch had the cheek to call me *a headache...*

The walls separating our houses were vibrating from the sheer volume of music playing in the adjoining house. The picture hanging over our mantel piece, the one of my mom, actually rattled from the power of the bass. And the worst damn part was they had no taste in music.

I secretly hoped Ellie was the one in charge of the music, because whatever slither of Noah that was still attractive, personality excluded, in my eyes would wither and *die* if I discovered he was the one who had chosen to play *Man, I Feel Like a Woman.*

Grabbing the house phone off the coffee table, I dialed my uncle's cell phone number and waited impatiently for him to pick up. He'd better have some pretty good calming remedies stashed in the house or some top shelf liquor, because I was so not putting up with this crap.

Uncle Max's phone rang three times before going to voicemail. *Great. Lovely. Love you, too, asshat.*

Hanging up without leaving a message, I stood and paced the lounge as I mentally tried to rein in my emotions. Every fiber of my body demanded I go next door and confront them, have it out once and for all. *But what good would it do?* That was my rational side talking, the superior part of my mind I hated listening to because it was usually right.

Checking the time on my watch, I realized it was just after eleven. I would give it an hour, I decided. If they were still making noise after midnight, then I would give myself full permission to go next door and kick some ass.

I hated to admit it, but I was feeling lonely and bitter.

And weirdly enough, the majority of the bitterness festering inside of me wasn't because of the party next door, it was because *I* was sitting here while there was a party going on next door. *His* party.

Liam.

That's it, I could talk to Liam. Distract myself from the debauchery happening next door.

Whether Liam and I were together or not anymore was irrelevant. The facts were, I'd spent three years of my life as his girlfriend. He was the first boy I'd ever loved, the first and only boy to stick his tongue down my throat – in the back row of the cinema when we were thirteen – and the first and only boy to put his penis in my mouth. Granted it was a one time occurrence and he dumped me straight after, but still...

Opening my laptop, I decided to log onto Facebook to message Liam. Facebook was a lot like a fake tan; time consuming, completely pointless, and utterly addictive. It was the lair of a few billion elite 'socialites' who preferred to conceal their real lives with perfectly concocted propagandas. I still used it, you know, because I had no willpower, and I still used fake tan because I was Irish. I guess I wasn't much of a rebel after all.

To: Liam Harte
From: Teagan Connolly
Message: So... I know we agreed not to do the long distance relationship thing, but that doesn't mean we can't be friends, right? How's school? Please say you're awake and can talk. P.S what time is it back home?

The second I pressed the send button I had an attack of second thoughts. When I'd told Liam I was moving to America, the night Uncle Max dropped the bombshell on me, Liam had made it clear that he wasn't interested in having a long-distance relationship. But when we didn't break up straight away, and continued seeing each other, I'd thought... I wasn't sure what I'd thought. But if I'd have known the outcome, I wouldn't have done what I did with him.

Maybe I should let it be? The night we broke up was not a pretty one, with plenty of tears – on my behalf – and almost five months had passed since then.

My inbox pinged causing my stomach to erupt with butterflies.

To: Teagan Connolly
From: Liam Harte
Message: It's 05.30 in the morning. I can talk for a while. School's school. Got a nice American fella yet?

Wow. Okay, so he was in a pissy mood. Well, at least he'd messaged me back. Cracking my knuckles, I began to write back.

To: Liam Harte
From: Teagan Connolly
Message: Don't be a dick, Liam. You're the one who decided to end things. It's not my fault I'm here and you're there. I'm suffering, too. L

I held my breath until my inbox pinged and then I dived into the message.

To: Teagan Connolly
From: Liam Harte

Message: I'm sorry, Teegs, for everything. The way I left things... It was a shitty thing to do to you. I know I hurt you and I know you may not believe me when I tell you that hurting you was something I **never** wanted to do.

Liam's words of apology didn't quite erase the rejection I still felt because of the way he'd treated me – and the horrible feeling I had that he'd used me – but they helped. Another message pinged while I was replying to his first one.

To: Teagan Connolly
From: Liam Harte
Message: I can't be your fella anymore, Teagan, but I can be your friend. Tell me about school and your neighborhood. Have you joined a gym yet, or a soccer team?

Comfort flooded through me, making me feel a little less lonely.

To: Liam Harte
From: Teagan Connolly
Message: School is okay, and I made a couple of friends. The Hill isn't so bad, but my next door neighbors are awful. There's this girl Ellie, and she hates my guts. God only knows why. But her stepbrother Noah is worse. He thinks he's so tough. I mean he's eighteen, but the guy is covered in tattoos, Liam. And he smokes and gets into fights...

And that's how I fell asleep, curled up on the couch, messaging my ex-boyfriend about the boy next door.

NOAH

I was going to lose my shit over the girl next door.

It was Saturday night and I was still brooding over her antics this morning. Who the hell did she think she was? No, scratch that, who did she think *I* was? Some junked up asshole who would slash her tires? It pissed me off something fierce to think she held that low an opinion of me.

Teagan Connolly was getting under my skin like a goddamn itch that needed to be scratched and no amount of alcohol seemed to be able to force the image of her face from my mind.

Dammit.

Our house was crammed with people from school, courtesy of Ellie and her impulsive nature, and my brain was like a broken record, replaying this morning's events until I was thrumming with pent-up frustration.

"You're awfully quiet tonight," Ellie mused as she sidled up to my side. "What's up?"

"Did you slash Teagan's tires?" I straight out asked her.

Ellie's face was a mask of innocence for a moment

before a sly smile crept over her lips. "Has someone been telling tales?"

Teagan was right – she'd been dead on the fucking money.

Folding my arms across my chest, I glared down at her, feeling furious. "Why the hell would you do that to her?"

"Why the hell would *you* care what I do to her?" Ellie shot back, her glare mutinous, as she copied my movements and folded her arms over her chest. "In case you've forgotten, she wrecked your car, Noah."

"I haven't forgotten," I snapped. "And I care, Ellie, because she's under the illusion that I'm somehow responsible."

"Well, maybe that's for the best," Ellie sniped before disappearing into the crowd of people, leaving me fuming.

The sooner this school year was over, the better. I didn't think I could stand much more of this bullshit.

"Dance with me, Noah," Reese Tanner, Ellie's cousin and bff, slurred as she rubbed herself against my body.

Her red hair was loose and flowing freely over her barely concealed breasts, nice breasts I remembered, and the sparkly, black little number she was wearing hugged her curves enough to rouse my interest.

"I don't dance, Reese," I told her as I stood in front of the bay window looking out onto the street. I was not in the mood to deal with clingers. And I knew Reese was a clinger. She was a nice girl, unbelievable with her tongue, but had been like a permanent marker to get rid of the last time. "Walk away, sweetheart," I told her. The fact that Reese worked part-time in reception at Low's dad's hotel made it especially hard to avoid her since I used the gym at least four times a week.

"I'm sure you can make an exception," she purred, dropping her hand to my belt buckle. Her fingers slipped under the waistband of my jeans and she tugged me closer. "For me."

I gazed down at the stunning redhead and found myself weighing my options. Stand around brooding over the girl next door who hated my guts and treated me like I was the fucking pariah of Colorado, or get my dick sucked.

Dropping my mouth to hers, I pressed a soft kiss to her lips. "My room," I murmured, pushing everything else to the back of my mind. "Now."

I led Reese up to my room and, after locking my door, I walked over to the shelf that held my stereo and switched it on. Anything to drown out Ellie's shitty taste in music.

Good Charlotte's *Little Things* bellowed through my ears and I felt some of the tension zap away.

Tugging my shirt off, I dropped it on my bedroom floor before turning around, pleased to see Reese already naked and spread eagle on my bed.

"This is a one-time thing, Reese," I told her as I climbed up and leaned over her. "No strings."

She nodded enthusiastically, wrapping her arms around my neck. "No strings, Noah," she agreed with a breathy moan, adding, "I know the rules," before pulling my face to hers.

7

TEAGAN

"So, you've made it through almost two whole months of high school," Hope teased Monday evening after school as she sat on my kitchen counter, swinging her legs back and forth and helping herself to my Ben and Jerry's. "How do you feel?"

"Accomplished," I chuckled as I grabbed a spoon from the drawer and took a scoop of ice-cream before Hope cleaned out the entire tub.

In the short time I'd known Hope, I had to admit her appetite impressed the hell out of me. I'd never met another girl who could put food away like I could and not gain weight. Well, she was luckier than me in the shape department, being that she actually had one. Hope had killer curves, whereas I had hipbones – not that it bothered me too much. I was happy in my skin, skinny or not.

"Well, you should," Hope said with a grin as she hopped down from the counter and handed me the ice-cream. Taking a hair tie from her wrist, she pulled her hair back and tied it in a loose ponytail. "And hey, Colt already got himself suspended for exposing himself to the girls' swim team, which totally takes the limelight off you."

"What the hell was he thinking?" I asked through fits of laughter as I thought about Hope's baby brother being dragged out of the pool hall by Coach Johnson on Wednesday.

"He's Colton," Hope grumbled as she grabbed two cans of coke from the fridge and followed me out to the garden. "He doesn't think, period."

The weather had been fiercely warm all day, so Hope and I had made plans to laze around in the garden after school and hopefully catch some sun. "We don't get enough days like this," Hope mused as she rolled the legs of her jeans up to her knees before sprawling out on the grass. "I'm gonna miss this."

"What, lazing on the grass?" I asked as I lay beside her and slid my sunglasses on.

"The sun," she replied sadly. "Winter's drawing in which means jackets, hats, and scarves. I mean, Halloween is tomorrow."

"I can't wait for winter." I sighed in contentment. "I've never seen snow before."

"You'll see plenty of it here." Hope chuckled. "Oh yeah, I meant to tell you earlier..." Hope yawned loudly and folded her arms behind her head. "I overheard Logan and Noah talking last night."

My ears perked up immediately. Things had been quiet on the western front since my altercation with Noah over the tires. He hadn't looked in my direction since that day and that suited me just fine. I didn't care. I *didn't*.

"Noah told Logan that Ellie's throwing a party tonight for his birthday," she said with a lazy sigh.

"Don't they have parents to wrangle them into line?" I

asked in disgust. "It's Monday for Christ's sake. Who throws a house party on a Monday night?"

"Apparently, Ellie does." Hope sighed heavily. "And Noah invited my brothers to it."

"Isn't he a little old to be hanging with your brothers?" I tossed out airily, desperately trying to keep my voice level even though the mere sound of his name caused my body to coil tight. "They're juniors, right? Shouldn't Noah have some friends his own age?"

"Noah's closer to their age than mine," Hope informed me in a sleepy tone.

"How's that?"

"Dad suffered premature empty-nest syndrome the year I was supposed to start kindergarten," she told me in an amused tone. "He held me back; therefore I'll be nineteen before I graduate high school."

I turned my face to stare at her. "I've heard of mothers getting it, but fathers?"

Hope smirked. "What can I say about my dad," she mused. "He's an unusual guy."

"That he is." *And incredibly hot...*

"Anyway," she continued. "My brothers turned seventeen in early September, and Noah turned eighteen today, October thirtieth– the same month as my mom, who, by the way, is on a flight to New York with Dad."

"A belated birthday present?"

Hope nodded. "Apparently, Dad couldn't take time off work until this week, which means I'm stuck on my own with Dumb, Dumber, and Dumbest until December."

"Until December?" I shook my head. "That long?"

"Yeah," Hope mumbled. "I know they're up to something else," she muttered. "I overheard them talking about letters and release dates, but they're so damn secretive it's impossible to figure out." She let out a weary sigh. "I swear my parents live in their own personal little bubble. They're so wrapped up in one another it's sick."

"It's rare," I mused.

"So, anyway... Technically there's less than a year between Noah and my brothers."

"Where's his mother?" I surprised myself by asking.

"Whose?" Hope mumbled.

"Noah's. She's married to Ellie's dad, right? Well, I've had the misfortune of meeting Mr. Dennis, but I've never even laid eyes on Noah's mom. Where is she?"

"That's a very good question, Teagan," Hope muttered without providing any more information.

We lay silently after that, basking in the heat of the sun, and enjoying the peace and quiet. The sound of a door banging next door and raised voices burst our serene little bubble.

"...Get out of my face, Ellie, I'm not talking about this right now..."

My ears pricked up at the sound of Noah's deep voice and I sat up.

Resting my weight on one elbow, I nudged Hope with the other, but she didn't stir. She was breathing slowly and I realized she was asleep.

"Since when did you grow a conscience, Noah?"

"What makes you think I've grown a conscience?"

"The Noah I knew wouldn't take shit lying down..."

"I'm not lying down..."

"Hope?" I hissed. "Wake up. They're fighting."

"Go away, Cam," Hope mumbled as she rolled onto her stomach and tucked her face into her arms.

"Then when?" I heard Ellie demand and I lay back down

quickly, hoping they wouldn't notice me eavesdropping on their conversation.

Noah didn't answer her. Well, let me rephrase that to 'Noah didn't verbally answer her, but the sound of a punching bag being decimated was proof enough that the conversation was over for him'.

"If you don't then I will, Noah."

A door slammed again and then all I was left with was the sound of a punching bag being pulverized and some very masculine grunting noises.

Thoughts of Noah that I really didn't want to have while I was sprawled half naked with sweat trickling between my breasts plagued me.

I tried to push him out of my mind but he wouldn't fuck off. The more he punched that bag, the more I squirmed.

Dammit, I couldn't cut a break.

NOAH

I was regretting ever looking out my kitchen window.

I had been trying to keep my distance from the girl next door, but the view of her sprawled out on her garden lawn – with those killer fucking legs and that mane of unruly blonde hair – from my kitchen window was too much to ignore.

I couldn't cut a break...

"Looking good, birthday boy." Ellie's painfully irritating voice filled my ears, and I closed my eyes, willing myself to be calm.

"Thanks," I told her. Today was my eighteenth birthday and so far, it had been nothing short of a disaster. I screwed up on a biology test this morning because I had to work last night instead of studying. I'd been refused visitation at the hospital this afternoon and to top it off, Cameron Carter had shown an abnormal amount of interest in my after school activities during lunch. Worrying about that hot-headed idiot was something I could do without.

"So, I invited Reese, Abby, Pam, and Kate over tonight to celebrate – oh and Jason, of course."

"Of course," I mimicked, rolling my eyes in disgust.

Jason Graham was Ellie's latest string-along. He devoted himself entirely to her every need and demand and she, in return, fucked him on a regular basis. That was the only way I could explain their relationship because it sure as hell wasn't a monogamous one.

"Who have you invited, Noah?" she asked, placing her hand on my arm.

"Cam, Colt, and Low," I replied in a frustrated tone, brushing her hand off as I turned to look at her. I was fucking frustrated because I didn't want to talk to Ellie. I wanted to stare at Teagan and Ellie was preventing me from doing so.

"And Teagan and Hope?" Ellie asked in a sarcastic tone. "Did you invite them, too, or were you just planning on staring at them the entire evening?"

Busted.

"What are you talking about?" I grumbled as I stepped around her and made my way to the back door. *Shit, I hadn't even noticed Hope out there...*

"I'm talking about *you*, Noah," Ellie hissed as she followed me into the back yard. "And your twisted fascination with *her*," she grumbled. "It's been over a month and you're still without a ride because of that bitch. She's trouble for us. I can feel it..."

"Get out of my face, Ellie," I snapped as I stalked down the garden towards the plastic roofed, make-shift gym I'd built when we first moved here. "I'm not talking about this right now," I told her.

Unfortunately, Ellie followed me. "Since when did you grow a conscience, Noah?"

Grabbing a roll of tape off the bench, I quickly taped my

knuckles, all while ignoring a fuming looking Ellie. "What makes you think I've grown a conscience?"

"The Noah I knew wouldn't take her shit lying down..."

"I'm not lying down," I spat.

"Then when?" she demanded. "When are you going to make her pay?"

I didn't answer Ellie's question – I couldn't. Instead, I pummeled my fists against the punching bag, letting off some steam and letting her know this conversation was over for me.

"If you don't, then I will, Noah," Ellie warned me, and a flash of concern for the girl next door rushed through me.

TEAGAN

I slept badly last night, waking up around four in the morning with a crick in my neck from sleeping on the couch. Even though I went upstairs to bed and tried to get some shut eye, I became so restless that I ended up getting up and showering at five am.

Out of boredom, I had taken more care than I usually would in my appearance; straightening my ash-blonde hair so it fell artfully down my back and applying full make up before dressing in a sleeveless white chemise, black skinny jeans, and my chucks. By the time I was dressed and fed, I still had about an hour to spare before I had to leave for school, so I decided to sit on my porch and have a bash off Martin.

I played quietly, aware that I wasn't in a *swamp*, allowing my fingers to glide over the strings as I played an acoustic version of Florence and the Machine's *Kiss with a Fist*.

As I played, my mind drifted to the Facebook message I'd received from one of the girl's in my class back home.

She'd let it slip that Liam was seeing Katie Horgan now –

had been since the week I left. Three years together and he'd gotten over me in less than a week.

Well, fuck him.

Throwing my head back, I closed my eyes and allowed myself to become engrossed in the song I was playing, letting the music flood me, drowning out the pain of Liam's fickle love and his stupid penis.

A male voice boomed from nearby and I screamed, literally *screamed* at the top of my lungs. Jumping to my feet, I wielded Martin as a weapon. Swinging around, I locked eyes on the creeper who'd frightened me.

"You." Narrowing my eyes, I lowered my guitar and let out a shaky breath. "You nearly gave me a heart attack."

Noah smirked from where he was sitting on his porch before taking a sip from his mug. "You seem attached to that thing." He inclined his head towards Martin. "Good to know." The way he said it was menacing and I immediately stiffened.

"Don't even think about doing anything to Martin," I hissed. "I will hurt you if you so much as look at him crooked."

"Martin?" Noah snorted. "You do realize it's a guitar, right? Just a piece of wood with a hole in it."

"To you, maybe," I snapped as I placed Martin back in his case and closed the lid before tucking it against the wall of my porch. "To me it's a vessel."

"You're a strange type of girl," he said dryly.

"And *you* are a noisy-assed neighbor," I shot back angrily. "Belated birthday wishes and all, but other people have to live on this street, too."

"You could hear them last night?" he asked, and the way he said it bothered the hell out of me.

"Yes, I could hear *you* partying to your heart's content," I informed him. "I also heard the latest figures on the number of smokers dying of lung disease." I stared meaningfully at his cigarette. "It's not good news, I'm afraid."

"You're not what I expected," Noah mused as he got to his feet and made his way down his porch steps.

There was no wall separating our front yards. He tipped the remainder of what was in his mug onto the grass between our driveways and then took a long drag of his cigarette before flicking the butt onto my side of the yard.

I rolled my eyes and stalked down my porch steps towards him. "And what did you expect?" I asked haughtily as I picked up his cigarette butt, quenched it and then threw it back at him. Unfortunately, the breeze went against me, and the cigarette butt landed on my side of the driveway.

Noah laughed and I muttered a curse under my breath before chasing after it.

"Not you," Noah replied as he exhaled heavily. "I didn't expect you."

"You're acting stranger than usual," I told him as I marched back to where he was standing. "No sarcastic comments or crushing insults this morning?"

"Not yet," he replied as he stared at me, like *really* stared at me.

Hooking my fingers in the pocket of Noah's jeans, I stuffed his cigarette butt inside before wiping my hands on his black t-shirt. "Don't drop your shit in my yard," I said sweetly. I rested my hands on my hips and glared up at his stupid face. He was staring at me in such a way, I was beginning to get freaked out. "What are you up to?"

No reply, just more staring...

"Stop looking at me like that, Noah, I mean it," I snapped.

"I think I like looking at you," he finally replied with a sigh.

He sounded reluctant. How sweet.

You think? "Since when?" I asked, my tone a mix of annoyance and disbelief.

"Since now," he rasped before snaking his arm out and grabbing the back of my neck. His lips crashed against mine and I was momentarily lost in a burst of emotions and feelings.

A fierce blast of pleasure coursed through me, followed by a demanding pulsing in my groin. My body went pliant in his arms, clearly lost to sensation. The second his tongue invaded my mouth, I came crashing back to earth with a bang. Out of the pure shock of feeling Noah Messina's tongue down my throat, I did what any girl would do in my situation.

I bit down.

Hard.

"Fuck." Jerking away from me, Noah proceeded to dab his tongue with his thumb. "What the hell, Teagan?"

"It's your fault," I shot back, but the fight went out of me when I noticed the blood on his thumb. "Oh, my god," I mumbled. "You're bleeding."

"You're sharp," he snapped before wiping his mouth with the back of his hand and glaring at me.

"You better hope you've got a strong stomach."

"Why?" I asked warily.

Noah smirked. "My tongue bar." He opened his mouth and stuck out his tongue. "You must've swallowed it." Shrugging, he added, "Hope it doesn't pierce anything important."

"I'm going to die," I cried before clutching my throat. Coughing as hard as I could, I attempted to spit it out all while Noah laughed his ass off.

"It's not funny," I spluttered between coughs as I jumped up and paced the ground. "I could have internal bleeding. I could sever my bowel. Any number of things could happen to me."

"Calm down," he taunted. "Moving around could jostle it and cause it to *sever*..."

"Shut up!" I screamed before kicking his mug that had fallen to the ground during his assault of my mouth at him. "This was your plan all along, wasn't it?" I demanded as tears filled my eyes. "To get me back for damaging your car by murdering me."

Noah laughed and I wailed.

"Death from a kiss," I sobbed.

"Don't worry," Noah taunted. "I'll give you the kiss of life."

"You've done enough," I spat. "You verbally attack me with that *thing* on a regular basis, but that's not enough for you, is it... Oh no, since now I'm going to choke to death because you feel the need to put jewelry on it."

"Teagan, calm down."

"I hope it falls off," I hissed before groaning. "Mortally wounded by a piece of metal that's touched another girl's genitals...." My stomach heaved. "I'm gonna be sick."

"Teagan, you are not going to die." Grabbing my shoulders with his hands, Noah held me still, moving his face from side to side until he caught my eye. "You're not dying, okay?" he said in a noticeably softer tone as he rubbed my arms with his surprisingly warm hands. "You didn't swallow it."

I felt myself calming slightly and it became easier to breathe. "I didn't?"

He shook his head slowly, eyes locked on mine before opening his mouth to reveal the evil silver ball, pride of place in the middle of his tongue.

"You asshole," I said with a gasp. "I almost had a heart-attack."

"Revenge is sweet," he chuckled, still grinning at me. "Happy Halloween, Thorn."

"Yeah," I spat before lifting my knee and ramming it into Noah's crotch. "You too, ass bandit."

"You crazy bitch," he hissed as he dropped to his knees and groaned in agony.

"I hope it falls off," I roared again as I stalked back to my house. "And I don't mean your tongue."

NOAH

I was in a shitty mood by the time I made it to school. My lips were tingling and my tongue was throbbing.

What the hell had I been thinking by kissing that little fruitcake? She named her guitar *Martin* and talked to it like it was her favorite child for Christ's sakes.

You kissed that little fruitcake because she's the first person to set you on fire and make you feel something other than numbness.

Shaking my head, I tried to force all thoughts of Teagan out of my mind as I walked through the student parking lot, but the sight of her red Civic made it impossible.

My stomach sank when I saw who was standing beside Teagan's car, and it sank even further when I recognized what that someone was holding.

Oh shit...

8

TEAGAN

I was seriously regretting kneeing Noah Messina in the balls this morning – not the biting his tongue part because *that* he had most definitely deserved - but I'd gone too far. Thankfully, I hadn't seen him all day, but I knew my good luck wouldn't last forever. I felt on edge. He'd messed with my head by kissing me.

What the hell had that been about?

And why the hell had I enjoyed it?

My last class before break was dismissed early so I bought my lunch, sat at our usual table and waited for Hope and Ash to join me. The cafeteria filled quickly – and noisily – and I played with my apple while I waited for the girls, rolling it between my hands absentmindedly.

I found myself looking up when the chattering around me seemed to die away. Countless pairs of eyes were watching me, whispering and pointing at where I was sitting.

It didn't take a genius to guess someone was standing behind me, but I didn't bother turning. Instead, I continued rolling my apple around aimlessly, purposefully ignoring the hushed whispers and stares.

Someone cleared their throat behind me and then I felt an electric surge penetrate my shoulder when someone touched it.

Leaning over my shoulder so close I could feel his stomach against my back, he whispered in my ear, "Teagan, can I have a word outside?"

Noah's fingers lingered on my bare shoulder and I jerked away, the feel of his skin on mine too personal, before forcing myself to turn and face him. "There's nothing to talk about, Noah," I told him stiffly. "I shouldn't have kicked you. I know that. Move on."

Noah exhaled impatiently and his minty breath blew into my face. "Just come outside, will you?" he snapped before running his hand through his hair. "I need to show you something – explain something."

I wasn't going anywhere with him.

God only knew what trick he had up his sleeve. I had wrecked his car, his iPad, and his prospects of fatherhood. The guy was out to get me.

I could see Hope watching me from the cafeteria line, along with the rest of the room, and I didn't want to make a scene. "Not a chance," I replied slowly. "So go away and leave me alone."

"Fine," Noah spat before straightening up to his full height. "Fucking suit yourself." With that, he spun around and stalked out of the cafeteria.

"Hey, Teagan, how's it going?" Jason Graham, an arrogant blond douche from my English class, said seconds before sliding into the chair opposite me.

I didn't like this guy.

There was something incredibly off about him. Of course, my immediate dislike for him may have stemmed from the fact that I'd spent a huge chunk of the summer having to endure watching him suck Ellie's face off. He was all up in Ellie Dennis's space, which made him no friend of mine.

"What were you and Messina talking about?"

I stared back at him and gave him my best why-are-you-talking-to-me-we're-not-friends look.

"Looked pretty intense?" Jason added, clearly not getting my drift.

"It was," I responded dryly. "We were trying to decide which position to have sex in tonight."

"You and Messina were talking about sex?" Jason's eyes widened and I rolled my eyes at his sheer stupidity. "Are you..." his voice trailed off and he looked around the room before looking back at me. "Are you serious?"

"Uh-huh," I added sarcastically. "Noah says I won't get pregnant if we have sex standing up. I told him that wasn't true. What do you think?"

"I think you're too good for him and every other douche in this school," Colton Carter added with a chuckle as he slid into the seat beside me before winking devilishly, his blue eyes dancing with mischief. "Hey, beautiful."

"Hey, Colt," I said in an amused tone. I'd quickly learned in the short time I'd been in Colorado that Hope's brother was an incorrigible flirt.

For a junior in high school, Colton had an impressive way with the ladies. Along with the fact that he was drop dead gorgeous, as were his brothers, Colton had a way of making you feel like you were the only girl in his world. Thankfully I could see through his charm, thus making me immune to such lethal personality traits.

"Back off, Colt," Hope added, shooting her brother a warning look as she and her brother Cameron joined us.

"Jason Graham," Cam sneered as he flashed Jason a dangerous looking smile. "What the fuck do you want?"

I snickered and Jason's face paled.

Hope smiled sweetly at Jason's red face. "Seriously," she said with a grin. "What do you want?"

"I was talking to Teagan," Jason, clearly finding his balls, growled, glaring at the Carter siblings.

"Yeah," Colt chuckled, nudging my arm. "About Messina's dick."

"Screw you, Carter," Jason snarled, jerking out of his seat, red faced and fuming.

"No thanks, dude, I like pussy," Colt shot back with a teaspoon in his mouth as he tore the cover off his yogurt.

"Ugh. Christ, Colt, I'm trying to eat here," Cameron groaned before tossing a French fry at his brother. Colt caught it mid-air with his mouth and chewed with relish.

"What's up with him?" Ash, who'd just joined our table, asked, pointing at Jason as he stalked out of the cafeteria.

"It's his time of the month," Colt mumbled before putting a spoonful of yogurt into his mouth and groaning in pleasure. "Mmm," he purred. "This is the first half decent thing I've eaten since yesterday."

"Are you dieting, Colton?" Ash teased.

"More like protecting the lining of his stomach," Cam scoffed before explaining, "Mom cooked us a casserole before she and dad left for Vegas – and she put four more in the freezer."

All three Carter siblings shuddered.

"Poor Logan," Hope mused. "He needs to learn..."

"Excuse me."

A tall, curvaceous red-head stood at our table looking

obnoxiously smug. I immediately recognized her from Ellie's gaggle of geese. I think her name was Rice or Reese or something like that.

"Yes?" I responded in a tone as equally condescending as she'd used.

"You own the red car in the parking lot, right?"

"I'm sure there's more than just one red car parked outside, but yes," I replied drolly, knowing full well she knew exactly what car I drove.

"You may want to look *on* your car." She narrowed her eyes and smirked spitefully at me. "Looks like someone really did a number on it."

Dropping the spoon I was using to stir my coffee with, I shoved my chair back and stood up.

"And you wouldn't happen to know who that someone is, would you?" I snarled as I stormed past her towards the door, not waiting to hear her answer. *Goddammit, I'd only replaced the tires. What the hell had they done now?*

I knew the Carters and Ash were following me – I could hear them calling my name – and probably half the school, but I didn't care. A really bad feeling had settled in the pit of my stomach and I broke into a run when I reached the front door of the school, stumbling down the steps in my rush to get to the parking lot.

When I reached the back of my car, I was out of breath and panting. My car looked fine, the same as it usually did. I checked the back tires before walking around to check on the front ones.

Something on the hood of my car caught my eye and I glanced upwards. When I realized what was lying there, strings burst, wooden body smashed to pieces, a scream ripped from my throat.

"Shit," I heard someone say from behind me.

"Teagan," Hope said as she slipped her arm around me. I shrugged her off. I did not want to be touched or consoled right now.

Martin... My guitar, the last thing my mother had ever given me... All I had left of my mother... Destroyed. Smashed into pieces.

Anger fused through my body. I swear I could feel my heart cracking into pieces. This was so unfair.

All I had left of her...

I didn't need Rice or Reese or whatever the hell her name was to tell me who did this. I already knew.

I left Martin on the porch this morning.
I forgot to bring him inside.

"Son of a bitch," I screamed before grabbing what was left of my broken guitar and turning around, glaring at the crowd of students who were standing around watching me. I didn't care about any of their faces. I only cared about finding one, and when I found it, my lip curled up menacingly.

"Are you proud of yourself?" I demanded as I stalked towards where Noah was leaning against a car with his arms folded.

He didn't look proud.

He didn't look anything really.

He stared emotionlessly as I came towards him with my trashed guitar.

"You're jumping to conclusions, Teagan," Noah said coolly, about two seconds before I smashed my broken guitar over his head.

Well, I had aimed for his head but he was a lot taller than me, so I connected with his shoulder instead. Out of the corner of my eye, I spotted Ellie and her friends standing a few feet to the side of us.

"Goddammit, Teagan, calm down," Noah snarled as he jerked to his feet and grabbed me by my arms. "Stop it."

"You're a cruel, heartless bastard," I screamed, tears pooling in my eyes, as I shoved free from his hold and lunged for him.

"And you're a hypocritical little bitch who jumps to conclusions," Noah roared, chest heaving, clearly livid, as he glared down at me. "You automatically assume *I* did this."

"You're a foregone conclusion, asshole," I hissed as I scratched and slapped every part of him I could reach.

Someone grabbed me from behind and lifted me away from Noah, kicking and screaming. I realized that someone was Colton when he whispered, "Calm down, Beautiful," in my ear.

I tried to break free from Colt but quickly gave up when I realized his arms were like bands of steel around my body. All of a sudden, I felt so defeated that the fight went out of me and then I did something I really hated doing.

I cried.

I heard Colt sigh heavily before turning me and wrapping his arms around me.

Hope, who was standing nearby, stepped forward and picked up what was left of Martin before turning to Noah. "Did you do this to Teagan's guitar, Noah?" she asked him in a level tone.

"No, Hope. To put the record straight, I didn't do it," he snarled as he wiped blood from his cheek – where I'd scratched him, I realized. Noah looked over Hope's head and stared directly into my eyes. "But I wish like hell I had."

TEAGAN

I ended up with a week's worth of detention for my outburst in the parking lot – which I thought was pure crap considering Noah wasn't even reprimanded for his part. Apparently, broken guitars didn't constitute a good enough motive to attack a fellow pupil; regardless of how much sentimental value they had.

The principal had even gone as far as calling Uncle Max into school for a meeting about my *behavioral issues*, so along with a week's detention, I was also grounded and car-less.

I'd tried to explain to Max the reason why I reacted the way I did, but *apparently* I was too old to throw *tantrums* and until I could get my violent urges under control, I could walk my ass to school and back.

On top of all that, I was currently trending on most social media platforms. One of Ellie's disciples had recorded the whole damn thing and uploaded it to the internet. So yeah, between the damn online video and rumors raging about me at school, my day had gone from bad to disastrous.

Hope texted me after Uncle Max left for work, inviting me over for dinner, but I lied and told her I'd already eaten. Within minutes I felt like a horrible human being and decided to bite the bullet, and break my grounding.

There's no such thing as ghosts.
There's no such thing as ghosts.
There's no such thing as ghosts.

That was my mantra as I stood outside Hope's red-bricked house with my finger on the doorbell.

No one answered so I rang it again and again, and then I let my mind wander, completely psyching myself out.

It was Halloween night, pitch black outside, and I hated the dark, truly detested it, so when the front door opened inwards after ten minutes of constant knocking, and I was greeted by baby Carter, I bolted inside without a second thought for the ghosts – or an invitation.

"Come on in," Logan chuckled as he closed the door behind me.

I swung around to apologize to him for my lack of manners, but quickly turned my head again when I saw he was dressed only in a pair of gray sweatpants – which, by the way, totally complimented his gray eyes.

What the hell was it with these boys?

"You're half naked," I told him, and my voice sounded oddly accusatory. "And your eyes are gray."

"To be fair, I was in the shower when you started banging on my door," Logan replied dryly as he shrugged the t-shirt I hadn't realized he was holding over his head. "And I really don't know what to tell you about the whole eye color thing," he added softly. "I guess you can blame my mom?"

"Sorry," I replied lamely. "I'm not a fan of the dark. It makes me jittery."

"That's all right," Logan replied calmly as he gestured to me to follow him. "Everyone's afraid of something."

"Is Hope here?" I followed him into their kitchen, glancing around nervously.

"Nope," Logan mumbled as he rummaged in the fridge and handed me a can of coke. "She went to the hotel for dinner with Cam and Colt."

"Thanks." I took the coke from Logan and followed him back through the hallway towards the lounge. I knew that's where we were heading because the outlay of this house was exactly the same as my house. "Do you think she'll be much longer?" I asked as I stepped through the doorway, freezing to the spot when my eyes landed on...

"What are *you* doing here?" I demanded at the same time as him.

"First, you're on my street," Noah growled, dropping the Xbox controller he was holding onto the coffee table before climbing to his feet and stalking towards me. He folded his arms across his chest as he glowered down at my face.

The black wife-beater he wore was sewn to his ripped chest, and he looked entirely too sexy in the gray sweatpants that were hanging low enough on his hips. *I could see his man V – his very sexy man V...* "Then you're in my school, and now you're in my fucking friend's house."

The muscles in Noah's tattooed covered biceps rippled as he glared at me. "Are you intentionally trying to get under my skin, Teagan?"

"Sorry for breathing, asshole," I snapped, feeling wounded by his words, but unwilling to let him know that. "But you don't own the whole damn world, Noah. It's a free country."

"Where's my money?" Noah demanded, getting in my personal space. He had a nasty red scratch on his cheek, because of me, and I momentarily felt a smidgen of remorse until his words registered with me.

"The same place it was earlier," I snarled as I reached up and flicked his forehead. "In your imagination."

Logan, oblivious to the blistering tension between me and Noah, strolled over to the couch and picked up an Xbox controller before taking a seat. "You're both welcome in this house," he stated calmly. "So play nice, children."

I narrowed my eyes at baby Carter. "I wouldn't play with him if the whole of mankind depended on it."

Noah laughed darkly. "No, because you prefer to play with paint, don't you?" He smirked. "I gotta tell you, Thorn, you're a fucking terrible artist."

"Maybe I should try using a different canvas, ass-muncher," I shot back through clenched teeth. "Your face, perhaps?"

"Try it," Noah hissed, stepping so close to me our shoes touched. "I dare you."

Of course, I went one step closer and pressed my chest to his. "You're not worth the price of the paint."

"Goddammit," Logan muttered before pausing the game he'd been playing. "What the hell is with you two?"

"He broke my guitar," I spat.

"No. No, I *didn't*," Noah roared.

"And he slashed my tires," I hissed.

Noah's race turned purple. "Jesus Christ, how many times..." Noah cursed and ran a hand roughly through his hair. "I didn't slash your fucking tires."

"All right, I really don't care," Logan grumbled as he got up and stalked into the hallway. "Take your domestic issues to your own side of the street," he added as he glared at the big ape next to me. "Now, Noah."

Nodding stiffly, Noah made a low rumbling noise in his

throat before grabbing my elbow and pulling me out of the Carter's house.

"Get off me," I spat as I tried to free myself from his grasp. Noah wasn't hurting me, but he wasn't being gentle either. And I was burning mad. He seemed to bring the worst out of me.

"You're not happy with ruining my car," Noah snarled as he dragged me down the driveway, releasing me roughly when we reached the road. "You wanna ruin the one fucking friendship I have that's worth a damn."

"Awh," I mocked as I rubbed my arm, spitting daggers at the guy in front of me as I walked backwards in the direction of my house. "Poor big, bad Noah, should I get my violin out while you cry me a river?"

Noah stalked towards me, backing me up against something incredibly cold and hard.

"Don't come any closer," I warned him, but my voice was shaking.

"Or what?" he snarled as he leaned closer, pressing me onto what I now realized was the hood of my car. "What are you gonna do to stop me?" He pressed against me roughly. "Come on, tough girl," he hissed. "Stop me."

"I'll bite you," I panted, as I lay on the flat of my back, trapped under the weight of Noah's body as he pushed his legs between mine. His hands were on either side of my face, his mouth was less than an inch from mine, and if anyone saw us they would think we were having sex. Our bodies were touching in all the right places, and we were both breathing hard.

"Then fucking do it, Teagan," he roared. "I dare you."

Never one to back down from a challenge, and with the current streak of violence coursing through my body, I lifted my face to his, and then I bit him.

I was aiming for his nose, but caught his chin instead. His stubbly chin.

Baring my teeth, I locked onto his face like a piranha. Noah snarled and tried to pull away from me, but I didn't let go. Instead, I moved with him and ended up kneeling on the bumper of my car with my legs spread, Noah's body glued to mine, his hands wrapped around my throat, and my mouth attached to his chin.

"Let go," he snarled.

"...ake...ee..." I hissed back, jaws locked around his chin. I knew how it looked, I knew just how crazy I was being, but still, I couldn't stop.

Noah growled, literally growled like an animal, and I truly thought he was going to physically hurt me, but then he did something completely unexpected.

He dropped his hands to my butt and lifted me.

Instinctively, I wrapped my legs around his waist, and then we were moving.

Noah moved with such speed, the air left my lungs when my back hit the front door of my house. Then he did something only one boy had done before. Noah pushed his hand between our bodies and slid his hand into my underwear.

Then he was cupping me, all of me, eyes locked on mine, dark and dangerous, and I felt...oh god, I felt...

My eyes fluttered when he slipped two fingers inside me as he slowly pulled his chin out of my mouth before replacing it with his tongue. I sighed into his mouth and my arms wrapped around his neck of their own accord.

He was kissing me.

Noah Messina was...Ouch.

Motherfucker.

"If you ever bite me again," Noah snarled as he stood me

on my feet and backed away, eyes fiery and full of... Hate? Passion? I couldn't tell. "I'll do more than just put my fingers inside you."

I could do nothing but stare blankly and touch my throbbing lip with my fingers.

9

TEAGAN

School was torture for the next month. Most of the school ogled me and whispered about the parking lot incident. I ignored their stares as best I could, managing to keep my head down and, surprisingly, my mouth shut.

I couldn't count the number of times I had a phone shoved in my face over the past few weeks – the video of me whacking Noah with a guitar was a huge hit. One guy even had the balls to ask me for an autograph. Apparently, half the school had labeled me a badass for taking on the infamous Noah Messina and the other half had labeled me batshit crazy. To be fair, I was probably a bit of both.

Loner personified was my latest coping technique and the only person I felt comfortable being around anymore was Hope, who had been a noble friend by not mentioning any of my prior satanic antics.

But the memory of Noah on Halloween night caused my body to break out in a hot, muggy sweat. Weeks later and I was still reeling. He'd kissed me and then destroyed my guitar before putting his fingers inside my body.

"I'll do more than just put my fingers inside you..."

I felt like I was splitting in half because when I thought of Noah, my brain raised huge, giant, enormous red flags, but my body... My body was all kinds of slutty when it came to thoughts of Noah.

I managed to stay out of trouble for the next month, that was until I walked outside for gym class, minus Hope, who faked a headache to get out of class, and caught sight of someone who made my blood boil and my heart race.

Noah was standing at the edge of the field with a string of girls swarming him. He looked like his usual annoying self, showing off his tattoos in a gray sleeveless shirt, his muscular legs on display in a pair of gym shorts, and the wolf tattoo on his leg looked fiercer than ever.

Noah was giving one particular brunette his undivided attention as he stretched his arms over his head and smiled down at her.

Jealousy flowed through me and I balked.

What the hell was I feeling?

I wasn't jealous.

I hated him.

Layton, who had come to stand beside me, noticed my tension. "You okay, Teagan?"

I looked up at Layton and saw nothing but affability in his golden eyes. "Do you think I'd get off on diminished capacity if I killed him?"

"Ignore him," Layton chuckled, wrapping his arm around my shoulder as he led me onto the field. "He's not worth getting upset over."

Noah, as if he sensed we were talking about him, looked our way and the look in his eyes was one of pure rage.

"Yeah, I'm just going to..." I mumbled, letting my words trail off and I broke into a run, silently thanking the heavens above that it was track today. A nice isolated sport; plus, I was fast.

When Coach blew his final whistle, I was the first one off the field and into the locker rooms. I showered and dressed in record time, desperate to get out of the hellhole and avoid confrontation.

As I passed the door of the boys' locker room, a huge body stepped out, blocking my exit.

"What do you want?" I hissed, looking up at Noah with narrowed eyes.

"We need to talk," he replied harshly as he crowded me, invading my personal space.

"No, we don't." I tried to shoulder past him, but Noah grabbed my elbow and pulled me down the hallway before shoving me into the small alcove behind the bathrooms.

"You just don't learn, do you?" Baring my teeth, I made a snapping gesture and backed further into the alcove – basically backing myself into a corner. Space was limited and Noah was taking up most of it. "You know I have a tendency to bite when threatened by repulsive creatures," I told him as I pressed my hand against his chest and tried to claim back some of the space he was taking up.

Noah grabbed my forearm and held it roughly to the wall above my head as he stepped even closer to me, his face mere inches from mine. "And *you* know what I'll do if you bite me again," he snarled. "So shut the hell up and listen to me for a second."

"You shut up," I shot back petulantly.

Noah shook his head and exhaled impatiently. "I want to make it clear to you that I wasn't the one who broke your guitar."

"Whatever, Noah," I snapped, chest heaving. "I heard what you said – *you seem attached to that thing*." I did a terrible impersonation of his voice before rolling my eyes and glaring into his furious looking eyes. "I know it was you."

"I kissed you, Teagan," he spat, his tone incredulous. "Why the hell would I break your guitar if I ... Fuck," he growled as he looked up to the ceiling before glowering down at me. "You're the biggest fucking headache I've ever dealt with."

"Because I kicked you in the balls, that's why you would break it." Shaking my head, I planted my free hand on his chest and glared at the man beast in front of me. "And as far as headaches go, there's not an aspirin on this bloody continent strong enough to handle a pain in the brain like you."

Noah stared at me for what felt like an age before nodding stiffly and stepping away from me. "Just so you know," he sneered as he ran a hand through his thick black hair. "Ellie did that to your guitar. Not me."

My eyes narrowed. "Like I'd believe you..."

"I don't give a damn what you believe anymore, Teagan," Noah spat before turning his back on me. "That's the truth."

TEAGAN

"He's looking at you again," Hope chirped as she bumped her shoulder against mine. "He's been watching you all class," she added with a smirk before blowing a bubble with her gum.

"Stop saying that," I snapped as I reached up and stabbed her bubble with my pen.

We were sitting in English class on Monday morning and I knew Noah was staring across the room at me. He had been burning evil lasers at the side of my face for most of the class. I couldn't blame him. Not after what happened on Thanksgiving.

"I'm serious, Hope. Just pretend you don't see him." I wasn't feeling quite as brave around Noah as before, and last weekend's events made me even more uncomfortable around him.

Thanksgiving night, after swiping a bottle of Uncle Max's vodka, I'd gotten as drunk as a skunk and had been pumped with Dutch-courage. Having already made one poor decision that night, I had then decided – along with an equally drunk, equally pumped Hope – in my idiotic state of debauchery, to take revenge on the neighbors for their crimes against me.

Our first mistake had been egging their house.

Our second had been throwing the flour balls.

Our third mistake had been getting caught.

Screw it, I regretted nothing. Our only *mistake was getting caught.*

We'd stumbled back to the sanctuary of my house the second Ellie opened the front door, laughing our asses off, and we had then proceeded to finish off the bottle of vodka.

Of course, Ellie didn't go down without a fight and had sent the big guns after us. But I swear, I truly hadn't known it was Noah at the front door banging and neither had Hope when she tossed the dish of water out my bedroom window and onto his head.

I still cringed when I thought of how I'd flung the front door open and tossed that bag of flour in his face. And how close I'd come to peeing my pants when Noah punched the wooden panel of my door, *a millimeter from my face.*

Ellie had definitely stepped up her game, though. When I opened my locker this morning, I'd been verbally assaulted by Ellie and her gaggle of geese. Now I was no wimp, but when you have eight girls crowding you, taunting you, and taking your physical appearance apart, it kind of sucks the fun right out of a person's day.

And that was only Ellie.

I could only imagine what sick and twisted payback Noah had lined up for me...

"Me stopping saying it won't stop him doing it," Hope taunted.

"I thought you said he was bad news," I snapped. "Keep my distance?"

"Pssh, who am I to tell you what to do?" Grinning, she

leaned closer to me and whispered in my ear. "So, Ash was in the bathroom earlier and overheard Ellie talking with her friends."

"I'm listening," I told her, leaning closer.

Hope chuckled. "So, I think I know why little miss up-her-own-ass has it in for you so bad." Cupping her hand around my ear Hope whispered, "According to Ellie, Noah has a soft spot for a certain blonde Irish girl next door."

My eyes widened and I turned my face to gape at Hope.

"He hates me," I spluttered. "I broke his car...." *He kissed me...* "He threatened my life..." *And I bit him...* "He told me he's going to hurt me, Hope." *And then I kicked him in the balls and bit him some more...* I shook my head in denial. "If that's a soft spot, I wouldn't like to see how he treats his enemies."

"Think about it, Teegs," Hope said excitedly. "It would explain why Ellie-the-serpent has been more venomous than usual – she's always been crazy jealous of anyone Noah's been with. It would *also* explain why Noah hasn't retaliated against you for destroying his car." Shrugging, Hope added, "Well, you did do a number on him, babe. Cam said it's gonna cost three grand minimum to fix. And there's the small matter of you covering him with flour."

I gaped at her. "You helped me do that."

Hope shrugged nonchalantly. "I'm a Carter."

I stared with my mouth hanging open for a moment before swinging my head around to look at Noah. "Does that look like the look of love to you?" I demanded in a hushed tone.

"You know what they say," Hope mused as she watched Noah as he sat stiffly with his fists balled, glaring evilly at my face. "Hate is the closest thing to love."

"Save me," I whimpered as I clutched her sleeve.

"Miss Connolly!" Miss Andrews glowered at me from the

front of the classroom. "Given your inability to compose yourself long enough to complete your assignment with Miss Carter, I suggest you move to another desk and start again with a new partner."

Hope snorted and I reddened.

"I'll contain myself," I told her, knowing full well who was sitting next to the only vacant chair in class. "I promise?"

"Up," she snapped and pointed towards Noah.

Standing, slowly I did the walk of shame across the classroom while my legs shook like ivy leaves.

When I reached his desk, Noah did absolutely nothing to put me at ease, keeping his chair – and his body – sprawled out, forcing me to climb over his lap to reach the inside seat. The class erupted in wolf whistles and why wouldn't they? It only looked like I was giving him a bloody lap dance. I was as red as a lobster by the time I was seated.

"So..." I cleared my voice and focused all my attention on my desk. "What are you going to do after high school?" I tapped my pen against my notepad, desperate to complete the assignment Miss Andrews had doled out to us. "What's your preferred career path or college choice?"

Noah didn't answer me, he just continued to stare, his brown eyes boring holes through my skull. "Noah," I hissed, twisting in my seat to nudge him with my elbow. "Answer the bloody question."

"You know what, Thorn, for someone who likes to play the victim, you've got a nasty little habit of vandalizing property," he said in a low tone. "You're becoming as bad as her."

Ouch.

"You and Ellie started this war," I snarled. "I did *nothing* to deserve your crap."

"You were born, weren't you?" he shot back cruelly.

"You asshole," I spat.

"Miss Connolly. Mr. Messina." Miss Andrews did not look impressed. "Detention after school," she spat. "Both of you."

Noah shrugged like he didn't have a care in the world.

Meanwhile, I covered my face with my hands and prayed for death.

There were only two words in the English language guaranteed to send my heart into overdrive and set my body on fire. Two words that, when spoken in sequence, put the fear of god and the desire of Aphrodite into me.

Unfortunately for me, those two words had just come out of Coach Johnson's mouth.

"I'm sorry, Coach," I choked out before clearing my throat. "I didn't quite hear you properly. Who did you say was my partner for rubbish collection duty?" *Please be someone else, anyone else. A different person. Let it be my imagination.*

"Noah Messina," Coach repeated and my heart soared for a brief moment before sinking into my butt.

Oh, sweet Jesus no.

Please god no.

I dared a peek at the tattooed gimp across the room and discovered he had stood up and was walking towards me with a face like thunder.

This was the opportunity he'd been waiting for.

He could kill me and make it look like an accident.

"Miss Connolly and Mr. Messina," Coach continued, eyes alight with excitement as he handed us a pair of metal claws and a roll of bin liners. "Now off you go."

Clearing his throat, Coach began naming the other

paired students, but I didn't hear a word. I was still stuck – choking to death – on the words *partner* and *Noah Messina.*

Why did bad things happen to good people?

"This is all your fault," I snarled as I climbed to my feet and followed Noah outside where it was hammering down with rain. "And whatever happened to writing lines on a chalkboard?"

Noah ignored me and continued walking towards the student carpark.

"Noah," I snapped as I rushed after him. It was freezing cold and the raindrops landing on my skin felt like tiny razorblades. When I reached him, I grabbed his elbow and pulled him to a stop. "Where the hell are you going?" I asked him.

Noah flinched and pulled his arm roughly away from me. "Not now, Teagan, I'm late for something."

"For what?" I demanded, rolling my eyes. "Your parole meeting? Noah, you're supposed to be my partner." I knew that sounded dumb, but it was the first thing that came out of my mouth. "You at least owe me…"

"Don't," he shouted and I didn't. I shut my mouth as I watched Noah's entire frame stiffen. He turned around slowly and fixed me with a look of such seriousness and intensity that my entire body froze to the spot.

The rain was coming down hard, but I didn't move. If the sky decided to open at this very moment and rain puppies down on us, I was fairly certain I wouldn't move an inch. His hooded stare caused my muscles to lock into place.

"I owe you *nothing*, Teagan," he finally whispered before turning around and walking away from me.

NOAH

I walked through the parking lot, forcing myself not to look back at her, as the rain poured down on me, and willed myself to get a fucking grip and stop worrying about Teagan. She'd deserved my harsh words just now. She deserved a lot worse for blaming me for her guitar.

Jesus Christ, she was the reason I ended up with detention and was currently an hour late to meet JD. That girl was nothing but a huge thorn in my side and I didn't need any more complications and pain in my life.

That wasn't pain I saw in her hazel eyes. It couldn't have been.

Forcing all thoughts of Teagan to the back of my mind, I maintained an impassive expression even though my body was coiled tight and rigid as I approached the black hummer parked at the entrance.

"You're late."

JD leaned against the hummer with sunglasses covering his beady gray eyes and his mouth set in a tight line. I forced myself not to shudder when his beefy hand clamped down on my shoulder. Hatred like I'd never felt coursed through me, and it took a hell of a lot out of me not to turn around and pummel this prick's face in.

His fingers dug into my shoulder blade. "You were supposed to meet me at the Hub over an hour ago."

"I know," I replied in a tight tone as I shrugged off his hand. "I had detention."

"Not my problem, Messina," he snarled, opening the car door. "You know the rules by now. I say jump. You jump."

Grabbing the back of my neck, he slammed my forehead against the door before pushing me into the passenger seat.

"I say crawl on your knees like a bitch and that's what you fucking do," JD spat when he climbed into the driver's seat beside me. "You got that, kid?"

"I got it," I replied in a flat tone as JD cranked the engine and tore off.

I couldn't feel any pain in my head.

I didn't wipe away the blood that was trickling down my forehead.

My complete attention was fixated on Teagan's face, and the fear in her eyes as she stood in the parking lot with her hand covering her mouth, watching us drive away.

TEAGAN

"I'm not kidding around here, Hope. You need to call the cops. Noah's been kidnapped."

I was finding it hard to keep my phone to my ear as I ran the entire way home from school. I had a stitch in my side but I didn't stop. My fear and adrenalin pushed me forward. "A creepy, red-haired dude smashed his head against the car door, shoved him into the passenger seat, and drove off like a bat out of hell."

"If Noah has really been kidnapped then why haven't *you* called the cops?" I heard Hope ask in an amused tone and I almost lost it with her. "Why did you call *me* first?"

"Because I'm stupid and obviously not prepared for a crisis of such epic proportions," I screamed, puffing out a breath when I spotted my house a few hundred yards up the street. "Where I'm from, puppies are bundled into cars, Hope," I hissed. "Not six-foot, tattooed, muscle-heads."

Oh god, what if he was hurt.

I didn't like him but that didn't mean I wanted anything bad to happen to him.

I could feel tears springing in my eyes and I quickly

blinked them away. "The guy who took him was *huge*, Hope. I mean ginormous."

The line was quiet for a moment and then I heard her voice close by. "You're not joking around, are you?" she asked as I sprinted past her house in the direction of Noah's place.

I didn't answer Hope – I was too busy running up Noah's porch steps. "Help!" I screamed as I banged on their front door like a rip-raving lunatic. "Please help."

My knuckles were throbbing from the force I was using to knock on the door. "Goddammit, open the bloody door," I roared, feeling out of breath and soaked to the skin from the rain. "Your son has been kidnapped – whoa!"

The front door swung inwards and I jerked back.

"What do you want?" the man I'd come to know as Ellie's father asked in a tight voice.

"Your son," I gasped, panting as I bent over and held my side. "Noah... he's been... taken."

His face reddened as his green eyes narrowed. "You're mistaken."

I shook my head. "No," I puffed, straightening my back. "I'm not. There was this guy at school... In a black hummer... Red hair..."

Mr. Dennis stepped onto the porch.

His hand shot out and latched onto my arm, roughly squeezing my bony bicep. "I'm only going to tell you this once, girl," he snarled as he leaned close to my face. "Keep your nose out of my family affairs."

"Your family affairs?" I shouted in outrage. I tried to pull my arm free, but his hold was like a vice grip. "I'm telling you that your son was kidnapped. I saw it with my own eyes..."

"What's going on?"

I physically slumped with momentary relief when I

heard Noah's voice behind me.

"This one was sticking her nose in where it doesn't belong," Mr. Dennis hissed as Noah joined us on the porch.

Sure enough, Noah's eyebrow was caked in dried-in blood and my stomach sank. My fingers twitched with the urge to soothe his injuries which was insanity on a whole new level considering what an asshole he'd been during detention.

Oh crap, I ran out of detention...

Noah didn't look at my face and he didn't look at his stepfather's face. Instead, he kept his gaze on the arm Mr. Dennis was still squeezing. "Let go of her arm," he told his stepfather in a deathly quiet tone. "Now."

Mr. Dennis let go of my arm and he let go quickly. "We need to talk, *son*," was all he said before storming into his house and slamming the door.

"What the hell are you doing, you little nut?" Noah demanded the second the front door shut and the momentary relief I'd been feeling was quickly replaced with heated anger. "Telling George I was kidnapped?" he shook his head and glared at me. "What the hell is the matter with you?"

"Little nut?" I stalked forward and cusped the back of his neck, pulling his face down to my level. "You *were* kidnapped, you fool."

I touched the cut on Noah's face and his eyes blazed with something other than anger. I quickly let go; the surge of electricity tingling through my body was too much. "Who was that guy in the hummer?" I asked him. "Where did he take you? Why didn't you kick his ass for doing that to you?" I shook my head and stepped closer to him. "Noah, what's going on with you?" *I want to help...*

"You need to stay away from me, Teagan," Noah rasped in a husky tone as he brushed past me. "As far as you can."

NOAH

I stood outside the red-bricked, two-story house across the street, feeling more pain than I'd ever imagined I could feel – or endure. I had waited until well after midnight before I dared leave the house. It was pitch black outside now and I could only hope they hadn't noticed me leaving.

The rain battered down on me but it did little to cleanse the feeling of dread looming in the pit of my stomach. Pressing the palm of my hand against the timber frame of the door, I managed to keep upright as I closed my eyes and prayed for a do-over life.

The door opened inwards and I was greeted by a pair of intense gray eyes.

"Hi," I mumbled, red eyed and hoarse. Using one hand to hold my aching ribcage, I used my other to push my drenched hair out of my eyes, shivering violently from the cold. "I need somewhere to crash for the night."

Low lunged forward, grabbed onto my slumping body, and helped me inside. "Jesus Christ, Noah," he hissed as he led me into the living room and sat me on the couch. "What happened this time?"

"Thanks, man." I sank onto the couch and watched as Low disappeared from the room only to return a few minutes later with a towel, an icepack, and a first aid kit. "What do think happened this time, Low?" I held the ice pack to my swollen jaw and leaned back. Logan knew what happened to me as well as I did. "Life happened."

"I can't sit back and watch much more of this, Noah," was all he said as he sank onto the couch and dropped his head in his hands. "Remember what I told you – about graduation?"

I nodded. That was all I thought about. I clung to Logan's words like a lifeline.

"I think it needs to happen now," he replied quietly.

"No." I held the ice pack to my eyebrow. "No goddamn way, Low." There was less than three weeks until Christmas. "I'm not having *that* on my conscience."

"Nobody's asking you to have anything on your conscience, Noah," he shot back evenly. "I want to help you."

"You are, man," I sighed. "More than you know."

"Goddammit, Noah," he hissed as he jerked to his feet. "Why did this have to happen to you?"

"I had the bad luck of being born into a family of fucking predators," I replied in a weary tone.

"That's not your fault, Noah," Low countered as he ran a hand through his hair and paced the floor. "You didn't choose this life. It was chosen *for* you."

"You think?" I let out a shaky breath and blocked out the mental image of several pairs of fists pummeling into me tonight. "And then I had the unbelievable misfortune of having Teagan fucking Connolly move in next door."

"Are you saying Teagan had something to do with you getting the piss knocked out of you?" Low asked me as he stood with his back to me, staring out the window. "Because I find that really hard to believe, man."

I balled my hands into fists. "I'm saying *they've* somehow come to the conclusion that Teagan is my weak spot."

"And is she?" Low turned and looked me square in the eye. "Is Teagan your weak spot?"

"Look at me, Logan," I shot back, gesturing to my smashed up face. "What do you think?"

10

TEAGAN

"Do you want to go home for Valentine's weekend, Teegs?" Uncle Max asked me on Wednesday evening, completely out of the blue. We were sitting in the lounge. He was watching a documentary on pregnant elephants and I was attempting some trig homework. When those words came out of his mouth, my jaw pretty much hit the warm furry mat I was sprawled over.

"It's December," I reminded him.

Max smirked and gave me an *'obviously'* look before saying, "I'm asking you now because I need to arrange some time off work and book our tickets. I'm working all through Christmas so the best I can do is Valentine's." Even though the man was curing sick kids and healing the world, I knew I was too selfish to ever think of a career as a doctor. There was no way I could dedicate ninety percent of my time to the job like Max did.

A trickle of excitement coursed through me and I grinned like a lunatic. "Hell, yeah I want to go home for Valentine's weekend." I'd been feeling miserable for weeks because of Martin and this was the best news to drag me out of my funk. "You mean it?" I narrowed my eyes and studied my uncle's handsome face. "We're going home in February, to Galway?

Max chuckled and nodded. "I mean it," he told me fondly. "But we won't be able to stay more than two or three days," he warned. "Work is hectic and I'll need to come back before..."

"I'll take it," I shouted happily before springing to my feet. "Oh man, I knew there was a reason I loved you, Maximus." I danced out of the lounge and grabbed my coat off the back of the door. "I need to tell Hope."

"You have ten minutes," Max called out. "You're still grounded."

OKAY, SO HOPE WASN'T AS EXCITED FOR ME AS I'D ORIGINALLY thought.

"You can't be serious," she snapped, cheeks flushed and eyes narrowed. "You're leaving." She folded her arms over her chest and sighed. "I can't believe this crap."

"Don't be such a princess," I shot back with a chuckle. "It's only for a few days, I'll be back before you know it."

"You say that now," she grumbled, leaning back in her chair with a huff. "But when you get there and fall in love with being back home, it will be a different story."

I rolled my eyes and took a sip of my hot chocolate. "Well, come with us if you're so worried." Smirking, I added, "But I warn you now, there's not much to do there."

Hope's eyes lit up. "Do you think your uncle would mind?"

I shrugged. "Doubt it," I chuckled. "He's fairly easygoing." Sliding my phone out of my jeans pocket, I sent Uncle Max a quick text asking if he'd be cool with Hope coming with us.

He texted me back a couple of minutes later.

Max: Fine by me if her parents are okay with it. Tickets are booked. Be home in 5. You're still grounded.

I GRINNED AND SHOWED HOPE THE MESSAGE.

"This is excellent news," she chirped. "I can't freaking wait."

"You don't know if your parents will let you go yet," I warned her.

Hope gave me a look that said '*fool, please*' before handing my phone back to me.

"I've always wanted to go to Ireland," she sighed dreamily as she rested her chin on her hands. "Uncle Derek's been, so have my parents."

"Good luck trying to get your daddy on board, Hopey-bear," Hope's grandmother chuckled as she carefully iced some cupcakes at the counter.

"Grandma, please," Hope scoffed as she smiled lovingly at the short, white-haired woman. "This is the opportunity of a lifetime." Frowning, she added, "Dad won't ruin this for me."

Grandma Tracy wiped her flour encrusted hands on her little pink apron and sighed. "You four are seventeen and eighteen years old, and your daddy still has me come over and watch you guys when he and your momma go out of town."

I gaped at my friend. "Your grandmother is *babysitting* you guys?"

Hope flushed and I burst out laughing.

I shook my head and tried to stop grinning. "You're eighteen."

"Have you met her daddy?" Grandma Tracy asked me, chuckling, and she shuffled towards the kitchen door. "Boys," she called out. "Dinner's ready."

A stampede erupted from somewhere upstairs, so I rose from my chair and said my goodbyes, ready to make myself scarce.

"Oh hey, Teegs, don't worry," Hope called out after me when I reached the front door. "I'm going with you to Ireland, come hell or high water."

TEAGAN

By the time school finished on Friday, I was looking forward to locking myself away from the world for two whole days.

Unfortunately, Hope seemed to have other plans.

"Sorry for barging in, Uncle Max," Hope called out as she sauntered into my kitchen. "But I kinda need to borrow your niece for the evening."

"In case you've forgotten, I'm kind of grounded," I muttered, casting Max an evil look from where I was perched on the countertop, dressed in my ratty old sweats, waiting for the kettle to boil.

Max had extended my grounded sentence when Ellie – the rat – went straight to him, sobbing her little heart of stone out over the whole flour bombing incident at Thanksgiving.

Hope frowned and worried her lip anxiously. Her blue eyes were round as saucers as she swung around to stare at Max. "Please?" she asked softly.

Uncle Max sighed heavily from where he was sitting, watching us. "You can go," he grumbled as he closed the lid of his laptop and leaned back in his chair. "You've suffered enough."

Hope clapped her hands and grinned. "You're the best," she squealed. "I promise we won't be out too late."

"Keep her as long as you like," I heard Max chuckle, and I shook my head in mock disgust as I hopped down from the counter and followed Hope to the kitchen door.

"Keep the tomfoolery to a minimum though, Teegs," Max said in a stern tone. He stood up and unplugged his laptop from its charger before sliding it into a brown leather case. "And *no* fighting with the neighbors."

"So, what's up?" I asked, prying my arm out of Hope's grasp when we stepped outside. It was dusk on the Hill and the sky looked darker than normal. I was hoping this was a sign of snow. I couldn't freaking wait for the snow.

"I need you to come with me somewhere," she mumbled as we crossed the street towards her house.

Hope pushed the door inwards and I froze when it creaked spookily.

There's no such thing as ghosts...

There's no such thing as ghosts...

Hope, noticing my reaction, rolled her eyes and pulled me inside. "Who told you?" she asked as she pushed me up the staircase.

"Layton," I whispered, clutching her sleeve.

Hope huffed. "He's such a gossip."

"Is it true?"

"All of it and more probably," she mused as she pushed me down the hallway, stopping outside the last door on the right. "Relax," she added as she pushed the door inwards. "There are no ghosts in this house, Teagan. They wouldn't get a minute's peace with my brothers," she added dryly, gesturing me into a yellow painted bedroom.

"Besides," she grumbled as she walked over to the closet and pulled the door open. "We've got bigger problems."

"Like what?" I tentatively took a step into her bedroom, and when nothing bad happened, I took another step.

I was halfway between the door and the bed when Hope turned around and glared at me. "No one died here, Teagan."

"Right," I chuckled nervously and forced myself to walk over and sit on her bed. "Sorry."

"Don't sweat it." She smirked. "They died in the kitchen."

I jumped off the bed and Hope burst out laughing. "That's not funny," I snapped. Grabbing a pillow from her bed, I chucked it at her. "I'm a little superstitious, okay?"

Hope cackled for a few more seconds before sobering. "On a serious note," she said as she forced herself to stop smiling. "I need you to come to the Ring of Fire with me."

Now I was the one laughing.

"I'm serious," she added before holding three fingers up. "Scouts honor."

I rolled my eyes. "I'm not Katniss Everdeen," I told her, pointing at her three-fingered gesture. "And I'm more of a *Walk the Line* kinda girl."

"I love that book," Hope said with a grin. "And I'm not joking. Ash texted me saying she heard Cameron talking about going to the freaking Ring of Fire with Noah tonight. And low and behold, the douche is now M.I.A, therefore I need to go and bring him home before he lands himself in the middle of Noah's crap – *again*."

"How is it I'm not one bit surprised to hear Noah Messina's involved in something called *The Ring of Fire*?" Folding my arms over my chest, I let out a calming breath before asking, "I'm probably going to regret asking this, but is this *Ring of Fire* an actual place and what happens there?"

"It's a real place, all right," Hope replied, her tone laced with disgust. "And from what the boys have told me, it's like..." She paused and twirled her finger around as if trying to remember a word. "A playground for the shady and reckless."

"Meaning?"

"*Meaning* some bad, illegal shit happens there, shit I don't want my brother involved in," she snapped. "And my parents are due home tomorrow night."

Lovely.

Sounds very enticing.

Rummaging in the bottom of her closet, Hope started tossing item after item of clothing behind her. "And I can't risk driving my car up there," she grumbled as she eyed a red boob tube dress skeptically before throwing it in a separate pile than the others. "Because dad more than likely has someone watching my movements." She sighed in disgust. "He's a serious control freak, I don't know how my mother puts up with him.... Ah, that's it." Hope grinned at what looked like a piece of cloth.

"Put this on," she told me, flinging it in my direction. "We need to blend in. Don't want anyone thinking we're cops."

"You can't be serious," I muttered, picking up the tiny, white piece of stretchy fabric.

"Oh, I'm deadly serious." She tossed a beautiful pair of black leather boots in my direction. I caught them with ease before tossing them down on her bed.

"An illegal ring of fire?" I shook my head and gaped at her. "Let me get this straight. You want *me* to go with *you* into the middle of no-man's land so you can spy on *your* idiot brother, who's most likely in the company of *my* arch enemy, and make sure he doesn't get arrested?"

"Yeah," Hope replied as she blew a curl off her face. "Sounds about right."

"There's no way in hell I'm going anywhere Noah Messina will be, unless it's someplace mandatory like school or the footpath outside my house."

I forced myself to believe that Noah hadn't hurt my feelings in the slightest when he tossed my concern for his well being back in my face the other day. I'd have to care about what Noah thought in order for it to hurt me. I'd have to care about him. And I didn't. I refused to.

"Are you hiding?" She laughed loudly, pointing her skinny finger in my face. "Oh my god." She leaned back in her heels and studied me with an astonished look on her face. "You're hiding from Noah Messina." She shook her head and mused, "You're letting him beat you."

"I am not hiding from him," I spat, my tone of voice defensive – *way* too defensive. "And I am not letting him beat me, I just... We were... And he just..." I wasn't sure what I was trying to tell my friend.

Hope's perfectly shaped eyebrows rose in surprise and I could feel the heat rising in my cheeks.

"He disturbs me, all right?" I snapped. "He makes me nervous. Happy now?"

"Ecstatic," she shot back, clapping her hands. "Put that skirt on and make *him* nervous."

I shook my head. "I'm not going. No way, no how, it's never gonna happen. I promised Max I wouldn't fight with the neighbors." I stared meaningfully at my friend's face. "A promise I'm sure to break the second I lay eyes on Noah Messina." *Ugh.*

"Please, Teagan," Hope begged. "I really need your help."

I felt my will buckling under her persuasive kneading. I knew that I was going to cave in and she knew it, too.

And then Hope used an evil-bastard trick.

She used the *puppy eyes*.

11

NOAH

Winning isn't enough tonight. Put him out of commission and I'll arrange Christmas visitation.

With great effort, I reread the text message I'd received from George once more before deleting it and tossing my phone into the passenger seat of Tommy's Subaru.

Keep your eye on the donut, Messina, and not the hole...

"You ready for this, dude?" Tommy asked as he leaned against the side of his car, watching me with a hooded expression etched on his face.

The quarry was packed tonight and Tommy's adrenalin was obviously pumping. He was jittery as fuck. Why, I had no clue because he wasn't the one who was about to take a beating.

"That guy Kruger looks pretty intense," Tommy said with a frown.

He was.

Last time I came up against Kruger, I was sixteen and the guy handed my ass to me. Shawn Kruger was like a fucking tornado in the ring; blowing his opponents to smithereens.

The only advantage I had tonight was the fact that Kruger had his girl with him tonight.

Big mistake.

You *never* brought your weak link to work.

I knew the second I saw the curvy brunette sidling up to Kruger's side that I was onto a winner.

Pulling my shirt over my head, I tossed it into the car with my phone. "It is what it is, T," I replied, holding my hands up for him to tape. "I appreciate you being here tonight."

Tommy rolled his blue eyes in exasperation as he concentrated on taping my knuckles. "Dude, we're friends. That's what friends do – they help one another out in shitty situations."

"Yeah," I said with a sigh, flexing my wrists. "But you know the drill." I stared into his eyes. "No matter what happens tonight, don't get involved."

A vein ticked in Tommy's neck, but he nodded stiffly and I sighed in relief. *He understood.* The last thing I needed was someone I cared about getting involved in this mess. It was bad enough that I had brought him here in the first place.

TEAGAN

We took my car to the Ring of Fire, which, may I add, was in the back ass of nowhere. Hope drove, which was probably for the best since I lost feeling in my toes by the time I reached the bottom step of her staircase.

I'd never looked skankier or felt shadier than I did right now.

I had on a skin tight, white mini skirt that was so short I was fairly certain the cheeks of my butt were on display, and a pair of black, thigh high fuck-me-boots.

My top, if you could call it that, was worse. All that covered the girls was a silver, sparkly bandeau that literally *just* covered my chest. I was bare from my ribs to my hip bones and from the bottom of my ass to my thighs.

Boy did I feel good about myself.

We traveled away from the Hill, the city, the street lights, and basically all human civilization. Hope pointed out a few different places as we traveled higher into the mountains. Where she used to live, where she used to camp; none of which I remembered because I was too nervous. It was dark,

I was freezing, and we were traveling into the unknown. The unknown didn't bode well with me.

After spending twenty minutes driving in silence down a secluded dirt road, Hope took another sharp left and, suddenly, a huge abandoned quarry pit came into view.

The further we drove into the quarry, the more suffocated I started to feel. Walls of resolute rock over eighty feet in height surrounded us. Burnt out shells of cars lay scattered on either side of us as we drove and within seconds, my eyes locked on... Oh yeah, we were here.

I was staring at a ring of fire.

I kid you not, a circling blaze of red hot flames blew high into the night air. Several smaller bonfires were scattered around the clearing surrounded by crowds of people, and I really did *not* want to get out of this car without a fire extinguisher.

"Are they insane?" I hissed as Hope parked my car at the edge of the clearing where all the other cars were parked. "I mean, really, are they seriously crazy?" I gaped at the side of Hope's face. "This place is a death trap." Hope was right.

This *was* the playground for the shady and reckless...

"I guess they don't care," she whispered, staring straight ahead at the scene unfolding in front of us. I wasn't sure if we'd landed ourselves into the middle of a brothel, a fighting ring, or a bloody car chase.

Shit was happening... Like everywhere.

Nickelback's *Burn it to the Ground* was blaring from the humongous pair of speakers sitting on the back of a truck, pumped, no doubt, by the huge generator next to them.

Women wearing far less clothing than us were parading themselves around in front of men. There were people in cars doing donuts and all types of dumb shit, and a huge mob of people were forming a circle in the center.

"You owe me, Hope," I grumbled as I climbed out of the passenger seat and adjusted myself as best I could. I caught my reflection in the car window and glared at the back of Hope's head. "You really, *really* owe me."

"I know," she replied in a serious tone as she tried to walk in a pair of sky high, black stilettos. She was wearing a flimsy red dress, and the only thing comforting me in this moment was the fact that there was as much of Hope on display as there was of me. But as much as I detested what I was wearing, and I *loathed* it, Hope had been right to make us dress up. At least we blended in. And the way I saw it, blending was good. It meant we could get in and out of here without being noticed.

"Can you see him?" I asked, taking the key to my car from Hope and popping it into my top, while I spied the crowds for Cameron and prayed I wouldn't see Noah, or worse, Ellie.

Jesus, knowing my luck she was here, too.

"No," Hope muttered as she bit down on her lip nervously. "He looks tough, Teegs," she whispered, clutching my hand in hers. "And he is, but he's got this horrible temper that makes him vulnerable. That temper fueled with his ADHD makes for a very unpredictable Cameron."

"We'll find him," I coaxed, feeling a huge chunk of sympathy for my fiery friend. Hope acted so tough and carefree, but I could tell by her eyes that she was scared to death for Cam.

The ground was littered with stones and I was finding it incredibly tricky to keep my balance. I spotted something, or more like heard, someone's name being called out to the left and groaned. "Hope." I caught her attention and pointed over to where a group had formed a circle around two guys fighting.

The stench of cigarettes even outside in the fresh air was overpowering, and I had a feeling these people were smoking more than tobacco. Everyone was rowdy, jittery even, and there was this buzz in the atmosphere.

We made our way over to the crowd and I could have wept when I saw who was in the circle fighting.

"Messina!" people screamed and cheered, meanwhile I swallowed some vomit. There was blood on the ground, mixed in with dirt, and Noah... Noah was bleeding from his eyebrow.

Without thinking twice about what I was doing, I let go of Hope's hand and pushed forward, butting several other spectators out of my way until I got to the front.

The other guy looked so much worse off than Noah, and a tiny part of my body sagged in relief briefly.

Very briefly.

My relief ended the second the other guy began punching Noah repeatedly in the face.

But Noah... He just didn't seem to feel it, smirking with each blow as if he was feeding off the pain.

And then he let rip and the crowd went berserk.

I'd seen boys my age fight before. Liam had been in plenty of scuffles over the years, both on and off the football pitch. I'd seen blood drawn in fights, hell even a broken rib or nose.

This was different.

Noah was like the Terminator. I'd never seen a man's fists move like I did at that moment. He was everywhere, the crowd was deafening, and I realized pretty quickly that I was in the middle of something I really didn't want to be involved in.

The display of brutality I had just witnessed wasn't normal. There was a level of viciousness in Noah's dark eyes as he pounded his knuckles into opponent's face that chilled my blood.

Turning my back on the fight, I tried to push my way through the mob, but no one would budge. I banged off some huge guy's chest and twisted around, trying to steady myself, but I was shoved in the back and then I did something incredibly unattractive.

I fell forward into the makeshift ring and face planted on the ground.

I tried to climb to my feet, but the people behind me surged forward, either too engrossed in the fight or too ignorant to care that I was still on the ground, leaving me with no choice but to curl into a ball and protect my head with my hands.

People rushed forward, some stepping on me, and I held my breath in fear. I felt a sudden sharp spike of pain as some asshole's boot connected with my face. Another one stepped down on my ankle, hard enough to make me cry out, and I braced myself for the stampede, every muscle in my body locked and coiled tight in fearful anticipation. You could imagine my surprise when I felt a hand wrap around my arm and drag me along the dirty, blood stained gravel and out from underneath the masses.

"Have you got a goddamn death wish?" Noah demanded as he dragged me roughly to my feet.

The second he let me go and stepped away I fell forward, unable and unwilling to put any weight on my ankle.

It was hurting so bad, and I was having a mini breakdown.

I nearly died.

I could have died.

I almost died.

Oh, Jesus...

Noah cursed under his breath and caught me again, slipping his arm around my back to hold me up. "You're a goddamn thorn in my side," he snarled as he walked me over to where a small group of men were standing beside a sweet looking, wine colored Subaru.

I tried to limp along with him but failed miserably and after another muttered curse, Noah lifted me into his arms.

"She yours, Messina?" I heard a man ask but I couldn't hear Noah's response.

To be honest, I was still in shock that he'd dragged me to safety in the first place. Noah hated me enough to leave me there. He'd said it himself; I was a thorn in his side, and I doubted I would have helped him or Ellie if I'd been in his position.

With my chest heaving, I tried to catch my breath, but I could feel the blood trickling from my lip and that did *nothing* to calm my emotions.

When we reached the men, Noah sat me down on the hood of a car. The metal was cold against my bare thighs, and I welcomed the feeling. The backs of my legs were burning from being crushed, the fronts of my thighs were stinging from being dragged over gravel, I was covered in dirt, and my hair was knotted and hanging limply over my breasts.

Yeah, I wasn't a pretty sight.

Noah clutched my jaw for a brief moment as he studied my face with eyes full of anger. He gently ran his thumb over my lip and wiped some blood away before dropping his hand from my face. He growled and ran a hand roughly through his thick black hair.

His chest was bare, his knuckles were swollen, and the white tape covering them was blood encrusted. He had a nasty looking cut over his eyebrow that had started to clot, and the faded jeans he had on were covered in a mixture of blood and dirt.

"Do you mind telling me what the hell you're doing here?" Noah demanded, eyes wild and frantic as he pushed his black hair out of his eyes.

I opened my mouth to respond, but a sharp stinging sensation caused me to shut it fast.

Noah shook his head in disgust and stalked around me. He opened the door of the car I was sitting on, and rooted around for a couple of seconds before coming back to where I was sitting and dropping a white shirt on my lap.

I immediately picked it up and pressed it to my mouth, desperate to rid myself of the horrible taste of blood. Blood that I suspected was coming from my lip. "I'm looking for... Cameron!"

I spotted Hope's brother less that ten yards away from us and tossed the t-shirt at Noah before shimmying off the hood of the car. "Hey, Cameron, get back here."

Landing awkwardly on my ankle, I bent forward and placed my hands on the ground to stop myself from falling. I tried to stand but my ankle wouldn't hold me, so I stood there for a moment with my butt in the air, contemplating what the hell I was going to do next.

"Where'd you think you're going, Messina," I heard a deep, male voice demand. "You're not finished here. Get your head in the game."

"And how exactly do you expect me to do that," I heard Noah snarl, "when she's got her fucking ass in my face?"

"I don't give two shits how you do it," the man warned. "Just fucking do it. You know better than to bring pussy here."

Moments later, a large hand clamped around on my lower hip, holding me still. Another hand grabbed the fabric of my skirt and pulled it downwards, covering me I realized, and I reddened in embarrassment.

"I'm done for the night, JD," Noah stated coldly.

"We'll talk later, Messina." I didn't catch a glance of the man Noah had called JD because he had already turned around and was walking away.

"Thank you for helping me," I whispered, knowing I owed him my gratitude. He'd saved my butt – big time.

"Don't talk to me," Noah hissed as he lifted me into his arms and carried me over to where the cars were parked. "I mean it, Teagan. I'm so fucking angry right now I could strangle you."

That was not a comforting thought considering my sore ankle would hinder my chances of escaping. I remained silent and rigid in Noah's arms as he walked over to my Honda Civic and dropped me on the hood.

"Who did you come here with?" he demanded, standing between my legs, looking fierce and furious.

"Hope," I replied as I gingerly rubbed my lip with my thumb. "She's looking for Cameron."

Noah's brown eyes widened in surprise before he threw his face up to the sky and muttered a string of curse words.

"So, you didn't come here with Cameron?"

"No, I didn't come here with Cameron. The idiot must've..." Noah snapped his mouth shut and glared at me, a look of pure disgust.

"Must've what, Noah?"

"Let's get something straight right now," he hissed, leaning towards me until his face was only inches from mine. "You don't get to question me. In fact, you don't fucking look in my direction again unless I tell you to."

"Fuck you," I shot back heatedly, feeling hurt and angry. "You don't get to tell me what to do."

"Your little stunt cost me a lot tonight, Teagan," he roared. "A lot more than what you already owe me for my fucking car." Backing away from me, Noah clenched his jaw and balled his hands into fists. He glared at me like I was the most disgusting creature he'd ever seen. "That's a long list of things you owe me for, Teagan. One of these days, I'm gonna come looking for payment."

"Teagan? Oh my god, where the hell have you been?" The sight of Hope walking towards us did little to comfort me.

"What happened to you?" Hope demanded when she reached us. I must've looked a mess because she flinched when she studied my mouth. "What the hell did you do to her?" Hope demanded as she swung around and glared at Noah, jabbing her finger in his chest.

"Hope, he didn't..." I began to say, but Noah exploded before I had a chance to explain.

"What did *I* do?" Noah roared in outrage before running a hand through his hair. "I just saved her ass from being trampled on!" Noah paced around in circles, clearly furious. "Because your girl here can't seem to keep out of my business."

Hope took a step back from him.

I leaned back a little further.

"I lost a shit load of money tonight because of *her*," Noah roared. His eyes were black as coal and locked on my face. "She cost me... just keep her out of my way, Hope," he snarled before stalking back towards the bonfire.

"Are you okay, Teegs?" Hope asked with a sigh as she leaned against the hood and watched Noah walking away from us.

"No," I managed to grind out through clenched teeth. "I'm not."

"I'm sorry," she mumbled as she reached over and wrapped her arm around my shoulder. "I shouldn't have dragged you into this crap."

"What's done is done." I wasn't going to make her feel worse than she obviously did. "Did you see Cameron? I saw him earlier. He was watching Noah's fight."

"Oh, I saw him all right," Hope snarled as she helped me into the car. "About ten seconds before he sped off in a car with Amy Valentine."

I scrunched my nose up in distaste. I'd only met the girl once or twice, but Amy Valentine wasn't the type of person I would like my brother to date. *If* I had a brother.

"What are you going to do about him?" I asked as I fastened my seatbelt and glanced over at Hope.

"I was going to ask you the same thing about Noah," she replied in a worried tone as she slipped into first gear and pulled out of our parking spot.

I have no idea... "Men suck," I grumbled.

Hope chuckled. "Amen to that, Sugar."

12

TEAGAN

Thankfully, my ankle wasn't broken; just badly bruised. My brain was the part of me that hurt most though, from listening to Uncle Max's two hour lecture on the dangers of bouncing on a trampoline without a safety net.

Yeah, that was the best I'd managed to come up with.

The weather took a turn for the worse on Saturday, with torrential rain settling over The Hill, so I spent all day at Hope's house, watching movies and eating junk food with her and Ash. There wasn't much else to do and the girls were good company. Besides, I felt safer on this side of the street, away from Noah.

"I still can't believe Noah did that," Ash chuckled as she placed a fresh bowl of popcorn on the table before taking the seat beside me.

Grandma Tracy, who was obviously not as over protective as Mr. Carter, had kindly excused herself for the afternoon, granting us some privacy.

Hope and I had filled Ash in on the shenanigans of last night, much to her delight. And, of course, Ash had her own theories for Noah's actions. "Swooping in and carting you off to safety." She winked at Hope, who was making the hot chocolates, before fanning herself. "Told you he likes her."

I stared blankly at her. "*Likes* me." I shook my head and muttered, "He's more likely to *kill* me. You should have seen the way he looked down his nose at me, Ash." I shuddered thinking about Noah's furious expression. Ash looked at me like I wasn't speaking a word of truth and I groaned in despair. "Help me out here, Hope."

"She's telling the truth," she told Ash, passing her a mug of hot chocolate.

Grabbing two more mugs from the counter, Hope took a seat at the table. "That guy is topping my shit list, Teagan," she growled as she pushed a mug towards me. "I'm thoroughly disgusted..."

The kitchen door flew open, causing Hope to stop mid sentence and me to glower at the guilty looking man-child. "I stand corrected," she hissed through clenched teeth. "*He* is topping my shit list."

"*You*." My eyes narrowed in disgust. "Do you have any idea of the trouble you caused me?"

Cam shrugged uncomfortably. "Uh, yeah," he mumbled, red faced. "About that..."

"I am so pissed with you right now, Cam," I told him, glaring. "I would've been trampled to death if Noah hadn't...." I stopped talking the moment I realized I'd mentioned Noah.

Cam's eyes lit up with mischief. "Oh yeah," he snickered. "I heard all about you flashing your ass to Messina. You cost him the fight," he added with a flirty wink. "Though I doubt anyone blames Messina for hauling your ass to safety considering the dude is bagging you."

"No," I snapped. "*You* cost him the fight... Hang on." My

head snapped towards Hope. "What the hell does *'bagging me'* mean?"

"It means the both of you have been *really trying*," Cam burst into song and I gaped at him in surprise.

"*Tryna hold back this feeling,*" Cam continued as he stalked towards me.

Wrapping his hand around my wrist, he pressed a kiss to my hand before swaggering over to the fridge. "*Whoo, let's get it on,*"Cam rasped with a shit eating grin etched across his handsome face. *"Giving yourself to Me...ssina..."*

"You just made a complete ass of yourself," Ash managed to choke out through fits of laughter.

"Unabashedly," Cam shot back with a cocky grin before winking at her. "You want a private concert, gorgeous?"

"Hot damn," Ash breathed.

"You ready, Cammy?" a female voice purred from the doorway and Cam turned his full attention on the raven-haired beauty standing in the doorway.

"Amy," he purred as he swaggered towards her with a hungry look in his eyes.

"Ugh," Hope muttered as she cast a disapproving look towards Amy Valentine. "Can you please stay away from my brother?"

"Sure." Amy nuzzled into Cam's side as he wrapped his arm around her shoulder. "If you can stay away from my cousin," Amy shot back with a smirk before turning her attention to me.

"Your ass is nothing short of amazing," she stated calmly before asking, "How do you keep it so tight?"

I spat a little of my hot chocolate back into my mug with shock. "Excuse me?" I sputtered, wiping my mouth.

"There's a photo of you online with Noah Messina," Amy

tossed out airily like it wasn't the huge deal it was. "And I would *die* to have your figure. What's your secret?"

"Kettlebells and cardio... Hang on..." Shaking my head, I held a finger up. "What photo of me and Noah Messina?"

Amy looked at me like I was stupid. "You know, the one with you twerking all over a very sweaty, half naked Noah."

Twerking?

The memory of Noah fixing my ass-ridden skirt as I balanced on my hands with my ass cocked in the air impaled my mind and my blood boiled.

Rising quickly from my chair, I grabbed my bag and stalked past the couple, stopping when I reached the kitchen door. "I wasn't twerking, you twat, I was trying to remain in an upright position."

"Tell that to everyone at school," Amy snickered. "Everyone's talking about it."

I rolled my eyes and waved at Hope and Ash before turning back to the guileless one. "At what point in time did I give you the impression that I gave two shits about what *everyone at school* thought of me?"

Amy stared blankly at me and I decided to leave it be. She wasn't worth wasting my breath on.

"I'm off," I muttered before stalking out of the kitchen.

NOAH

"Let me get this straight," Ellie hissed as she paced the kitchen floor, clearly livid. "You threw the fight for *her*?"

"I didn't throw the fight," I shot back calmly. "It was as good as over before Teagan showed up." Ellie's disgusted expression proved she either didn't believe me or wasn't satisfied. Either way, I didn't care. I'd done what any guy in my position would have done.

"And the consequences?" Ellie snarled, nostrils flaring as she stood in front of me with her hands on her hips. "What about those, Noah?" She shook her head in disgust. "Or have you forgotten what kind of a psychotic freak my brother can be?"

"Fuck the consequences, Ellie," I muttered wearily. "And fuck JD." I'd already had this lecture. I didn't need another, and if it wasn't for the blatant concern in Ellie's eyes, I'd tell her a few home truths on what a psychotic freak her precious *daddy* was.

"Oh my god, Noah," she screeched, throwing her hands in the air. "You can't be serious?"

"What do you care, El?" I mumbled, shifting awkwardly in my seat. "It's not your problem."

Dropping to her knees beside my chair, Ellie grabbed my hands and squeezed. "I care," she whispered with tears in her green eyes. "And I won't sit back and watch you destroy everything because of that girl."

"I picked her up off the ground," I growled in anger. "She was being fucking trampled on. How is that destroying everything?"

Ellie didn't answer my question. Instead, she wiped her eyes, climbed to her feet, and walked away.

Stopping at the doorway, she turned her dark head in my direction and sighed. "You have a visitor," she mumbled, lip warbling. "In the living room."

My body stiffened. "A visitor or *visitors*?"

Ellie nodded sadly. "Plural. You know the way my family works, Noah," she choked out. "It's called remuneration for damages owed."

Yeah, I knew, but that didn't mean I was ready for what was about to happen to me.

Shit.

TEAGAN

I was having the week from hell.

First thing Monday morning, when he returned from his trip, Hope's dad killed our dream of spending Valentine's together in Galway, thus spiraling Hope into a meltdown of epic proportions. Seriously, the girl was not nice to be around when angry and Hope was still *very* angry with her dad.

And yesterday, I ended up with lunchtime detention for using inappropriate language in History class when I called Reese *'a thundering whore'* for purposefully pulling my chair back just as I was about to sit down.

Then I woke up late this morning and started my day by having a huge altercation with Ellie over my guitar – which had resulted in her creepy father intervening and threatening me by saying, and I quote, *to stay on my side of the fence.*

The fact that Ellie fully admitted to trashing Martin – and slashing my tires – made both my blood boil and my cheeks flame. Noah had been telling me the truth which meant I bashed him with a guitar for no reason.

He was right, I was a judgmental bitch.

I'd stupidly left my car keys in Hope's bedroom and had to power walk my ass to school in the pouring rain, which resulted in missing my first class. Thankfully, I made it to my second class before most of my classmates and scooted inside, pleased I saw a friendly face at the back of the room.

Layton.

"Hey, can I sit with you?" I asked with a smile.

"Hey." Layton looked at me before quickly looking away. "Sure," he mumbled.

What's up his ass?

"So... Did you have a nice weekend?" I asked, more out of discomfort than curiosity.

Layton shook his head slowly before clearing his throat roughly. "Nothing worth mentioning."

"You're awfully quiet," I said evenly.

"I'm a little tired," he replied, not meeting my eyes.

"Do you want me to move seats?" I asked him straight out. "Is that the problem? You don't want me to sit with you?"

"No," Layton replied loudly, and a little too squeaky, before clearing his throat again. "You can sit wherever you want, Teagan. It's a free country."

"Right..." I folded my hands and stared at his beautiful face. "So, how's life? Are you looking forward to Christmas? It's right around the corner."

"Teagan, can I give you a little advice?" Layton didn't wait for me to respond. "Keep your distance from Messina." Sighing heavily, he added, "You're a nice girl and he's..." Layton paused and ran his hand over his shaved head. "You're playing with fire," he mumbled. "And you know how that saying goes."

I shook my head and raised my brows in confusion. "Layton, what the hell are you talking about?"

Layton didn't answer me. Instead, he turned his head and stared out the window, purposefully ignoring me.

A group of Ellie's friends walked into class and stopped dead when they saw me. All eyes locked on me and one even went so far as to point at me.

I raised my brows and stared back at them defiantly, but inside I was having a huge case of the WTF's. What the hell was going on around here? Had I somehow become the school leper?

"There's a photo of you online.... You know, the one with you twerking all over a very sweaty, half naked Noah."

Amy's voice drifted into my mind, and I scoffed loudly to myself. So, I was being treated like a disease because of the whole twerking business. Fabulous.

"That's *her*," one of the girls hissed to her friend as they passed by my seat.

"You have no class," one of the girls spat before sitting at the desk behind me.

"I hope you're happy with yourself," muttered another – Reese, I recognized. Her eyes were bloodshot. "You're destroying everything."

"Come on, come on, get seated, everybody. We have a lot to get covered this morning," Mr. Trammel, the biology teacher, called out as he rambled into class.

I opened my text book and tried to focus on what Mr. Trammel was saying and *not* on what the rest of the class were whispering.

Biology, and every class after that, passed painfully slowly and by the time I made it to the cafeteria for lunch, I was exhausted and tossing around the pros and cons of homeschooling.

"What the hell is happening in this place?" Hope growled as she dropped her lunch tray on the table before digging my car keys out of her jeans pocket and taking a seat beside me. "People have been acting strange as hell," she muttered with a sigh as she handed me the keys.

"Cheers."

"No probs." Tearing off the lid, Hope dug into her yogurt with a vengeance. "Thank god it's..." she stopped midsentence to lick the yogurt from her spoon. "...almost over. I need a break from this crap."

"Thank god," I said, relieved, as I stirred my coffee aimlessly. "I thought I was the only one being treated like a pariah."

"Jealousy *is* an ugly trait," Ash offered in a supportive tone before sliding her phone towards me. "On the bright side, Amy was right. Your ass is amazing."

"Good to know," I muttered with a heavy sigh.

Placing my elbows on the table, I rested my forehead against my palm before picking up Ash's phone, holding it away from my body like it was a poisonous snake. "Do I really want to see this?"

I didn't wait for the girls to answer.

Raising the screen to my face, my eyebrows shot up in surprise. "How the hell can anyone tell this is me?" I asked, feeling acutely relieved that my face was hidden. "This was taken from behind us. All you can see is my ass and the back of my legs." I mentally patted myself on the back for keeping my body tight and trim, and for having the good sense to shave. "You would've had to be there to know it's actually me."

"Maybe so, but it's not hard to put two and two together," Ash goaded with a chuckle.

Fair enough, it was pretty obvious that the guy in the picture was Noah. You could easily make out the side of his face as he... Cupped my butt cheek?

A male arm swooped over my shoulder and grabbed the phone before letting out a whistle. "Messina looks like he wants to take a bite out of you." Cam handed me back the phone before sliding into the seat beside me. "Do wolves eat p..."

"Shut up, you little pervert," Hope warned him before slamming her spoon on the table in frustration. "Oh, for the love of all that's holy..." she grumbled before jerking out of her chair and marching over to where a group of girls were blatantly staring and pointing at us. Of course, Ellie Dennis was one of those girls. Reese was another. All four girls seemed to grow nervous as Hope approached. "Gotta problem, girls?" Hope asked, eyebrows raised.

"Not with you," Ellie replied, cutting a dark look my way.

Hope noticed the evil looks I was receiving. "You see that girl over there?" She pointed to me before looking back at Ellie. "She's my friend. If you've got a problem with her, then I've got a problem with you. You got it?"

"Have you seen the state my brother is in?" Ellie demanded. Shoving her chair back, she stood up and stepped right up in Hope's personal space. It looked quite comical really considering Hope had a good four inches on her. "Because of *her*," Ellie spat, pointing her finger at me.

"What exactly are you accusing me of, Ellie?" I demanded as I jerked out of my seat and stalked over to where Hope and Ellie were standing. "*Because of me.*" I glared at her. "I have nothing to do with your brother."

"*Exactly*," Ellie hissed. "You are nothing to my brother, so stay the hell out of his way and stop making problems for him."

Actually, I said *'nothing to do'* and not *'nothing to'* but Ellie looked so pissed I didn't bother correcting her. Both statements were true.

"Listen to me carefully, bitch," Ellie growled as she stepped closer and wrapped her hand around my wrist. "I'm only going to tell you this once." Her green eyes burned into mine. "Noah has a lot of people depending on him, a lot riding on him staying focused and doing what needs to be done." Her nails bit into my skin. "Stay away from him or you're going to get hurt."

Tightening her grasp on my wrist, Ellie tugged me so hard I stumbled forward. "And stay away from the Ring of Fire," she whispered in my ear. "I knew you were going to cause trouble for us the minute I laid eyes on you," she added, her tone laced with disgust. "Stay. Away. From. Noah."

"If you don't take your scabby little hand off my friend, you're the one who's going to get hurt," Hope warned her menacingly.

Ellie dropped my wrist and stepped back slowly. "Take my advice, Teagan," she warned, eyes locked on me.

"I'm really not interested in taking advice from the school Barbie," I said in a bored tone, even though I was feeling a little rattled. "I enjoy thinking for myself."

I waited for the queen bitch to sit back down before I left the cafeteria.

Thankfully, Hope didn't follow me. I think she realized I needed space. I was in a foul mood, tired, and seriously pissed off with Ellie for making a fool out of me, and with Noah for being the root of all my problems.

"Hey, Beautiful."

I groaned internally when I reached the parking lot and was faced with Hope's baby brother. "Hey, Colt," I muttered, not making eye contact, hoping he'd get the hint that I wasn't feeling particularly sociable right now.

"How's your day going?" he asked as I walked past him.

Reluctantly, I stopped and turned around to face him, pulling the hood of my coat up to protect my hair from the rain. "You know," I said dryly. "A little ass and a lot hole."

Colt chuckled and then ran a hand through his soaking wet hair. "Well," he mused. "Don't let the *assholes* drag you down to their mundane level."

I pursed my lips and grimaced. "Right about now, Colt, I'm striving for normal. Mundane is sounding pretty damn appealing."

"Don't strive for normal, Beautiful," he said with a full dimpled smile. "Reach for yourself."

I shook my head in amusement. "Reach for myself?"

"Yeah." Colt grinned as he continued to walk backwards. "The best part about reaching for the best part of you is that it's completely attainable because it's already inside of you." He winked at my confused expression. "You already have the key, Beautiful. Find the lock inside of you it fits. And the best part of it all is you're the only one with a key, therefore no one can take the best of you *from you*. It's yours. For keeps."

What the...

I stood in the pouring rain, watching Colton as he strolled into the school building, feeling totally confused and surprisingly uplifted.

Yeah, Colton Carter was a strange guy.

NOAH

"Four grand, Messina," Mortico Gonzalez rasped down the line. "Consider it a little side earner."

"Are you for real?" I growled as I stalked around my living room like a madman with my phone welded to my ear.

After the beating JD and his henchmen gave me over the weekend, I hadn't even considered taking another fight for at least a couple of weeks. Shit, I hadn't been able to get out of bed until yesterday with the pain in my head. But with George away on business... Shit, what Gonzalez was offering me was fucking insane, but he'd planted the seed of hope in my mind.

Four thousand dollars would go a long way come graduation – if Logan's idea went to plan.

Gonzalez chuckled. "Absolutely, kid. Money's yours. Take out Cortez and I'll throw in a little sweetener for your troubles."

"What kind of sweetener?"

"Your debt to Lucius for the paint job?" Gonzalez mused. "Consider it paid."

My brows rose in surprise. "That's over three..."

"Grand," Gonzalez offered. "You're worth every penny, kid. Now, do we have a deal?"

Gonzalez's offer was complete bullshit, but it was bullshit I couldn't afford to turn down. "I don't have a ride to get up there," I told him as I stared out the bay window. I couldn't ask Tommy or Low. They'd been seen with me before. It was far too risky. If anyone got wind of the fact that I was doing a job for George's nemesis I, and anyone with me, would be a dead man...

"You're a resourceful kid," Gonzalez told me. "Find a way."

If JD found out I was doing side work for his father's opposition, he'd kill me with his bare hands. But like I said, Gonzalez's bullshit was too good to refuse.

My eyes fell on Teagan as she stalked up her driveway soaked to the skin and then to her cherry red civic, and suddenly I heard myself saying, "I'll be there."

TEAGAN

Uncle Max had left for work by the time I skulked back to the house.

Last night's dinner plates were exactly where we'd left them on the coffee table, so after finishing my homework, I set to work on straightening up the house before heading upstairs for a shower.

After showering and dressing in a t-shirt and pajama shorts, I spent a few moments ogling my plane ticket home that Max had left on my nightstand – *pretty little shamrock* – before sending Hope a text to let her know I'd managed to crack question three in our Trig homework. She didn't respond to my text, and I presumed she was on the phone to the *wonderful* Jordan.

The rest of the evening dragged painfully on and by nine o'clock, I was bored stiff. There was only so many times a person could recite the thirty-two counties before turning slightly suicidal, so with nothing better to do, I decided to terrorize myself with some horror movies.

I was pretty sure the storm was picking up outside and I wanted to be sound asleep before it got any worse.

As I lay curled up on my couch in my pajamas, watching *Friday the 13th* on my laptop, I closed my eyes and tried to empty my mind from all thoughts of my infamous ass jiggling. It was surprisingly easy and within minutes, I was dozing off.

It could have been minutes later or hours when the sound of a door banging startled me from my sleep. A hand covered my mouth, stopping me from screaming out.

"Payback's a bitch," a male voice whispered in my ear seconds before I was dragged off the couch.

I heard my laptop crash to the floor but I couldn't see a damn thing. Everything was black, I mean pitch black dark, but I knew exactly whose shoulder I was tossed over. Exactly whose back my face was pressed against.

I could smell *him*.

"If you broke that, you'll be sorry," I spat as I flayed my legs and struggled furiously to free myself from his clutches. "I know karate." *And seven other Chinese words.* "Let me go."

"You fight like a bitch, *Thorn*," Noah taunted as he slapped me hard on the ass. I was in a pair of light cotton pajama shorts and the slap really stung. "Where are your car keys?"

"Like I'd tell you," I snarled.

Don't look at the back of the door. Don't look at the back of the door.

"And if you hit me, I'll hit you back," I added before reaching my hand under the waistband of his sweats and digging my nails into his butt cheek.

"Jesus, you really are a thorn," Noah grunted and for a moment I thought he'd drop me, but then he straightened up and stalked through what I presumed was my hallway, stopping at the front door to remove *my keys* from the lock. Dammit.

"What happened to the lights?" I asked out of morbid curiosity. "What are you going to do to me?"

"Nature happened," he replied smugly. "And not nearly as much as I want to," he added before dropping me onto the floor. "Thanks for the wheels."

The minute he opened the front door I started to scream the place down.

"Thief!" I screamed at the top of my lungs, but Noah was too damn fast. He moved like a ninja, getting from my front door to my car within seconds.

"Hey," I screamed as I rushed down my porch steps to where Noah was climbing into the driver's seat of *my car* and then cranking the engine. The wind was vicious, blowing me backwards, and I was drenched almost instantly from the heavy rainfall.

Now, I know fear should have been my strongest emotion, considering I was being car-jacked and standing outside in a storm, but anger was what coursed through my veins.

Lightning forked in the sky above me.

And then I made the stupidest decision of my life.

I got into the car with Noah Messina.

13

TEAGAN

"Get out of the car, Teagan," Noah growled as he revved the engine menacingly. "I'm not joking around here. I need to leave."

"I wonder how many years the judge will give you for abduction and grand theft auto," I hissed in a spiteful tone as I fastened my seatbelt. I may have just put myself in a dangerous situation, but I wasn't suicidal. Seatbelts were a given in any circumstance.

"They'll have to catch me to sentence me," he shot back, casting me a sideways smirk as he took his foot off the clutch and accelerated, slipping into second and then third gear as he tore down Thirteenth Street. "And I'm very fast, Teagan."

Noah Messina looks good behind the wheel of my car, I begrudgingly thought to myself. His dark hair was mussed up in an effortlessly sexy way and the way he absentmindedly ran his tongue over his lower lip as he drove was wickedly distracting.

I folded my arms over my chest and stared defiantly ahead.

"So, what's the plan?" I asked when the silence got the better of me. He'd taken us away from The Hill. We were heading into the mountains and I was growing anxious. It pissed me the hell off that he could make me feel anxious. I wasn't afraid of him. *I wasn't*. "Drop me off in the middle of nowhere? Set fire to my car? Hold me for ransom in some secluded shed?"

Rain beat against the windshield and Noah flicked the wipers on full speed to clear it. To be honest, I didn't have a clue how he could drive in these conditions and I was truly surprised we were still in one piece and with four tires on the ground.

Noah laughed softly as he changed gears before taking a sharp corner. I was forced back in my seat from the speed he was driving and I thought I might pee. "You know, for a little girl who's all alone in a car in the middle of nowhere, with a strange and insanely attractive man..."

"Strange is a good word for you," I said, interrupting him. "Also, the word kidnapper comes to mind."

"Oh please," Noah snorted. "I didn't kidnap you. It was your choice to get in. I needed to borrow your wheels."

"What?" I turned in my seat to gape at him. "Hang on, let me get this straight. You break into my house in the middle of the night, almost smother me to death with one hand and sexually assault me with the other..." I inhaled a calming breath. "Because you want to *borrow* my car?"

Noah shrugged nonchalantly. "Pretty much."

"You're crazy," I mused as I studied the side of his face.

"And you're a huge fucking thorn in my side," he shot back, not taking his eyes off the road. "Because of your little *tantrum* with the paint, I'm still without a ride."

Holding the wheel with one hand, Noah used his free

one to pull a box of cigarettes and a lighter out of his pocket. "If I don't have a ride, then I can't work," he continued as he sparked up and took a deep drag from his cigarette before exhaling slowly. "And If I can't work, I can't keep the wolves from the door." He looked over at me, his brown eyes dark and meaningful. "Now can I?"

"You broke my windshield first..." I tried to argue, but Noah cut me off.

"What's worse, Thorn?" he asked in an eerily calm tone of voice. "Me accidentally cracking the windshield of your mediocre Honda Civic, or you purposely destroying the paintwork, and windshield, of my Lexus I.S 200?"

I opened my mouth to defend my car, but he had a point. *Dammit.* "Your sister started it..."

"I'm not Ellie," he all but roared before adding in a husky voice. "I'm worse."

"I'm beginning to gather that," I whispered before swallowing deeply. "If you needed to use my car to get to work, that's fine, but take me home first. *Please.*"

"No can do," Noah replied calmly. "I'm already running late. You chose to get in the car with me." He shrugged. "You're gonna have to suffer the consequences."

"What do you do?" I asked nervously. It didn't take a genius to know it wasn't good. We were in the middle of nowhere and he'd stolen my car. *Oh, sweet merciful Lord...*

Noah gripped the steering wheel a little tighter, a vein in his neck throbbed, and when he spoke, the fury in his voice was obvious. "I do what I'm told, when I'm told, no questions asked." Turning his face to look at me, he stared straight into my eyes and for the second time he said, "Let's hope you can swim, Thorn."

We didn't speak again for the remainder of the drive.

I chose to keep my mouth shut and stop asking questions.

I had a feeling the less I knew, the safer I would be.

But the minute Noah took a left and headed down a familiar dirt road, my heart sank into my stomach. I suddenly knew exactly where we were going, and that knowledge made me want to cry.

NOAH

She was going to cry.

She was going to cry and I was going to kick myself in the balls for being the cause of those tears and for putting her in danger. Because she was in danger. And I was in danger of losing my goddamn mind if those hazel eyes welled up any more.

The image of Teagan sitting beside me in her drenched pajamas with her tiny, sock covered feet planted firmly on the dashboard was almost too much. She sniffled, and I thought I might lose it.

I dared a peek at her and could have fucking groaned when I saw how unbelievably vulnerable she looked. She hugged her knees as she stared straight ahead, her hazel eyes wide and fearful. Her blonde hair was soaking wet and draped around her shoulders like a golden curtain. When she started to shiver, I felt like someone had physically sucker punched me in the gut.

I'd fucked up.

How had I ever thought it would be easy to borrow her car?

Nothing was easy when it came to her.

Jesus Christ.

TEAGAN

I was back at the Ring of Fire.

The huge walls of the quarry loomed above us as Noah drove further inside. It seemed different than the last time – quieter. There were maybe fifty or so people scattered around one lone bonfire.

Killing the engine of my car, Noah unbuckled his seatbelt and sat quietly for a moment before turning to face me. "Don't talk to anyone out there," he said in a serious tone. "Keep your head down and *do not* leave my side, do you understand?"

"Noah, I'm sorry for wrecking your car, and for kicking you in the balls," I blurted out as I clutched the seat nervously and eyed a huge, beefy man in a wife-beater walking towards our car. *My god, it was the month of December. Did he not feel the cold?* "And for biting you and ruining your fight, but can we just... Can you please take me home?" I could feel my body trembling. "Please don't make me get out of this car."

The brown in Noah's eyes noticeably softened. "Teagan," he said gently. "It's alright..."

"Seriously," I rambled on nervously, digging my nails into the fabric of my seat. "We need to get out of here, Noah. This place is..." I looked around and exhaled a sharp breath. "Treacherous."

Memories of being stomped on flooded me and I grimaced. "We shouldn't be here, Noah."

"Messina."

The sound of Noah's name being called came moments before my car door was opened and I was staring into the face of a dark-bearded man with arms the size of tree trunks.

"You brought me a present, Messina?" he asked as his eyes dropped to my bare legs. "Fresh." He smiled, revealing a mouthful of yellow-stained teeth. "And ripe."

"You couldn't handle her, Gonzalez," Noah replied, his tone a lazy drawl as he unbuckled my belt and dragged me onto his lap.

I went willingly, anything to get away from the creepy, bearded guy with the greasy black hair and paunchy beer gut. "W-what are you doing...?"

Noah's hands were surprisingly gentle as he clenched my hips and touched his mouth to my throat. "Play along," he whispered, low enough so that I was the only one who could hear him. His lips touched the skin covering my pulse. "And I'll keep you safe."

I nodded, terrified, and clumsily wrapped my arms around Noah's neck.

Pulling back, Noah looked at me almost apologetically. "Don't bite this time," he warned me in a gruff tone before covering my mouth with his

What the...

And then he was kissing me.

His lips were surprisingly tender against mine, guiding me deeper, taking me further...

The wolf whistles and suggestive comments coming from the men outside the car were drowned out by the sound of my pulse pounding in my ears, and when Noah slipped his tongue into my mouth and massaged my tongue with his, I forgot all about playing along. I crushed my body to his, pressing myself hard against the rising bulge beneath me.

His hands were clamped on my hips possessively as he thrust upwards and I pushed downwards. My body was aching, throbbing for something more, and I had no clue of what was happening.

The taste of him was heady; the feel of him like nothing I'd ever experienced before. Noah was everywhere; dominating, giving, tormenting, tasting, taking. I completely submitted to his touch, my body trusting him completely.

As fast as it had started, it ended and Noah pulled back, lips swollen and wet.

"She's *mine*," he said in a deathly calm tone as he dragged my hips forward. "And I don't share."

The man who Noah had called Gonzalez held his hands up in retreat. "No problem, kid," he chuckled before hacking up a phlegm ball and spitting it on the gravel. "Bitch is yours."

Everything happened so quickly after that, and I kind of lost myself in the mayhem.

Noah and I got out of the car, he kissed me hard on the lips before taking my hand and half-dragged me off in the direction of the bonfire.

I went with him, because, well let's face it, it was either stick with him or take my chances with the fifty other horned up dudes around me and, right about now, I was all about sticking with the devil I knew.

I stood like the good little doormat I was supposed to be as Noah spoke to a few men around the bonfire. I kept my head down, I didn't speak to a soul, and I never once let Noah out of my sight. I had no idea of what was happening, the atmosphere was incredibly frigid, or what Noah was doing with those shady looking men, but for the first time in my life, I truly felt pathetic.

Here I was, scantily clad in pajamas and slipper-socks, staying like a dog for a boy whose sister had purposefully made my life a misery since the summer. And to top it all off, I was soaked to the skin, courtesy of Mother Nature who had decided to turn into a moody, rainy bitch.

When Noah reappeared at my side, he gently took my elbow and led me back to the car. "I have something I need to wrap up," he said in a low voice. "Stay here and wait for me."

He opened the car door and waited for me to obediently climb in.

I didn't.

I'd reclaimed my lady balls and wasn't taking his shit.

"What the hell are you involved in?" I demanded. My mind was throwing all kinds of crazy theories about. "What's an eighteen-year-old guy doing hanging around with these kinds of people?"

"Get in the car and wait for me," Noah ordered fiercely. "And keep your goddamn voice down."

"No," I hissed as I held my palm out. It was pouring rain, but I refused to get in that car.

"Either get in with me and take me home right now, or give me my keys and I'll drive myself."

"Teagan," Noah warned. "I'm not asking you."

"I'm not sitting around here, Noah," I spat, glaring up at him. "I'm not staying here a second longer, so if you're not gonna take me home, then give me my goddamn car keys."

"Jesus fucking Christ, Teagan." Noah cursed and kicked the wheel of my car. "You're a fucking thorn in my side."

"That's ironic," I spat, shoving him hard in the chest. "Because you're the biggest prick I've ever met."

"Get. In. The. Car," he seethed, pressing his forehead to mine.

"Go. To. Hell," I shot back, staring up at him defiantly. "I'm out of here."

I really had no idea where I was going when I turned on my heels and marched off in the direction we'd come, but I knew it couldn't be as bad as where I'd been.

"I won't tell you again, Thorn," I heard Noah call after me.

"Fuck you." I flipped him the bird as I stalked down the dirt road. My emotions were everywhere. Why was I behaving like this?

Because of him, that's why. Ugh, because he made my blood boil.

"Argh," I roared and felt a little better.

A pair of strong arms clamped around me and lifted me off my feet. "I'll take you home soon, Teagan, I promise," he whispered in my ear. "But If either of us leave now they're gonna smell a rat."

I stiffened and Noah sighed heavily against my neck. "Just... Listen to me," he muttered before turning our bodies around and walking back towards the bonfire.

"What are you doing with these people?" I asked him, and my voice sounded young – young and terrified.

"I told you," he said in a gruff tone. "I do what I'm told."

"And tonight?" I asked him. "What have you been told to do tonight?"

"Tonight, I fight." Noah looked me directly in the eyes when he spoke. "I didn't want you to have to watch, which was *why* I told you to wait in the car."

"Why?" I tried to shake off his hold. "I've seen you fight here before. Why is this different?"

"It just is," Noah snapped. "There's a lot at stake."

"So that's what this place is?" I asked him as I looked around nervously. "A fighting ring?"

Noah nodded stiffly, not meeting my eyes. "Amongst other things."

"And that building back there?" I pointed in the direction we'd come. The huge warehouse a half a mile back the dirt yard with trucks and bikes scattered around it hadn't escaped my attention either. "Is that..." I paused and pinched the bridge of my nose, desperately trying to keep my nerve. "Is that a part of this?"

"Yes."

"You shouldn't have brought me here, Noah," I croaked out.

"You brought yourself here," he snarled, chest heaving. "I thought I could f... I didn't think... Fuck."

"Messina," a man shouted. "You're up."

"It's gonna be okay," Noah whispered in my ear before he pressed a kiss to my cheek. "I promise."

I grabbed his wrist when he moved to walk away from me and held on. "Noah." I begged him with my eyes. "Don't." God only knows why I was panicking like this, but I couldn't help it. "Please."

He looked torn.

He opened his mouth as if to say something, but dragged his hand through his hair and cursed instead.

Finally, Noah shook his head and pulled free from my grasp. "I have to," was all he said before walking away.

I stood, with my heart in my mouth, watching as Noah tugged off his t-shirt and dropped it on the hood of a car before balling his hands into fists and settling into his fighting stance.

The man Noah was fighting, if he was even human, was twice his width and a good two inches taller than him, which made this man-beast at least 6'5". The crowd of people erupted into madness the second Noah punched the man-beast in the ribs and suddenly, I couldn't look at this anymore.

This was it – his job.

Noah hurt people for money.

This was sick.

This was so wrong.

Turning around, I waded through the mass, not stopping until I reached the car, and collapsed into the passenger seat. I wasn't stupid, I knew what kind of trouble came with guys like him. It was at that moment I realized just how stupid men were. Testosterone filled idiots, fueled by sex, booze, and the thrill of the chase.

I was out.

I'd rather enroll myself into a convent than have any part of this farce. I should have guessed he was into all things bad the second I set eyes on him. For god's sake, the very first time we met, he'd just thrown a man through my windshield. And Friday night, when he pulled me out from under the crowd... God, he was vicious that night. He was eighteen and drove a top of the range Lexus. Who the hell owned a Lexus in high school?

Someone involved in illegal fighting drives a Lexus in high school, apparently.

Ugh. Screw this. Once Noah dropped me home, I would keep my distance from him.

"Pretty little thing, ain't you?" a voice said from close by, and my whole body stiffened. I couldn't move – I could barely breathe.

Getting a hold of myself, I grabbed the door and tried to swing it shut, but a beefy hand stopped it halfway and pulled the door outwards. I let go from the sheer force of his strength, and then I saw who owned the arm and my heart sank.

"I've seen you here before." Yellow Teeth grinned down at me. "Yeah, you're the bitch who's got JD's boy's head all fucked up." He tapped his finger against his temple. "That makes me curious."

Grabbing my arm, he pulled me out of the car and slammed me against it. "He ain't brought no other bitch here before," he growled in my ear as he clutched my throat with his hand.

"I'm not his *bitch*, asshole," I hissed. Fear spiraled inside of me as I desperately looked around for anyone who could help me, but came up empty.

Yellow Teeth smirked cruelly and tightened his hold on my throat. "What makes you so special, blondie?"

"Get your hands off me," I spat as I tried to shove him away from me. "Or they'll have to surgically remove my shoe from your ass."

Yellow Teeth laughed loudly, peering down at me with dark eyes and a sickeningly crooked grin. "Maybe he likes 'em feisty."

I opened my mouth to answer him, but Yellow Teeth squeezed hard, cutting me off. "You a good fuck, huh?" He clutched my throat tighter. "Is your cunt as tight as your asshole?"

"Don't touch me," I choked out. A whimpering noise ripped from my throat when he pushed his hand inside my shorts and cupped me roughly.

Tears pooled in my eyes and he laughed cruelly. "That's it," he sneered, stroking me vulgarly.

I clamped my thighs together but the bastard shoved his knee between my legs and forced them open. "Messina's got himself some tight virgin pussy..."

"You need a hearing test, asshole?" I heard Noah snarl, and I'd never felt so relieved to hear anyone's voice in my life. "I already told you she's mine."

Yellow Teeth stepped away from me and I sagged against the car in relief.

"I was only playing around, Messina," he chuckled, but it was a nervous sound. "No harm done."

Noah walked right up to him, not stopping until his forehead connected with Yellow Teeth's nose.

Blood sprayed everywhere and I thought I would vomit.

"Touch her again and I'll break more than your nose," Noah roared, chest heaving. "Comprende, asshole?"

Swinging around to where I was leaning against the car, Noah walked right up to me. The gentleness in his touch as he cupped my face, his thumbs stroking my cheekbones as he checked me over, was in direct conflict to his actions less than a minute before.

I didn't think twice about clutching his shirt and pulling him closer to me. I breathed in slow and deep, finding sanctuary in his mere presence.

Then Noah did something I wasn't expecting.

He cupped my face in his hands, let out a shivering sigh, and kissed my forehead.

It was such a tender, affectionate thing to do that it baffled my brain and accelerated my heart rate.

I was petrified while Noah looked wholly enraged. He had my front pressed to his chest, his hand was stroking my lower back as he glowered over my head at Gonzalez and his cronies.

"Mine," he said coldly, swinging around to stare at the half dozen or so men who were now surrounding us, flanking Yellow Teeth.

Thankfully, nobody seemed to want to fight him, and they gradually nodded and backed away from us.

Opening the car door, Noah helped me inside before walking around to the driver's side and climbing in. Neither of us spoke as Noah drove out of the quarry and back onto the dirt road. I didn't know what to say. To be honest, I was kind of flummoxed.

Noah looked mutinous as he fiddled with the car radio, flicking through songs before finally settling on Bruce Springsteen's *I'm on Fire*.

"So, this is what you do," I choked out when I was finally able to speak again. "You fight for money. You're a fighter."

"I told you," He replied in a cold tone. "I do what I'm told – and I told you to stay."

I chose to ignore that sexist remark and asked, "Was that man your boss?"

Noah glanced at me. "Who, Gonzalez?"

I nodded.

"No," he replied quietly. "He's just the asshole who was in charge of the fight tonight."

"Are you going to be in trouble?" I asked him.

Noah shrugged noncommittally. "He shouldn't have touched what's mine."

"Except I'm not yours, Noah," I reminded him. "And now you've punched one of your bosses..."

"Thorn, it's fine," he snapped. "I'll figure this out."

Tightening his hold on the wheel, Noah cleared his throat roughly. "You shouldn't have gone off on your own." Frowning, he added, "You could've been hurt."

"*Could've* been hurt?" I shot back sarcastically. "Oh, yeah, because Gonzalez putting his hands in my knickers was so much fun. *That* didn't hurt at all." I shuddered and leaned my head back against the seat. "I need to shower."

Noah didn't reply to that, but the way the car swerved slightly proved he was listening.

"Why do you do this?" I asked him when the lights of the city came into view.

"I do this for reasons you'll never understand," he said stiffly.

"Why do you fight?" I pressed, not satisfied with his noncommittal reply.

"Why do I fight?" Noah repeated my question, and he seemed to think about it for a moment. "Because I don't know how to do anything else."

"Yes, you do." I sighed heavily. "You're a senior in high school for Christ's sake. There are other jobs and sports you could be doing – legally."

"I need the release, Teagan," Noah grumbled as we pulled onto Thirteenth Street. "I need it to take the edge off of... Life."

"That's a really pathetic reason," I told him as we pulled into my driveway.

Hissing out a sharp breath, Noah jacked the handbrake and slammed the palm of his hand against the steering wheel. "I've been through more shit than you could *ever* relate to, Teagan." He was staring straight ahead, breathing fast and hard. "So don't fucking dare call me or anything I do pathetic. You have no idea what I've..." He stopped and clenched his fist. "Just don't."

There was something about the way Noah's voice rose, the deep pain in his voice, that touched something raw inside of me. I realized I was worried about him, even though a huge part of me hated his guts.

"Tell me, Noah," I urged. I knew I should walk away right now, leave him to it, but I couldn't. We were on the verge of something – what, I had no clue, but I could feel it in my bones. "Make me understand..." My words trailed off as I studied his closed off expression. *Piss him off... Get him to talk by pissing him off.* "Or is your real reason for beating people to a pulp as *pathetic* as your fake one?"

"Teagan, back the fuck off," he snarled. Opening his door, Noah climbed out and slammed the door before leaning against it. "My reasons are my own which means they – *I* – have nothing to do with you. Get that through your head. Fuck."

Anger boiled in my veins and I unfastened my seatbelt and scrambled out of the car. "Fine," I spat. Leaning over the roof of my car I narrowed my eyes and glared at him. "I'm just the girl who was almost *raped* because of your need for a *release*."

Noah flinched and I was glad.

"Teagan, I'm..." Noah stopped abruptly and tossed my keys over the roof of my car instead. "Just go home."

I caught them mid-air and shook my head, feeling hurt, angry, and weirdly emotional. "I'm not doing this anymore, Noah," I told him, detaching my car key from the rest of the bunch before shoving my key across the roof of the hood towards him.

Noah picked up my key and frowned at me.

I held my hands up in retreat. "I'm out," I told him, feeling crazed and irrational as I backed up the steps of my porch. "I'm not going to fight with you anymore."

"Your key?" His face was a mask of indifference, but I could have sworn I saw pain in those brown depths for the briefest of moments.

"I don't give a damn about my car!" I screamed dramatically, pushing my wet hair back from my face. "And if it means you'll leave me alone, then have the fucking thing. Consider it my white flag. I'm bowing out of this war." I turned my key in the door before looking back at him. "Tell your sister she won," I said coldly as I stepped inside. "You both have."

14

NOAH

"Tell your sister she won," Teagan shouted, eyes filled with tears. "You both have," she added and her voice broke.

I knew I should go after her. Stop her. Apologize. Convince her that I wasn't the heartless bastard she thought I was. But the truth wasn't something I could talk about. Not to her. Not to anyone.

The girl... Dammit, she meant something to me. I was still reeling from that kiss we shared in the car. *Jesus, her lips felt like heaven.* I felt a huge urge to protect her, shelter her from the bullshit of my life.

How the hell would she understand something I didn't understand myself? And her knowing the truth would put her in worse danger than she already was in. I couldn't allow that.

I couldn't fucking bear it.

Instead, I stood like a dummy with the key of her car in my hand, feeling more useless than I had in years as Teagan walked away from me.

The house was eerily quiet when I let myself inside and

the power still wasn't back. The storm had probably blown down a pole or something.

After lighting a shitload of candles, I grabbed my phone, slipped outside, and walked down to my makeshift gym, bracing myself for the phone call I had no doubt was coming.

TEAGAN

The second I closed my front door, I stripped my pajamas and socks off in the hallway, desperate to be rid of the icky sensation before switching on the light.

Nothing happened.

I tried the light switch in the lounge and then the kitchen before admitting defeat.

I was in the middle of a power cut.

Panic tore through me.

Here I was, naked as the day I was born, in the dark....

I managed to find a clean t-shirt of Uncle Max's in the laundry hamper and shrugged it on before feeling my way over to the sink to root for a flashlight. Thankfully I found one and switched it on.

The relief I felt from that tiny yellow orb of light was huge and I sagged against the counter. The wind was picking up outside, the sound of trees swaying against the heavy breeze was growing louder and louder, bringing with it a whole truckload of memories I didn't care to entertain.

What the hell was I supposed to do now?

Sit in the dark and wait for daylight?

I wasn't afraid of a bit of wind and rain, it was a given where I came from, but I *was* terrified of the dark – especially being alone in the dark.

The walls of the kitchen began to close in on me, crushing my windpipe, pressing hard against my skull, and I didn't think twice about reaching for the backdoor and escaping outside.

It was pitch black when I stepped outside, the night air was sharp and cutting, but the relief of not being enclosed was enough to calm my nerves.

A loud noise to the left of the bed of petunias startled me, and I froze. The sound of a man's voice broke through the silence and I found myself drawn to it. *Noah.*

Without thinking twice about what I was doing, I closed the door behind me and crept over to the far end of the wall that separated our gardens and crouched low, shifting around until I found an upturned plastic flower pot to sit on.

"...Don't you think I know that, T..."

I stopped breathing. Was he on the phone or was someone out here with him?

"...broken rib..."

Who had a broken rib? Did Noah have a broken rib? I hadn't realized.

"...Yeah, me, douchebag..."

I dropped my flashlight with fright and had to cover my mouth as the fear of god spread through me. I'd thought Noah was answering my thoughts but, thankfully, he rambled on.

"...No, he doesn't know about it..."

He sounded annoyed.

"...She's not for you, T..."

Who? Who wasn't for him?

"...I mean it..."

I cracked the flower pot I was sitting on.

I cracked the fucking flower pot.

"...Hang on, I think someone's out here."

I clenched my eyes shut and stayed as still as a statue for the longest time.

"...No, must've been a bear or a mountain lion," I heard him say and my heart froze in my chest.

They had bears and mountain lions?

Of course, they bloody did and now I was going to be nom-noms for one of them.

Fuck that. Run. Run. Haul ass to the house.

Dropping onto my hands and knees, I crawled as quietly as I could though the mud and leaves towards the house, trampling the bed of petunias in my bid to survive. I made it to the back door and felt around for the door handle.

It wasn't bloody there.

Where the hell did it go?

Dammit, I could have kicked myself in the ass for dropping my flashlight in my rush to safety.

"Curiosity killed the kitty," I heard a voice say, and I could have wept.

A light shone down on my head and I ducked my face in shame.

It wasn't a bear or a lion.

It was worse...

"Noah," I sighed heavily. "I was just..." I racked my brain, trying to think of a good enough lie to explain why I was outside in the dark on my hands and knees and covered in compost.

"You were just eavesdropping on a private conversation," Noah offered, his eyes dark, brows set in a deep frown.

"What're you... Where'd you..." I looked up and glared at him. "You're trespassing on private property – *again*."

Okay, not the right thing to say.

Noah clenched his jaw and I felt a sizzle of fear burn through me. "Get up," he growled.

"No." I shook my head. "I'm good where I am, thanks."

He sighed in annoyance. "It's freezing cold. The whole street's power is out," he grumbled, gesturing to the sky with his flashlight. "And you, genius, have locked yourself out by the looks of it."

"I have not," I said defensively. "I just don't see well in the dark, that's all. I can't find the handle. If you shine your torch on the door, I'll be out of your way in a jiffy."

"You can't see what isn't there," he grumbled. "That door?" He raised his brows. "Its key-accessible only."

I glared at the door. "You tricky bitch."

"You like talking to wood, don't you, Thorn?" he mused.

"Oh yes," I snapped as I climbed to my feet. "I can't wait to talk to the wood surrounding your dead body."

"Nice," he chuckled. "But you'll be waiting a while."

"I wouldn't be so sure if I were you," I spat.

"What makes you say that?" he asked in an oddly curious tone.

"Hmm, let's see." I pretended to check the reasons off with my fingers. "You fight violently, you smoke constantly, you drink excessively, you more than likely consume illegal substances and you most definitely sleep around."

I looked him up and down in pure disgust. "The cheerleaders talk, Noah." They didn't. Well, not to me at least, but it was an educated guess. "I'll give you 'til you're thirty-five – thirty if that nasty temper gets the better of you."

"Thanks for the morbid checklist," Noah said flatly. "I was going to help you out, but considering you're still a judgmental bitch, you can help yourself."

Noah turned to leave and a sudden burst of fear flooded me.

"Wait." I grabbed his elbow. "You're going to leave me here?" I swallowed deeply. "Alone?"

"You'll survive," he said mockingly, pulling free from my grasp. "A tough girl like you," he taunted. "You can talk to some trees if you get lonely. Oh, and watch out for the bears," he added spitefully.

"Wait... Noah, please wait." I raced after him, clutching onto the back of his t-shirt with a death grip.

He took pity on me and stopped walking, causing me to smack into his back. I staggered backwards as I tried to regain my balance.

Surprisingly, Noah reached out and caught me and, when I felt his hand cover mine, my pulse thumped so hard I was almost certain he could feel it.

Nemesis or not, Noah Messina was currently the only thing standing between me and isolated darkness. "Please don't leave me on my own."

"You're a fucking thorn in my side," he told me for possibly the hundredth time, but he didn't let go of my hand. Instead, he held my hand as he walked. The feel of his hand covering mine caused my stomach to twist and flip around.

"Let go for a sec," Noah ordered when we got to the bottom of the garden.

"No way." I held onto his hand with both of mine. Knowing how much bad blood was between us, he would disappear and leave me on my own out here.

"Teagan, let go," he repeated, clearly annoyed. "I'll help

you over, but I need to jump the wall first."

"I can't," I hissed. It was true. My hands were glued to him in fear. "Please..."

Noah growled and muttered a swear word before crouching down. "Climb on my back, *Thorn*," he ordered and I did, choosing to ignore the jibe. I wanted to live; name calling and snarky retorts weren't a priority right now.

I wrapped my legs around Noah's waist and held on for dear life. "Dammit, Teagan, move your hands," he grumbled.

"Sorry," I whispered and moved my hands from where I was covering his eyes.

"Hold on tight," he ordered, and I tightened my grip on his neck. I felt his Adam's apple bob against my fingers. "Not... That... Tight," he complained, gripping my bare thighs firmly.

A hot flash of desire hit me directly in the groin, and the way Noah moved; jostling us as he climbed over the wall, wasn't doing anything to ease the tension in my body.

The throbbing increased and I moaned when he jumped to the ground, my clit receiving some serious one on one from his back.

"You're really scared, aren't you?" Noah asked in a softer tone when we reached his back door. His breath tickled my forearm. "Your entire body is shaking."

"Mmm," was all I replied, all I dared to allow myself to say as I climbed down from his back and shifted around nervously from foot to foot.

"Where's your family tonight?" I asked him when Noah opened his door and let us inside. I was pleasantly surprised to see his kitchen, which was similar to mine, was lit with several soft glowing candles. "Are they here?" The silence was eerie, and I remembered the murders in the house across the street.

"Stop asking questions," he mumbled, closing the door behind me.

"Are you home alone?" My eyes followed his movements. "All by yourself?"

"Yeah, I'm home alone, please don't call CPS," Noah mocked before rolling his eyes. "I'm eighteen, Teagan, not eight."

"I didn't mean..." I felt my cheeks redden. "Forget it."

"What were you doing outside?" His brown eyes studied me closely and I could feel my cheeks reddening.

"I'm afraid of the dark," I blurted out.

"You're afraid of the dark so you go outside, in the *dark*," he stated in an irritated tone as he stood with his back to the door, frowning at me. "You're wet."

"What? N-no, I'm not," I argued, my voice squeaky and high pitched as I discreetly crossed my legs.

"You're soaking," he corrected me. "It's dark in here, but I'm not blind, Teagan."

I automatically looked down, which was about the worst thing I could do, because not only did I confirm that I was wet, but I also learned Noah was right about something else. I was soaking wet.

Yes, droplets of rain covered my skin, but *I* was drenched, my thighs sticky, and my only saving grace was the fact that Uncle Max's red t-shirt fell to my thighs.

Die, die, dear god let me die.

You hate him... right?

It's okay, you're both mature people.

It's a natural occurrence. Just...shake it off.

And that's about when I realized another thing.

Noah had given me a piggyback.

A freaking piggyback.

A high pitched whine slipped out of my mouth, and I

truly felt like lifting my face towards the sky and howling like a wolf. Because of Noah Messina's exceptional ability to summon a tsunami from my vagina, I was going to spend the rest of the school year being tortured. Mortification and sexual frustration festered inside of my body. I would never live this down. *He* would never let me live this down – *if* he knew...

Did he know?

I studied his face.

He didn't look like he knew.

He looked... Well, he looked rigid. He was frowning, nothing new there, and his hands were balled into fists at his sides.

I wondered if it was possible that my vagina could have a mind of its own, because the signals she was flashing out were all kinds of crazy. And then I wondered why the hell my core was pulsing so much?

He was a bastard – a mean, cruel, sarcastic, oh-so-beautiful bastard. I knew this.

Get with the program, vagina.

How was I supposed to get his top off without him knowing my true intentions? *Without him* smelling *my true intentions.*

"Can I have your t-shirt?" *Smooth, Teagan.* "I mean, will you take your top off for me?" *Ugh... I loathed myself.*

Noah raised his brow in surprise. "I'm not a complete bastard, Teagan, I'll get you a clean shirt."

"No," I shouted before letting out a nervous giggle – more like cackle. "No..." I tucked my hair behind my ears nervously. "I want yours. Uh, please?"

"You're the strangest creature I never knew existed," he mused thoughtfully as he studied me with his razor sharp eyes.

Whatever Noah was looking for on my face, he obviously didn't find it because he hissed in frustration before sucking in a sharp breath. "Wait here," he ordered in a tight voice as he roughly ran a hand through his hair. "I'll get something for you to wear."

Noah brushed past me and I could clearly see, even in the dim lighting which made being able to see it ten times worse, the stain of my err... *girlie juices* on his white shirt.

Oh, sweet merciful lord...

Think, Teagan, think...

"Noah, wait," I yelped as I lifted the hem of the t-shirt I was wearing and pulled it over my head. "I'm naked."

Noah froze, his whole body tensed, and then he slowly turned around and looked at me.

Covering my breasts with my hands, I shifted around awkwardly. "And I *really* need your shirt."

Okay, so maybe I hadn't thought this *entirely* through.

My goal was to get Noah's shirt, not lose mine in the process. Now I'm butt naked in the middle of the man's kitchen and all I was concerned about was getting that damn shirt off him.

My priorities were all kinds of messed up...

Noah was breathing hard through his nose as he balled and then un-balled his fists, his entire focus riveted on my body – my very naked body. His eyes never left me as he reached one hand behind his head and tugged his shirt off.

Biting down on my lip, I allowed myself to eyeball his skin; taking in the toned plains of his stomach, the dark trail of hair, those rolling pin abs, and the nasty looking bruise on the left side of his torso.

My nipples puckered tight. My skin prickled with goosebumps and my legs, my stupid, traitorous legs were shaking like ivy leaves.

Holding his plain white shirt in his hand, Noah made no move to pass it to me. Instead, he lifted his gaze to meet my eyes, his expression hungry.

I let out a shaky breath when I saw the intensity in his eyes.

"Do you think I'm stupid, Teagan?" Noah rasped, taking a step towards me.

My body stepped towards him without my brain's permission, and I watched as Noah's stomach muscles rippled. It took all my self control to stay where I was and not step closer and touch that smooth, toned skin. My hands dropped to my sides, and I thought I heard Noah growl.

"No," I breathed, trembling. "I don't think you're stupid, Noah."

He stepped closer, causing me to swallow deeply. "Do you think I couldn't feel you when we were outside?" He tilted his head to one side and took another step until we were chest to chest. "Pulsing against me?" His hips caged me in. "Throbbing?" Bending at the waist, he grabbed my thighs and hoisted me onto the kitchen table.

Closing my eyes, I let out a soft moan as my legs wrapped around his hips.

"You're aching right now," he purred as his hands slid up and down my bare thighs. The friction of his jeans against my clit was torture. "Aren't you?"

"Not for you," I moaned. The pressure in my core was so tight, I thought I'd explode if I didn't come.

Noah pressed against me hard and my mouth fell open. His dark hair was soaking and falling into his eyes; charcoal eyes that were burning into me.

I suddenly realized that I didn't dislike Noah, and that was a huge problem for me. I didn't dislike him and I definitely didn't trust him, but my god did I want him.

"*Only* for me," he corrected as he slipped a hand between our bodies and slowly thumbed my clit.

"How can I trust you?" I whispered, rocking against him. He felt so damn good, all I wanted to do was let go of the grudge I'd been holding and embrace what Noah was offering me. "I make you angry. You're... Always mad at me..."

"You make me hard as fucking rock," he corrected me in a husky tone. "Jesus, you smell so good." Noah pressed himself against me, his hardening cock bulging in his jeans. He felt so very familiar, his touch on my skin so incredibly right, like his was the only touch my body would ever need – ever crave.

My mind knew this attraction, and my behavior, was all kinds of fucked up and irrational, but there was this draw I hadn't felt before; or maybe I had and refused to consider it as anything other than my body's heated response to his assholeness.

"Goddammit, Teagan, you've been driving me crazy for months," he rasped, running his nose up and down my jawline. "You're a thorn in my goddamn side."

I groaned loudly but was silenced by Noah's lips as he devoured me. I wasn't sure if I was dreaming, because Noah kissing me and rubbing my clit was causing sensations inside my body that were entirely too good to be true.

"You know what this means," he purred as he licked and nibbled my neck, tracing his tongue all over my jaw, plunging into my mouth to duel with mine. "I win," he said against my lips. "And you're the prize."

I moaned when Noah's lips claimed mine, barely noticed the sound of the wind howling outside or the bright flashes of lightning when they lit up the room. My fingernails dug into his back, my heels pressed against his ass, urging him on.

"I always knew *she* was desperate, but this is a new low for him,"

A horribly familiar voice sneered, followed by another snickering voice. "Well, if it's handed to the guy on a plate..."

I froze before a huge wave of humiliation engulfed me.

Pulling my face back from Noah's, I blinked rapidly, clearing my vision before seriously wishing I hadn't.

Ellie, Jason, and a red faced Reese stood in the kitchen doorway staring straight at us, and the only thing protecting my naked body from being a full display was Noah's partially naked body– though all three still had a pretty good view. To top it all off, I was indeed sitting on a dinner plate.

Oh god...

"What the fuck do you think this is, a peep show? Get the hell out of here," Noah roared as he lifted me off my back and pressed his body tightly to mine.

I wanted nothing more than to shove him away and run for the hills, but that would involve me giving Ellie and Jason full view of my puss and that was something I was unwilling to do.

"Wow, Noah, I didn't think you'd actually go through with it," Ellie snarled.

"With what?" I asked, staring up at Noah's face. "Go through with what, Noah?" A horrible feeling crept over my skin as I continued to stare up at Noah. "Well?"

"His own execution," Ellie spat. "Because that's what you represent, slut." She turned on her heel and sauntered out of the room with Jason hot on her heels.

My attention fell on the red-headed pervert still

standing in the doorway. "Do you mind?" I glared at Reese's face. She looked furious. "This is kind of private."

"How could you do this to me, Noah?" Reese demanded, glaring at Noah. "And with that skinny freak...."

"You knew the rules, Reese," Noah said in a weary tone.

"And do your rules apply to her?" she shot back cattily.

"No," Noah replied coldly, tightening his hold on me. "They don't apply to her."

"You'll be sorry," Reese sobbed before rushing from the room. "You both will."

"They were here," I stated coldly as I pushed him away and got to my feet. I wasn't prepared to delve into the whole Reese conversation. It was pretty obvious what was going on between them, or at least had been.

Picking up my soaked t-shirt, I slid my arms through the sleeves and covered myself. "You said you were alone, but you weren't. They were all here. You lied to me."

"Teagan, calm down and listen," Noah said in a husky tone as he pulled on his jeans before holding his hands up as if he was dealing with a wild animal. "I didn't plan any of this, baby."

"Baby?" I shook my head in disgust as I backed into the hallway. "Have I got a pacifier in my mouth or something? I'm not your *baby*."

Noah looked sincere, his eyes burned with the truth, but I just couldn't be sure.

He stepped closer to me. "Come on. I was with you all night. I didn't fucking plan this."

Reaching a hand out, he snagged the hem of my shirt and pulled me into his arms, snaking them around my back before coming to rest on my hips. "Don't jump to conclusions again," he whispered, dropping his lips to my neck and kissing me softly. "Come upstairs. I'll find you something dry to wear."

His fingernails dug into my skin so erotically that I almost agreed. Almost. But then I remembered the summer of hell I'd endured because of the members of this household and the darkness looked oddly appealing.

"I need to go," I muttered as I pulled away and rushed for the front door. "This was a huge mistake."

"Teagan," Noah growled, slamming his hand on the door just as I opened it.

A deep guttural growl rolled deep in his chest. A sound that caused the muscles in my pelvis to tighten as he turned me around and pressed me against the door. "I'm not done with you," he rasped before lunging at me, kissing me fiercely. His lips were severe, hungry, and it cost me a lot to push him away.

"I'm not," I gasped, "doing this." Ducking under Noah's arm, I rushed through the hallway and swung open the front door.

A cry of relief left my body the moment my eyes landed on the headlights pulling into my driveway.

"Keep running, Teagan," he called after me. "Because you're not worth the fucking hassle," was the last thing I heard Noah say before I took off, running towards the sanctuary of my uncle.

NOAH

"Keep running, Teagan," I roared with my chest heaving as I locked my muscles into place so I couldn't chase after her.

Rain poured down on me as I stood in my driveway shirtless, watching the most beautiful fucking creature I'd never known existed run away from me. Frustration, wounded pride, and a huge amount of terror made me call out, "Because you're not worth the fucking hassle."

She was worth the hassle. Dammit, she was worth a lot more than I'd sanctioned and that *terrified* me.

I almost nailed her on my kitchen table. What the hell was wrong with me?

Reese, Jason, and Ellie... goddammit, this night had gone to hell.

Confused didn't come close to explaining how I was feeling. I was up in a heap, smothering in a concoction of scorching emotions for the girl who pissed me off worse than anyone.

I liked her.

Holy shit, I liked her a hell of a lot and the sudden realization of my feelings for Teagan was something I could have done without. I didn't need another person to worry about. I didn't *want* to need her or like her or even fucking think about her. But fuck, she was there now, stuck in my head, causing all types of anxious feelings to grow in the pit of my stomach until I felt I would puke. She was the one person who could shake me. Fuck, she was the one person who could ruin it all.

"Leave me alone, Noah," Teagan cried, running through the rain towards her uncle. She threw herself into her uncle's arms and jealousy swirled inside of me. *She shouldn't be running from me, ever...*

"What's wrong, Teegs, what the hell happened to you?" her uncle demanded.

The light coming from his car head lamps illuminated the concern etched on his face.

He seemed to register that she was wearing nothing but a t-shirt, because even in the darkness I saw him visibly stiffen. He looked around and locked eyes on me.

"What did you do to her?" he hissed in a menacing tone of voice.

Not enough by half, I thought to myself as I stood still as a statue as Teagan's uncle looked me over like I was a piece of shit.

"Nothing," she sobbed, pushing her uncle up the porch steps towards their front door. "He didn't do anything to me, I locked myself out. It's too dark. Let me inside, please, Uncle Max."

Regret churned inside of me. I needed to know she was okay, and I needed to apologize for being a prick to her.

"Teagan, I didn't mean that..." I started to say, but she cut me off quickly.

"Yes, you did, Noah," she spat, rushing past her uncle as he held the front door open for her.

"I don't know what happened tonight between you and my niece," her uncle said in a tight voice, waiting until Teagan was inside to speak. "But stay away from her," he snarled. "She doesn't need the likes of you sniffing around her."

His words struck a nerve inside of me and my hackles rose. "Isn't she old enough to make that decision for herself?"

"She's seventeen years old, you little shit," he hissed. "She has a bright future ahead of her. I know your score, Messina, and she doesn't need you dragging her down to your delinquent level."

Know my score? "What's that supposed to mean?"

"It means I know who your mother is," he snarled. "And who your father is."

"*Was*," I managed to grind out through clenched teeth. "Who he was."

"Keep your poison away from my niece," he warned me. With that, he slammed his front door and left me standing in the driveway feeling smug as shit that he'd left his car lights on.

A dead battery was the least he deserved for being a judgmental snob.

15

TEAGAN

I learned pretty quickly that there wasn't enough body wash in the world that could rid Yellow Teeth's groping hands. No amount of scrubbing erased the dirtiness I felt from allowing Noah to touch me the way he had. But the worst part was knowing deep down that I liked Noah touching me like that – *and I wanted more*. I was sick. How the hell could I have enjoyed something as degrading as what had happened?

When the power finally returned, I must have sat on that shower floor for hours, at least until the water ran cold. And then I wrapped a towel around my body and moved on to the guest bathroom before filling the bath with scalding hot water.

I felt disgusting, and I was fuming because I had let him win.

Noah Messina had hurt me.

I had sworn to myself I wouldn't let him in, and the bastard had crept under my barriers anyway. Now Noah was on my mind constantly and I couldn't stand it. He was not good for me, not good at all. He was involved in an illegal fighting ring, dammit, that alone should've had me running for the hills. So why was I obsessing about him?

Because he kissed you and made you feel it...

Because when he was touching you, it wasn't fake, and you know it.

Because he saved you, twice, even though you've been a grade-A bitch to him.

Because he put your key through the letterbox...

Uncle Max stayed at home with me on Wednesday night, and gave me a very thorough talk on the evil mind of the teenage male, but he was gone again by breakfast time Thursday. I knew that because I had to hide in bed until he left for work. Max was a pretty cool guy, but he'd lose his shit if he thought I was skipping school.

I avoided Hope's texts and calls.

I avoided everything.

Someone rang the doorbell a couple of times on Thursday, but I didn't answer. I wasn't interested in talking. Instead, I stayed in my bed, under the covers, with my headphones on my ears and the most depressing music playing on my phone.

To be honest, I wasn't sure how I was ever going to be able to face school again, especially now there were *four* people in my class who had seen me naked. I felt mortified, guilty, and a huge chunk of me wanted to rock in a corner. I'd been exposed...

So much had happened in such a short space of time that I felt like my life was railroading.

When people are told to define the word fear, it usually drudges up some deep, dark secrets from their past, whether it's the drunken kiss they shared with a colleague in the corner of the stuffy cloak room at the New Year's Eve office party, or the folded up credit card statement in the bottom of their purse with the *final reminder* stamp etched in bold ink. Yeah, sure, some people had phobias of spiders or heights or heck, even public bathrooms, but for me fear was never something I had to internalize or think too much about. I craved adventure and I had a very nice newspaper folded up and ready for every furry, eight-legged freak that dared come too close.

There used to be only one thing that could scare the life out of me.

The darkness.

Now there was something else.

The boy next door.

NOAH

Teagan wasn't in school on Thursday or Friday.

She wasn't answering her phone or the door to anyone, and knowing she was hiding because of me caused the guilt and frustration inside of me to fester to epic proportions. The entire weekend passed without me catching a glimpse of her blonde hair, and by the following Wednesday, I was growing anxious as hell.

Logically, I knew I had bigger problems than Teagan being pissed with me. George was currently out of state visiting relatives with Ellie, which for me was like a fucking holiday, but I knew the shit would hit the fan when he got back. And he would be back before Christmas.

I needed to concentrate on watching my back. I needed to worry about the fallout from doing a job for Gonzalez, that was sure to be coming my way any day now, but logic wasn't taking precedence in my head right now.

Teagan was.

"You look like you've been thoroughly sunk," a familiar voice said, rousing me from my daydream.

"What?" I asked in an amused tone as I climbed to my feet and jogged down the porch steps.

Kyle Carter stood at the end of my driveway dressed in sweats and ready to run. For a man in his forties, Kyle had some serious stamina. I'd been running with the guy for about a year now, ever since Cam and Colt decided their father was attracting too much female attention. Low usually joined us, but he had one of his appointments in Denver this morning which always drained his energy for a few weeks.

"You do realize that makes no sense, right?" I mused as I fell into step beside him as he pounded the pavement.

"Usually when a man looks like that, it's because of a woman," Kyle taunted as he jogged beside me.

"Looks like what?" I muttered. Teagan's face infiltrated my mind and my step faltered.

"Confused, frustrated, and undoubtedly petrified." Kyle laughed loudly as we rounded a corner. "So, who is she?"

"Believe me, you don't want to know," I grumbled.

Kyle stopped abruptly and swung around to face me. "Is it Hope?" His blue eyes were livid as he stalked towards me. "Are you messing around with my daughter, Messina?"

"No! Jesus, no, she's like a sister to me." I held my hands up and backed away slowly all the while, feeling a huge amount of sympathy for Hope's boyfriend, Jordan. *Poor fucker.* "It's Teagan, Kyle," I admitted, knowing I needed to spill the beans or take an ass-kicking.

Kyle's whole demeanor changed the second I said Teagan's name. "I *knew* there was something going on with you two back in the summer," he chuckled, picking up pace once more.

I tentatively jogged along with him. "How so?"

Kyle chuckled. "I was young once, too, and there's only

one woman who could've gotten away with doing that to my truck."

I stared at him. "Oh yeah?"

"Yeah," Kyle said with a smug grin. "My wife."

"*Anyway*," I muttered, moving on from that awkward statement. "Things are... Complicated in my life right now. It wouldn't work out between us." It couldn't. Teagan would be used against me and I couldn't let that happen. I needed to keep my eye on the donut, and ignore the stupid voice inside my head telling me *she* was the donut. "Not that it even matters considering she hates me most of the time."

"You know what they say," he laughed. "Hate is the closest thing to love."

"I'm not good for her, Kyle," I told him quietly. "I don't want to...." I paused and stopped running. "I don't want to break her."

Kyle stared at me long and hard before finally speaking. "Be careful, Noah," he told me in an oddly serious tone. "It's a very long drop, kid, and there's no coming back up. I hope she's worth the fall."

NOAH

"What do you want, Gonzalez?" I asked in a flat tone as I mentally scoped the area. It was the middle of the day, a week before Christmas, and he'd shown up at my house with my perfectly polished car in tow.

Either I'd earned the gang leader's respect the other week, or I was about to be taken up the mountains and kneecapped. Neither boded well with me. Mortico Gonzalez wasn't the type of person I intended doing business with again.

"What's with the face, Messina?" he chuckled, shoving his meaty hands into his jean pockets as he leaned against my car that was currently parked in my driveway. "Are you still tripping over the girl?"

A vein ticked in my neck. "My girl," I said in a cold tone, hoping like hell Teagan went to school this morning, because if she heard me calling her *my girl* she'd more than likely have a conniption fit. "And yeah, G, you can bet your ass I'm still tripping." *And he was tripping my fucking fuse box by making light of what he'd done...*

"I get it," Gonzalez coaxed as he raised his hands in the air. "She's yours. You don't share. I went too far."

"Looking in her direction was going too far," I snapped, filling with rage as the image of *him* with his filthy hands on Teagan tortured me. "Putting your hands on her took it to a whole new level."

He ran a hand through his greased back hair and sighed heavily. "Well, tripping or not, a deal's a deal, kid. You upheld your end," Gonzalez rasped. Raising his hand, he smirked and tossed my keys towards me. "And unlike your step daddy, *I'm* a man of my word."

I caught them mid air but remained exactly where I was, on my porch, stoically silent and not trusting his *word*.

A man's word meant nothing to me.

"You'll find your bread in the glove compartment," he added before taking his phone out of his pocket and pressing a few buttons. "Such a shame," he mused as he studied my face. "Such a wasted talent. If you ever get tired of being your step daddy's bitch, you phone me up."

"Am I missing something here?" I asked him, not having a fucking clue of what was going on. Yeah, I'd upheld my side of the deal and put Cortez out of commission, but hell... I'd lost my shit with him. None of this was making any sense to me. "I hit you, Gonzalez. I threatened to kill you."

He stared up at me with dark, intense eyes. "And would you do it again?" he asked.

"For her?" I nodded my head and folded my arms across my chest. "Absolutely."

"Then you're missing absolutely nothing," he chuckled. "Loyalty, Messina," he mused as a black Harley pulled up at the curb beside my house. He climbed on behind the driver. "Is a rare attribute – something your daddy didn't have enough of."

Gonzalez shook his head and patted the driver's shoulder. "You're not Antonio Messina," he called out. "So why do you still pay for his mistakes?"

TEAGAN

"Forget it happened?" Hope asked in an indignant tone as we walked towards the student parking lot Friday afternoon after school.

Courtesy of the school principal, Mr. Lafferty, my uncle had gotten wind of my absenteeism and had personally driven me to school this morning and had even gone as far as *walking* me into the building. I thought this was pretty pointless considering we were starting our Christmas holiday from school after today, but what the hell did I know? According to my uncle, attendance was essential.

I had hoped to avoid everyone I knew, but that plan had gone bust the moment Hope caught me in the bathroom and demanded answers. I'd spilled my guts, telling her everything about the ring of fire and Noah.

An entire school day had passed and the girl was still like a freaking detective trying to suck information out of me. But to be fair to Hope, she was the bearer of good news this morning when she informed me that Jason and Ellie were both absent. Apparently Ellie was out of state with her dad for Christmas and Jason had contracted chickenpox.

Reese was in school, but she hadn't said a word about the events of that fateful night. Instead, she just glared evilly at me whenever we'd passed one another in the hallway.

"You can't be serious, Teagan?"

"It really wasn't a big deal, Hope," I muttered as I popped an earplug in my ear and stared down at the screen of my phone, flicking through songs. "Forget about it – I have."

Ironically, Maroon 5's *One More Night* blasted through my earplug and I immersed myself in the lyrics.

Hope reached over and grabbed my phone out of my hand, preventing me from dutifully ignoring her. "You and Noah have been tormenting each other for months," she hissed.

Hope looked even more beautiful than usual, clad in a red coat, black skinnies, and white high heeled pumps. Her black, curly hair was pinned in an elaborate half up half down style. I looked like something old and moldy next to her in the workout clothes I'd changed into after last class and a huge padded coat. I had plans to hit the treadmill after school and work off some of the tension burning inside of me.

"You finally get down to business and *screw* it out, pun intended, and now you're saying you want to forget it ever happened?" Her blue eyes were narrowed in disbelief, proving she knew I hadn't forgotten a damn thing.

"We didn't *screw* it out, Hope. We kissed," I hissed, upping my pace as I stalked towards her car. It still hadn't snowed and I was feeling seriously let down.

"Yes, you *kissed*," Hope countered as she pressed a button on her car key and her white Jeep lit up. "And a hell of a lot more – while you were *naked*. This is huge, Teagan, you can't tell me it's not."

"Whatever." I didn't want to talk about this anymore. I

walked over to the passenger side of her jeep and flung the door open. I clenched my eyes shut and tried to block out the memory of Noah kissing me, and just how good it felt, but I couldn't block out Noah's words that had stung like the lash of a whip

"You're not worth the fucking hassle..."

Yeah, that still hurt something fierce.

"I'm over it," I muttered, climbing inside. Truth was, I was nowhere near over it. I hadn't seen Noah in days. He wasn't in school today and I forced myself to believe that I was happy about this, ignoring the dull ache in my chest. Maybe he had chickenpox, too? Ugh, it didn't matter to me because I didn't care about him.

I *wouldn't*.

"Do you like him?" Hope persisted as she climbed into the driver's seat. "Seriously, Teagan, do you have any feelings for him at all?"

"Does hatred count?" I offered sweetly as I rooted through a pile of CDs and placed a disc I wasn't familiar with into the car stereo. "He's good," as a voice I was familiar with blasted through the speakers. "Is this his new one?"

"Yes, he is, don't change the subject." Turning down the volume on her stereo, Hope turned to look at me. "Well?"

I exhaled heavily, knowing she wasn't going to let this go without a full confession. "He sets me on fire," I reluctantly admitted, leaning back in my seat, the memory of Noah touching me causing my entire body to heat.

I closed my eyes and shivered. "Noah Messina lights me up like a firework and I can't even begin to explain the multitude of emotions he rouses inside of me."

Hope's eyes widened but I carried on now that I was on a roll. "It's terrifying and addictive and wrong and right all at the same time. My brain can't stand him, and my body can't get enough of him." I let out a sigh. "Happy now?"

Nodding, she grinned and wiggled her eyebrows at me.

I automatically blushed and Hope's grin widened. "He's so bad for me, Hope," I confessed quietly. "The things he's involved in. He's so... He's..."

"I *knew* you were hot for him," Hope said smugly. "How far would you have gone with him? If Jason, Reese, and Ellie hadn't interrupted you?"

All the way... "I'm going to pretend you never asked that question," I shot back quickly.

"Dude, you have no idea how lucky you are having Noah live next door to you."

I rolled my eyes. "As opposed to?"

Hope's face was suddenly serious. "The object of my desire lives in a different state, Teegs," she huffed. "And won't touch any part of my body that's covered with clothing." Her brow wrinkled in confusion as she stared down at her hands. "I don't get why Jordan won't sleep with me."

"Okay," I chuckled, shaking my head. "Talk about a subject changer..."

"I'm serious, Teagan," Hope snapped before letting out a pained groan. "I've loved him my whole life." Hope's shoulders slumped and she rested her forehead against the steering wheel. "And he *won't* give it up, which makes me feel like a huge, virgin slut because *who* thinks like me?" She exhaled dramatically. "It's supposed to be the man who's desperate to take the next step, but Jordan..." Hope threw her head back and slammed her palms against the wheel in frustration. "He's like a freaking priest."

"Maybe he's trying to respect you?" I offered lamely, not knowing what else to say. "You said he's older than you, right?"

"Twenty-one," Hope replied immediately. "He is *twenty-one* years old, Teagan." She stared at me like I was missing something crucial. "Name another twenty-one year old man who wants to *wait*."

"Edward Cullen?" I offered, struggling to keep my face straight.

Hope glared at me. "He was one hundred and nine," she snapped. "And I know we're supposed to be talking about your screwed up tryst with Noah, and I am interested, I swear I am, but Jordan's coming home this weekend for the holidays and I'm done with the waiting. He *has* to have sex with me." Hope blew a curl off her face. "Please help me make my boyfriend have sex with me, Teagan," she begged.

I stared at her determined face with a horrified look on my own. "Well, this is the most uncomfortable conversation we've had in a while," I muttered, shaking my head.

Hope didn't have a chance to respond because the back doors of her jeep opened and three testosterone fueled triplets piled in.

"This conversation isn't over," she mumbled before shifting her car into gear and tearing off. "You're still sleeping over tonight, right?"

"Yeah," I mumbled. "I'll swing by after my workout."

"Great," Hope muttered. "We'll hatch a plan then."

16

TEAGAN

My plan to hit the gym after school had seemed like the perfect stress reliever, until I realized I wasn't the only one with the idea.

"We need to talk, Thorn," a deep, husky voice hissed from behind me and I momentarily tensed before running through the foyer of the Henderson Hotel in the direction of the elevators. The gym was underground, so that was where I was going, if he would just disappear.

The elevator doors opened and I rushed inside, only to pale when he followed me.

The doors closed and I was trapped.

Trapped with a guy whose car I destroyed with paint. A guy who riled me up more than anyone else on the planet. A boy who looked entirely too tempting in sweats. A boy who'd seen me naked. I swallowed deeply.

Oh, shit...

"If I didn't know any better, I'd swear you were trying to avoid me," Noah said dryly as he dropped his gym bag on the floor and folded his arms across his chest. "What are you doing here, Thorn?"

"What do you think I'm doing here, Noah? I'm here to work out... Oh, but don't worry, I'm here for more than just the *release* of punching the crap out of things," I sneered as I purposefully avoided looking at the way his t-shirt was glued to his chest, or the way his black tattoos looked fucking fabulous against his tanned skin.

"You're not gonna get over that anytime soon, are you?" he asked in an annoyed tone.

"The fact that you beat people up for money?" I shot back sarcastically. "No... I'm afraid not."

"What the hell is that?" Noah demanded, pointing his finger accusingly at my chest.

"It's called a *sports* bra," I spat. "You should learn the word. It's what people do for fun... They take up a *sport*."

I wasn't sure if I wanted to hit him or throw myself at him, and the memory of him kissing me did little to calm my frazzled nerves. I needed to keep my guard up with this one. I knew that now, all I had to do was make my body understand.

"So, this is the way it's gonna be between us?" he asked in a level tone. "Ugly?"

"Looks like it," I shot back.

"Fine." Reaching over, Noah pulled the strap of my sports bra before letting it snap back against my skin. "So are you working out or going *to work*?"

"You know what, screw this." I was either going to scream or cry. Suspecting the latter, I made a decision. I shoved past Noah and slammed my hand on the keypad. "Keep your bloody gym. I'm out."

"Stop pressing it," Noah snapped. "It's already moving. Teagan, stop, you're going to get it—"

"No!" I roared, pressing all the buttons just to piss him

off. "I won't stop. *You* stop. Stop telling me what to do. I want out of here, Noah. Now."

"Teagan," Noah warned as he moved towards me and tried to shoo my hand away from the keypad. "You're going to break it."

The words weren't out of Noah's mouth when the lift suddenly jolted, causing me to press up against him.

A few seconds later, everything went dark, and I didn't need a jolt to press against Noah; I practically climbed up his body.

"You just don't listen to a damn thing anyone says," he snarled, wrapping his arm around my waist. "I goddamn told you not to press them all at once."

"Oh, shut the hell up, Noah," I hissed, wrapping myself around him like ivy, squeezing his neck for dear life. "This is your fault."

"*My* fault?" he demanded in outrage as he clamped his hands on my thighs, which were currently wrapped around his waist, and held me tighter. "Please tell me how you came to *that* conclusion when you're the one who went nuclear on the goddamn keypad?"

"You touched my bra," I snapped, flustered.

"You grabbed my dick on the very first day of school," he shot back angrily. "What's your point? And besides, I've touched more than your bra, Thorn."

"You shouldn't have said that about going *to work*," I shot back, furious. "You hurt my feelings."

"Oh, I'm sorry." His tone was highly sarcastic. "If you're that fucking sensitive, then take care of yourself."

With that, Noah dumped me on the floor, in the dark, on my own.

"Why weren't you in school today?" I demanded, desperately trying to distract myself from the suffocating feeling engulfing me. "We had a test in English."

"I was supposed to be," I heard him say. "But something came up." He paused before adding, "I had... An appointment."

"At the STD clinic?" I shot back, breathing in through my nose and slowly through my mouth.

"Funny," he grunted.

"And another thing," I snapped, clinging onto my anger. Anger was good. Anger was better than fear. "Tell your asshole dad not to threaten me again."

"What?" Noah asked flatly.

"You heard me," I snarled. Why I was bringing this up was beyond me, but I was desperate to clutch at any straw that kept me angry with Noah because the alternative... The alternative terrified me. *"Stay on your side of the fence."* I mimicked the creep's deep voice from weeks back. "You take after him."

"George is my stepfather," Noah corrected me in a soft tone. "He's not my real dad. That title goes to the scumbag who left me to clean up his mess."

"Go scumbag dad," I muttered and immediately regretted my horrible words.

"Noah, I'm sorry," I told him, but I already knew it was too late to apologize.

The atmosphere around us changed. Chilled.

Noah was breathing hard and fast and was silent for so long I thought he would never speak to me again. But then he let rip. "Do you have *any* idea what it feels like to have a stepfather just shoved on you when you're fourteen? One that hates your goddamn guts?" His body stiffened beside mine and I shifted away. "A guy who uses your mother's *treatment* as a goddamn bargaining tool?"

"Noah..."

"Do you know what it feels like, Teagan?" he roared. "To be fucking alone in a family you don't belong to, with people who make you sick to your goddamn stomach?" Noah jerked away from me and then I heard the sound of his fist pummeling the wall of the elevator.

"Do you know what it's like?" he roared. "Having to pay back the debt of the woman who spent the best part of your childhood shoving you into cupboards and locking you away in a basement for weeks on end because she's convinced the fucking world is against her?"

"Noah, please stop..."

"Or being the one to console her every time one of my *daddies*, and those were a dime a dozen, left in the middle of the night?" he sneered. "Have you ever been afraid, Teagan, truly afraid of your parents? Have you ever been cold or felt the absolute fucking agony that is hunger pains?"

"No," I replied quietly.

"*No*," he sneered. "Of course you haven't. A good little girl like you wouldn't have a clue."

"Is that where your mom is?" I asked him nervously. "Having treatment?"

"Yes, she's *having treatment*," he spat in a mocking tone. "George is out doing god knows what, fucking god knows who, and Ellie's probably following suit. Is that enough information for you, Teagan, or would you like to know some more so you can ridicule me and talk down to me like I'm a piece of shit?"

"I don't know why I said that about your dad," I confessed, burying my face in my knees. I wasn't good with the dark. I was less than good in enclosed spaces. I was two seconds away from having the mother of all panic attacks.

"I do," he muttered. "You said it because you're a heartless bitch who gets off on hurting me."

"No, I don't get off on hurting you," I whispered softly, burying my face against my knees. "I'm sorry for what I said about your dad," I choked out. "I have a tendency to run my mouth off when I'm agitated."

My throat felt like it was closing up and I truly tried to stop what I knew was coming next. The second the first sob tore from my throat, I felt a wave of bitterness settle over me. I wasn't a crier, and I really hated that Noah got to see me weak.

"Dammit, Teagan, don't cry," Noah's voice wafted through the darkness. I heard his heavy sigh and that pissed me off even more.

"I'm not crying," I managed to grind out through clenched teeth as I wrapped my arms around my legs and buried my head in my knees. "I'm dealing with something."

"What?" I heard him ask from somewhere close by. An arm wrapped around my shoulder. "What're you dealing with, Thorn?"

God only knows why I said what I said next. "When I was fourteen, I was in a car accident," I confided, feeling a little dumb to be exposing myself to a guy who could crush me with his baby finger. I exhaled shakily and allowed him to pull me closer to him. "The car I was traveling in hit a tree and flipped over a ditch. I ended up being trapped in that car all night."

I was opening up to Noah Messina, the boy who terrified me beyond all frontiers.

The boy whose sister made my life a living hell for pleasure.

He was touching my hair and I was letting him do it. I was enjoying the feel of his arms around me.

What the hell was wrong with me?

"No one found us until the following morning," I explained quietly. "By then it was too late."

"Too late for what?" Noah asked softly as he pulled me onto his lap and held me there.

"My mom," I whispered, reveling in the warmth of his embrace. His arms were like a safety net around my body, forcing the fear away. "She died in that car, right in front of me."

I closed my eyes and took a few minutes to get a grip before I spoke again. "I couldn't see her, it was pitch black, but I could hear her. Calling for help, begging for mercy, and I *couldn't* get to her. My seatbelt was jammed. I couldn't free myself to get to her. I was completely trapped and had to watch my mother die. The feeling of being *that* helpless is something I never want to experience again. But the dark," I admitted, not knowing why I was telling Noah things I still couldn't speak about with my uncle. "The dark brings that feeling back."

"Jesus," Noah muttered as he shifted me on his lap so that I was straddling him. "I'm sorry," he whispered as he held my face to his chest. I could feel his heart hammering against my ear.

"So, yeah, that's why," I mumbled shakily as I lifted my face and rested my shaking hands on his shoulders. "I'm not good with the dark or enclosed spaces." The last few words escaped my lips in a huge breath.

"*This* is not the same thing," he whispered and his lips touched my ear when he spoke, his hand cupping my neck, fingers knotting in my hair. "You're safe with me."

"Promise?" I asked, leaning into his touch.

"I promise," he rasped.

"Where did he go?"

Noah's arms tightened around me. "Who?" he asked softly.

"Your dad," I replied quietly. "You said he left you and your mom. Where did he go?"

Noah let out a deep breath. "He's dead, Thorn," he said in a gruff tone. "He died when I was just a kid."

"What was his name?"

"My dad?" Noah asked.

"Yeah."

"Antonio Messina," he replied. "What about your mom?"

"Olivia," I whispered. "Her name was Olivia, and she was wonderful." My throat felt tight, and I had to breathe slowly to keep hold of my emotions. "My dad... my dad's name is Patrick." I clenched my eyes shut, feeling the usual agony rip through me. "He's in Cork, serving a prison sentence."

"A prison sentence?" Noah's voice was gentle and understanding. "So that's why you..."

"Live with my mother's brother? Yeah," I mumbled. "Dad was driving the car that night. He was completely intoxicated. He got four years," I told Noah. "He should have been given a lot more." I didn't mean that, or maybe I did... Ugh, it still crippled me. *Torn between the two people who raised me.*

"That's a shitty hand of cards, baby," Noah whispered, and the comfort I got from his words was immense. He didn't try to make light of what had happened, he didn't fuss or freak out. He simply called it as he saw it.

"Teagan, I didn't mean what I said about you not being worth the hassle," Noah added. "You ran out on me and I was pissed. It was my pride talking." He shifted slightly, pulling me closer.

"Noah, you were right," I whispered, feeling a sudden urge to clear my conscience. "I am a judgmental bitch."

"I was venting when I said that, Teagan," Noah said with an uncomfortable sigh. "I shouldn't have called you a bitch."

"You were being honest," I replied. "I've been a bitch to you – I *am* a bitch to you." Shaking my head, I let out a shaky breath. "Ellie admitted to me that she was the one who broke my guitar and slashed my tires."

Noah's body tensed but he didn't reply.

"I'm sorry for blaming you, Noah. I just thought... I thought you were like her," I whispered. "When you slammed that guy through my windshield, I saw red. I didn't think about anything except getting revenge." I sighed heavily. "She was making my life a misery. I just wanted it to stop."

"Teagan," Noah spoke softly, causing my heart to flip around in my chest. "I had *nothing* to do with any of the crap Ellie pulled on you."

"But you were her brother," I told him. "So in my eyes, that made you enemy number two."

Noah let out a heavy sigh. "That *made* me enemy number two... as in, past tense?"

Raw lust and anger fueled inside of me, and I wasn't sure if I wanted to hit him or kiss him. It was a very unsettling feeling. "I feel like slapping you and kissing you all at the same time," I admitted in a torn voice. "And it makes me feel crazy, Noah, because I know you hate me..."

"Hate you? I'm fucking lost in you, Teagan," he hissed, and I think my heart stopped in my chest.

"You're lost in me?" I asked, barely breathing as my heart thundered against my ribs. "You like me?"

"Yeah, Thorn, I do." I felt his touch slip away and opened my eyes. "If any other girl treated me the way you have, believe me, I'd have walked away by now."

"But at the Ring of Fire you were so horrible..."

"I was close to losing my goddamn mind that night," Noah replied, his tone suddenly angry. "There you were, stuck underneath all of those people." He let out a sharp breath. "I couldn't fucking breathe when I saw you lying on the ground, and when I saw him touching you... Jesus, Teagan, you came into my life and it's like... I'm so fucking caught up in you and all your drama," Noah admitted in a gruff tone. "For some reason, unknown to myself, I like you a hell of a lot – even though you're a goddamn thorn in my side and enjoy inflicting pain on me."

"Noah..." I let out a breathy sigh as I contemplated what the hell I'd just heard. "You can't like me..." I shook my head and shifted closer to him. "It's not feasible... We fight like cats and dogs."

"What can I say, I'm a fucking glutton for punishment." Noah chuckled.

I shook my head, sighing heavily, but Noah, quick to notice my mood change, pulled my face to his. "Stop fighting this. I know you feel it, too," he rasped against my lips. "This burning heat between us." He pressed his lips to mine. "This primal rawness," he purred before trailing his tongue over my bottom lip and pulling it into his mouth.

"Noah..." I moaned loudly when he sucked on my lip and released it with a pop.

"I've been aching for you," he whispered against my mouth. "Say it, too, Teagan, " he groaned, slipping one of his hands between our bodies. "Tell me you have an absolute fucking urge to feel me inside you as much as I have to be inside you."

What the hell could I do except nod like a demented dog and wrap my arms around his neck. I wanted him and I was tired of fighting my feelings.

"Noah Messina, you are *treacherous*," I whispered before crushing my mouth to his.

Rolling me onto my back, Noah covered my body with his, thrusting his tongue inside my mouth while his fingers undid the clasp of my sports bra and freed my breasts. Sliding the straps down my shoulders, Noah tugged the rest of my bra away in one swift movement before wrapping his warm mouth around one of my pebbled nipples. His mouth devoured my breasts as his fingers dug hard into my skin, trailing lower.

"This is crazy," I mumbled as I pulled his face to mine and ground my hips upwards, rubbing myself against his bulging erection. "What the hell are we doing?" I clutched him tighter, kissed him harder. I sucked in a shaky breath and Noah's scent filled my nostrils, making me dizzy. "You're so... Wrong for me."

The electric sensation I felt when Noah touched me caused me to tremble. I didn't know how far he was going to take this, and I couldn't breathe properly. His weight was pressing hard on me, but I knew however far he went there was no way I would stop him.

"Your body knows I'm *exactly* what's right for you," he rasped through kisses.

"Well my mind thinks you're a jackass," I breathed as I writhed under Noah's sweet caress.

"So gutsy," Noah purred. "You make breathing easy, Teagan," he added in a surprisingly soft tone.

"I do?"

Noah nodded and I couldn't stop my grin from widening.

Chuckling, Noah curled his fingers around the waistband of my shorts and raised himself above me before sliding both my shorts and thong down my thighs.

"You're a fast mover," I panted, breathless and nervous.

"I just know what I need," he replied huskily. "I've been craving you underneath me ever since you went head-to-head with me in that black thong and t-shirt."

My brain was screaming about the impracticalities of involving myself with a guy like Noah Messina, while my body was relishing this like I'd won the national lottery. "I don't roll like you," I whispered as I writhed in pleasure. I was denying his words while my body thrummed to his touch. "My uncle's a doctor and you... You inflict pain on people for kicks."

"Believe me, Teagan, I didn't want this, either," I heard Noah reply as he drew himself above me. His hand cupped my cheek and his nose touched mine. "I still don't."

"Wow, thanks," I muttered sullenly, feeling heated and rejected.

"But it's not about *want* when it comes to you," he said, stroking my cheek with his thumb. "It's fucking need, Teagan. The crazy inside of me *needs* the crazy inside of you."

I nodded and dragged his face down to mine. The second our lips touched, I groaned into Noah's mouth and arched myself upwards, wrapping my legs around his waist.

Noah growled against my lips before pushing my face back gently, holding me inches from his mouth with his hands.

"I don't want to rush you, Thorn," Noah whispered. He was breathing hard and fast. "But if you put your mouth on me again, I'm taking you."

Those words were enough to send me into a frenzy.

Crushing my lips to his, I pressed myself hard against Noah's growing erection, desperate for some physical comfort. He needed no other encouragement. His movements were wild, his kisses animalistic. He wasn't joking around. Noah Messina was going to fuck me. Right here, on the floor of the elevator, I was about to lose my virginity to the boy next door, and I couldn't be fucking happier.

Noah pushed my thighs apart before lowering his head and taking my clit into his mouth. When he suckled me, I arched upward, thrusting my hips into his face shamelessly. I didn't care how I looked. I wanted him.

He spread me open with his fingers and lapped me up with his tongue. He was vicious and rough and I loved every second of it.

A tightening sensation spread over my body, signaling I was about to come. But Noah stopped and leaned his body over me, staring down at me like an animal about to devour me.

"Wha... Wha... Why'd you stop?" I moaned.

"If I do this, then no one else does" he whispered, clutching my jaw in his hand. "Be sure you want me."

There was a hint of warning in his voice, and I couldn't stop myself from lifting my mouth to his. The carnal urge I felt to put my lips on his was overwhelming and overruled all common sense.

The sound of clothes shedding, followed by Noah's lack of contact, proved he was getting naked and I pushed my fingers inside myself, the need to come unbearable.

The tearing of a condom wrapper was all I heard before Noah's hands grabbed my hips, pulling me towards him. Pushing my legs apart with his knee, Noah pressed himself hard against me and I could feel his *erection probing me.*

"Are you sure you want this?" he asked, pressing the head of his sheathed cock against my entrance.

"Uh-huh." I nodded and rolled my hips erotically.

"Open your legs, Thorn," he whispered as he dragged my hips towards his.

I rested my elbows on the floor and spread myself further.

"Wider," he told me as he placed the palm of his hand on my pubic bone and began to massage my clit.

My eyes rolled back as the tightening came to a head.

And just as I started to come, he pushed into me, all the way to the hilt.

Noah's frame trembled above me, his weight came down hard seconds before he stilled. "You have no idea how badly I've needed this," he groaned as he thrust himself deep inside me. "How badly I've needed you."

It stung, and I cried out in shock, but my orgasm over-rode the pain, and my body sucked him in, welcoming his intrusion. I'd given him my virginity.

He won and I didn't care.

He could have whatever he wanted so long as he kept making me feel this good. It felt like he was my mate in some gutturally primal way. Yeah, we fought like cats and dogs, but there was no denying the way our bodies worked together; in sync with the others' needs and limits.

"Are you okay?" he whispered against my ear through breathless pants.

Was I?

I'd never felt better, spread open with him deep inside me. Somewhere in the back of my mind, a niggling doubt telling me I'd lost a little of myself to Noah fluttered around and echoed, but the unbelievable sensations I was feeling told me I didn't care.

I nodded and lifted my face to his.

I didn't even know how to describe the feelings that were coursing through me as Noah plunged his erection into me.

I felt exposed, vulnerable, and incredibly breakable for the first time in my life because I'd given him all of me.

The feel of his hard, pulsing cock sliding into me, pushing into me, taunting me, was too much.

It was so...

Oh Jesus...

A sudden jolt beneath me caused me to cry out as a wave of ecstasy rolled through me. Noah shuddered as he emptied himself inside me and I trembled beneath him. He bent his head and claimed my lips with his.

And then the lights flickered on.

I blinked rapidly, adjusting to the sudden brightness.

"Shit, the elevator's moving," Noah groaned as he slowly pulled out of me and reached for his duffel bag. Pulling a black shirt out of his bag, Noah slipped it over my head and helped me pull my arms through the sleeves before lifting me to my feet.

Noah dressed in record time. "You okay?" he asked in a gruff tone as he passed my shorts to me.

"I..." I shook my head and held onto his shoulders to steady myself.

Was I okay?

I looked into his dark brown eyes and chewed on my lip nervously. My thighs were drenched, but I didn't dare look down as I quickly slipped my shorts on. "I'm not sure."

That was the truth.

I wasn't sure of a lot of things right now. Like how I was feeling or how I should behave around him now.

Oh, sweet Jesus... Noah Messina got me on my back... in the elevator of a hotel... owned by my best friend's father.

Bending down, I grabbed my sports bra off the floor and my... underwear. My slutty behavior had surpassed anything else I'd done lately and I groaned in shame as I climbed unsteadily to my feet.

My hands were shaking, my entire body was shaking.

I felt like bawling like a baby.

What the hell had I done?

Feeling acutely embarrassed, I edged away from Noah until I reached the other side of the elevator and then stared straight ahead, willing the doors to open and provide me with an escape route.

"You can't be serious?" Noah said in an incredulous tone as he stared at me. "You're really going to pretend that *nothing* happened between us just now?"

I wasn't sure what I planned on doing, but I avoided answering Noah.

I avoided looking at him altogether.

"Teagan," Noah said with a sigh as he stepped towards me. "Come on, don't do this."

I stiffened and shook my head. "Don't touch me." I had no idea how to deal with the turbulence of emotions ripping through me. I needed space. A little time to think this fucked up situation over.

Noah threw his head back and growled. "Jesus Christ, Teagan," he hissed, bowing his head in obvious frustration. "All I want to do is take ..." Noah stopped talking and looked up at my face as if he'd solved a huge puzzle.

"You were a virgin."

It was an assumption; a completely accurate, dead on the money assumption, that I furtively denied when I saw his expression soften.

"You were so tight, but I just thought..." He shook his head and stepped closer. "I didn't realize..."

"I was not a virgin, Noah," I taunted, lying through my

teeth. "I was with my last boyfriend for three years. We had..."

"Stop talking," Noah snapped. "Don't talk to me about other guys."

"Sex," I continued, ignoring his protests. "He fucked me. A lot." Why was I being like this? Why was I trying to fight with him? "Sorry to burst your little virgin bubble."

"Your blood is on my cock," he said flatly, gesturing to his crotch. "And your thighs are smeared with it," he continued. "So stop fucking lying about who's been inside you, Teagan, when it's perfectly clear the only person who has had the pleasure of fucking you is me."

I think I died a little when he commented on my thighs.

"Go screw yourself, Noah," I spat, focusing so hard on the elevator door that my eyes became crisscrossed, and my vision blurred, and that's exactly the way the control panel guys found us when they opened the doors.

"You already took care of that, Thorn!" Noah called out after me as I rushed out.

17

Noah

"If I do this," I told her, clutching her jaw in my hand. "Then no one else does." It was a warning – one I hoped she would hear because I had no intentions of letting her go. "Be sure you want me."

I'd never felt so exposed in my life. Hell, I'd never told anyone about what I went through with my mother. Low didn't even know the half of it.

But Teagan... Jesus, it felt like she just shoved her hand through my chest, clutched onto something vital inside of me and wouldn't let go. I was still fucking reeling in emotions as I held her face in my hand and waited for her answer.

She touched my lips with hers and that was the only sign I needed.

Lifting off her, I quickly stripped my clothes off and rooted in my pocket until I found a condom in my wallet.

Jesus Christ, my hands were trembling as I rolled it on, the thought of being inside her was making me go a little crazy and the sounds she was making as she writhed on the elevator floor were close to making me lose it.

Grabbing her hips, I pulled Teagan towards me and settled in between her legs. She was so soft and warm and fucking perfect. Too good for me, but I wasn't letting her go now. Teagan had driven me crazy for months, frustrated the hell out of me, but the way she was making me feel right now made everything else just fade away.

"Are you sure you want this?" I managed to croak out, pressing the head of my cock against her entrance.

"Uh-huh," she moaned as she rolled her hips enticingly.

"Open your legs, Thorn," I whispered.

She rested her weight on her elbows and spread herself further.

"Wider," I purred as I began to thumb her clit. Jesus Christ, she was so smooth and tight. The moment I heard her breathy moans, I couldn't wait any longer and buried myself inside her heat.

Teagan cried out and bucked her hips upwards. Her fingernails dug into the skin on my back and I had to bite back a groan as I slid out slowly before pressing deep inside her.

"You have no idea how badly I've needed this," I confessed. She was so goddamn tight and snug that I had to calm myself or I was gonna fuck it all up. I'd been with other girls, many, but no one had ever felt like this – like Teagan.

She mewled and groaned as her hands wandered all over my skin, and I swear I'd never felt a sweeter touch. The eagerness in the way she moved against me gave me comfort on a level I never knew existed.

"Noah..." she sighed, arching upwards. "Yes..."

Resting my weight on one elbow, I used my other arm to hitch her thigh up. "Are you okay?" I panted against her ear as I plunged into her. I knew I was close to coming. I'd been close since I pushed inside her, but the noises she was making and the way her tight little pussy clamped me made it impossible to hold off any longer.

The elevator floor jerked beneath us, causing Teagan to cry out and me to shudder in pure fucking pleasure as I came hard inside of her. Teagan trembled as my orgasm flooded into her and I couldn't stop myself from claiming her lips with mine.

And then the lights flickered on and I saw her lying underneath me, looking into my eyes with such innocent confusion that my heart constricted in my chest. "They must've fixed the elevator," I told her in a voice thick with emotion. She flinched as I slowly pulled out of her. *Damn, she was so tight...*

I reached for my gym bag and pulled a black shirt out, sliding it over Teagan's head before helping her stand. I dressed myself quickly before grabbing her shorts. Teagan was being abnormally quiet, and I was growing concerned. "You okay?" I asked her, holding them out for her to step into.

"I..." She shook her head and held onto my shoulders as she stepped into her shorts. Her hazel eyes were wide and she nibbled on her lip, studying my every move as I pulled her shorts up her thighs.

"I'm not sure," Teagan finally replied in a small voice. Brushing her hair behind her ears, she bent down and grabbed her bra and panties and slipped her feet into her sneakers before letting out a whimper.

Her entire frame was shaking and I had no clue of what

to do. I wasn't used to this response. I didn't get it. Had I hurt her? Fuck. Concern churned inside of me.

I went to put my arm around her, but Teagan shimmied away from me and stood in the far corner of the elevator with her nose cocked in the air.

"You can't be serious?" I said flatly as I gaped at her. "You're really going to pretend that *nothing* happened between us just now?"

She didn't answer me.

"Teagan," I snapped as I took a step closer to her.

She shook her head "Don't touch me."

"Jesus Christ, Teagan," I hissed in frustration as rejection coursed through me. "All I want to do is take ..." I stopped talking, I stopped fucking *breathing* when I noticed the blood smeared on her thighs. I glanced down at myself and bit back a curse. "You were a virgin."

I'd taken her virginity on a goddamn elevator floor "You were so tight, but I just thought..." I shook my head and stepped closer to her, as a mixture of remorse and delight coursed through me. She'd only been with me. "I didn't realize..."

"I was not a virgin, Noah," Teagan spat, red-faced. "I was with my last boyfriend for three years. We had..."

"Stop talking," I warned her. "Don't talk to me about other guys."

Why was she being like this?

Why the hell was she trying to pick a fight with me?

"Sex," she taunted. "He fucked me. A lot. Sorry to burst your little virgin bubble."

"Your blood is on my cock," I said in a flat tone, gesturing to my dick. "And your thighs are smeared with it," I added, furious. "So stop fucking lying about who's been inside you,

Teagan, when it's perfectly clear the only person who has had the pleasure of fucking you is me."

Her face paled and I immediately felt like a dick. "Go screw yourself, Noah," she spat.

The doors opened and Teagan rushed past the control guys as I roared, "You already took care of that, Thorn!" regretting each poisonous word as it spilled from my lips.

TEAGAN

Striding towards the front door of the hotel, I willed myself not to look back at Noah, even though he was calling out my name at the top of his lungs.

What the hell had possessed me to give Noah Messina my virginity? Oh god, my heart was racing so fast I felt faint, but the butterflies fluttering around in my stomach were much worse. They were huge, demented, Noah-loving butterflies that went bloody berserk whenever I thought of him, which was *constantly*.

"Teagan, will you just stop for one damn minute..."

Oh god. I upped my pace.

Keep going...

Almost there...

Reaching the exit, I swung the door open forcefully before marching outside.

The sharp sting of the night air hit me full force in the face and I wrapped my arms around myself before starting off in the direction of The Hill, though I wasn't one bit surprised when Noah's hand wrapped around my arm and pulled me to a stop.

Even the slight touch of his fingers on my elbow caused my skin to burst out in a serious case of goosebumps. I couldn't stop my body from shivering, nor could I stop the teeny, tiny part of my brain that was pro Noah from reveling in the fact that he came after me.

"You're not walking in the dark, a week before Christmas. I'm taking you home," he said sharply before leading me down the street towards his Lexus. His sparkling, *paint free* Lexus.

My eyes narrowed as awareness hit me full force in the chest. I stopped walking and swung around to glare at Noah. "Is this why you had to *work* that night?" I demanded, pointing at the car and then at him. "You fought to make enough money to fix your stupid car?"

"One, my car is not stupid." Noah unlocked the car, opened the passenger door and gestured impatiently with his hand for me to get in. "And two, what I do is *my* concern, Teagan." He let out a discontented sigh. "My business is exactly that. *Mine*. Nothing to do with you. Now get in the car."

I didn't move.

Noah raised a dark, perfectly curved eyebrow at me and I met his stare head on. "Christ, Teagan, just trust me and get in," he finally muttered in exasperation.

"Trust you." I snorted, probably not the most attractive move, and folded my arms across my chest. I was still internally reeling from the sex. "Uh... Yeah, trusting you is what I'm gonna do," I retorted sarcastically. "It's right up there with shaving my head and swimming with sharks."

"You sure as hell trusted me earlier when I was buried to the hilt inside you," he snarled.

"Classy," I hissed, red faced and mortified. "Very classy, Noah."

"I didn't mean that. God, you make me say things... I need a filter... Shit..." Noah shook his head in frustration before sighing heavily and waving his hand between me and his car. "Just get in the car and I'll take you home."

"Keep shaking your hand in my face and I'll show you where you can put it," I warned him. "It rhymes with pass, so keep on doing it. I *dare* you."

"God, you're a fucking handful," he muttered, exhaling heavily. "I pity your poor uncle."

"Yeah, well I pity myself for ever letting you touch me," I hissed through clenched teeth. "No, scratch that, I don't pity myself because that would involve me having to actually feel something for you. And I don't."

"God, you can be such a bitch, Teagan." Noah let out a harsh laugh, clearly frustrated with me, and moved closer. His chest rose and fell quickly as he towered over me. "Why don't you just admit how you feel about me so I can kiss you already?"

"I have no idea what you're talking about," I lied.

"You care about me," he accused me as he stared down at me. "I make you vulnerable and that scares the hell out of you."

"No." I shook my head, refuting his accusations. "I'm not... I don't care about you."

"Admit it, Teagan," Noah urged as he stepped towards me. "You're vulnerable and you're pissed off because I do that to you." He let out a sigh. "You ran out of there because you hate the fact that you want me. You hate the fact that you were *wrong* about me." He stepped closer. "I'm exactly what you want, crave, and that rebellious streak inside your brain fucking hates it."

"Shut up," I snapped. "You have no idea how I... I wasn't wrong."

"You *want* me to be the asshole you've concocted in your head," he taunted, interrupting me. His tone of voice was one of anger, but his eyes, they told me a different story. His eyes showed his confusion, and his... Hunger?

Heat.

He made my skin burn by just looking at me.

I was in serious trouble.

"And now you've realized that I'm *not* that guy and you're reeling because that changes everything," he growled as he reached up and stroked my chin with his thumb. "*Tonight* changed everything."

"I'm not sure why I ran back there," I admitted, curling my fingers around the back of his head, still reeling from what had happened between us.

I had a list of things that, logically, I knew I should be feeling. Shame, disgust, and regret were the three big ones that should be present, but they weren't.

Instead, I felt exhilarated, confused, and incredibly reckless. My body was hosting a gymnastics competition between the contents of my stomach and my heart seemed to be winning, fluttering like a crazed butterfly inside my chest. "I'm just... I'm confused as hell about you, about how you make me feel," I admitted in a torn voice. "You scare me."

Noah's eyes softened as he pulled me closer.

Cupping my cheeks with the palms of his hands, he pressed a toe-curling kiss to my lips and I couldn't stop myself from sagging against him. "I really don't think you have a clue of what you're doing to me," he said gently as he looked into my eyes and tucked a tendril of hair behind my ear. "Of how far astray you're leading me." His eyes danced with humor. "You're a bad influence on me, Thorn."

"I'm the good one here," I told him with a smirk. "You're

the one who partakes in criminal activities in a place ridiculously named the *Ring of Fire*..."

"That's not my choice, Thorn," Noah replied in a serious tone. His brown eyes burned into mine. "I *have* to do that."

"Why?"

The street lights illuminated a faint scar above Noah's right eyebrow, and I couldn't stop myself from raising my hand and cupping his cheek.

"Noah," I sighed as a heavy weight settled on my chest. "You're worth more than this bullshit life you're living," I told him, surprising us both when my voice cracked slightly.

Noah visually shuddered from my touch. He stared down at me like I was some strange creature he couldn't remember the name of.

"Why do I..." I paused and asked myself what the hell I was doing, but the words just slipped out. "Why do I get the feeling that you need someone to fight for you as ferociously as you fight those men?"

The words were barely out of my mouth when Noah was pulled backwards and dragged away from me.

"We've been looking for you," a huge red-headed man snarled as he grabbed Noah by the back of his neck.

"Teagan, get in the car," Noah managed to say before he was shoved face down on the sidewalk by the huge man who'd dragged him away from me.

I didn't get in the car.

Instead, I screamed like a banshee and prayed someone somewhere would have the common sense to call the police.

"My father wanted us to remind you what happens to defectors," the man added before nodding his head in my direction. "Consider this your first, last, and only warning."

He then held Noah down as another three men came forward and formed a circle around his body.

"Hey, get the hell off him!" I roared, my tone frantic, as I rushed towards the men who were now kicking and punching him.

"Noah!" I screamed as I thumped my fists against one man's back, desperately trying to break through and get to him.

My stomach lurched when I saw Noah being held face down by the scruff of the neck and beaten to a pulp.

Blood caked all over his hair and face.

An overwhelming feeling coursed through me, urging me to shield him. To *save him*. Without thinking twice about it, I scrambled over to where he was laying and, shoving the man's hand away from Noah's neck, I covered his head and shoulders with my body.

Some asswipe managed to catch the side of my face with his boot and I cried out in pain, but remained exactly where I was.

"You got your pussy fighting your corner, kid?" One of the men, the one whose legs I managed to squeeze under, sneered. "George told you..."

"You can tell *George* to go fuck himself," I snarled, not having a goddamn clue who I was talking about. I looked up at their faces and grimaced. My eyes locked on the man in the blue shirt with the red hair. He looked familiar, but I just... I couldn't remember where I'd seen him. "Because if I ever meet the man in the flesh, he's going to be walking like a constipated cowboy with a boot shoved up his ass."

"Teagan," Noah warned in a quiet tone as he slowly pulled himself to his feet, taking me with him. He warned me into silence with one look and the slightest shake of his head.

"*Teagan?*" Blue Shirt whistled in surprise. "The next door neighbor, *Teagan?*"

Noah stiffened beside me.

"You've got more balls than brains, kid," the man chuckled. "You saw what happened to Kruger's career when he got involved..."

"*This* has nothing to do with her, JD," Noah said stiffly, limping forward so that he was blocking me from the men's view. His stance was protective more than aggressive. "And you can tell your father that I haven't forgotten a damn thing."

Blood was dripping down Noah's face, and all I wanted to do was wrap my arms around him and protect him from this crazy fucking world he seemed to have fallen into.

"I'm sure George will be *very* interested to hear about your little *friend* here," Blue Shirt said with a grin as he leered at me briefly before returning his gaze to Noah "We'll be seeing you, kid," he chuckled before turning around and walking away with the other men.

"Call the cops," I blurted out the second the men were out of sight.

Swinging around to face him, I looked up at Noah expectantly. "Noah, call the cops now. They can't get away with this." I moved to cup his cheek, but he pushed my hand away, backing away from me.

One of Noah's eyes was practically swollen shut, his cheekbone was flecked with ugly, dark bruising, and blood was flowing from the gash above his right eyebrow.

"No cops," was all he said before limping back to his car and opening the passenger door.

I dropped my hand to my side and bit down hard on my lip, desperate to hold back the tears that were threatening to spill.

Temper tears, I assured myself.

"Why the hell not?" I managed to choke out. "Noah, those men could've killed you..."

"Just drop it, Teagan," Noah snapped, cutting me off mid sentence, and I flinched from the coldness in his voice. "The cops can't do a damn thing to help me."

"But you're bleeding!" I screamed. "Your face is destroyed." I shook my head in disgust. "Those men just beat the shit out of you, Noah."

When he didn't reply, I kind of lost it.

"Oh my god, there is something very wrong with you," I screamed in frustration. "You're a complete disaster, Noah. Why the hell are you allowing those creeps to get away with attacking you – us?"

Noah's facial expression changed the minute those words passed my mouth, a vein in his neck throbbed, and he stared at me like I was a stranger.

"You're absolutely right, Teagan," he said, rubbing a hand down his face. He stared hard at me for a moment before laughing humorlessly. "There is something *very wrong* with me, so why don't you just fucking walk away before I infect your perfect little existence with my bullshit life."

"Fine," I spat as I folded my arms around myself protectively and turned to walk away from him. "Watch my back as I walk away from your bullshit life."

"Goddammit, Thorn," I heard Noah hiss seconds before he bundled me into his car and slammed the door.

"Buckle up," he snapped as he slid into the driver's seat and cranked the engine. Blaring the radio to the maximum volume, Noah tore off without as much as a backwards glance. The Stunning's *Brewing up a Storm* blasted from the speakers and I fastened my seatbelt and submerged myself in the lyrics.

"You don't understand what happened with those men

back there, Teagan," Noah muttered after ten minutes of icy silence. "It's not as simple as calling the cops."

"No, I don't understand," I replied stonily, feeling wounded and pissed off. I clenched my fists against the leather interior and inhaled through my nose. Bad idea since Noah's scent; sex, man, and body wash, flooded my senses. "Why don't you get a real job?"

Noah changed gears and sighed. "I have a record."

"For being a dick?" I offered dryly.

"Funny," Noah shot back in a flat tone. "Look, I've been in trouble with the law, Teagan. On more than one occasion."

Slowing down to take a corner, Noah dropped his hand to the gear stick, his fingers accidentally brushing against my thigh. I squirmed on the cool leather seat. "Nobody in their right mind would hire me," he added in a melancholic tone.

"I would," I blurted out, turning my face to look at him. Noah glanced sideways at me and frowned. "Hire you, that is," I clarified quietly.

"You see what I mean," he said as a reluctant smile spread across his lips. "Nobody in their right mind."

Now I was the one to say, "Funny." Shifting in my seat, I folded my arms and stared at his side profile. "What about Kyle?"

His jaw ticked. "What about him?"

I rolled my eyes. "Ah... The guy's *minted*," I said in a sardonic tone. "Couldn't he give you a job?" Shrugging, I added, "You're friends with his kids, I'm sure Kyle would help you if you..."

"No," Noah snapped. "I'm not asking Kyle for any more handouts."

"What do you mean *any more* handouts?"

"Exactly what I said," he shot back coolly and I could've howled in frustration.

"They were talking about your stepfather, weren't they?" The more I thought about it, the more certain I was that his stepdad was somehow responsible for Noah's fucked up lifestyle...

"George is my stepfather. He's not my real dad. That title goes to the scumbag who left me to clean up his mess..."

"Do you have any idea of what it feels like to have a stepfather just shoved on you when you're fourteen? One that hates your goddamn guts? A guy who uses your mother's treatment as a goddamn bargaining tool?"

"Do you know what it's like having to pay back the debt of the woman who spent the best part of your childhood shoving you into cupboards and locking you away in a basement for weeks on end because she's convinced the fucking world is against her?"

"Have you ever been afraid, Teagan, truly afraid of your parents?

"What's he got you involved in, Noah?" I asked him. God, the guy was trouble with a capital T. Dammit I *knew* this, but instead of feeling fear for myself I felt it for *him,* because deep down, I knew he wasn't bad. Lee had been right when she said Noah was troubled. "Tell me," I urged him. "Let me... Help you."

Noah let out a heavy sigh but didn't reply. Instead, he rested his elbow on the car door, placed his head in his hand, and used only his thumb on the other hand to steer the wheel. I swallowed deeply and focused on the speedometer that was showing we were doing eighty in a sixty zone.

This made me nervous.

Very nervous.

"You can't help me, Thorn," he whispered, finally breaking the uncomfortable silence. "You can't change me either. I'm never gonna be the kind of guy you take home to meet the family."

"So, what's the plan?" I snapped. "Fight for those men for the rest of your life?"

He shrugged nonchalantly but didn't answer me.

"Tell me why you fight." My voice was shaky and I couldn't stand that Noah could make me feel this unbalanced. "Tell me; what's he got over you?" Because I just *knew* his stepfather and those men at the hotel were connected. "Tell me, Noah."

"Teagan, I..." Noah paused and inhaled deeply before speaking, "Stop asking questions you know I'll answer with lies."

"So don't lie," I pressed as I folded my knees beneath myself and turned my body to face him. "Because I won't stop asking."

"I got mixed up in some bad shit when I was younger," Noah admitted, his tone gruff, his eyes dark and focused on the road. "This is my way out."

"What kind of shit?" I asked, leaning closer into him. I was physically drawn to him. I couldn't help it.

"The kind girls like you only read about," he whispered. "You wouldn't understand, Teagan," he added, "so there's no point trying."

Anger bubbled to the surface. "That's so stupid, Noah," I hissed, both worried and agitated. I was feeling anxious, for him, and the knowledge of that was incredibly unsettling. "Don't you care about yourself? About your body?"

Again, Noah didn't answer me.

"What about me?" I clamped my mouth shut the second those three pathetic words slipped out.

NOAH

"What about me?" she blurted out and I sucked in a sharp breath. I felt more pain the moment those three words fell from Teagan's lips than I'd felt when JD and his gang were kicking the crap out of me.

"What *about* you, Teagan?" I managed to say as I turned onto our street, even though I was finding it hard to speak. I pulled into her driveway and killed the engine. It was hard to breathe with her sitting next to me, so vulnerable, so fucking beautiful it hurt.

"You and me," she mumbled, red faced, shifting onto her knees to face me. "We just... You said you... You know I... But I don't want any part of *that*."

Teagan didn't deserve this.

She deserved better than me.

I needed to let her go, but I knew in my heart I wasn't going to.

I closed my eyes and inhaled a deep breath.

"I do what I do to keep my mother in rehab. She's schizophrenic and a recovering heroin addict." The words just spilled from my mouth in a rush and I couldn't look at

Teagan to take her measure. I kept my eyes closed as I told Teagan more than I'd dared tell anyone in my life.

"My stepfather runs a disreputable business that I've been dragged into. I'm his best fighter, and if I win my fights, George pays the monthly fee it costs to keep my mother facilitated." I couldn't believe she'd managed to get me to talk. Fuck, I should know better than to tell her, but I just... I *wanted* to open up to her. I wanted Teagan to know I wasn't all bad. I couldn't tell her everything, all my reasons, but I needed her to know that I didn't have any other choice in this. "If I don't fight... Well, let's just say they have ways of making me."

I kept my eyes shut, waiting for the sound of a car door slamming to let me know Teagan had left.

It didn't come.

Instead, I felt two small hands touch my shoulders seconds before a body landed on my lap. "Thank you, Jesus," she whispered before pressing her lips to mine, and I opened my eyes in surprise.

"Thank you, Jesus?" I asked in confusion, pulling back to stare at her. Teagan was sitting on my lap with her hazel eyes wide and locked on mine.

She nodded her head and sighed in relief. "You have no choice," she said in a relieved tone. "This isn't who you are, who you want to be."

"No, it's not," I rasped, pulling her closer. "But it's my reality."

Teagan shook her head in obvious confusion. "But, Noah, I had a neighbor," she told me, "back home in Ireland – Clare. She's schizophrenic and lives a good life with her husband Joe. She has a career and a mortgage and a..."

"A three grand a day heroin habit?" I offered dryly, knowing Teagan wasn't getting it.

She could never get it unless she'd lived my life and witnessed what I had.

"No," Teagan mumbled, red faced. "She doesn't have that..." Her voice trailed off as her eyes locked on mine. "Why would he do that?"

"Why would *who* do that?"

"George," she told me in an impatient tone before sighing in obvious frustration. "Why would he do that to his wife? To you?"

"Because he can, Teagan," I muttered, feeling both angry and uncomfortable. Her questions were skirting dangerously close to a topic I was not willing to talk about. "Can we leave it at that?"

"But none of this makes sense, Noah." Teagan shook her head and frowned. "Why would he treat her that way?"

TEAGAN

I was trying really hard not to freak out, but the more I thought about the shitty way Noah had been treated for quite possibly the majority of his life, the angrier I felt. "If you're mother's as sick as you say," I mumbled, "you know, with the drugs and stuff, then why did they get married?"

"Why do old guys marry younger women?" Noah shot back tightly. "Looks and submission, Teagan."

I'd been wrong about Noah. All this time I'd thought... When he was *nothing* like Ellie or her father... Wait. "Is Ellie really George's daughter?" I asked him all of a sudden.

Noah brows rose in surprise. "Yes," he drawled slowly. "Why would you ask that?"

I shrugged awkwardly. "After what you've just told me, it wouldn't surprise me in the slightest if she was his second wife or something screwed up like that."

Noah's eyes darkened, but when he blinked he was back to me. "That's gross, Teagan," he grumbled. "She's his youngest child, daddy's little girl, there to do her father's dirty work and get all the *staff* on board..."

"He has more children than just Ellie?"

"Several more littered across the country," Noah replied dryly. "But only two that he acknowledges. Ellie and JD."

"Who's JD?"

Noah sighed heavily. "JD is the overgrown bastard you thought kidnapped me that day we had detention. The guy in the blue shirt who kicked my ass back there."

"I knew I saw that guy before tonight," I hissed in disgust.

Noah shrugged and said, "JD will be George's successor, when the scumbag eventually kicks the bucket."

"His successor of what?" I dared to ask.

"The Ring of Fire, the Hub, the business – everything George owns," he bit out.

"And you?" My hands tightened on his shoulders. "What about you, Noah?"

"And me," Noah confirmed with a sigh. "The Dennis family fucking owns me, and they know it."

"How can your mom allow this?" I demanded, feeling outraged for him. "Why the hell did she marry that scumbag?"

Shaking his head, Noah rubbed his face with his hand and let out a weary sigh. "She's forty-six and beautiful, Teagan. He's sixty-eight and powerful. It's a match made in hell. Besides, she has no choice in the matter. It's this or end up like..." Noah stopped abruptly and turned his face away.

"Like who?"

"Look, Teagan," he snapped. "There are some men out there who are desperate to dominate. And some women who are desperately dominated."

"How did they meet?" I asked him cautiously, aware that he was growing more agitated by the minute.

Noah's body stiffened beneath me and I watched as the shutters closed in his eyes. "My dad worked for him." He didn't meet my eyes when he spoke and his jaw was clenched tight.

"Is that all?" I asked in a level voice, knowing deep in my bones he was lying to me.

"Is that not enough?" he sneered.

Defensive... Yeah, there was definitely more. "You tell me, Noah."

"There's nothing more," he replied, again not meeting my eyes.

"Liar," I hissed.

"Believe what you want," he snapped. "That's all you're getting from me."

"I'm an all or nothing kinda girl, Noah," I told him. "Complete disclosure, or nothing at all."

Noah got my meaning because his eyes narrowed. "Don't give me an ultimatum, Teagan," he warned me. "You won't win."

"I just did, Noah," I shot back heatedly.

"I'm not the type of guy who takes orders from his girl, Teagan," Noah muttered, jaw clenched.

"Well aren't we lucky I'm not *your* girl?" I spat as I opened the door and climbed out.

Swinging around, I leaned back into the car. "You told me earlier you weren't the kind of guy a girl brings home to meet the family."

Noah frowned at me in confusion. "Yeah... And?"

"*And* just so *you* know, I'm not the kind of girl who asks her family for permission," I told him before slamming his car door and marching up my porch steps. "Congratulations, Noah," I called out shakily. "You've won and you've hurt me all in one night."

"What did that door ever do to you?" Uncle Max asked when I slammed the front door and stalked into the kitchen.

As soon as I reached the table, I sank onto the chair closest to me and dropped my head in my arms.

"Teagan?" Max demanded from somewhere behind me. "What's wrong?"

"Just leave it, okay?" I mumbled, feeling thoroughly confused.

What the hell had just happened? *Too much in one night, that's what...*

"No, I won't leave it. You're upset, something has obviously happened," Max continued, playing the role of the concerned uncle superbly. "And I want to know what it was."

Well, let's see; I let the next door neighbor fuck me in an elevator shaft... Oh yeah, and get this, his stepdad is some major crime lord who gets off on abusing sick women and blackmailing their sons. My heart feels like someone took a razor to it. My virginity is driving off in a black Lexus. My body is throbbing and all I want is a hug from a guy who won't tell me the truth... "I have a headache, that's all." I lifted my head and forced myself to make eye contact with him. "I'll be fine after a shower."

"A headache," Max repeated in a disbelieving tone. He stared at me for a long moment before shaking his head. "Whatever you say," he grumbled as he shrugged on his coat. "I have to go to work. Oh yeah, and don't forget to call Hope," Max added as he grabbed his keys and made his way towards the door. "She wants to know if you're still planning on sleeping over."

Great, that was all I needed...

"I'll do that," I called out, but the sound of the front door slamming let me know Max hadn't waited for my reply.

18

NOAH

I watched Teagan storm into her house and slam her front door, knowing full well I couldn't go inside my house tonight. JD showing up outside the hotel meant I needed to steer clear of the house until he calmed down.

Hell, I'd taken a risk even coming back to the street, but there was no way I *wasn't* dropping Teagan home after what had happened between us in the elevator.

I sent a text to Low, asking if it was okay to crash at his place as I sat in my car staring up at Teagan's house until her bedroom light came on. And then I had to clench my eyes shut and force myself to stop imagining what she was doing up there.

A virgin.

I hadn't been expecting that, hadn't even realized it until afterwards when I saw her thighs. I'd never been with a virgin before and that knowledge did nothing to stem the confusing emotions raging inside of me.

Dammit, I screwed up big time by taking that job from Gonzalez. George was going to make me pay for it and that was fine. I had no problem paying for my mistakes, but I fucking knew in my heart that the stakes had changed.

Tonight had changed everything and I'd unintentionally managed to put the one person who meant something to me in danger.

Reluctantly cranking the engine of my car, I reversed out of Teagan's driveway and decided to drive the familiar route eastwards, the one I both craved and dreaded, to the Haven-Bay Clinic while I waited for Low to reply.

As I sat in the visiting room of the Haven-Bay Rehabilitation Center, my mind kept drifting back to Teagan and what she'd said to me.

"Why do I get the feeling that you need someone to fight for you as ferociously as you fight those men?"

God, those words caused me to shudder and I dropped my head with a sigh. Teagan didn't know how right she was.

"Hello, Noah."

My entire frame stiffened from the sound of *her* voice.

Exhaling slowly, I stood and faced the frail blonde woman standing in the doorway. The woman who was partially responsible for my train wreck of a life.

"Hello, mom."

"What are you doing here?" my mother asked me as she looked around the room. Her gaze landed on my face, and she looked through me with indifference; there was no love or even fondness in her eyes and that hurt something fierce. "Where's George?"

"Fuck George," I snapped, feeling infuriated beyond belief. It was a fucking disgrace that I had to ask his permission to see my own mother, but then again that was her fault the bastard had so much power over us. "I needed to see you," I told her in as calm a tone as I could muster. "We need to talk."

Her brown eyes were wide and cautious as she pushed the rim of her glasses higher on her nose, a nervous trait, and slowly moved further into the room. "Why didn't you write to me?" she asked as she lowered herself onto the brown leather couch opposite me. "You know I don't like seeing you."

You would think after eighteen years of hearing shit like this, I would be immune to her lack of feeling towards me, but no, it still stung like a bitch.

"There's a lot of things I don't like doing either, mom, but I do them *for you*," I shot back tightly as I studied her emotionless expression. "And what I want to talk to you about isn't something I wanna write in a fucking letter."

My mother's dark eyes flared with resentment. "You grow more like your brother each day," she spat, wrapping her arms around her knees. "That dirty mouth." She scratched at the back of her hands and I noticed her nails weren't taped up tonight. "I should wash your mouth out with soap."

"I'm eighteen now, Mom, not eight, so I'd like to see you try," I replied dryly. "And please don't start with the brother shit again. It's getting really old."

I didn't have a brother. I didn't have a sister, either, for that matter. I was my parent's only child, but when my mother got angry, she would always accuse me of being the reincarnation of my phantom *brother*.

"I don't want you here," she snarled.

"And I don't want to clear up yours and dad's mess for the rest of my life," I snapped, chest heaving. "I can't do it anymore, mom," I choked out. "I need out."

"You can't," she screeched, eyes wild with panic. "You have to do this..."

"Look at me," I countered in an even tone. I gestured to my bloodied and bruised face. "Is this the life you want for me..." I paused and forced myself to get a grip before finishing. "I'm gonna die if I don't get out soon, mom."

Images of Teagan flooded me and I flinched. I didn't want this life anymore. I wanted a fucking shot at a future like everyone else. I wanted to be able to take that girl to the movies and not fear every second of it. I wanted her to know me, the real me. And I wanted the absolute fucking guarantee that spending time with me wouldn't put her in danger. I had to get out of this.

"You're just like him," Mom snarled. "He used me for my body, same as you."

Clutching her forehead with her hands, mom began to shake her head rapidly, digging her nails roughly into the skin covering her forehead. "Toxic. Another one of his spawn is growing inside of me... Tainting me..."

"Mom, stop," I begged as I stood up quickly and moved towards her.

Dropping onto my knees in front of her, I gently pried her fingers away from her face. "Please don't do that," I managed to choke out, the pain of watching her hurt herself as cutting as ever. "Please."

It hurt to see her in this state considering before she'd had me, she'd once had a stable life and a good career. But something had happened to my mother, something more than her illness. I blamed my dad for introducing her to drugs, but it was more than that. She was so secretive, so lost, and I couldn't figure it out.

"The things I've done, Noah," she rambled as I held her hands in mine. Tears streamed from her eyes, trickling down her cheeks, and I couldn't stop myself from pulling her onto my lap. "The things I'm responsible for... because of *him*. Because of *you*."

"Shh," I coaxed, wrapping my arms around my mother's frail body. "It's okay. You're safe."

"You can't stop, Noah," she cried. "There's no way out."

"Kelsie, what are you doing out of bed?" A soothing female voice asked from behind me and my mother froze in my arms.

"Do as you're told," she hissed into my ear. "Don't let what happened to him happen to me. *You* let him die."

My mother's words impaled me and I staggered backwards, landing on my ass. "Mom, that wasn't my fault," I whispered.

"Come on, sweetie," the nurse coaxed, helping my mother off the couch before turning to me. "You need to leave, Mr. Messina," she ordered as she shuffled my mother towards the door. "Your mother is having a bad day. She had a visitor earlier today and she's been agitated ever since."

I bet.

I needed to leave this place, but I knew in my heart I was as trapped as her. "Okay," I muttered, climbing to my feet. "I'll talk to you soon, Mom," I told her, but it was too late.

My mother was gone.

TEAGAN

"Do you ever sleep?" I muttered as I pulled my pillow out from under my head and draped it over my face. "Seriously, Hope, turn it off."

It was three in the morning, we were still awake, and I was seriously regretting agreeing to sleep at Hope's house – and regretting introducing Hope to the Irish television show *Love/Hate*.

I managed to doze off at some stage, but the sound of screaming woke me. When I asked Hope what the hell was happening, she just shrugged and told me her mom had nightmares, which had totally freaked me out.

"Shh," she mumbled, eyes locked on the screen. "One more episode."

I discovered Hope was one of those people who had to see something through to the end, which was why we were currently on season *three* of the show, and I had a pain in my brain from listening to her imitating the characters' accents. But I was thankful to *Love/Hate* for distracting my friend from her infatuation with losing her virginity, because I was still pretty hung up on the fact that I'd lost mine tonight to a criminal gang's *muscle*.

Jesus Christ, I'd had sex with Noah Messina, and I'd done so on an elevator floor in the fanciest hotel I'd ever stepped foot inside. Oh god, my cheeks flamed thinking back, and my toes curled.

"Ugh." Tossing my pillow on the floor, I climbed off my makeshift bed and stretched awkwardly. "I need a drink," I whispered. I couldn't lay there a second longer with my brain tormenting me, throwing images of Noah's face around. I had to move, go... Anything to distract myself.

Hope waved me off. "Help yourself to whatever," she muttered.

Shaking my head, I crept out of Hope's bedroom and crept down the staircase.

Thankfully, someone in the Carter household didn't seem to like the dark, either, because the place was lit up like a glowworm. I had to steel myself before I walked into the kitchen and even then, I screamed my head off.

"Jesus," I gasped, holding my hand to my chest. "You nearly gave me a heart attack."

"Sorry, sweetheart," Cam chuckled as he poured himself a cup of coffee. "You want some?"

Cameron's piercing blue eyes locked on the *gorgeous* shiner I was sporting on my cheekbone, courtesy of the big ape wearing the size twelve boots, but thankfully he didn't ask questions.

"Yeah," I replied as I lowered myself onto a chair and forced myself not to stare at my best friend's brother like he was a piece of meat. "Thanks."

"How's the foot?" Cam asked as he placed a steaming mug of coffee in front of me before taking the seat opposite mine. "By the way, I really *am* sorry about the whole Ring of

Fire thing, Teagan," he added in a surprisingly serious tone of voice.

"It's better, and apology accepted," I told him, looking anywhere but his naked chest. "You're up late – or early..." I shrugged. "Whatever way you want to look at it."

"You heard my mom, didn't you?" was all he replied in a quiet tone.

"Yeah... I heard her," I said quietly as I studied his rarely troubled face. "But it's not a big deal," I told him, feeling a strange need to comfort the dark haired, bare chested giant beside me. "Everyone has nightmares, Cam."

"Yeah," he said with a sigh. Curling his fingers around his mug, Cam blew into his coffee before taking a sip. "But not everyone has *lived* their nightmares."

"What do you mean?"

"Nothing." Cam shook his head and jerked out of his seat. "Nothing, I'm talking shit. Night, Teegs."

"Goodnight, Cameron." I watched him leave and felt strangely saddened.

Cam turned when he reached the door. "I should warn you." He jerked his thumb in the direction of their lounge. "Lover boy is crashed out on the couch."

I shook my head at a loss.

"*Noah*," he explained drolly.

"He is?" My heart dropped into my ass and then decided to skyrocket up into my mouth. "*Why?*"

Cam shrugged casually. "Maybe he has the same reasons for being here as you have."

"What? He wants to have a sleepover with your sister, too?" I asked dryly but my comment backfired when a huge swell of jealousy rose inside of me.

"You're a spunky little thing, aren't you?" Cam mused

fondly as he scratched his bare chest, eyes twinkling with mischief.

A thought popped into my head all of a sudden and my head snapped up. "Do you know much about his family?"

Cam's brow burrowed. "Whose family?"

"Noah's." I rolled my eyes with impatience. "Do you?"

Cam sighed heavily. "Teegs, you really shouldn't..." His voice trailed off and he glanced at the kitchen door before walking back towards me.

Returning to the chair he'd vacated, Cam leaned towards me. "I really shouldn't be discussing this," he said with a sigh as he rubbed his face with his hand. "And with you, of all people."

With you, of all people...

"Why?" I asked in annoyance. "Am I not privy to that sort of information because his sister has decided to hate me?" I let out a heavy, defeated sigh.

"No one's privy to that sort of information, Teagan," Cam replied softly. "And indifference is worse than hate," Cameron pointed out. "Personally, I'd rather be hated than not cared about at all."

"That's comforting," I muttered sullenly.

Cam shrugged. "There's emotion in hate. A lot of feelings go into hating someone."

I shook my head in confusion. "Okay, that makes no sense, Cam. How does any of what you've just told me have anything to do with Noah's family?"

"It doesn't," he said with a cocky grin. "I just said the first thing that popped into my head, which was more than likely complete bullshit."

"Well, thanks for your bullshit advice," I grumbled as I stood up and placed my mug on the draining board.

Cam stretched his arms above his head before getting up

and walking over to the door. "Sorry, Galway girl," he chuckled. "But if you wanna know about Noah's personal life, then you're gonna have to put your big girl pants on and ask him yourself."

The sound of Cam's footsteps descending down the hallway made the thought of Noah sleeping in the next room a sudden and huge temptation.

Crap... I wanted to see him.

Oh god, I was so screwed.

Shuffling out of the kitchen, I tiptoed down the hallway and placed my hand on the door handle, turning it ever so slowly. Pushing the door of the lounge inwards, I held my breath and allowed my eyes to adjust to the dimly lit room.

The television was on mute, but the light coming from the screen and from the lit up Christmas tree standing in front of the bay window was enough to illuminate Noah stretched out on the Carter's couch with one arm resting over his face and the other placed atop his bare chest.

A navy afghan was pooled around his hips and I couldn't move my eyes from the spot. There was something incredibly stunning about Noah's hips – his whole body in fact. I would never admit it to another soul, but I was pretty sure his was the most beautifully sculpted male body I'd ever seen in real life.

I felt an intense urge to trail my finger over the grooves on his stomach just to check if they felt as hard as I remembered.

Dammit, stop thinking about him like that.

Closing my eyes, I turned my head and urged myself to calm the hell down. One more look and then I would go back upstairs and pretend to sleep. I was veering dangerously close to stalker central but I figured one more peek wouldn't hurt. Then I'd go to bed.

I'd have to.

Because what was the alternative? Wake Noah up and ask him to take up where he left off in the elevator? Yeah, I had bigger issues than Hope. At least she wanted to sleep with her loving boyfriend. I wanted... I wasn't sure what I wanted.

"Teagan."

Holy shit. I let out a startled cry and clutched the door handle with both hands.

Moving his arm away from his face, Noah stared at me, his dark brown eyes roaming shamelessly over my body. "You gonna stand by the door all night or are you gonna come in?"

He's bad news wrapped in beautiful packaging, Teegs, I chanted in my head as I ogled his magnificent body. *Be wary. Keep your guard up...*

Noah pulled himself up to rest on his elbows and I swallowed deeply when the afghan moved lower on his waist, revealing white boxer shorts. Fitted and extremely *snug* white boxer shorts. "You're letting the heat out, Thorn," he rasped, twisting his neck from side to side. He dropped his feet to the ground and sat up before patting the cushion beside him. "Decision time."

Did he just...

How did he...

Hang on, why were my feet moving towards him?

Against my better judgment, I trotted over to the couch and lowered myself down.

"Why are you sleeping on the neighbor's couch, Noah?" The question just burst out of me, and I worried my lip as I looked at his injured face.

Noah let out a heavy sigh and I was suddenly and acutely aware of the heat of his body as the coarse hairs on his muscular thigh brushed against my smooth, soft skin. "Sometimes it's..." he paused and pinched the bridge of his nose, shifting on the couch so that our bare legs were touching before saying, "it's just safer this way."

"Safer?" A slicing pain tore through me. The thought of something bad happening to Noah caused my chest to restrict, making it hard to breathe. I stared up at him, a dozen different emotions at war inside of me. "Is it because of those guys? Are they going to come back for you?"

Blowing out a sharp breath, Noah's shoulders sagged and accidentally rubbed against mine, setting off fireworks inside my body. "Not tonight," he finally replied.

"I want you to say never," I admitted, my voice torn.

All my earlier anger had evaporated and all I was left with was this raw, unpolished feeling of affection pooled with an unnerving amount of helplessness. "Tell me that what happened to you tonight will never happen again," I blurted out, feeling weirdly emotional. I was so afraid for him. "Please, Noah."

Noah's hands shot out and clamped down on my hips, drawing me onto his lap so that I was straddling him. "I can handle this, Teagan," he whispered against my ear, wrapping his arms around my waist.

I felt the lightest of pressure when his forehead touched mine. My body was thrilled at the touch. "I don't want you to handle this," I told him. "I want it to stop." The heat emanating from his skin was causing my body to burn. I could feel him strain against me and my heart raced erratically. "I *need* it to stop..."

"I shouldn't have told you," Noah grumbled as he leaned back. "I should've kept my goddamn mouth shut because now all you'll do is worry, and want..."

"Want to know more?" I filled in, nodding my head. "Absolutely."

"I told you more in one car ride than I've told anyone else in my entire life, Teagan," he admitted.

Noah's eyes burned with sincerity, and I couldn't stop myself from asking, "Why me, Noah? Why tell me?"

"Because we match," he admitted with a sigh and my heart skipped a beat.

We match...

Noah's fingers tightened on my thighs. "We're joined, Thorn," he rasped. "Connected. We just are."

"We just are?" I repeated slowly, eyes locked on Noah's. Hell, I felt like I was drowning in the darkness of his eyes. I lowered my face to within an inch of his. "What does that mean, Noah?"

"Sometimes things are unexplainable because some things don't need an explanation," he told me in a gruff tone before covering my lips with his. "I can't give you a definition, Teagan," he whispered against my lips. "I can't answer the why's or how's of what's happening between us because honestly, what you're making me feel is fucking alien to me."

Noah's tongue trailed over my lower lip before he pulled it into his mouth and sucked. I was lost to sensation as my tongue dueled erotically against his.

My all time favorite Florence and the Machine song drifted through my ears, and I pulled my lips away. "Kiss with a fist," I stated, highly amused by Noah's choice in ringtone as I pulled back and grinned at him.

"What can I say?" Noah shrugged nonchalantly as he leaned forward, with me still on his lap, and grabbed his phone off the coffee table. He switched it off and tossed it back on the coffee table. "It's been stuck in my head since I heard this insanely hot Irish girl singing it at the crack of dawn right outside my house."

"Insanely hot?" I raised my brow in amusement. "You're full of it, Messina."

"Well, here's more of it," he chuckled softly before pressing a kiss to my lips. "Someone once asked me if I had to choose one song, one three or four minute piece of music to explain my life, what would I pick?"

Noah leaned back against the couch, wrapping his arms around my waist and when he smirked, my heart rate spiked. My body seemed to go on high alert. I was coiled tight with a fucked-up mixture of lust and terror.

"Could I choose," he explained, tone husky. "Or would the music choose me?"

"What did you say?" I asked, thoroughly enthralled.

Noah stared at me, his brown eyes dark as night. "At the time, I thought the question was pretty random," he chuckled. "But now, now I'm beginning to wonder if it's pretty genius. To have one piece of music to explain your life..."

"Would be extraordinary," I agreed with a sigh. "Four minutes to sum up the course of a lifetime... What did you choose?" I asked, suddenly and desperately needing to know.

Noah smiled but didn't tell me.

Instead he rolled me onto my back and covered my body with his before thrusting his tongue inside my mouth while his fingers pulled at my nightie. "Something I heard you sing once," he whispered through kisses as he managed to rid me of my nightdress.

"What... When?" I moaned, writhing underneath him. I arched myself upwards, wrapping my legs around his waist. All that separated our bodies were his white boxers and my pink thong.

"Back in the summer," Noah rasped between kisses. "It was the most beautiful fucking sound I ever heard."

"I want to be with you, Noah," I admitted against his lips, clutching him tightly to me. "But I'm scared," I admitted. "I'm terrified of losing myself in your world when I know it's wrong."

"I won't let that happen, Thorn," he whispered, pulling my lip into his mouth and sucking gently. His forehead touched mine, his breath fanned my face, and I closed my eyes, inhaling deeply, reveling in his scent. "I'll get us both out of this. I promise."

The sincerity and emotion in his words struck something deep inside of me. "Okay," I whispered. "I admit it. I care, and you make me vulnerable."

"About damn time," he groaned before lowering his mouth to mine.

Someone cleared their throat loudly.

Oh shit.

My body froze and I was almost too afraid to open my eyes to see who was there.

Noah obviously didn't hear them because he continued to kiss me, devouring me like an addict would his drug of choice.

"I *really* wouldn't if I were you," a deep male voice said and finally Noah caught on and froze, eyes blinking open with shock, lips still pressed to mine. "That couch is like a fertility shrine," the same voice added in an amused tone. "If you knew half of what's been conceived on that thing..."

"Jesus Christ, Dad," another male voice muttered.

"Yuck," I whispered, cringing.

Noah muttered an impressive array of curse words before reluctantly craning his neck. "Do you mind?" he asked in a flat tone.

I peeked over Noah's shoulder quickly and saw not one, but two men standing in the doorway of the lounge. One of the men was of average height, muscular build, with a Christmas hat on his head and his arms laden down with presents.

The bald-headed uncle, I realized.

"Not really," the bald uncle chuckled. "But the control freak upstairs will... Hey – isn't she the one who tossed paint on your car? You guys are together now?"

"Yes, we're working things out, Derek," Noah replied dryly. There was reluctant fondness in Noah's voice letting me know that he knew this Derek guy. "So, if could you please fuck off and let us work things out, it would be much appreciated."

My eyes locked on the other guy who was clocking in at well over six four with curly black hair and that guy was...

"Jordan!"

I heard Hope's sequel of delight seconds before she barreled into the lounge and threw herself upon the curly haired giant.

Jordan caught her easily and the hug they shared, the intimate way he shuddered when she pressed her face into his neck, was so intimate and beautiful.

"Merry Christmas, Keychain," Jordan whispered against her neck as he knotted his hand in her curls. "I told you I'd make it."

"No way," Colton's familiar voice chuckled, followed by Cam's booming voice as he cheered, "I knew he was bagging her."

"Goddammit, Noah," Hope screamed, obviously just noticing our naked presence. "I can't believe you brought a girl into my... Oh. My. God. *Teagan*? What are doing underneath Noah? And *naked?*"

"Nah," Colt chuckled. "I can see lace panties."

"Pervert."

Let me die...

Let me die...

"Hi, Hope," I mumbled, twiddling the tips of my fingers that were wrapped around Noah's neck while I buried my face against his chest. "Please get me out of here," I begged Noah in a hushed tone as I clung to him in pure mortification.

Noah pulled back to look at me. His eyes burned into mine and the affection I saw in them caused my skin to tingle with heat. "Hate to break up the family reunion," Noah said, eyes still locked on mine. "But could you guys take this into the kitchen so we can get up and out of your hair?"

"Yeah," a distinctively commanding voice ordered.

Noah's entire frame stiffened and I think I shriveled a little inside.

"Everyone go back to bed," Mr. Carter ordered as he stood in the doorway, his angry blue eyes locked on Noah. "Now."

Everyone, including Derek, scampered out of the room like chastised rascals.

"This isn't as bad as it looks, Mr. Carter," I muttered, red faced.

"You." He glared at Noah. "Get off that girl and get your ass on the other side of this room."

"And you," he snapped, pointing at me. "Get your clothes on and your explanation ready. I'm calling your uncle."

"Kyle, you need to..." Noah began to say but Kyle stopped him.

"Kitchen, Teagan," Mr. Carter snapped as he turned around and stalked out the door. "One minute."

19

NOAH

"You're a glutton for punishment, dude," Colt told me from where I was currently sitting on the couch between him and Logan. Hope and Jordan were sitting on the armchair opposite us and Cam was pacing the floor with a shit-eating grin on his face.

"Apparently, I am," I grumbled as I tried to sit still and not fidget.

Teagan had been marched into the kitchen about fifteen minutes ago by a pissed looking Kyle and I was growing anxious as hell. Shit, I was two seconds away from stalking into that kitchen and the only thing that was holding me back was the fact that I had a hell of a lot of respect for Kyle.

The disappointment in his eyes when he caught me on the couch with Teagan was something I wouldn't forget easily. But if I left now, I'd be proving I deserved that look. I *didn't* deserve that look, even though Teagan deserved a hell of a lot better than me.

"Dad told you to go home," Colt added in an amused tone. "He's gonna hit the roof when he realizes you're still here."

"I would take the get out of jail card if I were you, man," Cam offered, stopping to adjust the star on the top of their Christmas tree before resuming his pacing. "There's nothing fucking chivalrous about waiting around to take an ass-kicking from an overprotective parent."

"Like you'd know anything about chivalry," Low snorted.

"Actually, I would," Cam snapped, glaring at Logan. "Have you forgotten about the time Danny Valentine caught me in Amy's bedroom?" Cam shuddered and cast an evil glare in Jordan's direction. "Thanks to that douchebag, my face got up close and personal with a part of the toilet that my ass knows intimately."

"Sorry," Jordan said with a smirk. "My uncle's a little..."

"Insane," Cam spat. "I believe the word you're leaning towards is insane, Jord."

"What's going on with you and Teagan?" Hope asked in a level tone, her blue eyes locked on my face. "If she's just another girl you're planning on messing around with or using for sex..."

"She's not *just* another girl," I told her, meeting her stare head on and meaning every word that was coming out of my mouth. "She means... More than that."

"What the hell are you talking about, you big vagina?" Cam shook his head and gaped at me like I'd spoken a foreign language. "She means *more* than that..." He glared down at me with a look of disgust. "Don't fucking tell me that girl managed to sink you, Messina? What the hell has Galway girl got underneath that nightdress? A golden pus..."

"If you wanna keep your mobility, I suggest you shut your mouth and not talk about her like that," I snarled heatedly. "*Ever.*"

"Oh dude, he's completely pussy whipped," Colt laughed and made the sound of a whip cracking.

"Colton," I warned.

"You guys are so immature," Hope snorted. "Seriously..."

The sound of Kyle's raised voice caused me to jump to my feet.

That was it. I couldn't sit here a fucking second longer without her.

Every fiber of my being demanded I go into that kitchen and protect what was mine.

And that's exactly what I did.

TEAGAN

"What the hell were you thinking, Teagan?" Hope's father demanded as he stalked around his kitchen like a mad man. "Have you lost your damn mind?"

This was the tenth time Kyle Carter had asked me that question and again, I didn't bother answering him. I, like everyone else in the room, which consisted of a pale faced Lee Carter and a grinning Derek, knew he wasn't finished ranting.

Besides, if I told him what I was really thinking; that I was mad as hell that Derek and Jordan had interrupted us, I doubted it would be appreciated.

"Seventeen," Kyle groaned, rubbing a hand over his face. "She's seven-fucking-teen, Princess," he growled as he looked at his wife, despair evident in his eyes.

"I'm sorry," I mumbled, not knowing what else to say, as I sat at the kitchen table. "I'm eighteen in a few days..."

"See," he hissed. "She's a goddamn baby." He let out a sigh. "They're kids – kids, for Christ's sake." His gaze locked on his wife. "The world is going to shit, baby. Kids..."

"Kids." Derek snorted. "You're a huge fucking hypocrite, dude."

"Don't you start with me, douchebag," Kyle shot back, nostrils flaring.

"Calm down, Kyle," Lee replied in a soft tone as she trotted over to where her husband was turning purple and patted his chest. "Breathe," she coaxed.

Kyle seemed to relax under his wife's gentle coaxing and I silently thanked god that there was someone on this earth who could tame the wild beast.

"What the hell am I supposed to tell your uncle when he gets here?" Kyle asked me. He ran a hand through his thick, dark hair before dropping his hands on his hips, towering over me with a look of horror etched on his face.

The kitchen door swung inwards, and my entire body froze when Noah stepped inside – thankfully fully dressed in faded jeans and a navy hoodie.

"I thought I told you to go home," Kyle snarled, eyes flaring with anger as he stalked towards Noah.

"And I'm going," Noah replied in a level tone, standing head to head with Hope's dad. Mr. Carter was taller, but only just, and when Noah's gaze flickered towards me I felt dizzy. "But she's coming with me."

My heart somersaulted around in my chest.

She's coming with me...

Noah shot me a meaningful look and I quickly climbed to my feet.

Oh, I was so going with him...

When I reached Noah's side, he wrapped his hand around mine and squeezed.

"You know, what, Noah," Kyle said in a disappointed tone of voice, shaking his head, distracting me from reveling in Noah's touch. "I thought more of you, kid, I really did."

Noah's jaw clenched and I had a feeling Kyle's words had hit a nerve. "It's not what you think," he replied stiffly.

"I've been where you are, Noah," Kyle continued. "And this..." He gestured towards me. "Her... In my house? You think it's no big deal, but it is." Kyle shook his head in disgust. "Because she's..."

"*She's* my girlfriend," Noah announced, shocking the hell out of me. I squeezed his hand and Noah looked down at me, smiling. He met Kyle's stare. "She's *my* responsibility. I'll walk her home."

The front door slammed behind us. "Actually, she's not your responsibility," an achingly familiar voice growled from behind us and I wanted to cry.

Uncle Max stalked into the Carter's kitchen and shook hands briefly with Kyle before turning to glare at Noah.

"Until the twenty-fifth of this month, when she turns eighteen, she's mine," Max said tightly, eyes locked on Noah. "So keep your grubby little hands off her."

Noah's hand tightened around mine and I could tell he was as pissed as I was. This was unbelievable. We had no luck.

I glared up at Hope's father, feeling completely betrayed. "You sold me out."

"If you were my daughter, I'd want to know," Kyle replied as he ushered Lee and Derek from the room. "We'll leave you three to talk it out."

"I'm not your daughter," I muttered under my breath. "Or his."

"Well, let me tell you something, Teagan." Max looked down at me and I could see the disappointment in his eyes; could hear it in his voice. "I'm glad Kyle called me about this. It's called being a responsible parent and I, for one, am extremely thankful because I have absolutely no intentions of wasting my life raising *another* kid that's not mine."

I stepped back, feeling physically winded from his words. I gaped at my uncle like I'd never seen him before in my life, and in a way, I hadn't. This version of Max was completely new to me.

"Do you really believe that?" I asked, biting down hard on my lip, as I stared up at my uncle's face. "That you wasted your life raising me?"

"Absolutely, if the first thing you do is spread your legs for that piece of shit the minute my back is turned," Max shot back heatedly.

"The minute your back is turned?" I shook my head in disgust, hating the way my voice was trembling. "You're back is *constantly* turned, Max. Since we moved here you're never around for me. I'm on my own ninety-nine percent of the time. And he's not a piece of shit..."

"So, you're acting out for attention?" Max roared into my face. "Behaving like a tramp? For god's sake, have you no respect for yourself? Or for me?" Stepping forward, Max did something that he'd never done before. He put his hands on my shoulders and shook me like a rag doll.

"Hey man, back the hell off," Noah growled, stepping in front of me, shielding me from my uncle's menacing glare. "Don't touch her like that."

"And who the hell are you, *man*?" Max shot back in a condescending tone before shoving Noah in the chest. "Only the jumped-up little shit who's been bullying her for months."

"Don't touch him, Max," I surprised myself by saying.

Both Max and Noah swung their gazes on me and I realized in that moment, I'd taken sides.

I'd taken Noah's side over my own uncle.

"Are you serious, Teagan?" Max asked in a disgusted tone of voice. "You're actually going to defend this... Loser?"

"He is *not* a loser," I snapped, feeling acutely protective of Noah. "And you are overreacting here, Max. You don't know anything about him."

"I know more than either of you do. He's bad news, Teagan," Max roared. "I know he's been admitted to the ER more times in the past six months than any other eighteen-year-old." Max leered at Noah like he was a piece of trash. "I know that every time he's brought in by those men, so is another misfortune – *always* in much worse condition than him," Max hissed. "And I know his mother is a..."

"Finish that sentence and I will bury you," Noah snarled, chest heaving. "Uncle or not..."

I stepped forward and grabbed Noah's hand, squeezing it gently to calm him down.

Max, noticing my actions, shook his head and laughed humorlessly. "Well, I've seen it all now," he sneered.

"You have no idea what you're getting yourself into," he told me as he pushed between us and stalked towards the door. "But I'll tell you the same thing I told your mother when she was your age," he choked out in a pained voice. "Don't come crying to me when he breaks your heart. Because he *will*."

"What the hell does that mean?" I called after him.

"It means, do as you damn well please, Teagan," Max roared. "You're just like your mother. You're not going to listen to a word of sense while you've got love tinted glasses perched on your pretty nose, so I'm not standing around here wasting my breath."

The door slammed shut and I stood frozen in the middle of the Carter's kitchen, eyes wide and locked on Noah's.

"Well that was a little excessive," I finally muttered,

feeling like my world had just pulled out from underneath me. "I've never seen him so angry."

Noah's jaw ticked as he stared down at me with a stormy expression in his eyes. "He's right you know," he bit out. "I'm bad news."

"I know you are," I told him as I stepped closer and wrapped my arms around his waist. I didn't need Noah or Max to tell me something I was completely aware of. I'd been to the ring of fire and I'd been with him tonight. I wasn't stupid. I knew he was involved in dark and shady things; he'd told me as much. "But just because you're bad news doesn't mean you're a bad person."

"Teagan..." Noah clenched his eyes shut and exhaled heavily.

"Did you mean what you said to Kyle?" I asked Noah as he pressed his forehead to mine. "That I'm your girlfriend?"

"Yeah," he confirmed huskily, and my heart soared in my chest. "But there's more stuff you should know about me before you decide to be with me," he whispered. "And I can't tell you..."

"Why can't you tell me?" I asked him.

"Because I want to keep you safe," he admitted in a vulnerable tone. "And I'm terrified the more you know the more danger you'll be in."

A tremor of fear rolled down my spine.

He was warning me.

I should listen to him, to my gut instinct that was screaming danger.

But I didn't.

Ignoring the spasm of fear, I wrapped my arms around his neck and let out a sigh. "I'm happy I did what I did with you tonight." I closed my eyes and bit down on my lip. "I just wanted to tell you that."

"If we do this, Teagan," Noah said in a gruff tone as his hands smoothed over my hips. "It's not going to be easy – being with me..." He paused and trailed his thumbs against my cheekbones. "It's gonna be rough, Thorn. I'm the worst kind of wrong for you."

"I'm well aware of that," I admitted honestly. "But, I also know there's more good in you than there is bad, Noah."

Noah looked at me for a long time before letting out a weary sigh. "How the hell did we get here?"

"Get where?"

Pressing his lips to my throat, Noah ran his tongue over my pulse. "To the point where I can't fucking breathe without you."

His words shot a tremor through my body and I let out a sigh. "You broke my windshield," I breathed, tilting my neck sideways to accommodate his lips. "And I..."

My words were smothered by Noah's lips as they crashed down on mine, searing me, and I was sure I'd never be the same again. I would never understand him, and maybe that was okay. I only had to accept him, and my heart seemed to do that without consulting my brain, so I figured that would be enough. I was taking a gamble with Noah, on being with him, but I knew in my bones I'd never feel like this with anyone else.

"Okay, break it up," a male voice I recognized as Derek's said in an amused tone. "I've been given instructions to walk this one home."

Reluctantly, I pulled away from Noah. "I guess I'll see you... Tomorrow or something?" I muttered, feeling flustered and a little unsure.

"You definitely will," Noah told me with a reassuring smile.

20

TEAGAN

"Pass the milk, Teagan," Max grumbled during breakfast Sunday morning as he stirred his mug of coffee with a spoon. "Today if possible."

We were sitting opposite one another at the kitchen table. Max was testing my patience, and he was also marginally closer to the milk than I was, and he damn well knew it.

Reluctantly, I shoved the carton an inch closer to my uncle, with as little enthusiasm as humanly possible, before resuming my post of ignoring the enemy.

The jackass had grounded me for the duration of my Christmas holiday, and had even taken two weeks leave from work to watch me. The stipulations of my punishment included not leaving the house, no sleepovers, and the confiscation of my car keys, phone, and laptop. Max also made it perfectly clear that I was to have absolutely no physical contact with the boy next door, be it fighting or fondling – his actual words.

So, I'd basically spent the past two weeks staring out the window longingly. I hadn't seen Noah since that night and the only thing keeping me slightly sane was the fact that he'd knocked on my front door every single day. I thought it was pretty great of him, considering Max always answered and hurled abuse at him. But Noah always told him the same thing; *you can try to keep her from me, but I'm not going anywhere.*

On the upside, Max's *emergency leave* was up and he was due back at the hospital today.

On the downside, the tension between us now was palpable and I knew in my heart and soul that we'd lost a part of our relationship that could never be repaired or replaced.

I was mentally counting down the minutes until Max left for work. I didn't want to be around him anymore, not since the words *'I have absolutely no intention of wasting my life raising another kid that's not mine'* came out of his mouth two weeks ago. Betrayed didn't even begin to explain how I felt around him now.

"For a girl who turned eighteen last week, your behavior is incredibly juvenile," Max muttered, and I had to bite my tongue to stop myself from shouting out a string of F-bombs that would only prove how juvenile I truly was.

"No need to remind me about my fabulous eighteenth," I replied sarcastically. "It was such a joyous occasion." Not really, since I spent the entire day in bed feeling sorry for myself.

"I'm due back at work today," he said. "But don't for one moment think that changes the stipulations of your punishment. I'm speaking to you, Teagan," he snarled in a condescending tone and I snapped.

I'd had all I could take.

"I'm eighteen now, Max," I hissed, glaring across the table at the man I'd once worshiped. "And luckily for me, that means you don't get to tell me what to do anymore."

"While you're living under my roof I do," he shot back, cheeks flushed.

"Maybe I should move back home and live under my own roof," I tossed back angrily.

"Well then, maybe you should," Max growled before letting out a heavy sigh.

Shaking his head, he stood slowly and picked up his mug. "You may not believe this, Teagan, but I'm doing this for your own good."

"Doing what?" I snapped. "Tossing me out on the streets? Gee, thanks a bunch."

Max sighed heavily. "No one is tossing anyone out. Teagan, all I'm trying to do is protect you from making the same mistakes your mother did," he told me. "With that waste of space."

My hackles rose. "Patrick Connolly may not be your cup of tea, Uncle Max, but he's still my father – my flesh and blood."

I hated my dad for what he'd done, for the absolute fucking agony of not having my mother in my life every day, but he was still my dad. The bond was still there, buried deep, and I sure as hell wasn't going to sit here and listen to Max talk shit about him. And comparing me to my mother was just sick.

"And he's still the reason your mother is in a grave," Max spat as he stalked towards the door. "Four years today, Teagan. December thirty-first that man you call your father put my sister in her grave." He let out a shaky breath. "Don't make the same mistakes she did. Seeing that boy could put you in yours."

"Noah is a *good* person!" I all but screamed as tears welled up in my eyes. I didn't need Max reminding me what day it was. I was fully aware New Year's Eve was my mother's fourth anniversary.

"Ask Noah who his father is," Max snarled. "Or better yet, ask him what price is on his head."

"I know who his dad was," I shot back, furious. Closing my eyes, I inhaled slowly and tried to keep calm. "I know enough about him to know he's who I want to be with."

The sound of the front door slamming provided me with a minuscule amount of relief, though the damage was done and I felt truly shattered.

Climbing to my feet, I hurried up the stairs and reached my bed before the tears flooded me.

Dammit, I hated New Year's Eve.

NOAH

I watched from my living room window as Teagan's uncle stormed out of their house before tearing off in his car. Miraculously, Ellie and George were still away and, according to a text I'd received from Ellie, wouldn't be back until school resumed.

My heart hammered in my chest as I watched his Focus drive out of sight.

This was it, the moment I'd spent the past two weeks waiting for. Only now I was suddenly nervous.

Shit, what if Teagan didn't want to see me as badly as I wanted to see her – *needed* to see her? Hell, it had been two weeks since we'd slept together. What if she regretted it, regretted me...

I stood at the window, freaking the hell out of myself, relaying to myself everything that could possibly go wrong until the sky turned dark and the street lamps came on.

Across the street, Low's house was lit up like the fourth of July and I knew just how much food I'd be consuming and alcohol I'd be swiping if I walked across the street and joined the Carter's New Year's Eve party. I'd been to the previous four, but the gorgeous blonde in the house next door kept my feet firmly on this side of the street.

Dammit, I needed to see her.

I had to.

I couldn't wait a minute longer.

Inhaling a deep breath, I straightened my shoulders and made my way next door.

TEAGAN

"Why are you crying, Thorn?" Noah's voice penetrated the silence and I stilled.

My bedroom door creaked shut and I felt the mattress dip beside me seconds before his warm hand pressed against my cheek, wiping away my tears.

"Please stop crying," he whispered. Wrapping an arm around my waist, Noah pulled me flush against him. His thumb brushed over one of my eyelids and then the other.

Sniffling, I forced myself to stop crying and open my eyes. The moonlight pouring through my bedroom window highlighted Noah's beautiful face, his eyes were black as night, and I scrambled closer to him, the need to touch him almost unbearable.

"Happy tears?" he asked in a soft tone as he stroked my cheek.

"No," I replied. "I got into a fight with Max earlier and today is... my mom's anniversary." I closed my eyes and inhaled slowly. "New Year's Eve is the one day of every year that truly gets to me."

"On a brighter note," Noah announced and I sagged in

relief. He got it. *He got me...* "There's something in the kitchen that needs naming."

"What?" I stared at Noah and tried to gauge his expression, but the guy had an excellent poker-face.

I tried to downplay my burning curiosity, but that lasted all of five seconds before I leapt off the bed and scrambled out of my room. Rushing down the staircase, I skidded to a halt when I reached the kitchen door. When I saw what was in there, my jaw dropped.

"Well?" Noah chuckled, wrapping his arms around me from behind. "It's not the same as your old one, but it was the best I could get. The guy in the shop said a Gibson was the next best thing. What do you think?"

"I think it's a guitar?" I gaped at the six-string and then at Noah's beautiful face. "Noah, why did you buy this for me?"

"I bought it for you because I'm the reason Ellie smashed your... Martin," he told me, smirking on the last word. "Happy birthday, Thorn."

"I want to keep you," Noah whispered hours later as we lay on my bed, so quietly I wasn't sure if I was supposed to hear.

I opened my eyes and stared into his.

"If I could wrap you up and lock you away, keep you someplace safe where nothing and no one could touch you, then I would. I just want to have you, Teagan."

"I missed you these past few weeks," I choked out as I lay on my side clutching the front of his hoodie, gripping it tightly. "I mean, I really, *really* missed you, Noah," I admitted, feeling better now that he was with me. "Like *desperately* missed you. I mean, how messed up is that? I've spent the last six months forcing myself to believe that I hate you and now..." I paused and let out a shaky breath. "And now that I've admitted the truth to myself, how I really feel about you, I feel like I'm..."

"Drowning?" he offered before pressing a kiss to my lips, causing my whole body to spark to life. "I know the feeling, Thorn," Noah added. "There wasn't a thing I could do to stop you from getting inside me," he added in a gruff tone. "You just were. You came. You... Stayed."

There was something incredibly sexy about a man with strength. A man who could express himself. I could see the strength in Noah's brown eyes. I heard it often in his words, I felt it every time he touched me. I wanted to see how that strength felt inside me again.

"I want to remember this moment forever," I breathed, feeling right for the first time in weeks. "Being here. How it feels... How it smells. The taste of you. The weather." I curled my toes up and sighed in contentment. "I think I'm quite possibly falling in love with you."

"Jesus, Teagan, don't say it if you don't mean it," Noah warned me in a hoarse tone as he clutched my body to his. "Not that. Don't say it if you're not categorically sure."

"Categorically?" I raised my brows and smirked. "Swallow the dictionary before you came over, Noah?"

"I'm serious," he growled.

"So am I," I teased.

Rolling me onto my back, Noah leaned over me, eyes hard and locked on mine. "Don't mess with me, Teagan," he warned. "Not about something like that."

"I wasn't..." I whispered, feeling suddenly anxious. Raising my hand, I cupped his face. "I'm not messing with you, Noah," I heard myself saying. "I meant every word."

It was the truth.

I meant it.

Holy shit, *it was the truth*....

I closed my eyes and inhaled a slow, calming breath before I spoke. "I shouldn't have said that."

"Yes, you should," Noah countered, pressing a kiss to my nose. "If you meant it..."

"I meant it. Oh, sweet Jesus, I *meant* it," I hissed, feeling incredibly vulnerable. "Shit, I love you."

Noah laughed and I opened my eyes and glared at him.

"Stop laughing at me, asshole," I growled. "I just told you I love you. This is serious."

"I know," he growled. "Can't you feel how happy you've made me?"

Noah pressed his bulging erection against my thigh and I clenched my eyes shut before letting out a whimper. "Oh, dear god, it's too soon for that kind of talk..."

"Says who? The media, Dr. Phil, your uncle?" Noah chuckled before dropping his mouth to my neck. "Love doesn't have a specific time frame, baby," he purred as he trailed kisses up and down my skin.

"Well, it should," I moaned as I writhed under him. The weight of Noah's body on mine was ecstasy and I was finding it harder and harder to concentrate. His lips had that effect on me. "And stop calling me baby."

"You said *in*," Noah whispered as he held himself above me, smiling down at me. "You said you're *in* love with me."

My cheeks reddened. "Yeah, so?"

"That's the most important word," he told me gently.

"Wow," I teased. "You're sprouting more crap than usual."

Noah smirked and pressed a kiss to my lips. "You love your uncle, right?" he asked.

I nodded. Max was an ass, but I loved him.

Noah's smile widened. "You've loved your pets, maybe a favorite teacher or a certain brand of candy." Frowning,

Noah continued, "You've used those three words at some time or another to describe those objects and people?"

I nodded again as heat crept up my neck.

"Which of those have you loved?" he asked me as he brushed his nose against mine.

"All of them at some stage, I guess," I replied.

"Exactly," Noah said with a smile. "But which one of them are you, or have ever been, *in* love with?"

"None," I admitted.

"That's because of the *in*, Thorn..."

The alarm on my phone went off, signaling the start of a brand new year and I smiled up at the boy next door. "Happy New Year, Noah."

"Happy New Year, Teagan." Noah bent his head and pressed his lips to mine. "And for what it's worth, my *in* belongs to you," he whispered.

"It does?" I asked, barely breathing as my heart hammered in my chest.

"Of course." Noah scorched me with a kiss that ignited a fire and burned a hole right through the center of my heart. "You're my Thorn," he rasped between kisses. "If you leave me, I'll bleed out."

21

TEAGAN

New Year's Day and the remaining week of our Christmas holiday passed in a beautifully snowy – yes, it *snowed* – blur, and consisted mostly of stolen moments of passion and intimacy between me and the boy next door.

Noah would either sneak over here when my uncle went to work, or if Max was home, I'd wait for him to fall asleep before sneaking outside and meeting Noah in his car. Thankfully, Noah's so-called family stayed away and we were able to remain in our little bubble for a little longer. With George out of town, Noah's knuckles were in semi-retirement mode, which was absolutely fine by me. I didn't want him fighting anyway.

I was slowly coming around to the idea that I adored the tattooed, muscle head next door. It was a terrifying feeling, though, because I'd been in love before with Liam, but the burning intensity and hunger I felt for Noah was pungent. It was smothering, overwhelming, and completely enthralling. And, to be honest, I was pretty sure I'd never be the *me* I was before I met him again.

My stomach felt like it was going to fall out of my butt as I walked into English class on Monday morning. The prospect of seeing Noah without sneaking around, and as an official couple, had my stomach twisting in knots. I was both nervous and excited as I scanned the classroom for his familiar face.

I spotted Noah's empty desk, and my heart sank.

It sank even further when I noticed who had recovered from his chicken pox epidemic; Jason grinned at me and I wanted to gag.

Oh god.

"THEY HATE ME," I TOLD HOPE AS WE WALKED THROUGH THE cafeteria towards our usual table. "I'm serious, Hope. I can *never* show my face inside your front door again."

"Stop being such a drama queen," Hope chuckled, wrapping an arm around my shoulder. "My parents do not hate you. They've had weeks to get over it, and they have. So stop being a baby and come over sometime. I really want you to meet Jordan – *clothed*."

I slumped down on the chair beside Ash and let out a heavy sigh. "Do you think it's possible for a person to die of embarrassment?"

"Depends on the circumstances surrounding the case," Ash shot back in an amused tone.

"Oh, well how about Hope's entire family catching me stark naked, with the exception of my knickers, and underneath Noah back at Christmas. Does that constitute a good enough reason or should I add my uncle throwing a conniption fit to the list?"

"You and Noah?" Ash squealed, dropping her spoon onto the table. "When... How... Where?"

"The *how* I'm still unsure of," Hope chuckled as she took a seat opposite us. "But the *when* was a few weeks ago and the *where* was my couch."

Ash's eyes gleamed with delight. "You little skank."

"Yes," I mumbled, casting Hope an evil glare. "I'm all of that and more."

"So, what does this mean?" Ash demanded excitedly. "Are you two, you know, a couple now?"

"Yeah," I muttered, red faced. "But I thought he'd be here today and he's not. I hope... It's just... Ugh god, this sucks." I buried my head in my hands and groaned. "I'm so confused. He makes me so confused and flustered. I don't feel normal."

"Well you are," Hope cackled. "You're having a normal reaction. Just a perfectly normal teenage girl, whose hormones are raging, reaction to her hot, teenage boyfriend who has equally raging hormones... Err... Hey, Noah."

My entire body froze and Hope's whole face reddened as a pair of strong hands clamped me under my arms and lifted me out of my chair.

The sound of catcalls and wolf whistles was drowned out by the frantic beat of my pulse as Noah turned me in his arms and crushed his lips to mine. He did that thing with his tongue bar and I was putty in his hands.

I could hear people whispering loudly around me. I could feel eyes boring into my skull as the majority of students were lapping up the gossip we were providing for them. And in that moment, I couldn't have cared less. The rest of the world seemed to slip away when he was this close to me.

"I could eat you," he whispered against my mouth. "You smell fucking awesome."

I knew we were in the middle of the cafeteria, with a fully engaged audience, but in that instant wild horses couldn't have dragged me away from him. "Where were you this morning?" I asked against his lips.

"I overslept," he rasped. "This little nymph next door kept me up half the night. But I'm here now."

Noah's hands moved to my waist, tugging me closer as he sat on the table with me facing him on his lap. "Let's get out of here," he purred, his voice seductive and his offer extremely enticing. "We need to talk about something."

"Can't," I breathed. "I have a practical test in biology after lunch. We're dissecting a cow's heart."

"I'll test you," he teased. "I'll give you a practical lesson in human reproduction."

"Noah..."

"And I'll give you an A plus. I'm very thorough. All you have to do is bend over and spread your..."

"That's quite enough, Mr. Messina," a stern voice ordered, cutting Noah off mid-sentence. "Put Miss. Connolly down."

Noah growled against my lips before reluctantly placing me on my feet. He kept his hands on my hips and I buried my face in his neck, feeling like I was about to die of shame.

While I was contemplating how much trouble we were in for our public display of affection, Coach Johnson said, "In the future, please refrain from copulating until you're on your own time."

"Sure thing, Coach," Noah replied before looking down at me in confusion.

Mortified, I looked up at Coach and smiled sheepishly. "Sorry."

Coach shook his head and stared at us with a look of total dismay. "I just can't figure kids out nowadays."

"Copulating?" Noah mouthed, looking down at me. "The fuck's that mean?"

"Mating," I clarified, red faced.

"Oh, goodie. A new, fun word," he declared in a sarcastic tone, showing me a side of him I hadn't seen before. "Sweetheart, would you care to join me in the janitor's closet? I'm feeling a very strong urge to copulate with you."

Humorous Noah... Wow, this was kind of a revelation.

I raised my brows in amusement. "Sweetheart?"

Noah's face broke into a huge smile and my chest tightened. He didn't smile enough. It was a truly beautiful sight. "Well, I'm kinda scared to call you *baby*," he told me in a teasing tone. "But I feel like I should have an endearing name for my girl."

For my girl...

Oh Jesus...

Taking his outstretched hand, I waved to the girls and followed Noah out of the cafeteria. "Teagan," I told him, forcing my lips not to smile at him as my lungs played havoc with my oxygen supply. His words squeezed something deep inside of me. "You can call me Teegs or Teagan."

"Okay, my little Thorn," Noah replied sweetly before pressing a kiss to my nose as we wandered outside into the bitter cold.

I liked the snow here in Colorado. Back home, the closest I'd been to snow was in the form of a can – the horrible sticky kind people sprayed on window panes for Christmas ambiance purposes. Here, snowflakes fell from the sky in abundance and it made me feel all squiggly inside.

"Why do you always say that? That's like the millionth time you've called me *Thorn*," I asked Noah, shuffling closer to his body for warmth from the arctic air.

"I told you," he chuckled, smoothing his thumb over my knuckles as he led me down the snow-covered steps towards his car. "You're my thorn, if you leave me I'll bleed out."

My heart skyrocketed when those words left his mouth and I felt kind of dizzy.

Deep breaths...

"Oh... Hey, I told you I have a test after lunch," I reminded Noah when he unlocked his car, opened the passenger door, and gestured for me to get in. "I'm not skipping, Noah. I'm in enough trouble because of you as it stands."

"Relax," he coaxed. "I need a smoke, that's all." He shrugged and smiled lazily at me. "Thought you could keep me company."

"And partake in some second hand inhalation," I grumbled, watching as Noah walked around to the driver's side. "Wow, Noah, you sure know how to treat a girl."

"Don't you just know it," he shot with a smirk before climbing inside.

Didn't I just...

I sat in the car with him but I pretended it was because I was cold. I was a liar though because I was fairly certain I'd inhale the fumes of a jumbo jet if it meant I could keep him company.

God, I was a very sad girl.

"So, what did you want to talk about?" I asked him as I watched him flick cigarette ash out his window. "You said there was..."

"Ellie's back," Noah announced before exhaling a cloud of smoke. Turning his face, he looked directly into my eyes and sighed. "Which means George is en route."

My heart sank.

Everything had been so perfect these past few weeks and Noah's so-called family returning would ruin it.

"Ellie's back. Yay," I muttered sarcastically. "I was missing our little sparring sessions."

"Can you do me a favor and try not to antagonize her?" he muttered in an irritated tone and his irritation seemed to set off mine.

"No, actually I can't," I shot back petulantly. "She's a bitch and I happen to be deathly allergic to that particular breed."

Noah snorted and I looked over at him and smirked. His eyes darkened as he stared intently at me.

This lunch could be salvaged yet...

"You know, you're turning me into a rule breaker," I purred. A seedy image of the two of us sparked to life in my vivid imagination and I blushed. "I'm still not supposed to have contact with you – of *any* kind."

"Well, it's lucky your uncle doesn't know about the elevator then, isn't it?" Noah crooned as he flicked his cigarette butt out the window and dragged me across the console so that I was straddling his hips. "Or our nightly get togethers... He might try to keep you away from me until your twenty-first birthday."

"He might," I agreed, wrapping my arms around his neck.

"Thorn, you know what George returning means for me, right?" Noah whispered and my heart shriveled inside my chest. "You know what I'll have to do for him... For her?"

I nodded slowly.

I knew what it meant. Noah would have to fight again and it put the fear of god inside of me.

"I don't have a choice, Teagan," Noah added, noticing my sudden deflation. "You know that."

"I hate this," I told him, burying my face in his neck. I

knew Noah didn't have a choice, but that didn't mean I had to be okay with George Dennis using him as a human punching bag. "I hate *him*."

"Me too, baby," Noah coaxed, pressing a kiss to my collarbone, and I didn't bother correcting him. "That's why I need you to not argue with Ellie." He let out a heavy sigh as he trailed his lips up my neck. "We don't need to draw unwanted attention to..."

The driver's door flew open, causing Noah to trail off and me to yelp in surprise.

"So, it's true?" Ellie sneered, holding the car door open, wrecking our private moment and boiling the blood in my veins. "You're *with* her now?" She looked at me straddling Noah and shook her head in disgust. "You idiot."

"Walk away, Ellie," Noah shot back in a tight tone of voice. "Now."

"You should take your own advice," Ellie hissed, "and walk away – from *her*."

"What the hell is your deal?" I snapped. Enough was enough and I'd taken all I could from Noah's skanky sister.

"Stay out of it, Thorn, I'm handling this..." Noah began to say but I shut him up with one look.

He had my hips clenched so tightly I had to physically remove his hands from my waist so I could climb off his lap and out of the car.

"No," I warned him in an even tone as I stood outside his car. "I may be your girlfriend now, but I still have a mind of my own, so *I* will speak for myself, thank you very much."

Noah looked up at me with reluctant admiration shining in his dark eyes before nodding his head slightly.

"Well, isn't this a Kodak moment, El?" A familiar voice laughed. "Noah's breaking all of his rules these days." Reese walked over and stood beside Ellie, glaring daggers at me.

"You're telling me," Ellie replied coldly.

"Jesus fucking Christ," I heard Noah grumble as he got out of the car and came to stand beside me. "Come on," he said, wrapping his hand around mine. "Let's just leave."

"You know he'll get bored, right? You're just a fresh challenge for him," Reese sneered, flicking her red hair behind her shoulder. She looked me up and down slowly before scrunching her small nose in distaste. "You're no different than me, Ellie, and dozens of other girls at this school."

Ouch...

"Wow," I replied, keeping my tone light and carefree even though I was anything but. "Thanks for the heads up and all, but you're kinda reeking of jealousy, Rice." Shrugging, I added, "It's a very ugly trait, you know."

"It's Reese," she hissed. "And you won't be so smug when you see what we've got..."

"Reese, let's go," Ellie interrupted, staring meaningfully at her friend before stalking off.

Reese's whole face lit up and without another word, she rushed after Ellie.

"Let me guess," I sneered when the girls were out of earshot. "You slept with both of them?"

"Teagan..."

"She's his youngest child – daddy's little girl, there to do her father's dirty work and get all the staff on board..."

He was staff. "You slept with your own step sister?"

Noah's words last night flooded my mind and I felt physically sick.

"Did you take her virginity, too, or was that just me?" I hissed, feeling outrageously pissed. "And what about Reese and the *dozens* of other girls at this school?"

"Thorn, just calm down and listen to me," Noah coaxed, tugging me closer to him. "I never claimed to be a saint..."

"Don't talk to me, you man whore," I hissed. Breaking free from his grasp, I turned on my heels and stalked back towards the school.

"You're jumping to conclusions without hearing me out again," Noah growled as he chased after me and tried to hold my hand.

"I told you not to talk to me, slapper," I shot back, slapping his hand away. "And it's not so much jumping to conclusions as it is putting two and two together." The thought of Noah with any other girl, not to mention dozens, drove me freaking crazy. "Go run after your little brothel buddies," I hissed. "I'm done."

"Teagan..."

"Fuck you," I snarled.

"You already did that," he shot back.

"Go away, Noah." Ugh, jealousy was an ugly trait and right about now I was bursting to the seams with it. "That's obviously why Ellie's been such a bitch to me," I hissed. "You're with her."

"I'm with *you*," Noah growled.

When Noah tried to grab my hand again, I swung around and pointed my finger in his face. "Back up, buddy," I warned. "I'm pissed as hell with you right now, so just respect my personal space."

"No," Noah snapped, stepping forward. He grabbed my hips and pulled me flush against him. "I won't respect your space, because it's my space, too."

"What the...?" I shook my head and began to protest, but Noah interrupted me by pressing a rough kiss to my lips.

"I'm either fighting with you or I'm *fucking* with you," he growled against my lips. "There's no middle line, Teagan. Not between us."

"But you slept..."

"I understand why you're mad, Thorn," Noah told me, snaking his arm around my lower back. "I do, and we can hash it all out later, but first you need to understand this."

Raising one hand, he clasped my chin and lowered his face to within an inch of mine. "There will be no storming off and breaking it off with me," he said slowly. "I've risked too much to fuck this up on a tantrum, so if you've got an issue, Thorn, you better raise it with me because you're *not* walking away from me."

"I wasn't having a tantrum," I muttered sulkily. My cheeks were burning and I felt like a grade A idiot. "I didn't have one..."

"There will be no break-ups," Noah continued, stroking my chin with his thumb. "In fact, there will be no breaks of any fucking kind."

"We've been boyfriend and girlfriend for less than a month," I managed to choke out, my voice thick with emotion. "Don't you think you're being a little full on?"

"We've been a lot more than this for a lot longer than that, Thorn," he purred, pressing a kiss to my lips. "You know it as well as I do."

I nodded and wrapped my arms around his neck

Noah was right. I knew it, too, and that knowledge scared me to death.

Max's face when I climbed out of Noah's car after school was one of pure, unadulterated rage. He stood on our porch glaring down at us as Noah rounded the car and pulled me into his arms.

"Your uncle sure looks chipper this evening," he chuckled before pressing a kiss to my cheek.

"Yep," I replied with a sigh as I wrapped my arms around Noah's waist and hugged him tightly. I knew I was going to hear about this from Max, but to be honest, I really didn't give a damn what he thought anymore. I was quickly discovering the only thing I truly cared about was the boy whose arms were wrapped around me.

"I'll see you tonight, okay," Noah whispered, stroking my cheek with his thumb. "After he falls asleep..."

"I'll leave a key under the mat," I told him before reaching up and covering his mouth with mine.

When Noah eventually stopped kissing me and went inside his house, I remained standing in my driveway, staring at the front of his house.

I needed to help him.

I couldn't sit back and wait for George to return and ruin his life all over again.

I needed to fight for Noah Messina just as viciously as he fought for his mom.

22

NOAH

"We need to talk about where your loyalties lie, kid," was the first thing I heard when I opened my front door Tuesday morning, and my heart sank.

He was home.

Back to reality.

"I'm late for school, George," I replied stiffly as I closed the front door and made for the stairs. Ellie had returned from their trip two weeks ago and when George hadn't returned with her, a tiny part of me had hoped – fucking prayed, he never would. "We can talk about my *loyalties* later."

I'd spent most of the night fooling around with Teagan, but I'd slipped out of her room at the crack of dawn before her uncle came home. Besides, I needed to go home and grab a shower before school.

Now I was wishing I had just gone stinking and bookless. It would have been a hell of a lot easier than having a confrontation with my stepfather.

The sound of the staircase creaking behind me confirmed George wasn't in the mood to wait.

"You don't make the rules around here, Messina," George rasped as he hurried after me, also confirming to me that I had a fifty percent chance of making it out of here unscathed. "JD seems to be under the impression you're seeing that little bitch next door," he snarled. "He reckons she's been spotted at the quarry, twice, and was with you at the hotel."

"Yep," I muttered through clenched teeth, pushing my bedroom door open. "She was." There was no point in lying. He would find out either way.

"What's going on with her, Noah?" he wheezed, standing in my doorway. "You know better than to stick your fingers in the goddamn cookie jar. Her uncle's a doctor for Christ's sake – that's almost as bad as a cop."

"*She* is none of your business," I warned him, reeling from the emotions that were seeping into my body. "I fight for you. That's the agreement, and I do it when I'm told, no questions asked. But you sure as hell don't get to tell who I can spend my time with," I added as I rummaged in one of my dresser drawers for a clean pair of socks and boxers.

"Spending time with her?" George sneered as he took a step into my room. "So that's what Ellie saw you doing, spending time with her, when you were screwing her in my goddamn kitchen?"

"Be very careful, G," I seethed. Walking over to my closet, I grabbed a clean pair of jeans, a t-shirt, and hoodie. "I'm feeling really fucking reckless right now. One more word against her and I'm gonna lose my shit."

His hand clamped down on my shoulder, nails biting into my shoulder blade, and I had to force myself to remain still and not pulverize the creep into next year.

There was no doubt in my mind that I could. George knew that as well as I did. But the bastard held the trump card, the one thing that assured my submission, and he wielded it over me any chance he got. "And how was your pretty little *mommy*?" he sneered, green eyes narrowed and full of poison. "I heard you paid her a little visit over the holidays."

"Like you don't know," I hissed, roughly shaking his hand off. "Her nurse told me about the *visitor*." I shook my head in disgust. "What was it this time, meth or coke?"

"What can I say? She called me begging for it," he chuckled. "Your sweet little momma's crazier than a bag of frogs, Messina, but she's one hell of a great fuck."

"You make me sick." My fists clenched with the urge to knock him out. "You're scum, George. Fucking scum." I was shaking as I watched him step out of my reach.

"Sooner or later, I'm going to get her away from you," I vowed. "Someplace you and your scumbag cronies can't get to her. Can't poison her body."

George's eyes lit up with amusement. "But what would be the point in that, Noah?" he asked in an innocent tone. "Now that I know about your little soft spot for the doctor's niece and can easily use her instead of your mother to keep you in line."

My blood turned to ice in my veins. "Don't even think about involving Teagan in this."

"You already did that, you little shit," George snarled. "When you fucked me over with Gonzalez. Be glad that your body's not rotting in the fucking mountains next to your father's."

I watched George walk across my bedroom. "You fight Gonzalez's boy, Javi, Friday night – the thirteenth," he informed me and my stomach churned.

Gerome Javi was a fucking butcher. No one *survived* a fight with the guy, let alone beat him. Javi was a fight to the death kinda guy; no remorse and no way out. Step into the ring with him and you were signing your own death certificate. I didn't have a prayer of beating him and George knew it.

"This is different, isn't it?" I questioned, feeling more fear than I had felt in years. "This is it – my punishment." I could feel the vein in my temple throb as I glowered down at the man I hated more than anyone else on this planet.

George nodded his head, confirming my worst fears, and my legs felt weak.

This was bad.

This was so fucking bad.

"The rules have changed, Messina," he told me. "Because of your defection, I can't trust you anymore."

"My defection," I repeated flatly. "I fought to make some extra cash and get my car fixed. I'd hardly call it defection."

"That's because you don't have a loyal bone in your body," George snarled, red faced, as he stepped towards me and poked my chest. "You don't have a clue of what loyalty means, just like your piece of shit father."

"I'm not my father," I snarled.

"Not yet," George sneered. "But lose against Javi on Friday and you'll be spending a whole bunch of time with him."

"So that's what this is?" I hissed, forcing my voice not to shake even though the image of Teagan's face was making me feel faint with fear. "You want rid of me, but you want Javi to do your dirty work for you?"

"I demand allegiance from my men," he roared. "And you, my boy, knew exactly what would happen when you took that job for my fucking arch rival." Marching past me, George turned when he reached my door and smirked. "Oh, and be sure to bring your little girlfriend Friday night, you know, for moral support... or for a final farewell."

"No goddamn way," I snarled, chest heaving. "She stays out of this, George."

George threw his head back and laughed. "What's wrong, Messina?" he goaded. "Don't you think you can win?"

"She's not going," I seethed. I could feel my temper peaking and I urged myself to calm down and breathe. "Leave her out of this, G. I mean it."

George studied my face with an amused expression. "You were always weak, Messina," he croaked. "Same as your father. He lost his head for a blonde."

Shaking his head, George opened my bedroom door and stepped onto the hallway. "Bring the girl," he sneered. "Let's see how focused you are with your piece of ass in the crowd."

"One of these days, I'm gonna kill you," I vowed, jaw clenched, eyes locked on his fat fuck of a face. "I promise you that much."

"Famous last words, Messina," he taunted. "Oh wait, those really *were* your father's *last* words, right before I put a bullet between his eyes."

TEAGAN

Max and I still weren't on speaking terms – not a single word to each other in weeks. So when I spotted his plane ticket in the trash this evening, I wasn't one bit surprised.

I'd assumed a family trip home for Valentine's weekend wasn't on the map considering the man was having a hard time looking at me these days. I still had my ticket, though, and with a little luck, I would be on that plane Saturday morning.

I hadn't spoken to Noah about it. He didn't even know I was planning on taking a trip home this weekend. I only hoped that when I did speak to him about it, he would be as enthusiastic as I was.

"He plays the gickar, too," Hope snickered, stirring me from my reverie. We were sitting in her lounge. Hope was sprawled out on her couch and her boyfriend, Jordan, was sitting on the floor beside her, and drooling all over my guitar.

"Come on, hot shot," she giggled, nudging Jordan's shoulder with her foot. "Show us what you've got."

I rose my brow in amusement as I watched the playful

couple from my perch on the armchair opposite them. "Gickar?"

Jordan caught her foot and dragged her off the couch, setting her on his lap. "It's a private joke." Jordan chuckled, not taking his eyes off Hope's face. "Isn't that right, *Keychain*?"

"How long have you guys known each other?" I asked, unable to stop the smile that was stretching my lips at the sight of Hope's beaming smile as she gazed lovingly at Jordan. This was my first real time spending time with Hope's beau and already I was completely won over. He was great.

"I was one," Hope teased as she tried to defend herself from Jordan's tickling fingers. "He was four."

"She dropped her keys at my feet," he added with a smirk.

"And he's been fetching them ever since," Hope giggled.

"Is that so?" Jordan purred, wrestling Hope onto her back.

I watched in extreme discomfort as Hope dug her hand into her pocket and pulled out her car keys.

"That's right," she crooned before stuffing the keys down her top. "Fetch."

"And I'm out of here," I squealed. Leaping to my feet, I covered my eyes with my hand and made a beeline for the door.

I guess she didn't need my help after all...

NOAH

Dammit, I was living in perpetual hell.

It seemed all of my previous wrongdoings and indiscretions had decided to clamor together and torment me just for the fun of it. Fucked up thing was, they had seemed to morph into my girlfriend.

"You're not going to the quarry, Teagan. Get it out of your head."

I was sprawled on top of her bed not even pretending to not watch her change. She was too tempting and apparently, I had zero willpower when it came to her. I was seriously regretting telling her about the fight on Friday – especially now that she was demanding she go with me. Jesus, I was stupid to even entertain the notion that Teagan might be capable of doing what she was told. Thankfully I hadn't let on what a big deal it was.

"Well, you're not going without me, Rocky Balboa," she shot back sarcastically as she shrugged out of the tight denim jeans she was wearing.

"I'm Rocky?" I cocked a brow. "We're not in a movie, baby, this is real life."

The thought of her in the quarry again caused every muscle inside of my body to coil tight with tension. Teagan being within touching distance of all those scumbags, and if I didn't win...

It wasn't happening.

No fucking way.

I couldn't risk it. I couldn't risk her.

"Well how's this for a plot twist; you can either take me with you or I'll drive myself there." Teagan tossed her jeans at me before continuing to prance around her bedroom in a bra and thong. "It's your choice." The girl was made of steel. She was breaking all the rules having me in her bedroom and she was breaking every piece of my self control by arguing with me.

"That's not a choice, baby," I grumbled. "That's tyranny and you damn well know it."

"Maybe it is tyranny," she replied airily. "But it's what's happening."

"Not if I can help it."

"What's your deal, Noah?" Shaking her head, Teagan let out a heavy sigh and folded her arms across her chest. "You've told me your secrets and I've told you I understand. I want to be with you, to support you." Her brows furrowed as she stared at me. "You think I'll be afraid because of last time or turned off if I see what you're capable of?"

Yes, I'm scared, I'm fucking terrified... "It's not something I want you to have to watch me doing," I managed to squeeze out.

"Before my mom died, I spent most of my childhood camping, Messina," she told me smugly. "You're a prince in comparison to the colorful camping companions I've had over the years."

I didn't respond, but the corner of my mouth tipped up.

She was trying to make me feel better.

"Um... Let's see." Teagan pretended to think about it for a second before grinning. "There was the particularly curious herd of cows who trampled on our tent and almost squashed us to death in third year, freshman year to you. And then there was the attack of the water rat the summer we camped in the field of maze."

Her eyes bulged as she used her hands to animate the shape of an animal. "I swear he was the size of a toddler. Oh, and the most memorable trip was the one I went on to county Kerry with our school and our History teacher was arrested for urinating on the wheel of our school bus on the side of the road."

The school bus tale caused me to chuckle, and Teagan grinned victoriously.

"So you see, Mr. Messina," she teased, strutting towards me. "You are like a little furry kitten."

Lowering herself onto the bed, she crawled up my body until our chests were touching. I couldn't stop myself from wrapping my arms around her. Jesus, she smelled so damn good.

"Nothing will ever terrify me quite like that water rat," Teagan whispered. "So stop overthinking things. I'm coming with you," she added before lowering her mouth to mine.

My heart swelled to the point of pain as I rolled her underneath me. Yeah, she wasn't coming with me, but the arguing could wait until later.

NOAH

"Do you have a passport, Noah?" Teagan asked me at school on Wednesday.

We had taken to eating lunch in my car. Well, what had started as me going out to my car for a smoke and Teagan keeping me company had turned into private lunch dates in my Lexus.

Swallowing a bite of my sandwich, I turned my face to look at her. "Yeah, baby, I do." Her pretty face flushed and when she smiled up at me, I felt physically sucker punched.

Jesus, there would be no getting over her.

The past few months had been the best of my life and I wasn't exaggerating or ashamed to admit I was head over heels in love with the girl next door. I also wasn't ashamed to admit that the girl next door had given me the one thing I'd always lacked and constantly craved.

Aspiration.

Teagan Connolly gave me hope every time she smiled at me, or cracked a joke, or played me a song on her guitar. Confidence oozed from her. Her laugh was infectious. I was drawn to her aura. She was gorgeous, stunningly beautiful, but then so were a lot of girls.

Looks were a lot of the hunt but they were never the catch.

She was the catch.

The whole package.

Teagan called me treacherous, but she was the one who could shake mountains.

She'd unintentionally lit a fire of hope and desire inside of me that seemed to burn brighter and grow stronger the more time I spent with her. To want someone so much that even when you have them, when you're with them, you're still hungry. Still craving them. I needed more of her and the more I got, the more I knew it would never be enough. It sounded weird, fucking crazy, but there it was.

The girl accepted me, all of me, and to have someone so good to love you back even when they know you're not perfect, even though you've done terrible things and *will* do terrible things... Well, that was an indescribable feeling.

It all ends on Friday...

The thought penetrated my mind and I had to force myself not to physically flinch.

"Can I see it?" she asked, and her Irish accent curled around me like a blanket of comfort.

Reaching over, I opened the glove compartment and handed her my passport. "Why?"

"I have a proposition for you," she told me as she twisted sideways to face me.

"Remember when you said that you and Logan were planning on hiding out at his grandfather's farm in Louisiana after graduation?" Her hazel eyes were wide and fixated on mine.

"Yes..." I coaxed, feeling like a douche for telling her and making her worry. I'd spent weeks trying to assure Teagan of this. Besides, that plan had gone to shit the minute I pushed myself inside of her.

She inhaled a deep breath before saying, "I think we should run away together."

TEAGAN

"I think we should run away together."

There, I'd said it. I'd admitted to my boyfriend the idea that had been plaguing me since he told me he was fighting on Friday night.

The look of shock on Noah's handsome face proved that was the last thing he expected me to say, but there it was. His brown eyes were narrowed on mine, his brow was creased, and I was fairly sure he hadn't taken a breath in over twenty-five seconds.

"Well?" I asked after a few minutes of stunned silence. "What do you think?"

A muscle in his jaw worked as he stared down at me. "Where would we go?" he finally asked, and his voice was thick with emotion.

"Ireland," I told him. I so desperately wanted to help him that I was prepared to do anything to free him from his stepfather's clutches.

George was back and had resumed control of my boyfriend. Making him fight; risking his life, his future.

I couldn't stand back and let that happen to him.

"Ireland?" he croaked out.

"I already have a ticket booked for Friday night," I told him quickly as I tucked his passport into my coat pocket, taking advantage of the vulnerability I saw in his eyes. The desperation I heard in his voice. "Well, three am Saturday morning, it's a red-eye flight. I can get you one, too. You'd be safe there. Free from George and JD... from everyone." I was rambling, I knew I was, but this was the biggest pitch of my life, and deep down in my heart and soul, I knew this was his only opportunity at freedom. *I needed to sell it to him dammit...*

"Come with me, Noah?" I whispered. Reaching over, I grabbed his hand and squeezed it tightly. "Run away with me."

"What about your uncle?" he asked me in a soft tone as he stroked my knuckles with his thumb. "What about my mother?" Shaking his head, he let out a heavy sigh. "We can't just run away, Teagan."

"Why not?" I demanded, climbing across the console to straddle him. Sitting on Noah's lap, I cupped his cheeks with my hands and forced him to look at me.

"You were going to leave after graduation," I told him. "You said so yourself. And Max knows I don't plan on staying here when school finishes." Leaning closer, I pressed my lips to his and kissed him hard.

"Three months, Noah," I whispered against his lips. "That's the only difference between Logan's plan and mine. Do this with me."

NOAH

I wanted to say yes.

I wanted to say fuck the consequences and leave right now with Teagan, but what would happen to my mother if I did that – if I didn't fight on Friday?

George would...

"Teagan, I can't," I choked out, eyes clenched shut. I didn't want to see the disappointment in her eyes. I didn't want her to see the pain in mine.

"Yes," she hissed before pressing her lips to mine almost savagely. "You. Can."

She wrapped her arms around my neck and pressed her forehead to mine. "You have to," she mumbled.

"I can't," I mumbled, chest heaving, as regret flooded me. "It's too far... my mom. I have to stay close."

"I'm going, Noah," Teagan told me. "And I'm booking you a ticket to come with me." She stroked my cheek with her small hand.

"You need to know you have options," she told me. "There's more to life than the Dennis family."

More to life than the Dennis family...

More to life...

Life...

"Don't make me watch that again," she whispered, and I swear my heart cracked when I saw her lip wobble. "I love you. I can't bear the thought of anything happening to you. It would destroy me..."

"Okay," I heard myself saying – fucking lying. *Why the hell was I lying to her?* "I'll come with you."

Teagan lifted her face and when I looked into her tear filled eyes, I realized exactly why I was lying to her. Why I would *continue* to lie to her and let her believe I was going with her. Because she deserved better.

Because Teagan was the one thing I ever did right and I wanted to keep her safe and untainted from the rest of my life.

And if I didn't win Friday night, I didn't want her to be here to find out. I wanted her safe. I wanted her on that plane and as far away from George as possible.

I needed her shielded.

"You will?" Teagan sniffled. "You really will come with me to Ireland?"

"Yeah," I managed to choke out. I loved her. I fucking burned for her. I would do just about anything to protect her, even if that meant I had to protect her from me. "I really will, Thorn."

TEAGAN

"If someone told me back at the start of senior year that you would be running away with Noah Messina, I'd have laughed in their face," Hope mumbled as she sat on my bed with a mixture of shock and disbelief etched on her face. I'd told Hope everything and she was surprisingly understanding, if not a little depressed. "I can't believe this, Teegs."

"Neither can I." But it was happening. I was getting on a plane in less than eight hours with Noah Messina and I knew in my heart and soul that it was the absolute right thing to do.

I loved him and, crazy as it sounded at eighteen, I knew it was the real deal.

I knew *he* was the real deal for me.

"I love him, Hope," I told her as I tossed my clothes into my suitcase. "And Noah needs this... He needs someone to save him."

"I know," she muttered. "I just wish you guys didn't have to leave."

"They're never going to let him be, Hope," I told her. "As long as Noah stays here, he's the property of George Dennis and his family. I love him too much to sit back and let that happen."

Shaking my head, I grabbed my slippers and shoved them into my case. "I've seen what they're capable of." The memory of those men beating Noah outside of the Henderson Hotel flooded my mind and I shuddered. "He *needs* this."

"And what do you need, Teagan?" Hope asked softly.

"Him," I replied simply. "I need Noah, and I need him alive."

"Where's Noah meeting you?"

"He's meeting me here in a few minutes," I mumbled, checking my watch. "We'll take a nap and then drive his car to the airport since Max still has my keys."

"And what about Max?"

"I'll leave a note." I couldn't think too much about Max and how what I was doing would make him feel. If I did, it was possible the guilt would break me down.

Hope stared at me for a long moment before sighing and nodding her head. "I understand why you're doing this," she told me as she got to her feet and embraced me in a hug. "Just... just stay in touch, okay? Don't forget me."

"Never," I replied.

The sound of someone clearing their throat alerted me to the fact that Hope and I were no longer alone.

Noah stood in the doorway of my bedroom, with one lone duffel bag in his hand and that fire he lit inside of me the very first day I laid eyes on him roared to life. My body seemed to hum with electricity when he was near.

"Keep in touch," Hope choked out as she pressed a kiss to my cheek.

"I will," I told her.

"And you, too," Hope added, stepping towards Noah.

Wrapping her arms around him, Hope stretched up and whispered. "Don't break her," before rushing from the room.

And then she was gone and I was left on my own with Noah.

"Have you got everything you need?" I asked him, my voice thick with emotion. It had been hard saying goodbye to Hope. I was really going to miss that girl.

"Come here," Noah murmured, taking a step towards me.

I didn't need to be asked twice. I rushed over to him and allowed him to envelope me in a hug that touched parts of me only he could.

"Any regrets?" Noah asked me in a soft tone.

"Nope," I whispered. "Not one."

NOAH

I needed to leave.

My fight was in less than an hour and if I didn't get a move on soon, I'd be late.

But Christ, I was fighting my hardest battle right now, trying to force my body out of her bed. Because my heart sure as hell didn't want to leave her. Teagan looked so innocent and carefree when she was sleeping, that I wished I could just melt into the duvet with her and disappear right now.

A million different thoughts and emotions were rushing through me, driving me close to insanity. But the worst thought was about Teagan, about what she would think when she woke up and realized I was gone. When she figured out I wasn't going to Ireland with her. Would she forgive me?

I hoped like hell she could, because I was going to win her back.

I wasn't losing the fight tonight.

I couldn't.

Not when I had a future with Teagan to look forward to.

I would find a way of getting my mother away from George and then I'd... And then I'd go get my girl.

"I love you," I whispered into her ear.

I pressed a kiss to her cheek before gently sliding off her bed and creeping out of her room.

I'd practically guessed George had a hidden agenda when he told me to bring Teagan to the fight. At the time I'd just assumed it was his sick attempt at kicking me when I was down, but the second I walked through the doorway of the Hub, it became perfectly clear what my stepfather's true ulterior motive was.

"Messina," George's raspy voice echoed through the bar and I had to steel myself before looking over. "Get over here now, kid."

Inhaling a deep, calming breath, I slowly made my way through the crowd until I reached the table full of George's *associates* at the far corner of the room.

JD was there.

So were Ellie and Reese.

Several other familiar faces looked up at me, but I didn't care about them because my heart felt like it had deflated in my chest the minute I locked eyes on George's ulterior motive.

"Mom."

I looked hard at my pale faced mother as she lolled against George's beefy shoulder. Her brown eyes were glazed over. Her skin was deathly pale and the veins in her arms were visible under her faintly bruised skin.

She stared straight through me like she was looking through a window.

"Mom," I said a little louder, ignoring the snide comments coming from JD and his dad, hoping to god she wasn't too far gone this time.

Again, nothing.

I stepped around the table, not giving a shit whose feet I stepped on, and knelt in front of her. "Mom, are you okay?" I rested my shaking hand on her boney knee and forced myself not to shake her. "Mom?"

"Noah, can I have a...." Ellie's voice drilled through my ears but I was having none of it.

"Don't talk to me," I warned her. She'd sat back and allowed this to happen. She was as bad as her father.

"What did she take?" I asked coldly, forcing myself to push back the fear of seeing my mother in catatonic mode to the back of my mind. If I didn't, the fear would fucking choke me. "What did you give her?"

"She's fine," George chuckled darkly, clapping me hard on the back. "She's in better shape than you are, or at least than you'll be in by the time tonight's over."

A cold sweat broke out on the back of my neck as I remained impassive. "What's she doing here?"

"Consider her presence *arrière-pensée*," JD growled from behind me.

"Or a strong incentive," George added before turning his attention to his guests. "Tonight, we have a special engagement," he announced with a cruel smirk. "My best fighter against Mortico's,"

"A fight to the death," a deep gravelly voice said from behind me and every muscle in my body coiled tight. "You sure about this, kid?"

Teagan's face penetrated my mind, and I found the strength to climb to my feet. Turning slowly, I faced the man I knew was Gerome Javi and smirked. "It's your funeral."

TEAGAN

"That bastard," I hissed as I stalked across the street and banged on the Carter's front door. I didn't care if Kyle answered, I was too bloody furious.

The Carter's front door swung inwards and Logan's face smiled back at me. "Hey there, jailbird," he teased. "How's the life sentence going?"

"Where's Hope?" I demanded as I rushed inside.

"Out on a date with Jordan," Logan said, closing the door after me.

"I need your help," I told him in a no-nonsense tone of voice before pushing past him and making for the stairs.

Noah had given me the slip.

The dirty snake must have crept out when I was asleep, after many hours of against the rules frolicking, because when I woke up my bed was empty and his car was gone. What the hell was I supposed to do now? Let Noah stay with those creeps and wreck his entire future?

I couldn't. I physically *couldn't* stand here and let that happen to him.

He was worth more than that.

He deserved better.

"Where's the fire?" Logan asked.

"At the quarry," I told him. "Noah's gone to the Ring of Fire to fight some guy named Javi and I need you to help me talk some sense into the idiot."

Logan's face paled, his entire frame stiffened, and then he let loose a string of F-bombs that would've made his brothers proud.

"Javi – Gerome Javi?" Logan roared as he followed me up the stairs. "Jesus fucking Christ, Teagan, why didn't you stop him? Javi's a butcher. He fights to the fucking death. He's a goddamn psychopath."

"I thought I had!" I shouted back as I rushed into Hope's room and began rummaging in her closet. "He lied to me, Logan," I snapped as I pulled out a pair of denim shorts, a white tank top torn at the midriff, and Hope's infamous thigh high black boots. "We're supposed to be leaving tonight."

"Leaving?" Logan stood in the doorway of Hope's bedroom with his arms folded across his chest and a look of pure rage on his face. "Where?"

"Ireland," I told him as I pulled off my clothes and dressed quickly. "I can't watch his life unravel like this a second longer," I grumbled. I didn't care that Logan was in the room while I was undressing. I presumed there was nothing I had that he hadn't seen before and he'd never looked at me like that, anyway. Besides, I had way bigger problems than Logan Carter catching a glimpse of my ass. "It's too unfair, Logan, and Noah deserves better. A shot at a future."

"I know," Logan whispered quietly. "I've been saying that for years."

"Our tickets are booked," I rambled. "He told me he was

coming..." Sinking onto the bed, I pulled the boots up my legs. "Why the hell would he go to the fight when I gave him a way out?"

"Because there's no way out, Teagan," Logan told me in a sad tone. "Not for him and he knows it."

"What the hell does that mean?" I demanded as I got to my feet and rushed over to Hope's closet and pulled out a black, tight fitted leather jacket. I took a quick glance at my reflection in Hope's mirror and cringed. Yep, I was all kitted out for the Ring of Fire – not that I relished the thought of going to that hellhole again.

"Do you know why he fights for George Dennis and his family, Teegs?" Logan asked me in a soft tone.

"Yeah," I grumbled. "To keep his mom in treatment. He fights for her." I was mad as hell at Noah actually, but pissed or not I wasn't going to sit back and do nothing. Doing nothing made me feel helpless and I didn't do helpless. I was an action type girl. "So get your keys," I told Logan as I brushed past him and made for the stairs. "Because that's where we're going – to fight for him."

"His mother's illness isn't his only reason, Teagan," Logan told me as he put the pedal to the metal and floored it.

I was sitting in the passenger seat of his dad's Mercedes and feeling completely badass as Logan navigated the beast of a car through the mountains like a boss.

"What do you mean?" I muttered as I kept my eyes glued to the windscreen. Logan turned onto the dirt road and a rush of fear trickled through me. Holy crap, I was about to barge into an illegal fighting ring and kidnap the star of the show.

Did I have a gun at my disposal, or a knife, or even a freaking nail file?

Nope.

But what I did have at my disposal was far deadlier to a man than a gun and much more alluring than the blade of a knife.

I had boobs and a vagina.

I figured those particular popular body parts would come in handy when trying to entice my boyfriend to leave with me, considering he spent as much time with his mouth on those parts as he did communicating with me.

"Did Noah ever tell you about his father?"

I stilled and turned to look at Logan. "I know his name was Antonio Messina," I told him. "I know he's dead."

"Do you know that George killed him?" Logan asked me in a level tone and I swear my heart stopped beating in my chest. "Do you know why?" he added in a soft tone, taking a quick glance at me.

"No," I whispered, clenching my hands together. "I didn't know that."

23

TEAGAN

"Wait. Let me get this straight." I pressed my thumbs against my temples as I desperately tried to take on board what Logan was telling me. "Noah's life was traded for his mother's?"

"Antonio Messina was George's right hand man," Logan explained. "His best fighter, his faithful dealer... the whole nine yards."

"Wait, George deals drugs, too?" I felt my body break out in a cold sweat. "Of course, he does." Laying my head back I let out a sigh. "I bet he sells women and murders puppies, too."

"He dabbles in prostitution," I heard Logan say and I felt like weeping. "But as far as I know, he's not into puppy slaying."

"How do you know all of this?" I demanded. "Did Noah tell you?"

"I have ways of finding out what I need to know," was all Logan replied before continuing with his tale of horror. "When Noah's parents met, their lives pretty much went up shit's creek without a paddle," Logan said with a sigh.

"Apparently, Antonio had a soft spot for blondes and Noah's mother was one hell of a prize. It was the affair from hell," he told me. "Two extremely impulsive people, with addictive personalities living in hazardous conditions with every type of lethal temptation at their disposal."

"What happened to them?" I heard myself asking. "What did they do?"

"Drugs happened, Teegs," Logan replied sadly. "They fucked up, got hooked on heroin, and then they made the mistake of shitting on their own doorstep." Logan rubbed his hand over his face and sighed heavily. "When Noah was fourteen, his mother and father stole a shipment of heroin they were supposed to be delivering for George. They were caught."

"What happened?" I asked, barely breathing.

"George was so pissed when he discovered their betrayal that he put a bullet in Antonio without thinking twice about it."

"Stop," I screeched. "Just... Stop for a sec and let me take this in."

Logan sat patiently beside me as I struggled to come to terms with what I'd just been told. We were parked a half mile away from the warehouse on the dirt road and I was having a mini breakdown.

"George killed Noah's dad?" I turned to face Logan, and looked him straight in the eye, praying he was bullshitting me. The serious expression on his face proved he was telling the truth. "I can't believe this," I muttered, shaking my head.

"Yeah, well neither could I when I discovered it," Logan replied calmly. "It's not every day a guy finds out his best friend's life is the price of his mother's."

"What?"

"You haven't figured it out by now?" Logan mused. "I thought you would've..."

"Uh, no, sorry, Dr. Evil, I haven't," I grumbled. "I'm from a small town in the back ass of nowhere. Things like this don't happen to people like me."

Logan smirked before shaking his head and continuing, "With his best fighter dead and a hugely important fight right around the corner, George found himself in a pickle, so to speak."

"A pickle," I repeated in a flat tone.

"George turned his sights on Noah." Logan shrugged uncomfortably. "He knew he needed Noah, he could see the potential in him, but he also knew he would need an... *incentive* in order to get Noah on board and fight for him."

"So, what, he used Noah's schizophrenic mother as an incentive?" I snapped. "Logan, that's sick."

Logan nodded slowly and I could see the anger in his gray eyes. "I know, and I couldn't agree more with you on that, Teegs, but it doesn't change the facts. In exchange for his mother's life, Noah agreed to step into his father's shoes. George married Kelsie, dumped her in a psych ward, tossed Noah a few bones in the form of visitation papers, and took total control of him."

"Why?" I demanded. "Why would George want Noah? He was only a teenage boy for Christ's sake."

"A teenage boy who was groomed from birth to follow in his father's steps," Logan informed me in a tight tone of voice.

"You didn't know him then, Teegs," he added softly. "Noah at fifteen was as ruthless in the ring as he is now. He was tossed in a ring as soon as he was old enough to block a punch. Bred to inflict pain and cause damage. Noah Messina's path was written for him before the guy was old enough to comprehend what was happening." Logan shook his head in disgust and let out a pained growl. "God, I hope he hasn't fought Javi yet. That guy is a killer, Teagan. The only way to beat him is to take him out permanently. There is no other way."

"If that's the case, then why is he *here*," I screamed, gesturing in the direction of the quarry, "instead of on the way to the airport with me?" My whole body shook as I stared at Logan, looking for answers. "Why didn't he run with me when he had the chance?"

"I don't know, Teegs." Logan stared at me for a long moment before finally saying, "I can only assume George has threatened him somehow. Maybe with his mom, or maybe with..."

"Me?"

Logan nodded. "It's possible. Shit, Teagan, get down..."

The passenger door of Logan's car flew open and I found myself looking into the cold green eyes of none other than JD Dennis.

"Oh shit," I whispered.

He smiled darkly. "We were hoping you'd come, blondie."

Everything happened so quickly then I didn't have a chance to scream before a sharp pain ricocheted through my temple and the darkness cloaked over me like a blanket of smothering fog.

NOAH

I couldn't look at my hands.

They wouldn't stop shaking.

Javi's blood was smeared across my knuckles, my face, my fucking bare skin.

My stomach retched even though there wasn't a damn thing left inside it. I'd vomited more in the past twenty minutes than I had in the past eighteen years.

I didn't think I could ever look myself in the eye again. What I'd done... oh, Jesus. Clenching my eyes shut, I leaned against the bathroom mirror and forced myself to breathe slowly, but I started to gag again.

"Are you okay?" a familiar female voice asked from somewhere behind me and I didn't have any fight left inside of me to tell her to go to hell.

"Noah," Ellie coaxed as she stepped up to me and placed a hand on my shoulder. "You did what you had to." She paused and sucked in a sharp breath before saying, "He would've killed you if you hadn't..."

"Killed him first?" I managed to croak out. "Is that what you were gonna say, Ellie?" I turned and faced her. I could see the tears in her eyes. "Is that supposed to make me feel better?"

"You didn't have a choice," she argued. I knew in some sick way, Ellie actually cared about me, that's why she was here trying to comfort me, but it wasn't enough. She was a part of them. I didn't want her comfort. And now, because of her father, I was no better than those scumbags in the bar. "You're a survivor," she told me. "You're..."

"I'm a killer," I snarled before shoving past her and staggering out of the bathroom. I couldn't breathe. I couldn't fucking think straight. My skin was crawling. I needed to get the hell out of here. Get some fresh air, anything.

Pushing through the crowded bar, I kept my head down as I forced my way towards the exit. A few more steps and I would be...

"This is crazy... What the hell are we doing?.... You're so... Wrong for me."

I stopped dead in my tracks as the sound of *her* voice resounded through me.

"Noah Messina, you are treacherous..."

As I turned slowly, I prayed with all my heart that I'd imagined her voice in my head. I was hallucinating. Fucking dreaming. I had to be.

But the image of Teagan's naked body writhing on the elevator floor projecting from a flat screen television bracketed against the wall at the far side of the bar assured me I wasn't.

My eyes were glued, fucking riveted to the screen in horror as I watched a naked version of myself plunging into my girlfriend, fucking her on the floor like a goddamn animal.

What the...

"I told you I'd make you sorry," Reese sneered as she

sauntered past me. "You fucked her," she sniggered. "And I fucked you both. Enjoy the CCTV footage," she added cruelly. "Consider it the perks of working at the hotel and having access to the security cameras."

That's why they wanted Teagan here tonight, to see this.

They wanted to rip my heart out of my goddamn chest...

The door of the bar opened inward then and JD came barreling through with Teagan in his arms. "Get your hands off me, jackass," she snarled as she kicked and lashed against JD's tight grasp. "You better run when I get my hands on you," she screeched before biting down on JD's arm.

"Bitch," he hissed, releasing her quickly, as he nursed his wounded arm.

"Noah," Teagan gasped the minute she saw me.

Staggering towards me in a pair of exceptionally high boots, Teagan threw her arms around my neck and let out a cry of relief. "Oh, thank god," she cried. "You're okay. You're okay..."

"What the hell are you doing here?" I demanded as I held her against my body as tight as I could. This was my worst fucking nightmare coming true.

"I came to save you," she whispered, and it was then the enormity of what I'd done impaled me. This girl had come to save me, but I wasn't worth saving. Not anymore.

"We still have time," she rambled. "Just come with me now. Logan's gone to get his...." Teagan's voice trailed off as her attention fell on the screen behind me.

"That's us," Teagan hissed as she covered her mouth with her hand and backed away from me.

The hurt in her eyes was crippling as she stared in horror at the television screen. And when she turned her gaze to me, the betrayal I saw in her hazel eyes caused my heart to split clean open.

NOAH

I was a pornstar, granted an unintentional one, but a pornstar nevertheless.

My head was screaming at me, pushing forward all the incriminating evidence against Noah to the forefront of my mind. Shame, mortification, and more dominantly, anger coursed through me.

He'd done this. It had to be Noah. He must have recorded us, or gotten access to the elevator footage. But why?

Oh god, I felt physically sick and gagged as realization dawned on me

How had I been so deluded, so wrong about him?

For Christ's sake, I was going to run away with him. I was prepared to do that for *him*.

I was here to help *him*.

"Thorn," I heard Noah say as I backed towards the door JD had dragged me through. His eyes were wild and frantic as he held his hands out palms facing me. "I didn't do this," he said quickly.

"Oh my god," I whispered when words found me again. I

gasped for air but couldn't get enough into my lungs, I felt winded. I felt so exposed, so violated.

Swinging around on shaky legs, I stumbled out of the warehouse and into the parking lot, desperate to get away. I had no idea where to go. Logan had taken the car to get help. He'd managed to fight off JD's men and break away, but for what?

"Teagan... Thorn, wait dammit, let me explain..."

The feeling of suffocation was urging me to move faster and further away from Noah and this fucked up arena. Yet there was another feeling festering inside of me that was even more unbearable. I felt like I was tearing my body in half, literally ripping myself apart by running from him.

"Wait," Noah rasped, seconds before his arms enveloped me. "Reese stole the CCTV footage from the hotel," he said in a panicked voice as he turned me in his arms. "It wasn't me. I fucking swear to you it wasn't."

"Logan told me everything," I choked out, though it was little more than a breathy whisper. "About your mom and dad, the drugs... Everything." My throat felt like it was closing up, severing my air pipes, suffocating me. "Did you fight him – Javi?"

"I..." he paused to brush a lock of hair from his eyes before whispering, "I did."

"Did you win?"

Noah's eyes met mine and I didn't need to ask any more questions. Noticing the horrible markings on his face, I sucked in a sharp breath. The answers were written on his face, the truth was in his eyes – naked and ugly and cutting me deep.

"He's dead?"

Noah nodded his head slightly and a scream ripped from my throat.

"Oh my god, Noah." I stared into his brown eyes, not bothering to brush away the tears that were spilling down my cheeks. "You *killed* a man."

"He's a survivor," Ellie snarled as she stalked towards us. The look of detest in her eyes was obvious and directed at me. "So don't you dare try to make him feel bad for wanting to live."

"Ellie, you better back the fuck away from my boyfriend right now," I snarled as I glowered at her touching Noah's shoulder. "I'm about three seconds past crazy and a hare's breath away from beating your ass."

"I had no choice," Noah choked out, brushing Ellie's arm off, as he reached over and grabbed my wrist, dragging me close to his chest. "I wasn't ready to let go of my life, let go of *you*..." Tears pooled in his eyes. "I know I've screwed everything up," he said in a gruff tone.

"You could go to prison for this, Noah," I cried. I felt like my heart was shattering into a bazillion pieces. "This is murder. Logan's gone to get the cops. You know that means..."

"I know," he rasped, backing away from me. "And I know what needs to happen next," he added, before pinching the bridge of his nose. "You need to get out of here, Thorn. Away from me. I understand you won't be able to love me after this, after what I've done."

"If I didn't love you, I wouldn't be here!" I screamed, kicking the dirt, dust and whatever the hell else that was on the ground by my feet. Stalking towards him, I grabbed him by the back of the neck and dragged his face down to meet mine. "I'm in love with *you*." I pressed a kiss to his lips. It was rough, hard, and everything I was feeling in that moment. He had blood on his hands. He was a killer. *A killer.* "Let's go," I heard myself saying.

"Go?" Noah shook his head in confusion. "Teagan, I'm going..."

"With me," I snapped, grabbing his hand. "You're going with me."

"Teagan," he rasped, clutching my face between his hands. "You can't get involved in this, baby. It's too big. You need to get out of here." Pressing a hard kiss to my lips, Noah broke free from my grasp and turned back towards the warehouse.

"Don't do this, Noah," I begged him as I watched him walk towards George and the gang of men who had formed a crowd outside the warehouse. Watching our spectacle no doubt.

"Get out of here, Teagan," Noah hissed as he continued to walk to them, to the dark side.

"No." Running after Noah, I grabbed his hand and pulled him towards me. "Please, don't do this." I hated begging, it wasn't in my nature, but I'd beg on my knees if it meant I could save him. "If you love me, even a little bit, then leave with me now. Forget about this."

"Messina!" George roared and I felt the muscles in Noah's arm bunch tight with tension. "Get your ass back here, boy, you're not done for the night."

"Let me save you," I rambled, holding onto his arm for dear life. "Turn away from them and come with me. Please, Noah. Please..."

Noah stood frozen for what felt like an age as he stared into the eyes of his stepfather. "You can still love me," he whispered. "Even though..."

"I can't *not* love you," I told him and it was the truth. I was quite possibly signing myself a first class ticket to hell, but I didn't care. I wanted him and I would do anything to keep him safe. "I'm your thorn," I added with a sob.

"I'm out," Noah called out as he wrapped an arm around my shoulders and walked me towards his car, and the weight of his hand in mine felt like the hugest gust of air filling my lungs.

"Thank you," I whispered in relief.

"I'll make this right," he told me softly before tucking me into his side, protecting me. "I'll fix this."

"You're out?" George roared as he stalked towards us. "I don't think you understand the way this works, Messina. There's no way out. We had an agreement – what about your mother?"

"Watch my back as I walk away from you, George. From *all* of you," Noah spat as he opened the passenger door and helped me in before rounding the car and climbing in alongside me. "Hold on tight," Noah instructed me as he cranked the engine and tore off.

"Do you have the tickets?" Noah asked as he shifted into fourth gear to take a sharp corner.

I nodded. "And our passports," I added as I watched out the back window. "They're in my boots."

The lone headlamp on what I presumed was a car behind us was blinding and catching up quickly. "Do you think that's them?" I asked nervously. "Do you think they'll follow us?"

"I wouldn't put anything past George," Noah growled as he took a glance in the rearview mirror and cursed loudly. "Shit... it's JD," Noah told me. "He's on his bike."

"Is that bad?" I demanded in a high-pitched tone.

"Well, it's not good, baby," Noah growled, speeding up quickly. "Shit, he's gaining on us."

"Go faster," I hissed, watching in horror as JD tailed us. "Hurry up, Noah," I screamed. "Fucking floor it."

"I am, Teagan, I am," Noah roared. "Fuck, you're a pain in my ass, woman."

"Well take an aspirin," I shot back, paling when JD's bike swerved right and out of sight of the back window.

"Oh god, Noah," I screamed as JD suddenly came into sight in my car door window. The black gun he was pointing against my window caused me to temporarily lose my mind. "Get down!"

Without thinking I grabbed Noah's shoulders and forced his head down, causing him to lose control of the car just as the deafening sound of a gun shooting off floated over our heads.

There was no sign of JD or his bike. All I could see was the rocky mountain wall we were heading straight for.

"Jesus Christ," I heard Noah hiss as he made a frantic grab for the wheel, but we were swerving out of control. "Teagan, I can't.... Hold on, baby." Noah's upper body was suddenly covering my face and I clenched my eyes shut, bracing myself for the impact we were sure to feel.

When it came, the pain that ricocheted through my body was like nothing I'd ever felt before and then there was darkness. Darkness and the overwhelming smell of gasoline.

"Noah, are you okay?" My head was thumping so hard it felt like a stampede of elephants had participated in a game of chicken limbo on my skull and the fat one lost. "Noah?" I croaked out as I twisted my body around to face him.

A rush of raw, unadulterated fear shot through me when I saw him. His face was covered in blood, he was twisted at an obscure angle, and his eyes were closed, but... His chest was moving. *Oh, thank god.*

I tried to unfasten my seatbelt and get to Noah, but like some twisted case of Déjà vu, the belt wouldn't budge.

And that's when the panic truly set in.

"No," I cried as I pulled at the clasp. "Dammit, no."

The darkness...

The smell of the fumes...

The fire blinding me... Wait, what?

"Noah," I screamed when the first pillar of smoke and flames erupted in front of my eyes. "Wake up." I frantically tried to free myself and then Noah but the stupid belts were jammed. "Noah, I love you," I sobbed in case I didn't get another chance.

"Don't panic, Thorn," I heard Noah say. His tone was commanding and, in that moment, I couldn't have been more relieved. Opening his eyes slowly, he turned his face to look at me. "I fucked up my car, baby."

"We're stuck inside a car that's on fire and you're worried about its condition?" A wave of hysteria flooded through me, and I found myself laughing and crying at the same time. "You're unbelievable."

"You really wanna pick a fight?" Noah growled as he leaned forward and grabbed a pocket knife out of his glove compartment. "Really, Thorn?"

"Okay, good point." I closed my eyes and tried to stay calm. I could feel Noah pulling at my seatbelt, sawing through the straps, trying to free me from the carnage.

Tears slipped from my eyes, trailing down my cheeks, mixing with smoke and dried blood. "I don't blame you," I added quietly. Noah's hand stilled briefly before starting up again. "For winning the fight," I explained. "I... I'm glad."

"I don't want to think about the fight, Teagan," Noah said quietly. "I need to focus on getting you out of here."

"I'm sorry," I whispered. It needed to be said. "This is my fault."

"No," he shook his head. His fingers worked frantically as he cut through the harness. "This is all on me, baby."

"I shouldn't have come here... I forced you into leaving with me..."

"Teagan, look at me. *Look* at me." Noah's eyes were red and pained. "This is *not* your fault. Do you understand me? This is *my* fault, baby, and you're not going down for it."

The sound of sirens blasted through my ears and panic tore through me. Noah hissed out a sharp breath. "The second this belt cracks, I want you to get out of this car and run." He caught my chin between his fingers. "Do *not* stop running. Do *not* wait for me."

He kissed me hard and I felt the belt give way.

"Do it," he hissed. "Run."

24

LOGAN CARTER

Deep down inside of me, I'd always known this would all end in a ball of flames.

The one regret I had was that I sat back and let it go on for as many years as I had.

"You did the right thing tonight, Logan," my father said as he stood beside me, watching as the paramedic's checked Noah over and the firemen extinguished his flaming car.

Except I hadn't done the right thing.

I hadn't done a damn thing.

Teagan had.

"What do you think's going to happen to him now?" I asked as I watched Noah being handcuffed by two policemen and ushered into the back of a squad car. "Will he do time?" I asked. "Can you help him, Dad?"

My father sighed heavily before wrapping his arm around my shoulder and leading me back towards the car. "I don't know, Low," Dad muttered as he climbed into his car. I got in beside him.

"I just wish you would've confided in me earlier," he said and I could hear the disappointment in his tone as we drove back towards the quarry. "I could have done a hell of a lot more for the kid if I'd known... Holy shit."

Dad slammed on the brakes so hard I thought he was going to jackknife the car, but then he did something I was not expecting.

He got out of the car and stalked towards the crowd of people handcuffed outside the warehouse and being monitored by several policemen.

"You," Dad roared, shoving past Noah's stepfather who was cuffed to a huge cop.

Dad stopped in front of a frail blonde woman. Noah's mother, I realized, and I climbed out of the car and chased after him. "Keep your head," I called out to my tempestuous father.

"Kelsie Mayfield," Dad snarled, chest heaving. "So, you've finally decided to crawl out from under the rock you've been hiding behind for seventeen years?"

"You know her?" I asked in surprise.

"Yes, Logan, I know her." Dad turned to face me. "Or at least, there was a time when I thought I did."

Raising his hand, he pulled his shirt away from his neck, revealing a stab wound he'd received before I was born. "She had a hand in this," he roared. "And in your mother's scars."

My blood turned to lava in my veins. "You're the lawyer?"

Kelsie ignored my question.

Instead, she kept her eyes locked on my father. "He betrayed me, too, Kyle," she sobbed. "Once you signed it all away, David threw me out like I was yesterday's paper."

"Are you surprised?" Dad demanded. "Goddammit, I told you what he was like."

"This way, miss," a deep voiced cop ordered as he grabbed Kelsie's arm and led her away from us.

"Take care of Noah," Kelsie shouted after us. "He's your brother, Kyle."

"What?" Dad and I both shouted simultaneously.

"He's your father's son," she cried out. "Not Antonio's."

"WELL SHIT," I MUTTERED, SEVERAL MINUTES AFTER KELSIE was carted away as we drove back to Thirteenth Street. "That changes things."

"I should be surprised," Dad told me as he pulled into our driveway. "But to be honest, I'm not."

"Do you believe her?" I asked him.

"Yeah, kid, I do," Dad replied quietly. "He's done it to enough of his women – and his sons."

Holy shit, Noah was my uncle... "So, what happens now?" I asked him.

"Not a word of this to your mother until I figure all of this out. She doesn't need the worry," he said in a sharp tone as he unfastened his seatbelt and climbed out of the car. "I need to phone your Uncle Mike and then I guess I better get a lawyer down to the station."

"You're gonna help Noah?" I asked, feeling nothing but admiration for my father. He was an amazing guy.

"Yeah," Dad said with a sigh. "It's not the kid's fault he has the misfortune of having Henderson blood running through him. It's not ours either."

NOAH

I didn't kill him.

Out of everything I'd learned tonight, and there had been a hell of a lot, the one thing that stuck out in my mind was the fact that Gerome Javi was alive – unconscious and suffering from extensive internal bleeding, but still alive.

The relief I felt when I heard this was like nothing I'd ever felt. Well, the relief I'd felt when I managed to free Teagan from the burning car was something close. She was safe, George was arrested, and I wasn't going to be spending the next thirty years in a prison cell.

Three to five years for grievous bodily harm sounded a hell of a lot more appealing than thirty to life for first degree murder. That was for fucking sure.

"You sure you wanna stay here tonight?" Kyle asked me as he helped me out of his car and up the porch steps of George's house. He'd arrived at the station with an army of attorneys and bailed me out on the spot. But I wasn't even close to coming to terms with the fact that the man was my half brother.

"Yeah," I said in a gruff tone as I hobbled inside. "I'll

manage." Truth was, I couldn't wait to be on my own. I needed to contact Teagan. I knew she was next door. She'd sent me a million texts and I'd spotted her watching out her bedroom when I was walking up the driveway.

"I'll watch him," I heard Reese say and I stiffened.

"I'll watch myself," I snapped as Kyle helped me up the stairs to my bedroom. "Why couldn't you have left her to rot in there," I muttered. Kyle had given Reese a ride home from the police station and I was pissed as hell because of it. I got that she was his employee, but the girl had caused me nothing but problems.

"Rest those ribs, kid," Kyle ordered as he helped me onto my back and covered me with my duvet. "They're gonna sting like a bitch in the morning," he added softly.

"They already do," I muttered, holding my side. I'd busted three ribs and the pain was something fierce.

Kyle's phone started to ring and he slipped out of the room before answering it.

"Here," Reese said softly as she handed me two pills. "For the pain."

"Thanks," I choked out. Taking the pills, I chugged them back and let out a sigh when they went down. "Now go."

"But..."

"Go," I snapped. "I don't want you here, Reese."

After about an hour, the pain started to ease and my mind became surprisingly light.

"Where's your phone, Noah?" I heard Reese ask and that confused me. I thought she was long gone.

"Go...aw...ay..." I managed to slur, but I couldn't move my lips properly. I couldn't open my eyes.

Something was seriously up with me, I could barely lift my hands.

I felt a sudden weight against my pelvis, but I couldn't move an inch.

A nervous tingle shot up my spine before everything became too hazy to worry about.

And then everything felt sweet and soft and warm.

I was dreaming.

TEAGAN

I'd been home for over five hours. I'd missed my flight, the sun was starting to rise, and I had spent every minute of those five hours waiting for the boys in blue to knock on my door.

I paced my bedroom floor for the millionth time feeling anxious as hell, and the only thing that was keeping me sane was the knowledge that Noah was okay.

He was more than okay... He was a freaking Carter.

I'd hidden and remained perfectly still in the backseat of Mr. Carter's car earlier and heard the entire conversation between him and Logan. When they went inside, I'd waited another few minutes before creeping out of the car and skulking back to my house.

Noah was in the house next door.

I knew this because I'd watched Mr. Carter walk him inside over an hour ago. Reese had been with them and that caused my good nerves to unravel. I had hoped she'd be keeping company with a jail cell right about now, but I guess wishes didn't always come true. *I guess there was no law against being a whore.*

I'd sent Noah over a dozen text messages, but he hadn't answered a single one. I was trying not to freak out, but it was virtually impossible considering the night we'd put down.

The sound of a door banging flooded my ears and I lurched towards my bedroom window and watched as Mr. Carter crossed the street to his own house.

A little while later, my phone beeped and I somersaulted onto my bed to grab it.

Noah: *Need 2 show u something. Front door's unlocked. I'm in bed. Come straight up."

Be there in 2, I replied as I threw open my bedroom door and rushed down the stairs.

"Noah?"

The house was deathly quiet when I slipped inside. I welcomed the silence. At least we could talk without being disturbed. Climbing Noah's staircase, I walked straight to his bedroom door and knocked lightly before twisting the doorknob and pushing the door inwards.

My heart dropped the moment I saw him lying there.

My stomach churned and a pained cry tore my throat.

Skin – *naked* skin –limbs and long red hair invaded my vision.

That's all I could see.

The blood rushed to my brain so fast, everything became cloudy. When I was eventually able to focus, the image that laid before me caused my stomach to churn.

Noah and Reese fucking like rabbits, right in front of my eyes.

Reese was straddling Noah, screwing him like a fucking Duracell bunny, bouncing up and down, grinding her naked body on top of *my* naked boyfriend.

"Noah," I cried out as disgust churned inside of me.

He didn't even incline his face in my direction. He kept his eyes closed, grunting softly as Reese fucked him.

"I'm leaving!" I screamed, frantic. "I can't... I... I... How could you do this to me?" I was losing control of myself.

Tears were spilling from my eyes. I needed to get a grip, but every time I tried to grab onto the ledge of something rational, *their* sweat soaked, naked bodies fused together impaled me and I felt like bursting into flames.

I could forgive a lot of things, and maybe I had my priorities all wrong, but I couldn't forgive this.

I could *never* forgive this.

Noah didn't respond.

But she did.

Twisting her head to one side, Reese glanced at me with a smirk. "Bye now," she sneered before lowering her mouth and claiming Noah's.

And that's when I ran.

"What the hell happened to you?" I demanded when I saw my best friend standing at my front door, drenched from the rain that was hammering down, with mascara running down her cheeks. She was shaking so badly I don't think she could answer me.

"Hope?" I asked softly as I wrapped my arm around her waist and led her inside. "Hope, what's wrong?"

"He's gone," she said in a flat tone. Her whole body shook violently. "He... He broke his promise."

"I..." I paused, unsure of what to say. She looked in shock, like she was in a daze of some sort, and I was terrified because I'd never seen her cry before.

"I'm leaving," I told her. "I can't... I can't stay here, Hope. Not now. I'm going home."

I bit down hard on my lower lip and forced my hands to stop shaking as I dragged my suitcase onto my uncle's porch and closed the front door behind me. The sun was rising and I wanted to be long gone before anyone woke up.

Taking one final glimpse at Noah's house, I inhaled a deep breath and held my head high as I made my way down the steps towards my taxi.

"This all you got, Hun?" The taxi driver asked me and I nodded. I couldn't speak. I was afraid I would break down and cry if I did. "You ready?" he asked me, and again I responded with a small nod.

"Teagan, wait up," a familiar voice sounded from behind me.

My mouth fell open when I spotted Hope running down her driveway with a suitcase in one hand and a duffel bag in the other.

"I'm coming with you," she puffed as she opened the back door and tossed her luggage in before climbing in.

"What do you mean you're coming with me?" I demanded as I climbed in beside her. "Hope, you can't be serious? What... What about Jordan?"

"Don't talk to me about him," she hissed before turning her attention to the confused looking taxi-driver. "Seriously, dude, put the pedal to the metal before my dad finds out."

He must have heard the warning in Hope's voice because he tore off without another word.

"Have you got somewhere we can stay?" Hope asked. Her eyes were bloodshot, but not one single tear fell from them

"You can cry, Hope," I said quietly. "It's okay to feel."

"The only man I'll ever cry over will be the man who is worth my tears," she snarled, chewing on her lower lip. "He's not."

I watched as she played with the ring on her pinky finger before slowly removing it and placing it in her pocket. I was burning to ask her what had happened between her and Jordan but she'd kept her mouth shut about Noah, so I let her be.

"Do your parents know where you're going?"

"My mom knows," she replied. "I guess she'll talk to dad when he's calmed down."

"We're really leaving it all behind?" I sobbed. "You're sure about this – about coming with me?"

"One hundred percent," she choked out. "I am leaving Thirteenth Street and I am *never* coming back."

SEVEN YEARS LATER

Noah

"How are you doing, man?" I heard my manager, Tommy, ask seconds before he landed in the booth beside me. Quincy, my trainer, who was sitting beside me, tugged a sweet little brunette down on his lap and pressed a kiss to her neck before raising his beer bottle and clicking it against mine. "How're the knuckles?"

"Still functioning, Q," I told him before taking a swig of my beer. I was sore as shit, but the adrenalin that was still coursing through me numbed the aching.

Quincy was celebrating tonight. So was the brunette on his lap and the other forty or so people crammed up in the private room of the Krash bar. I'd done it. Finally, after eighteen months of blood, sweat, and fucking tears, I was a contender for the belt.

Had been for months now, but this was it. I was going to get my shot soon. Tonight's win sealed that for me.

The irony that I was now at the top of the very same game that had gotten me thrown behind bars seven years ago didn't go unnoticed. I was twenty five years old and had spent the majority of my adult life behind bars, paying for a liar's mistakes.

"You good, Noah?" Lucky Casarazzi asked.

Turning to face him, I gave him a genuine smile. "All good, man." This fucker right here was my right hand man. He was my brother. We'd served some serious time together. Had shed blood together when we were inside.

"Smell that, Champ?" Quincy chuckled, bleary eyed and three sheets to the wind. "That, my man, is the smell of success – of freedom."

I wasn't sure if I could ever get used to the feeling of freedom again. It had been eighteen months since I was released and every day since still felt like I was living on borrowed time. But I didn't verbalize my thoughts. Instead, I stood up, tossed another shot down my throat, and headed for the bar.

A dark-haired woman caught my attention at the far end of the bar, and when I realized who she was, my world came crashing down on me.

"Hope?" I called out as I pushed past a drunk couple in my bid to get to my old friend. My heart was beating erratically in my chest. "Hope? Is she here – is Teagan with you?"

"Stay away from her, Noah," Hope warned me before rushing from the bar.

Like hell I was staying away from her.

Every fucking day since she ran out on me felt like I was hemorrhaging.

She was my thorn.

And I was getting her back.

TEAGAN

"What do I mean to you?" I blurted out, never one to mince words. My cheeks reddened, I could feel them burn, but I kept my eyes on his face.

"Everything," Jordan mumbled, never taking his eyes off the pad he was sketching on. His fingers moved so fast across the paper, so skillfully, as I stared at him, drinking him in.

He looked good, too good for my twin bed he was sitting on - too good not to touch and I was itching to touch him.

His hair was a mess, a sexy mess of curls, and his whole body looked entirely too tempting.

God, hormones had officially found me. This was only day three of summer vacation. We had *at least another month together. How the heck was I going to cope?*

"Everything." I tested the word around and decided that was a great answer. "You really mean that?"

"Of course," he added with a chuckle. "You're my little keychain..."

"This is really good," I muttered to myself as I studied the manuscript in my hands. Uncrossing my legs, I snuggled against the plush cushions on our super comfy couch, engrossed in my best friend's latest masterpiece.

..."Are you going to tell me what's wrong?" I asked, holding my breath, fearing his answer, hoping he would lie and tell me he was fine because that look in his eyes was petrifying me. He was hurting. I could feel it in the way his hands trembled, I could see it in his eyes. Something was wrong.

"Jordan," I whispered when he didn't answer.

He didn't look at me.

Instead, he stared downwards. God, I knew this conversation was going to end badly and if I was Ash, I'd know a number of different tricks to take his mind off his problems, but he wouldn't let me touch him.

God knows I'd tried...

"Hope, I don't..." he broke off and rubbed his face with his hand. "Just sit with me," he choked out.

Edging closer to me, he bowed his head, rested his knee against mine and shuddered violently. "This is all I can manage," he admitted. "Please don't ask me why."

"I won't," I told him, forcing myself not to throw my arms around him.

I never asked and I never touched. He would freak out if I did and I needed him close to me. I needed the smell of him in my senses, the weight of his knee against mine. I needed answers.

Dammit...

"I love you, Jordan," I whispered, hoping to god and every angel, star, and whatever the hell was up in the sky that he would open up to me. That today would be the day he would tell me his troubles.

"I'm never gonna be the right guy for you, Hope," he rasped, twisting his head to look at me. His green eyes penetrated me, burned me. "You'll figure that out soon enough, but it would be a hell of a lot easier if you'd let me go now. Your dad's right about me...."

...As you can tell, I've been in love before, but it was the first kind. The sweet, innocent, will-never-end kind of love that gently flickers over time but never completely burns out or fades from your heart.

It's a special sort of love really, and sometimes it's the one that lasts the longest. The one you remember when you're old and gray and drawing your final breath into your weary lungs. If I had one wish it would be that I was his. His one love, the one that burned brighter and harder than all the others. The love that lasted the lifetime of the heart it was embedded inside...

This would be Hope's sixth full length novel in four years and I fully believed this was her best work to date. She self-published a story she'd written back in high school on a whim and it had been *huge*. She had been offered a dozen publishing deals since, but she preferred to stay indie. So along with the help of her trusted agent/publicist – aka me – Hope's writing career was going from strength to strength.

I was also the person who quietly and dutifully changed her latest hero's name from Jordan – because it was *always* Jordan, without embarrassing her.

With every book Hope spat out, her stories became more tragic and profoundly despairing. I knew why this was happening, I only wished I could make it better.

The banging on our flat door startled me and I leapt off

the couch. The manuscript I'd been holding in my hand scattered to the floor and I groaned. *I hadn't numbered them...*

The loud rapping noise continued.

"Hang on," I shouted as I made my way over to the door. She was always doing this – going out for the night and forgetting her keys. Usually I didn't mind because I was out with her, but tonight I hadn't felt up to going clubbing. Even though it was the middle of July here in Cork, it was hammering down with rain outside and I'd had more than my fair share of nights gallivanting in the rain to last me a lifetime.

"Hope, I swear to god I am going to tie your key around your bloody..." My voice trailed off the moment I opened the door inwards and caught a glance of Hope's wide eyed, horrified expression.

"What's wrong?" I whispered seconds before she barreled into my arms.

"He's here, Teagan," she choked out, squeezing me so tight I could barely breathe. "In Cork... I saw him at the club," she slurred. "He's *here*."

"Who?" I demanded, hugging her tightly. "Who's here, Hope?"

"Noah," she hissed, and the ground fell out from underneath my feet.

All the emotions I'd felt when I was seventeen came back full force, smothering my heart and sabotaging my ability to breathe easily. "Oh my god," I choked out.

"You're my thorn, if you leave me, I'll bleed out..."

"And for what it's worth, my in belongs to you..."

"I'm either fighting with you or I'm fucking with you. There's no middle line, Teagan – not between us..."

My throat closed up. Every emotion and memory of him that I'd spent years forcing into the darkest parts of my mind were resurfacing – fucking flooding me. Noah Messina, the man who stole my heart, the man who shredded it right in front of my eyes.

"He saw me," Hope wailed. "Teagan, he knows you're here."

THANK YOU SO MUCH FOR READING!

Noah and Teagan's story continues in
Thorn, Carter Kids #2
Available now.

Please consider leaving a review on the website you purchased this book.

Carter Kids:
Treacherous
Always
Thorn
Tame
Torment
Inevitable
Altered

OTHER BOOKS BY CHLOE WALSH

The Pocket Series:
Pocketful of Blame
Pocketful of Shame
Pocketful of You
Pocketful of Us

Ocean Bay:
Endgame
Waiting Game
Truth Game

The Faking it Series:
Off Limits – Faking it #1
Off the Cards – Faking it #2
Off the Hook – Faking it #3

The Broken Series:
Break my Fall – Broken #1
Fall to Pieces – Broken #2
Fall on Me – Broken #3

Forever we Fall – Broken #4

The Carter Kids Series:
Treacherous – Carter Kids #1
Always – Carter Kids #1.5
Thorn – Carter Kids #2
Tame – Carter Kids #3
Torment – Carter Kids #4
Inevitable – Carter Kids #5
Altered – Carter Kids #6

The DiMarco Dynasty:
DiMarco's Secret Love Child: Part One
DiMarco's Secret Love Child: Part Two

The Blurred Lines Duet:
Blurring Lines – Book #1
Never Let me Go – Book #2

Boys of Tommen:
Binding 13 – Book #1
Keeping 13 – Book #2
Saving 6 – Book #3
Redeeming 6 – Book #4

Crellids:
The Bastard Prince

Other titles:
Seven Sleepless Nights

ABOUT THE AUTHOR

Chloe Walsh is the bestselling author of The Boys of Tommen series, which exploded in popularity. She has been writing and publishing New Adult and Adult contemporary romance for a decade. Her books have been translated into multiple languages. Animal lover, music addict, TV junkie, Chloe loves spending time with her family and is a passionate advocate for mental health awareness. Chloe lives in Cork, Ireland with her family.

Join Chloe's mailing list for exclusive content and release updates.
http://eepurl.com/dPzXMi